THE
NIGHT
DAHLIA

BOOKS BY R. S. BELCHER

The Six-Gun Tarot
The Shotgun Arcana
The Queen of Swords
Nightwise
The Brotherhood of the Wheel
The Night Dahlia
King of the Road (forthcoming)

THE NIGHT DAHLIA

R. S. BELCHER

TOR

A TOM DOHERTY ASSOCIATES BOOK
NEW YORK

THE NIGHT DAHLIA

Copyright © 2018 by Rod Belcher

A Tor Book
Published by Tom Doherty Associates
175 Fifth Avenue
New York, NY 10010

www.tor-forge.com

Tor® is a registered trademark of Macmillan Publishing Group, LLC.

Library of Congress Cataloging-in-Publication Data

Names: Belcher, R. S., author.
Title: The night Dahlia / R. S. Belcher.
Description: First edition. | New York : Tom Doherty Associates, 2018. | Identifiers:
   LCCN 2017039424 (print) | LCCN 2017044101 (ebook) | ISBN 9780765390141
   (ebook) | ISBN 9780765390127 (softcover : acid-free paper)
Subjects: LCSH: Missing persons—Investigation—Fiction. | Secret societies—
   Fiction. | Fairies—Fiction. | GSAFD: Fantasy fiction. | Occult fiction.
Classification: LCC PS3602.E429 (ebook) | LCC PS3602.E429 N53 2018 (print) |
   DDC 813/.6—dc23
LC record available at https://lccn.loc.gov/2017039424

Our books may be purchased in bulk for promotional, educational, or business use.
Please contact your local bookseller or the Macmillan Corporate and Premium Sales
Department at 1-800-221-7945, extension 5442, or by email at
MacmillanSpecialMarkets@macmillan.com.

First Edition: April 2018

Printed in the United States of America

0 9 8 7 6 5 4 3 2 1

To Robert B. Parker and Raymond Chandler, Jeff Rice,
Chris Carter, Warren Murphy and Richard Sapir.
To Elmore Leonard, Ambrose Bierce, John D. MacDonald,
Humphrey Bogart, and William Goldman, for bringing me up right,
and to Phil Rowe, the man who introduced me to most of them.

To the memory of John Weddle, for whittling and picking the guitar
and belly laughter, for the smell of sawdust, for being a kind,
patient, and gentle man.

To the memory of Paul Franco: solider, father, loving warden
of the Earth. You could make flowers grow in a desert.
So much strength and so much kindness in one man is truly a gift
to all who have the privilege to know him. Thank you.

And to the memory of my dad, Harrison Gordon Belcher.
Thank you for that one good memory. I know you tried. Rest.

To my mom, Mabel T. Belcher, who took me fishing when she hated
worms, camping when she hated bugs, and sat in warm silence
with me as we both read. You taught me how to be brave when
you are trembling, and to endure the unendurable.

You are all fathers to me.

To my godson, John Siegfried Peraro Santos.
I'm very proud of the young man you are growing up to be.

To my children, Jon, Emily, and Stephanie:
I love you all more than there are words to express. You are my light.

THE
NIGHT
DAHLIA

ONE

I watched the playground on the other side of the high, chain-link fence, trying to figure out which of the elementary school children had the gun. The kids were doing like kids do, running around, chasing each other in circles, laughing, screaming. A few climbed on the monkey bars, others jockeyed to get a turn on the swings or the slide; a few played hopscotch. I couldn't recall ever being that young, happy, or clueless. I hoped to hell I could keep them that way. "Hoped to hell," I'm a fucking riot. The sun was beating down on me, but no one had noticed I didn't cast a shadow on the sidewalk. I had hocked it a while back.

I was getting the stink-eye from the circle of teachers near the double doors that led into the school, probably into the school cafeteria if it was anything like my old alma mater, Welch Elementary, back in West Virginia.

The teachers' worried frowns as I stood at the fence, studying the children at play, insulted me. I had tried so hard to blend in. Jeans, steel-toed work boots, a maroon-and-black paisley button-down with the sleeves up and the tails out. An old army medic satchel hung over one shoulder as my "murse." My long black hair was pulled back in a tight ponytail. I was goddamned eye candy. Shit, I even left the *Aqualung* trench coat at home. It was too damned hot for it anyway. Late spring in Texas is kinda like autumn on the surface of the sun.

I saw one of the teachers raise a blocky walkie-talkie to her lips and speak into it as she bored death rays into me with her baby browns. I smiled my most sincere smile—*Aw, shucks, I'm jist a good ol' boy, standing here, minding my own beeswax. I mean no harm to y'all's planet*—and lit up an American Spirit. I needed to find the little darling quick, because I was sure I was about to get a visit from the school's cop, and I didn't have time to try to convince Officer Friendly I wasn't a perv or a psycho.

I tuned out the heat, the teachers' resting bitch faces, and the sounds of traffic behind me. I did catch a quick burst of a car's radio through a rolled-down window blasting "Nasty Freestyle" by T-Wayne, then I pushed that away too. I focused on the tingling pressure up and down my spinal column, the bone road to the seat of self. I felt a geyser of aggressive, passionate, and destructive crimson power wash over my root chakra and gush upward to guide my Ajna, my "third eye." My gaze was pulled to the far left, near the school's brick wall, and I found the source of the scarlet energy. It was a little boy, about nine years old, wearing a red-and-blue-striped T-shirt, jeans, and an Avengers backpack. He was pulling something out of it, looking about furtively as he did. His eyes were wide, unblinking, and glassy. His skin was like wax. He was licking his lips. We locked eyes, the child and I, and I knew, and so did the thing behind his eyes.

"Excuse me," a deep voice with a Texas twang next to my ear said. "Is there a problem, sir?" I knew from the tone, from the way he spit out "sir," that he was a cop.

"Yeah," I said, my West Virginia accent in full bloom as I blew smoke in the cop's eyes and ducked around him, running fast. "Call for backup! That kid's got a fucking gun!" I sprinted to the end of the fence, turned the corner, and passed through the open gate toward the boy. The teachers were reacting to my dash, and I had to put my shoulder into one of them to knock him out of my way. Two others grabbed at me, though, trying to stop me.

"Settle down, now!" one of them growled. He was sincere in wanting to protect the kids, but he didn't move or grab me like someone who's gotten into too many scraps.

"Hey! Don't you move!" the cop yelled after me.

There was a snap, like a firecracker, then another, then the screaming began. "Goddamn it!" I said, struggling with the two men grabbing my arms. The playground crowd began to part as kids ran. There were two children on the ground in widening pools of blood, near the nine-year-old who was brandishing an old Colt Army .45.

"Fistulae Globis dormiat," I shouted as I opened my Muladhara lens instinctively, gesturing at the boy's gun. It wasn't my most elegant working, but my close-to-a-carton-of-cigarettes-a-day habit was making my lungs feel like they were being grated like cheese as I struggled with the teachers in the oppressive heat. I felt my spell wrap around the pistol in the kid's hand and then felt the crimson power radiating from the boy tear my working like cobwebs. Muladhara-against-Muladhara energies usually meant the bigger predator won. Not a comforting thought—I was used to being the biggest predator on the playground.

The spell did get his attention, and the boy pointed the gun in my direction and fired. I twisted one of the teachers trying to pin me, wrenching him between me and the gun. The man jerked as a bloody hole exploded in his back. He slid to the ground, convulsing in shock. I watched the life leave his eyes as he slid off me. The kid's face twisted in anger. I tripped the other teacher struggling with me, and the kid shot him in the face as he fell forward.

The school resource officer who had hassled me at the fence was only a few steps behind me as the second teacher fell. He raised his gun and aimed at the boy. "Joey," the cop called out, "put that gun down right now, son. Do it, or I'll have to shoot you!" The kids were fleeing through the double doors back into the school, blocking the cop's shot. Joey decided to make a run for it with them. "Joey!" the cop shouted and began to move into the screaming stream of children. Joey was lost in the blur. There was a loud bang, and the cop fell onto his back. I knelt beside him and saw he was still breathing, probably a vest.

I picked up the cop's 9mm and continued after Joey. I don't like guns. They make it too damn easy to kill. Even psychotics and children can pull it off with their help. However, bullets are faster than just about any magic spell you can care to lob, and I, for one, was not going to be the brain donor bringing magic to a gunfight.

Terror was smeared across the air of the cafeteria—shrieks of sanity being pulled loose at the seams, and sobs of innocence dying. Another gunshot. I dropped low behind a table by the door and found three little kids looking at me with huge eyes, moist with fear.

"Stay here," I said. "Help's coming." In the grand scheme of things, it was the lamest shit I could utter, but it was all I had. That kind of bullshit still played with kids this age. They still believed in "Help's coming" and "Everything will be okay." I made my way up the brick hall to the double doorway that led out into Matthew Stone Elementary School's central corridor. A little girl, maybe five or six, lay by the doorway, her tiny chest dark and wet with blood, her eyes fighting to stay open. They were pretty eyes too.

"Why?" she asked me, weakly. "Why did Joey hurt me? I thought he was nice."

I knelt by her and brushed her hair, slick with blood, out of her hazel eyes.

"It ain't Joey, darlin'," I said softly.

"Am I going to die?" the little girl asked.

"No, honey," I lied. "There are going to be some nice people coming along in a little bit. They're going to want you to get up and go with them. You do that, and I promise you they will fix you right up, okay? No more pain."

"Okay," the little girl said. She looked past me. "Oh," she said. "They're . . . so . . . pretty . . ." She smiled at me, some blood drooled out of her suddenly slack mouth, and she died.

I set the gun down next to her. I didn't want to touch the damn thing anymore. I closed her eyes, crouched beside her there for a moment, waiting for some higher power to do the right fucking thing by this child and give her her life back. When that wasn't forthcoming, I got back to my feet. I didn't worry about fingerprints on the gun; I had cooked up an enchantment on my prints and DNA a long while back that gave computers and technicians fits.

I followed the sounds of fear and death to their source. It wasn't the first time I had heard those sounds, and it sure as hell wouldn't be the last. There were sirens outside now, lots of them. I saw news trucks as I passed a window, clustering around the cops and EMTs like fucking maggots squirming on a carcass. At least they were predictable.

I walked down dark, cool corridors of hastily locked doors decorated with big construction paper suns smiling down on stick-figure children. First names of students, written on little laminated clouds, denoted their homerooms. My boot steps echoed along the tiled walls. I smelled gun smoke and piss. Smeared finger paint art projects, book reports written on wide-lined practice paper with colored drawings to accompany them, were like chains of islands between the doors. I could hear trembling voices whispering behind those doors. The fear of the children and the adults sworn to protect them huddled in the classrooms, waiting, praying; it was palpable. Those voices, the words, the images on the wall. This place was custodian of the future, and the thing ahead of me wanted to murder it all for its own sick pleasure.

There was so much primal force at work here, so much relentless, inevitable death and so much desperate, aching life: the two surging, clashing, crashing. Someone like me—a magus, a shaman, fakir, medicine man, a miracle worker—could take those energies and stoke them, build on them to make themselves even more powerful, more like a god. The universe hits back though, and there was always a price paid for power culled from trauma. Believe me, I know all about that. I could teach a fucking class. Back home they called me a Wisdom.

The trail to Joey included two more dead bodies, another child and another adult, maybe a janitor. I was walking toward death yet again and I felt next to nothing, aside from a yearning not to be present in this awareness. The wider the doors of perception were thrown open, the more you began to wish someone would shut the fucking door and stop letting all the damned flies in.

Twenty feet from his last victim was an open door labeled STORE-ROOM. For a second, I wished I had kept the gun. I have never been big on dying for principle, but it was too late now. I stepped into the storeroom, more like a closet on steroids, shrouding myself in my own mystical and mental defenses as I did. Little Joey was sitting on the edge of a work table, the semi-auto .45 pistol in his hand. His skin was corpse-colored, glistening with sweat, and his eyes were fractured with broken blood vessels. He raised the pistol. The slide was locked back. It was empty.

"All out of bullets," the boy said. His voice was wrong, too deep, too mature to be coming out of a nine-year-old's mouth. He began to laugh as he dropped the gun to the floor. "Too bad. I was having a great time."

"Recess is over, asshole," I said. I aligned the energies inside my body, visualized them like jewels glittering in a vertical row, preparing them to begin. "Time to go back home, Dean."

"How the fuck do you know who I am?" the monster inside the child rumbled. The kid was running hot; I could feel the heat coming off his skin from ten feet away.

"You're also killing your host, like any good parasite does," I said. "Joey dies, you go back in, Dino."

"Then I'll take this little fucker with me," Dean said. "Last one for the road! Besides, it ups my kill-count."

"Okay," I said. "We're done here." I began to flex my Manipura chakra through my solar plexus, drawing all my personal energy in and the universe's raw fuel to boot. I visualized it as a cleansing white light, growing, building, a storm of pristine purity. I felt Dean's crimson Muladhara energy—his base, animal desire to survive at any cost—grow and thrash in reaction to my marshaling of powers.

"I claimed this child," Dean snarled; some sounds like dogs ripping apart meat issued from the boy's mouth. The temperature in the storeroom dropped to that of a meat locker as he stole its energy. Joey's eyes were now blazing as if they were made of red-hot metal. "I am one of the Hungry, the lonely ones, pushed from the accursed radiance by jealousy and hubris. Your petty magics are no match, little mortal, for one who has embodied hate against your kind since the human heart first beat."

I lowered my face. The boy was rippling with waves of heat, like hot asphalt, clashing with the numbing arctic cold. Dean hopped off the table's edge and took a step toward me.

"I am Zepar," he said, "the bringer of madness, and you are nothing to me, little cosmic speck."

I looked up into the possessed child's face; I couldn't help but grin. "Horseshit," I said, dragging the word out a bit with my drawl, and dropped my shroud of protective disciplines and gestured with a fist toward the child, launching a spear of pure cleansing light at the demon. The thing screamed, and I could hear the boy screaming too. "Zepar?" I said. "Really? Shit, Dean, that sounds like one of those medicines on the commercials where they tell you to seek medical help for a hard-on that lasts longer than four hours. 'Check with your doctor to see if Zepar is right for you.'"

"It burns!" the demon whined. The light was pinning it in place.

"Yeah, I'll bet it stings a bit. You're not Zepar, the bringer of madness. Does old Z even know that you're using his moniker up here? He's going to be pissed when you get back, Dino. They have trademark infringement laws in Hell? Probably got enough lawyers down there with time on their hands." The boy had dropped to the floor, first to his knees and then onto his back, writhing. His tongue was flickering in and out of his mouth, but the man's screams and the buzzing of insects continued issuing from him, unabated.

"Your name is Dean Corll," I said, "and you were a serial murderer of young boys. You raped, tortured, and murdered over twenty-eight kids before one of your scumbag accomplices shot you dead in 1973. You were a mortal speck, just like me, pal."

"Please make it stop! It hurts!" Corll said. "It's burning me . . . and the boy! It's tearing his soul!"

"You've been everyone's punk-ass bitch in the big empty for over forty years, Dino," I said, "and you decided to make a break for it when Joey here and his mother moved into your old house on Lamar Drive. Isn't that right? Now get your ass out of that mobile home and run on back to Hell. Your landlord's waiting for you."

"No," Corll hissed. "This sweet little thing is mine, mine! I'll not give him up. I've planted my roots in his tender essence, and I won't easily be pulled out. If you don't stop this, you'll shred his soul. Who are you anyway, to order me about, to have so much power tucked away at your call, to dare to face one of the fallen with no protections, no fear?"

"You're more like 'the stumbling' than 'the fallen,' and only a poser, a wannabe, would call themselves that anyway. I'm Ballard, Laytham Ballard, and if you really want the rough trade, man, you got it."

As the light held him fast, I began to intone the ritual of exorcism, one of the variations I was taught over thirty years ago from a gruff old demonologist and his sweet, gray-haired, hymn-singing wife. It called on the nurturing powers of creation to compel the Hungry to depart the innocent host. It could take days, months, or even longer, but with all this pure Manipura energy behind it, a lightweight like Dean here should be heading for the exit.

Instead, Corll began to laugh, even as tears rolled down poor, convulsing Joey's cheeks. "You have some balls even uttering those words, half-soul-man," Corll growled. "We know of you in the empty places, Ballard. Ballard, the corrupt Nightwise; Ballard, who supped with our Master and skipped out on the check. Ballard, whom both monsters and saints fear . . . and pity. You dare try to dislodge me from my meat with pretty, pretty holy words. You've bargained away pieces of your soul for petty powers and shallow favors. You're bound for a far greater hell than I, Ballard. You have no moral authority over me," the child-defiling demon said. "Keep trying to pull me out, and you'll add this boy to the endless roll of all those you have damned in your miserable life."

He was right, unfortunately, about all kinds of things. He'd have to willingly come out of there, and all that would be waiting for him was Hell, so I had to sweeten the pot a bit, or maybe more like piss in it. The spiritual light diminished and was gone. Corll guffawed, sounding for all the world like a rutting pig. Before he could rise off the floor, I took something from my shirt pocket and knelt beside him. It was a three-inch-long, dull, rusted needle. I placed it on Joey's chest and uttered, *"Malum, manere donec veniam ad hanc formam amotus fuero."* Then I grabbed an industrial-sized jug of bright blue window cleaner off the shelf next to me. "Fine," I said, "suit yourself." I unscrewed the cap of cleaner and took a whiff.

"What is that?" Corll said. He tried to rise but discovered he couldn't.

"If you're staying at the party," I said, "you might as well have a drink." I pinched Joey's nose and began to pour the window cleaner down his throat. The boy and the demon choked and hacked as the toxic gunk went down.

"What the fuck are you doing?" Corll sputtered as I tipped the bottle back up. "Are you actually trying to kill the boy?"

"Yeah," I said, "I am. That little needle there came out of the pelvis of a guy by the name of Albert Fish. He killed kids too, more than you. He thought God was telling him to do it, go figure. Old Al was a self-mutilator, besides being a homicidal fuck, and he would drive needles into his body. A buddy of mine who collects high-end weird shit got this for me. It's got some power to it, bad power, and I figured it would have a good resonance with you, Dino, and looky there, it does. You can't come out of that body until I take this off the kid's chest, and yeah, I'm going to fucking kill him, and his soul will fly off to a real sweet place, maybe back into the big old cosmic rinse cycle where hopefully he won't draw the 'get possessed by a C-list demon fucktard' card again."

I poured another big drink of the poison down the kid's throat.

Joey and Corll both gagged and coughed. I stopped pouring again. I heard shouts and bullhorns far away. I was running out of time. "You see, Dino," I continued, "wherever the poor kid's soul ends up, it's better than being with you. So happy ending for little Joey. I'm not sure what kind of ending for 'the mighty Zepar,' however. Hard to say."

"You're bluffing," Corll said. "You came in here, tried to stop me, because you wanted to save the boy. You won't kill him now."

"Actually," I said, pouring more of the poison out of the jug again into the struggling boy's mouth, "I'm here for you, Dino. I don't give a fuck what happens to this kid, or anyone else. You read me my bio. You think I won't? Stick around and find out, huckleberry. This is a contract job . . . for your landlord. Y'know, the one you call . . ." I tried to do my best Igor impersonation, which is kinda rough when you have a West Virginia drawl, ". . . the Master."

"Oh shit!" Corll gasped around more of the poison splashing into Joey's mouth. "Wait, wait!"

"The power of Windex compels you, fucker," I said.

"Jesus!" Corll screamed, squirming, "Stop, stop, please, don't!"

"I slip this needle into the boy's body somewhere, and you're anchored for good. My best guess is that after the agonizing stomach cramps and painful-as-shit death from his nervous system shutting down," I said, "you'll just be trapped in there until the body decays. Locked in that rotting meat jail, until everything that is Dean Corll just fades away into oblivion. It's a harsh ending, Dino, but it satisfies my employer, so . . ."

"I'll leave, I'll fucking leave," Corll said. "Hurry up, I can feel that shit starting to affect his nervous system!"

I put the cap back on the jug and placed the boy's hand around the plastic handle. I put my hand on Fish's needle. "I ever catch you in this world again, I'll finish the job, next time. This is my fucking house, bitch."

"I'll be waiting in line for you when you get to Hell, Ballard," Corll said. I lifted the needle off the boy's chest, and the thing that had been Dean Corll departed with a moan like a hot desert wind. It left the dank, cloying stench of rancid blood and candy in its wake.

"Yeah," I said, slipping open my satchel, "but your punk ass will be waaaay in the back of the line, Dino." I stood, tucked the needle away in my pocket, and slipped on a dark blue windbreaker I had removed from my bag. On the back in bright yellow letters was the word PRESS. I also removed a lanyard with an official laminated press photo ID, a baseball cap with the logo of the *Houston Chronicle*, a local newspaper, on it, and a very nice digital Nikon camera. I knelt down beside the kid and waited for what I knew was coming next.

Joey was breathing, a little ragged but still alive. Fun fact: you can drink a small amount of window cleaner, about two ounces an hour, and get wasted off of it, but too much does fuck up your nervous system and can kill you. You find out all kinds of neat life hacks like that when you vacation at rock bottom.

A pair of cops in tactical gear, probably the point on a SWAT team, appeared on either side of the open door.

"Don't move!" one of them shouted. I put my hands up.

"I think he's trying to kill himself," I said. "He drank a bunch of this blue cleaning shit. He was like this when I came down the hall."

"Keep your hands up, stand, and move over to the side," the other cop said. "Jesus, it's the shooter all right, we need medics in here now!"

One of the SWAT cops frisked me and spun me around, reading my press ID. "How the fuck did you get past the lines and get in here, asshole?"

"Hey, look, I'm sorry, man," I said. "I'm new and I was just trying to get . . ."

"Get him out of here," an older tactical cop with sergeant's stripes said as he entered the room with the EMTs. "Place is getting too damn crowded."

They confiscated my camera and ran my press credentials. My hacker, Grinner, had been good to his word and worth every penny. The fake ID stood up. In less than an hour, I was walking away from the school and dumping my career as a photojournalist in a trash can next to the bus stop.

While they were vetting me, they brought Joey out on a stretcher. He was handcuffed to it. He was awake and crying, calling out for his mother. I felt a cowardly relief pass through me at the thought that I didn't have to be the one to tell the boy his mother had been his first victim. I'd seen her body in the hallway of their quiet home.

I imagined the nightmare existence Joey was going to have now, the horrors outside and inside eating him until the day he departed this earth. Death would have been more merciful. Kid hadn't done a thing wrong, just got handed a shit deal. My job was done, I had done the best I could. I was never supposed to win this, never supposed to get there in the nick of time to make it all right for anyone except the manipulative bastard who sent me here. It was a cluster fuck from the jump.

I hailed a cab. "Drive," I said, handing the guy a hundred, and fumbling for a cigarette. I kept thinking that if I looked behind me, Joey would be there, staring at me.

"Where?" the cabbie asked.

"Away," I said, "fast."

TWO

The Voodoo Queen on Milby Street was a dive that tried a little too hard to be a dive. It made the hipster kids feel like they were really slumming without the need for paying gangland tolls and packing pistols. I liked the joint from my last visit to Houston because the music was good and the folks there didn't skimp on the alcohol in their drinks. I bypassed the voluminous menu of concoctions that came in hollowed-out pineapples and fishbowls with little totem poles of fruit spears and paper umbrellas for buying the lone bottle of Pappy Van Winkle Reserve they had up on the top shelf. The fetching lass that sold it to me had hair dyed white and a tapestry of tattoos covering her slender body.

"You're kidding," she said. "That's like a three-thousand-dollar bottle of twenty-three-year-old whiskey. You know that, right?" I handed her a wad of cash.

"Here's four K," I said. "It's a tip for being the prettiest sight I've seen all day, darlin'." The bartender looked at the money, back to me, and stepped to the back bar to count the bills and make sure they weren't fake by the light of the enormous fish tank full of brilliantly colored clown fish that adorned the back wall of the bar. She came back with the bourbon like she was cradling the Ark of the Covenant, and a glass tumbler.

"Ice?" she asked.

"Be like pissing in holy water."

"What's the special occasion?"

"It's my birthday," I said, getting up from the bar.

"Happy birthday!" she said and actually meant it. "Hey, I get off at eight. I've never tasted twenty-three-year-old bourbon before."

"Well, come find me," I said. "I'll introduce you to it, but I suspect that whiskey is older than you are."

She laughed, and I retreated to the shadows of the bar floor.

Funny thing, when you buy a bottle like this, they pretty much let you camp any damn place you please. I went around a velvet rope and sat myself down in a corner booth of a closed section. The only lights in here were the small round fills built into the ceiling, bright light under them, and deep shadow all around. I could still hear the music from the jukebox. It was playing the Swan's cover of "Can't Find My Way Home." I poured a drink and sipped it like the first kiss from an old lover in a long, long time. I had stayed dry for eleven months, Magdalena's influence on me. She was gone, little Joey was gone. Gone, baby, gone, like the song goes. But Dean-fucking-Corll would go on forever. That little girl was gone, but my evil ass sat right here in air-conditioned comfort, getting good and tight. Cheers. Seeing children's brains sprayed all over walls seemed as good a reason as any to take a flying leap off the wagon. I drained my glass; it was smooth as Sinatra, worth every penny. I poured myself another one, saw that little girl's eyes as she slipped away, and toasted the darkness.

"Happy birthday, asshole," I said.

Half a bottle or so later, a waitress came back to see how I was doing. I told her to bring me a bottle of the cheapest, nastiest tequila they had and a Budweiser in a bottle. I gave her five hundred dollars for her trouble. After that, I had no shortage of customer service.

The bottle of tequila was almost gone, and a forest of empty brown beer bottles covered the table. The afternoon crowd in the bar had mostly been office folks skipping out for a beer at lunchtime, a few

college kids with no classes and money to burn, and of course my
people, the barflies who didn't give a fuck about the décor or the crowd
as long as there was a seat for your ass and booze to whittle away the
hours of your life until the end. There is a certain Zen meditation
present in hard-core alcoholism.

The evening crowd was in now. It consisted of more sketchy locals
from the Second District, the surrounding neighborhood, and swarms
of hipsters, nursing the one PBR they could afford. There was a battle
over who was setting the tone for the night on the jukebox, the music
jumping from blues, to dance, to country. I did my part for the war
effort by tossing in Johnny Cash's cover of "I See a Darkness" and
followed it up with K.Flay's "Blood in the Cut." Take that, alt-folk
scum! I paid the club manager a grand to keep my section closed.
I wanted to be in a fishbowl, watching life, seeing how normal assholes spent their Friday night.

I had almost finished off the Pappy Van when the tattooed bartender walked up to my table with a stride like a panther. The black
lights made her white hair almost glow. "You didn't forget about me,
did you?" she said over the throbbing music and the traffic jam of
voices. She had a glass in her hand. I nodded for her to sit and she
did. I poured her a glass, the last of the bottle, leaving a single swal-
low for myself. She raised the glass, and I raised the bottle.

"Happy birthday," she said, "and congratulations on another successful fulfillment of your ongoing obligation, Laytham."

I paused in drinking the last of the bottle and cocked my head at
the bartender, who drained her glass and sighed. I looked across the
bar and saw the same bartender, same tattoos, same hair, waving
bye to the other bartender on duty as she headed for the door, her
purse over her shoulder.

"That," said the bartender sitting across from me, "is what sin
tastes like." I slipped a cigarette between my lips.

"Got a light?" I asked the Devil.

"You had two images prominent in your mind," the embodiment
of all malice said as she lit my cigarette like any good bartender

would. "This sweet young thing you visualized rutting with, and that dead little girl back at the school. Since it was your birthday, I chose, sorry for this, the lesser of two evils."

"What do you want?" I asked. "You are assassinating a very expensive buzz. I did your dirty work, and got you your AWOL scumbag back."

"You did, Laytham," it said. "I would have manifested sooner, but I had to wait until your consciousness was altered sufficiently for us to interact. I wanted to congratulate you on heroically saving that poor boy's life, Laytham. Bravo."

"Fuck you," I said, and drained the last of the bourbon. It tasted like ashes.

"Technically, fuck you," she replied, pouring herself a glass of the last of the oily tequila, "since you were the one who bartered away three years of your life in my service in exchange for those wishes you needed so desperately at the time." I watched the Devil drink the last of my booze. I think there was a metaphor in there somewhere. "Haven't we had fun these past few years? Me, breaking up the wearisome monotony of your plodding march toward self-induced oblivion with my little honey-do list of tasks. You, a villain most foul, given chances over and over again to act the hero, like you did today. Tell me, hero, how does it feel to be back on the side of the angels?"

I looked across the table for anything left to drink. There was nothing. I looked up at this thing of purest self-hate, conjured out of my own mind, and said nothing. There was nothing to say. The Devil knows you, because the Devil is you. She went on, taking one of my American Spirits out of the crumpled and almost empty pack. "I wanted to congratulate you," she said, lighting the cigarette between those full lips, "and let you know I was here to give you a little birthday present of my own. You have worked off about a year's worth of your debt in the past two. I am forgiving almost all of the remaining time on your account tonight, my dear Laytham."

"Almost?" I said, leaning across the table, knocking several beer bottles over as I did. I think a few smashed on the floor.

"I'm holding onto one minute," the Devil said. "That's all. One measly minute, and of course the ragged chunk of your soul invested in that time will remain in escrow until that minute is paid. Am I not a generous god?"

"You're what my granny would call a hoodooer," I slurred. My companion nodded.

"Well said. How is your dear grandmother these days? Don't hear much from her since you 'helped' her all those years ago, eh, hero?"

I roared and launched myself across the table at the son of a bitch. The table tumbled over as I fell. Bottles shattered everywhere. I was on the floor with all the other broken things, trying to get back up. The pretty bartender was gone; I was alone. I had been alone the whole time.

"Okay, big spender, time to call you a cab." Thick hands lifted me off the floor and to my feet.

"Letgoame," I said, articulately, and tried to pull away. It didn't work. The guy holding me was a good six inches taller than me and outweighed me by maybe eighty pounds. He had a hardness behind his eyes that told me the smile fixed on his face was a lie. If I pushed, he would beat the hell out of me. "You have any idea who you're fuhkin' with?" I said.

"Look, friend," the bouncer said, walking me out of the closed section, "Let's just go outside and talk about this, okay?"

"Fuhyou," I said and took a swing at him. "I'm fuhkin' Laythm Ballard, you muther fuhker!" It connected, but there wasn't anything behind it. I might as well have slapped him with a bar rag. I tried to put together a spell, some kind of spell, death spell? Fire-fall? My concentration was like mercury, and my energies were as scattered as any other broken-down old drunk's would have been. The bouncer snapped off two quick, tight jabs at me. He wasn't just a meathead that stood at the door and checked ID; he had training. There were bright lights popping behind my eyes, and I was falling. Then there was movement after some time in the dark. A female voice was near my ear.

"Who did he say he was?"

"Nobody, just an old, rich drunk," I heard the bouncer telling the girl, "celebrating his birthday a little too hard. He was back there talking to himself for the last half hour."

There was a hole in my memory after that. My next awareness was the smell of garbage. I climbed to my knees and looked. I was in an alley, next to a Dumpster overflowing with kitchen trash. I had no idea where I was or how much time had passed. I slid back down, and my face hit the sticky asphalt. I slept.

Someone was turning me over. The man's face was square and bland in its ugliness. He had short, thinning blond hair. He wore an expensive suit with his cheap haircut.

"It's him," square-face said to someone. He had a British accent.

"Fuck off," I said. It was still dark, and all I wanted to do was go back to sleep. Blondie grabbed me by my shirt and hauled me to my feet. I drove a right into his jaw, and this time it had a little something behind it. He staggered back, shaking his head. I was in another alley filled with Dumpsters. I had no clue where I was. There was a black SUV, a Mercedes-Benz, idling with its lights on. Square-face's companion stood by the car; he held his arms behind his back. He was black, taller than me, and dressed better than his partner. He wore the expensive clothes better than Square-face too. He had his black hair cut very short, almost military fashion, and he had a neatly trimmed goatee. His eyes were hazel, and his features were fine, with slightly pointed ears, a slender nose, and good cheekbones.

"There's no need for that, Mr. Ballard," Cheekbones said. It's been my experience that when someone says that, there's absolutely a fucking need for whatever "that" is. In this case, I threw a shaky upper cut at Square-face. He blocked it and planted a solid one in my gut. I dropped to my hands and knees and vomited on his Testoni shoes.

"Shit, mate!" Square-face snapped a kick at my face, which my booze-drowned brain registered as a Hapkido kick, in the instant prior to me blacking out.

"You sure this is the guy?" a voice asked. There was a reply and more talking, but I slid back into anesthetized slumber, bordering on poisoned coma.

Time passed. My face ached. My jaw ached. My ribs ached. My brain spun in the darkness of my skull. I smelled my own stale vomit and piss. I was placed in a comfortable seat and belted in. Cool air blew on my face. I slept. I awoke and asked for water through swollen lips to match my swollen eyes.

"Fuck you," a familiar British voice said. "Legend, my ass. This tosser's a fucking bum."

"You're just mad about your shoes," another voice without the English accent said, and I laughed.

Then, at some future point on the other side of dizzy, nauseous blackness, a cool glass was placed to my lips.

"Drink slowly," a voice that wasn't Square-face said. The tiny sliver of my brain that had avoided the deep fryer figured it for Cheekbones. I drank the cold water, swallowed, and then slept again. Time passed. I dreamed. I was talking to the little dead girl. She had lost her doll in a blood-painted maze. I wandered with her and tried to help her find it. The maze never gave up the doll or offered a way out.

I awoke to being carried by my two well-dressed keepers off some kind of airplane and deposited in the back of a limo.

"Where we going, fellas?" I muttered. Neither of them answered me. I sunk into the leather seats and sighed. "This thing have a bar?" I asked Cheekbones. If he answered me, I didn't hear it before I slept again.

THREE

Afternoon sunlight filtered through the antique lace curtains. I was in a bed with an excellent mattress and feather pillows. The thread count on the sheets was a number approximating the national debt. There was a pitcher of ice water on the bed next to me along with a small bell and several bottles of salt tablets, analgesics, and stomach medicine. There was also my crushed but serviceable brown package of American Spirits and my tarnished old Zippo. I sat up and winced a little from the soreness in my side and stomach. Had I gotten kicked? When I blinked, it hurt. I touched my face. My lips and eyes were sore and puffy, but the swelling was already receding. I had been in a scrap, but I'd had much, much worse. I did my requisite ten minutes of hacking and coughing, paying my tribute to the god of nicotine with an offering of lung tissue.

I slipped out of the clean, comfy sheets and discovered I was naked. I checked myself for any injuries other than the ugly green-and-blue bruise on my side. The old bod was still getting by, covered in tattoos and scars, my meat biography. For a fella of my advancing decrepitude, I was holding up okay. I was still cut like Iggy Pop, hold the heroin; still had all my hair, it was falling down to my shoulder blades, and the majority of it was still black. Still had most of my teeth, but not for lack of trying.

I looked out the window and saw endless, perfect green. A verdant lawn worthy of the Elysian Fields. I was either dead and in the wrong place, or the guest of someone who could afford to have his vast grounds manicured on a daily basis. I drank the better part of the pitcher of water, sat on the edge of the bed, and lit up a cigarette.

Whoever had me didn't want me dead or at a disadvantage. They had gone to some time and trouble to patch me up. That sounded to me like a job, so I stood up and checked the closet. My clothes were all there, cleaned, pressed, and perfect. I pulled up my jeans, put on socks and boots, and slipped on the shirt. My wallet was on the shelf above the clothes. Everything was still in it, about two thousand in cash; it should have been considerably more, but I chalked that up to my binge, not theft. There was also a bunch of credit cards, and an ID, all in names that weren't mine.

I gathered up my smokes and lighter, tried the door and found it unlocked, and walked out of the bedroom, buttoning my shirt as I did. The house was old; it smelled of well-oiled wood and was a little stuffy with heat. I walked down the hall past numerous doors and came to a foyer at the top of a grand staircase. I had an excellent view of a series of stained-glass mosaics that were capturing the afternoon sun. It was some of the finest glass work I had ever seen. The colors and the designs shifted and flowed, and I suspected there might have been a bit of subtle enchantment at work in the overall effect, but if it was, it was some of the most subtle working I had ever seen. The scene depicted was a beautiful autumn forest, alive with leaves of garnet, fire, umber, and salamander. A sun and moon presided overhead, circling each other in phase-dances of life, death, and rebirth. Tall, slender beings, cloaked in colors that put the leaves to drab shame, stood at the center of it all, their skin lustrous like diamonds, their eyes, trackless night. Above the mosaic was a family crest I recognized. I realized who had me, and something long-buried writhed in me, thrashing like a hungry eel in my guts.

"Ah, Mr. Ballard, you're awake. Excellent." The voice was Irish, gentile, and belonged to a man at my six. He was in his late sixties, maybe early seventies. He had a full head of white hair, thinning a bit on top, and a wrinkled, ruddy complexion with prominent laugh lines. I liked him almost instinctively; I think that was the point. He wore a suit and tie with a simple apron over them. "I'm Carmichael, sir, Mr. Ankou's butler. I trust you are feeling better than when you joined us, sir?"

I laughed. "Yeah, I'm good. Thanks. Sorry for the mess. I reckon you had to clean that all up, huh?" Carmichael kept smiling.

"Think nothing of it, sir. It reminded me a bit of earlier days here, when the house was a bit more lively and boisterous."

"Well, I don't care to have anybody clean up my messes for me," I said. Someone cleared their throat. It was Cheekbones, in another tailored suit, this one charcoal gray. He looked good, *GQ* good.

"Your history would suggest otherwise," Cheekbones said. "You seem to leave messes wherever you go and seem to have little care for the consequences to others."

"Mr. Burris," Carmichael said, "I was about to notify you that Mr. Ballard is up and about."

"Thank you, Carmichael," Burris said. "I'll take him down to Mr. Ankou." I nodded, waved bye to the butler, and followed Burris down the staircase.

"Where am I?" I asked, as I lit a cigarette. Burris kept walking.

"An estate outside London," he said. "You are a guest of the Ankou family."

"'Honor above,'" I said in a trilling language that didn't have its origin upon this earth. Burris looked over his shoulder but kept walking. "That's the house motto, isn't it?" I said in English, exhaling a cloud of smoke.

"It's more than a motto," Burris replied in the same language. It sounded like water babbling over stone. "Someone like you wouldn't understand."

Burris took me through the manor. I walked past a parlor with ancient Middle Eastern tapestries adorning the walls. In the room, an old, blind Egyptian with ram horns growing out of his temples was reclining on a mass of cushions, taking sips off a water pipe full of very pungent marijuana as he instructed a half-dozen serious-looking young men who rested on their knees with blades and guns arrayed ritually before them. Burris paused for an instant to look into the room, and a flicker of a recognizable emotion crossed his face, gone too quickly for me to get a bead on it.

We passed another room with very expensive antique furniture; a circle of ladies practiced needlepoint and spoke quietly among themselves. Their garb ran from Victorian-era gowns to modern-casual. The matriarch of the circle was an old woman, easily in her nineties with giant moth wings of dusty gray twitching at her back as she jabbed a bony finger at a young girl who was looking down, admonished and blushing.

Burris opened a glass door that led to a narrow corridor, also of glass. The corridor, like an airlock, opened into a large conservatory through a door at the other end. The glass walls and ceiling were buttressed with ornate beams of what appeared to be silver. The sunlight flashed off a few of the lower beams. There were plants everywhere, mostly orchids, and the floor was dark, rich soil. I saw a few plants, I was fairly certain, that were not native to Earth. The air was hot and moist to accommodate the flora, and sweet smelling, almost to the point of being cloying.

Burris led me along well-worn dirt paths through the foliage until we reached a clearing that contained a small rattan table and four high-backed rattan chairs. A man sat in one of the chairs, sipping a cold, sweating glass of white wine. He was an average-enough-looking fellow, with slightly prominent front teeth, big ears, and a mop of curly brown hair. His clothes cost more than most cars back in the States ran you. He regarded me and Burris with a look of practiced disdain, reserved for "the help," I'm sure. The man standing at the opposite edge of the circle was tall; he wore a white linen suit. I didn't recognize the tailor from the cut, but it made the other guy's clothes look like he shopped at Goodwill. He had a powder-blue dress shirt and no tie. He had his back to me and, for a moment, when

I first looked at him, he seemed . . . larger, too large to fit in this space, too large for my mind to fully comprehend. Imagine getting a glimpse of the ocean, the *whole* ocean, all at once. He seemed to squeeze the enormity of his being back into a human-sized space my monkey brain could wrap itself around. He turned to look at me with dark eyes flecked with silver and a warm smile. His hair was brown, straight, and fine, and fell to his collar. He had a widow's peak. He had the kind of real tan only the rich can afford to cultivate.

"Laytham Ballard," the cosmic force pretending to be the tan man said. "Please have a seat. You stay as well, Burris."

"Yes, sir," Burris said and sat in one of the rattan chairs. I joined him in another. The tan man sat down as well and crossed his legs. As if on cue, Carmichael appeared with a tray of drinks, refreshing the wine of the guy who had been sitting when we arrived. There was a chalice of something for the tanned man. The cup was covered in what I was pretty sure were real jewels. For Burris, it looked like ice water, and for me a double bourbon on the rocks. When I sipped it, I was surprised to discover it was more of the Van Winkle Reserve.

"How do you say it?" the tan man asked. "The hair . . . of the dog? Yes?"

I tipped the glass at him and nodded. "That is exactly how we say it, Mr. Ankou."

The tan man smiled and nodded as he sipped from his million-dollar pimp cup. "I am Theodore Ankou, Lord of the Isles of Albion, Baron of the Black-Light Realms, High-Minister to the Court of the Uncountable Stairs, and Patriarch of the Ankou clan. I trust you understand all that?"

"I do," I said. "You left out a few, I assume for brevity's sake. I am honored to be a guest in your realm, Lord Ankou." That last part I said in the slippery-sounding liquid language of the Fae that Burris and I had spoken on the stairs. My Fae was rusty, and it probably sounded weird as hell with a Southern accent. Ankou smiled and raised his cup in salute.

"So it's true; you know our ways and customs."

"You knew I did," I said. "You knew all about me before you ever sent your men to fetch me. The Ankous are well known for their . . . thoroughness."

Theo laughed. "Thank you for the compliment, Mr. Ballard. We found out as much as we could," he said. "Most of it is urban legend and well-promoted myth. There is very little hard data in this world about you, Mr. Ballard, a remarkable feat in this age of digital scrying. Humans seem only too eager to lay every detail of their lives out for the world to see. But men like you, Mr. Ballard, you understand the power and currency of secrets."

Ankou withdrew a Diamond Rose iPhone from his jacket pocket and pulled something up on the phone's screen. "'Laytham Ballard,'" he began. "'Born in Welch, West Virginia, United States. The exact date and time of birth has been obscured through both technology and ritual.'"

"I had this Coptic horoscope assassin on me for a bit," I said, "trigger man for the Followers of Montanus. If he knew your date and time of birth, you were dead. 'Sides, birthday parties get kinda lame. After your twelfth, it's all downhill."

Ankou continued reading.

"As for your childhood, both parents are reported deceased. Names and locations unknown. A persistent rumor is that you raised the dead at the age of ten. You were also supposedly an inmate at the Weston State Mental Hospital between the ages of eleven and twelve. Again, all the records regarding that story can't be found." I said nothing. "Ah," Ankou said with a seam of a smile. "Perhaps that one's a bit too close to home, yes?"

I drained half my drink.

"You were supposedly inducted into the Nightwise, a most prestigious honor for a wizard," Theo said, not even looking up from his phone. "You are the only member of that august circle to ever be dishonored and cast out."

"I wasn't fired; I quit," I said. "More pricks in that 'august circle' than on a cactus." Mr. White Wine chuckled at that. He covered his mouth as he did. Classy.

"It is claimed that you are the man who stole the philosopher's stone from the mobster and master alchemist, Joey Dross, in 1999, then lost it in a high stakes poker game, or over a woman, accounts vary. A few years ago, you and some accomplices broke into the U.S. Treasury Department in Washington, D.C.," Ankou said, putting his phone away, "and supposedly made off with rune-etched currency printing plates worth millions, infuriating the All-Seeing Eye in the process. Few men cross the Illuminati, the Secret Masters, and live.

"In 1996 you were the leader and sole survivor of a group of individuals that rescued dozens of Kolkata street children from a Brahmarakshasa lair. You are said to be the only mortal wizard to have ever harnessed the power of the Tianzi Tablets and not gone incurably mad. You are the subject of numerous documentaries, books, magazine articles, and social media 'fan pages,' and, if the myth has any truth to it, a cameo in at least one pornographic movie."

"*Hairy Boff-her and the Wand of Wonder*," I offered happily. Ankou crossed his legs, angling his body toward me.

"You have decades of similar anecdotes surrounding you, Mr. Ballard. Depending on whom you ask, you've either stolen from, conned, betrayed, saved, or avenged pretty much everyone associated with the occult underworld: 'the Life,' I believe you people call it. You're a legend."

"Okay," I said, taking another sip of my drink, "my turn, and I don't even need to check an eight-million-dollar cell phone for this one. The Ankous are one of the last of the original Fae clans to still reside on Earth. You were building exquisite architecture, creating literature, music, and art, and, oh, being worshiped like gods, demons, and ancient astronauts when humanity was scratching the fleas off our asses in caves and trying to figure out the whole agriculture gig."

Ankou nodded and sipped from his goblet. He seemed very pleased with himself. "These days," I continued, "your family is pretty diversified. You own media corporations and banks, you pull diamonds, gold, silver, plutonium, all kinds of goodies out of the Earth, and then you take profits from those and a bunch of other commodities all along the way, from inception to market. You are major players in the Court of the Uncountable Stairs and have treaties and trade deals with everyone from the Grays' massive collective colony to Rangi, the Polynesian sky god—y'know, the one you see on late-night TV, hocking his self-help books? You own factories, retail chains, and companies that make computers, cell phones, military drones, water purifying straws for the third world, and wind turbines. Oh, and heroin. Lots and lots of heroin. A major part of your bottom line, I'd guess. The Fae families, as a group, including the Ankous, are about the third-largest producers and distributors in the world of 'smack,' I believe you people call it."

The smug smirk slid from Ankou's face. "So," I said, finishing off my drink, "how can I be of service to the Sugar Plum Mafia?"

"You live up to your reputation, Mr. Ballard; that much is evident," Ankou said. "I want you to find my daughter, Caern. She's missing."

"You have more money than God's loan shark," I said. "You have your own army of house knights"—I nodded toward Burris—"you own security companies; you can buy whole detective agencies and put them to work on finding your girl. You can employ more hackers and data miners than the Chinese government and the Russian Mob combined, not to mention you have enough juice on the street to put a bounty out and have every lowlife, junkie, dirty cop, and street hustler looking for her. Why bring me in?"

"I have done all of that," Ankou said, "and more. My daughter's trail is completely cold. I understand you have acquired a reputation for finding things and people that seem to have vanished without a trace. I think Caern has been swallowed up by some part of the Life so deep and so foul that all my resources can't reach her."

"But you think I can?" I asked.

"You're Laytham Ballard," he said. "Just your name has cachet in some very, very dark places, places my people cannot go."

"I have unlocked the 'Master at Slumming' achievement," I said, "true." Ankou's companion with the wine looked confused by that. "How cold a trail are we talking about here?"

"Caern has been missing since 2009," Ankou said. "Nine years after my wife, her mother, the Lady Osperia, died in a car accident in Spain."

"How old was she when she disappeared?" I asked.

"Thirteen," Ankou said.

Memory bit into me. Thirteen was the age I'd left home.

"You've been looking for her for all these years? And not even a lead?"

Ankou shifted in his chair. I didn't know enough about this guy, except by reputation, to read him, but that squirm was the first tell I noticed. "If my people had made any progress, Mr. Ballard, you would still be in that Houston alley, nestled up with your garbage and your vomit and not drinking my good whiskey. I have exhausted every possible resource at my disposal, including a pilgrimage back to the Shining Lands of our creation to scry in the waters of Elphyne for her. Nothing."

"You know she's probably dead, right?" I said, leaning forward in my chair. "All these years, no word, no leads. It doesn't look good."

"Then we need proof to that end," White Wine said. His voice was exactly what I had thought it would be, nasally, like he was afraid to smell air contaminated by commoners.

"This," Ankou said, sounding a little pained, "is Lord Weer-asethakulakkinuoye, of one of the most prominent of the Equinox houses. He is Caern's betrothed."

"Ah, okay," I said. "So this new urgency in finding your daughter wouldn't have anything to do with an arranged marriage agreement between your house and Lord Snuffleupagus's here, right?"

"The girl is of age now," Weerasethakulakkinuoye said. "The agreement must be fulfilled or dismissed. I need proof if she's dead."

"I don't work for you, pencil neck," I said to Prince Pinot. I looked over to Ankou. "I'm not even sure if I work for you. You want me to chase down a girl and drag her back here for some bullshit marriage she had no say in"—I jerked a thumb at Weerasethakulakkinuoye—"and I'd lay good money on her not wanting any part of it."

"You may not believe this," Ankou said. "But I love my daughter very much. We Fae do not conceive many children. Caern is our only one. My wife, my love, is gone. Caern was all I had left of her. The happiest I've ever been in this world, or any other, was when the three of us were together." I saw some emotion pass behind those dark eyes; it was a mystery to me what it was. Ankou's perfectly modulated voice cracked a little as he spoke. "I want her home safe, Mr. Ballard. I promise, I will listen to her wishes about the wedding and abide by them." Weerasethakulakkinuoye didn't like that; he started to open his mouth to say so, but Ankou shut him down with a stern look. "I just want to know that she's safe. I'd like her home, but I won't force her."

"What's in all this for me other than a huge pain in the ass?" I asked.

"I could threaten you," Ankou said, "tell you how every person you've ever worked with or cared for would be dead in twenty-four hours if you refused." I leaned back in my chair.

"Fuck 'em," I said. "You go on and kill 'em. See if I give a damn."

Ankou smiled. "You mean that, don't you? I heard that about you too. Quite the mercenary, quite the loner. Many of those tales about you seem to end with you being the only one still alive. You really don't care if I were to kill every single one of your associates and loved ones, do you?"

"Only one way to find out," I said. "Folks who run with me and don't end up dead may be harder to grease than you think, Theo, and anyone stupid enough to love me gets what they deserve."

"I see," Ankou said. "Well then, of course there's money, but I know men like you acquire and lose it with great rapidity, and it is really more of a means to an end for your lot. So I won't insult you with an offer."

"By all means, insult away," I said.

"Name a price," he said, "I'll triple it." The look I gave him must have made him realize he shouldn't have.

"Well, lastly," he said, slipping his hand into his jacket pocket, "I can offer you this." He produced a small black glass bottle. The bottle had a rubber dropper–style cap, like you might see on eye- or ear-drops. I sensed power off the bottle without even trying.

"My grandmother told me never to accept potions from fairy folk," I said. "Those could be magical roofies for all I know."

"If I had wanted you glamoured, Mr. Ballard, you would be licking my shoe right now. No, I need you with your somewhat odious personality and faculties fully intact. What do your perceptions tell you about this bottle?" Ankou said as he unscrewed the top of the bottle. I opened my third eye to a tiny slit and felt the waves of the energy in the bottle sync perfectly with my own aura. *What the hell?*

"It feels like it's mine," I said. Ankou squeezed something out of the bottle by way of the dropper and moved the dropper and pipette over my palm. A drop of a glowing blueish-white liquid shivered at the mouth of the pipette.

"May I demonstrate?" he said. I nodded. He released the rubber bulb, and the glowing liquid dropped from the glass pipette. It fell toward my palm, and then stopped and hovered, then drifted downward lazily, like a dandelion seed. The light was brilliant blue-white like an arc of lightning at the instant it strikes. It flashed like a firefly, and I slowly raised my hand toward it. This . . . belonged to me . . . it was part of me, somehow.

I gently touched the drifting, flaring light with the tip of my index finger and felt . . . I felt . . . the emotion connected with the memory of my pa sitting me on his lap in his old, worn leather recliner. I could smell his hair tonic and his English Leather, the stale scent of tobacco—his coffin nails, he called them. He was reading to me from the *Encyclopedia Britannica*. Every night he'd let me pick a volume and then we'd randomly read an entry. It was the only good, solid memory of my pa I had, and it filled me with warm feelings of security and belonging, love and . . . joy. *Joy*, it was something I hadn't felt in a very long time, was incapable of feeling anymore. The tiny lightning droplet sizzled against my fingertip and was gone; the emotion faded just as quickly.

"That's . . . my joy," I almost whispered. Ankou nodded. The twist of a smile had returned to the corners of his lips again.

"Yes," he said. "It certainly is. This tiny sample of it was expensive, even for someone with my considerable means. To us Fae, the distilled emotions of humans are a very powerful drug, very valuable. You bargained away your joy to House Tycho, in exchange for their adoption of a human ghost into their demesne, I am led to understand. The girl had died in a car accident. She must have been very precious to you. Joy freely given is a very powerful narcotic indeed, Mr. Ballard."

I said nothing. I rubbed my index finger and thumb together, trying to feel any remainder of the tiny drop. There was none. The melting ice in my empty glass cracked and shifted slightly. "Find my daughter, and I will buy back every last drop of your joy from the Lunar Lords, and return it to you."

"Counterproposal," I croaked, trying to get my head back in the game. "You use your position in the Court of the Uncountable Stairs and your pull with the Tycho clan, and you get that ghost released from her duties. She gets a walk. No more doing shit jobs for you all. You do that, and I'll find your girl."

"Again, most impressive," Ankou said, putting the empty bottle away. "Most mortals given a drop of pure, undistilled joy would do almost anything for more. This little ghost must have been very special to you."

Her name was Torri Lyn and, a million lifetimes ago, we had loved. She had been one of the only people in this world to see the real me and still love me. She died.

"Joy's only worth something if you got a reason for it," I said. "We have a deal?" Ankou looked over to Weerasethakulakkinuoye, and the little fop nodded.

"Yes," Ankou said, "we have a deal."

FOUR

Two hours later we were in the air on Ankou's private jet, an Airbus A380. The thing was a fucking hotel with wings. Two levels, bars, conference rooms, a lounge, and a full kitchen with all the fawning staff to go with it. You could easily seat hundreds of people in here, crushed in cattle-car style like most folks have to fly. I wondered if the folks who flew this way could even survive a coach class flight without therapy for the trauma. I was a long-ass way from the trailer park in Welch.

I ordered a scotch, stretched my legs out—a luxury on most flights— and got comfy in the padded leather seat. I didn't buckle up, a rebel even in gilded luxury. Burris was sitting across from me. He looked at me like a cat that had just swallowed a mouse past its expiration date.

"What?" I said. His eyes flickered to the glass and then back to me. He said nothing. "Don't like this, huh?" I said, raising the glass and taking a sip.

"We were told you had dried yourself out," he said.

"Well, sucks to be 'we' then, don't it?" I said. "I'm officially off the wagon. What's your beef anyway, raised by warrior monks? Never touched the stuff? It will make Baby Jesus cry?" Something shifted behind Burris's eyes, but his face remained stone.

"It undercuts your performance, makes you sloppy and careless, and can leave you defenseless," he said. "As a wizard, you should already know that; as former Nightwise, they should have trained this juvenile behavior out of you before you ever hit the streets. I don't intend to carry your besotted ass through this. That's all." I noticed again that Burris had no British accent. He didn't seem to have any accent my ear could pick up.

"Shit," I said. "I can conjure like Doctor-motherfucking-Strange, Master of the Mystic Arts on crank, even with a snoot full," I said and took another drink.

"We'll see," he said and lowered the back of his seat to get more comfortable. "With that kind of attitude, why did you stop?"

"Trying to be something I fucking wasn't for someone who should have known better," I said. "Didn't take."

"Obviously," Burris said. He closed his eyes, and I assume he slept. Maybe he was meditating, or hibernating, or something. I don't know what the hell Vulcans do.

I was not happy to have a sidekick in this caper, especially one I didn't pick myself. Burris coming along was the one term I couldn't get Ankou to back off on. I had a large duffle bag stowed in my private freaking bedroom on this plane, which held half a mil of the Fae mobster's money, all washed and clean as a whistle. He didn't even blink when I told him I'd need that for walking-around money. In the seat next to me was a fourteen-thousand-dollar Solarin smartphone with better-than-military encryption, which Ankou handed me when I told him I needed ultra-secure communication to reach out to my people. But when it came to his knight, Burris, he simply ignored every argument I gave him.

"Burris is my insurance policy," Ankou said. "He makes sure you don't simply take my money and disappear or go on a long vacation instead of looking for Caern. You'll find him very unobtrusive, and he is not without his talents."

And that was that. So I was stuck with Burris. Swell. Talents my ass. If looking for a little girl lost comes down to a fucking firefight, I know enough on my own to get the hell out of that.

I picked up the black-and-gold Solarin and dialed a number I knew was to a KFC in Okinawa. It was routed and rerouted about two hundred times, bounced off a few satellites, and finally was answered.

"Talk," a gruff bass voice on the other side of the world said.

"Howdy, I wanted to pre-order a large twelve-piece bucket, original recipe, and large sides of chicken feet, rice balls, and squid ink for Christmas Day," I said.

"It's the asshole that walks like a man," Grinner said over the line.

"We clean?" I asked the best damned hacker on the planet. His name was Robert Shelton, but everyone knew him by his handle, Grinner. He was one of those handful of people that Ankou had been talking about who had ridden with me and lived.

"Affirmative," Grinner said. "Whatever you need, Ballard, it's already gonna cost you double, 'cause it's you."

"Oh come on, really?"

"After how you did Magdalena dirty, you're lucky I'm taking your calls at all," Grinner said. "She was the best fucking thing to happen to your miserable ass, and you pissed it away."

"Look, that was almost a year ago," I said. "Give it a fucking rest."

"Double," he said.

"Well lucky for me I got the money to handle that," I said.

"Yeah, this week," Grinner said. "You still owe me thirty K for debugging that shitty Herobrine thing that was killing people. I got mouths to feed, motherfucker."

"Calm your tits, Grinner," I said. "Add the thirty thou to my bill for this one; I'll wire you the money when we land. Okay?"

"What idiot is giving you his ATM card?" Grinner asked.

"The idiot I want you to dig up everything on," I said. "His name is Theodore Ankou."

"The fucking alien mobster!" Grinner said. "Have you lost your fucking mind, dealing with those ass-probing motherfuckers?"

"He's not an alien," I said, "he's Fae . . . okay, well, they're kind of like aliens . . . but not exactly." Grinner made a whistling flying saucer sound, like something from a fifties monster movie. "Knock that shit off," I said. "I want everything on him, his business, and his family, especially his daughter, Caern. She's been in the wind since 2009."

"Oh, don't make it too easy for me, Ballard," Grinner said. "Okay, fifty large plus the thirty you owe me. Hell, let's just go ahead and round that to a nice, even hundred thousand for that 'tits' comment . . . and how you walked out on Magdalena." I sighed.

"You're a fucking brigand," I said. "If I didn't know it was going to the baby and Christine, I'd tell you to piss off. How is your beautiful wife and little Laytham?"

"In your fucking dreams." Grinner chuckled. "Little Turing is doing great. His mom is still a fucking smoking-hot sexy kitten MILF, and for some god-awful reason she still loves the hell out of you, hillbilly."

I heard Christine shout out in the background, "Hi, Ballard! Thanks for paying for Turing's college!" I laughed.

"Better than you deserve, asshole," I said to Grinner, "both of them."

"Got that right," he said. "Okay, man, I'll get on it once I see the digits in my account. Try not to have a close encounter with a rectal probe if you can help it."

"Thanks, Mom," I said, "I'll send pictures. Talk soon."

"Out," Grinner said, and I was listening to flat, dead silence over the line. I called one of Ankou's people on the number he had given me and arranged for the money to be wired to Grinner's dummy account du jour. I asked one of the nice attendants for another drink and snuggled up across the aisle from my new bestest buddy. A few benzos from the bottle in my pocket, some more scotch, and I tiptoed past the sandman into the realm of drugged, dreamless sleep.

We landed at the Athens International Airport. It was pretty much like every other major airport I'd ever been through, a bland cross between a shopping mall and a subway station. It did my heart good to know that the birthplace of western civilization had three frozen yogurt kiosks. From here we'd take a hovercraft over to the island of Spetses, where the super-rich played, while the folks here on the mainland watched their life savings crumble like a temple to Apollo.

I made a quick stop at one of my drops in an airport locker here. I grabbed a few useful odds and ends, some of my clothes, fake IDs, and a fresh burner cell phone. I stashed a hunk of the cash Ankou had given me for a rainy day. Other people had houses, bedrooms, closets. I had dead drops: bus, rail, and plane lockers, and bolt holes. There was a photo of me and August Hyde taped to the door of the locker. We were laughing, sitting in a cafe in Rio. For a second, all the years folded like a paper fan, and I was beside him in that Thule bunker in the Argentinian jungle. His rune-covered Browning Hi-Power blasting away at the rustling things that had once been men, coming out of every shadow. I heard his voice, calm, like a teacher instructing a pupil, which I guess in a way he was: *Grab the brain slides, Laytham! Get the brain and go for the stairs, boy!* I pulled the picture off the locker door, crumpled it, and dropped it in a trash can alongside greasy Sbarro boxes and discarded luggage claim tickets. I wish memories were as disposable.

There was a bulletproof luxury SUV waiting for us on the tarmac. As we drove into airport traffic, Burris and the driver spoke softly in Greek. The knight leaned back to talk to me from the front passenger seat.

"They told me they have a boat waiting to take us over to the island. The Ankou family has a house overlooking a private beach on the northwest side of Spetses. We'll be staying there. Caern's apartment is in the city on the eastern side of the island."

"Yeah, I caught some of that," I said. "My Greek's not as good as my Latin, but it will do. Kind of weird for a thirteen-year-old kid to have her own place in the middle of party central, ain't it?"

"Not if you're this kind of rich," Burris said. "Caern was a very independent kid after her mother passed away."

"What was your read on her?" I asked. The driver had turned onto a congested central street. Thousands of protesters were clogging the entrance to a large skyscraper that was corporate headquarters to one of the nation's banks. The protest had spilled out onto the street, and cars were honking, drivers shouting and gesturing angrily as traffic had slowed to a crawl through the chanting, equally angry mob. Our driver swore under his breath.

"My opinions are not going to help you find her," Burris said.

I shook my head and looked out the window. Our dark little air-conditioned cocoon creeped along through a screaming, shouting sea of angry faces. First it was unemployment and corruption, then the austerity shell game, then the referendum vote, then the run on the banks, insane inflation, and then the fight over immigration of refugees. Through the tinted windows, I saw a kid probably in his early twenties. He was wearing no shirt and had tattoos of Greek football team logos on his chest, arms, and back. He was pounding his fists against the bulletproof glass. His eyes were glazed over, stupid with raw hatred. I doubted he had a clue what he was protesting, but it was an excuse to meet girls, get wasted, and wreck stuff—oh and blame somebody else—an ideal little vacation from the shit pile of his own life. It's sad how little history or people really change. We just keep doing laps. A thought occurred to me as we pulled free of the mob and the SUV accelerated again. All those times I saved the world with some snappy spell or daring last-second plan, I was saving it for a whole bunch of bullet-headed, mouth-breathing goons. No, that's not true. I was saving it for me, to save my handsome ass. It may be a fucking circus on fire, but at least I got good seats.

The "boat" waiting for us at a private slip was a forty-eight-foot Cantius speedboat. Like everything else the Ankous owned, it was expensive and high quality, just like yours truly, except he was only renting me.

We headed out to sea, and I had the onboard hostess fix me up with a cold Corona. I unbuttoned and took off my shirt, tossed it in a deck chair, lit up a cigarette, and felt the sun, the cool sea air, and the spray kiss me.

"I'm sorry we didn't think to drag the couch out here on the deck or run the Stars and Bars up the flagpole to make you feel a little more at home," Burris said. I looked over to the knight. He was standing with his arms crossed, scanning the horizon, his eyes hidden behind his Maybach sunglasses. He looked like a cross between Othello and the Terminator.

"Expecting an assassination attempt from seagulls?" I asked, burping a little from the beer.

"The Ankous have political enemies and business rivals," he said. "I have no doubt they all know about you since we scooped you up. They may decide to grab you to find out what you're up to, see if it gives them a tactical advantage, or they may decide just to kill you to derail whatever it is they think you are doing for the family. So relax, get drunk, and enjoy the ride. One of us has to do his job."

"I bet you are a fucking madman at the company Christmas party," I said, and turned back to enjoy the breathtaking view. We were crossing the blue, glass waters of the Saronic Gulf.

Four beers, half a pack of cigarettes, and plenty more stimulating conversation from Burris later, we were slowing and making our way along the Gulf of Argolis, toward Baltiza Bay on the eastern side of Spetses. Off to our starboard was a yacht so big it made our forty-eight-footer look like a dinghy. The ship was gliding along at a leisurely pace with hundreds of beautiful partygoers hanging off its rails, drinking, drugging, and dancing on its decks. The sound system on the yacht was throbbing as it blasted "BonBon" by Era Istrefi across the bay, probably killing aquatic life with the decibel level.

To port you could see the labyrinth of the city the isle was named for. Whitewashed, boxlike buildings were stacked side by side and seemingly atop one another, rising up the hillside of the island. Tiny terraces and colorful, shuttered windows breaking the almost-geometric solidarity of the cozy homes and shops. I could see tourists and locals streaming through the crowded, winding, cobblestone streets tucked tightly between the structures. At the water's edge were marinas with boats of every size and shape imaginable, bobbing gently in the turquoise waters, as well as seaside cafes with patrons enjoying seafood and beers under large, shady umbrellas. If thirteen-year-old me had been here, I'm pretty damn sure I'd never have left. It made me try to connect a little with Caern. Did she leave all this willingly, or was she taken? And if it was of her own free will, what had driven her out of paradise?

Our boat took us up the eastern face of the island, past crowded public beaches and pristine private ones. The sand on the shoreline gleamed like powdered gold, kissing water of liquid sapphire. I think I understood why Ankou had a home here. This place was as close to any I'd ever seen on Earth to match the otherworldly beauty of Faerie.

We went around the northern tip of the island, and I saw villas dotting the sides of the hilly island, nestled among the myrtle and pine trees. I saw groves of lemon and fig trees on terraces of land along the hills. Eventually we docked at the private pier that also housed a small and powerful-looking cigarette boat and a hundred-and-thirty-foot yacht. Men who looked more like soldiers than dock hands caught the mooring lines and helped tether us to our section of the pier. There was a winding set of wooden stairs that led up the hills to the rear of the beach house. Burris and I carried our bags up the winding staircase. Servants offered to carry everything up, but we both tacitly refused.

The house was a luxury fortress with a stunning view of the sea and the mountain the house rested at the top of. We were shown to our rooms and told that dinner would be ready around six. I dropped my single, battered, old canvas bag with the zipper that stuck some-times on the floor next to the bed. The bag was the color of sand and covered with poorly drawn runes and the logos of old bands like the Stones, Kiss, the DKs, and Lynyrd Skynyrd, all in black Sharpie. It was my bag of magic tricks, and it was the oldest thing I owned. It had left the trailer park in my hand when I was the same age Caern had been when she had disappeared, thirteen. Jesus, that was a long time ago. A lot of miles since then. Most folks who knew me well enough for me to give a shit about their opinion would say I was still in all the essential ways a thirteen-year-old. Sad, but pretty much true.

I figured one of the grotesque goodies in my bag would help me narrow down the search for the girl. First, I needed to check out her place, which Burris had assured me had not been altered in any significant way since her vanishing act in 2009. I unlaced and kicked off my steel-toed boots, fell back onto the bed, and was asleep in short order. I awoke with the knight standing over me, jabbing a finger into my chest.

"Dinner," Burris said and walked through the open door. He didn't bother to close it. I rolled off the bed, shut the door, and grabbed a quick shower. I finally changed out of the Houston clothes and traded them for a *Rick and Morty* T-shirt and jeans. As I sat at the edge of the bed and slipped on my boots, I thought about the problem of ditching my asshole chaperone. I retrieved a little something from my bag and headed down to eat.

The spread was as top shelf as everything else had been. I pushed some food around my plate and had a few glasses of wine. Burris ate sparingly and narrowed his eyes at me across the table. "Yes, I'll eat my veggies," I said, draining my glass of wine. The knight sighed and sipped his beer.

"You're a waste of time and money," he said. "Fortunately, Ankou has plenty of both."

"Never 'Mr. Ankou,'" I said, pouring myself another glass, "it's always just 'Ankou.' Why don't you kiss your boss's ass like all of his other drones, Burris? Burris . . . what the hell is your first name, anyway? Did they give you one when they grew you in the lab?"

The edges of Burris's lips curled a millimeter. "Vigil," he said. A hint of northern street accent slipped out as he continued. "My grandma told me my mamma named me that because it was a long, hard labor, and Mom and I both kept vigil. I'm loyal to my house. I'm willing to take a bullet for Ankou; I'm not here to prop up his ego. That's enough."

It was my turn to give him a smile. "Maybe you're not as big a tool as I thought you were, Vigil." I palmed the small bottle that I had taken out of my bag from my jeans pocket, hiding it with my linen napkin. I allowed my hand to pass over my wineglass, and a few drops of liquid from the bottle fell into my wine as I raised the napkin to dab my lips. I raised my glass with my free hand to toast as I put the napkin and bottle back under the table. Vigil raised his bottle of Mythos beer, in kind. *"Dulcis Bacchus sanguinem et sanguinem, Gaia, sensus vestri: ut mulgeatis mea implebitur. Hoc donum tibi."*

"Odd toast," Vigil said. "Sounds like a spell." I shrugged and drained my glass.

"It was on a little bottle I saw once. It was supposed to hold some of the god Bacchus's blood. I always thought it was like a prayer to the Greek god of partying."

"Well, no partying tonight," Burris said. "Tomorrow morning, we drive into the city and go over Caern's apartment. I want you straight. Time to start earning your pay, Ballard."

"I need to go over the place alone," I said, refilling my glass and gesturing to one of the servants with the empty wine bottle. The guy took the bottle, nodded, and went around the corner. "I'm good at doing this, but I have my own way of going about it, and my way is a solo act."

"It isn't now," Vigil said. I started to reply. Instead I drained another glass of wine.

"Whatever you say, partner," I said as they returned with another bottle of wine.

We retreated to the den. I made a play for the remote, but Burris snagged it first. I figured I was doomed to an evening of watching ESPN, but to my surprise, he stopped when he spotted *Reservoir Dogs*. "I love this movie," he said, stretching out on one of the couches with his second beer. "I've seen it a hundred times."

"Same," I said. An odd question tumbled into my brain. "So who do you think is the good guy in this? The cop or the thief?"

"Both," Vigil said, "and neither. They both have a code and they both honored it. Sometimes a code is all you have to keep you human, keep you standing upright and breathing."

"And sometimes it gets your ass killed," I said. A weariness settled over me and I realized how many oaths I had broken, how many promises I had failed or threw away on an altar of selfishness and self-aggrandizement. I knew who I was dealing with now and it made me a little sadder. I had hoped Vigil was an idiot, a drone. He wasn't.

Vigil glanced over to me on my couch, nodded at the screen where Harvey Keitel was being a total badass. "It ain't no *Pulp Fiction,* but this cool?"

"Yeah," I said, "cool."

I downed two more bottles of wine, a bottle of Sans Rival ouzo, and a few beers. Vigil stopped watching the flat screen, which was the size of a small movie theater screen. He looked at me, shook his head, and finally excused himself for the night.

"You're going to hate me in the morning," Burris said as he climbed the stairs.

"I already do," I said, waving as he disappeared upstairs. After he was gone, I waited about twenty minutes and then whispered the final trigger of the spell that was spun with the drops of god's blood. *"Hoc donum tibi."* Before the last syllable had faded, the working took, and I was sober, stone cold sober, and poor Burris upstairs had just inherited my drunken buzz I had spent all evening building for him.

I wandered over to the villa's garage and was not disappointed. Top-fucking-shelf. I decided to pass on the Lamborghini and the Bugatti parked there, opting to take one of the motorcycles, a sleek, black NCR M16 Streetfighter. I eschewed the helmet—yeah, yeah, I know, but we've already established that I'm an idiot—tying my hair back and out of my eyes. The instrument panel included a hands-free cell phone, GPS, and a compact but powerful-looking sound system. I wondered which button fired the phasers. This thing cost a hell of a lot of money, and it was a far, far cry from the old Suzuki dirt bikes I used to ride and race when I was a kid.

I pushed the ignition, kicking the bike in the guts. It snarled back at me. I snapped on the headlight, fiddled with the satellite radio until music spilled out of the speakers, and spun out of the garage into the darkness. I followed a bumpy private road for about a quarter of a mile. It finally connected to a main road with a stunning view of the island and the sea below. I accelerated the Streetfighter and felt the wind on my face, the dance of gravity and velocity pulling me toward oblivion or balance, life or death, when I took my first curve. Fuck, yes. I finally felt free and myself for the first time in days.

I had gotten Caern's apartment's address from Burris while we had watched TV, and I headed northeast, back toward the city on the other side of the island. I was going to enjoy the solitude on the way there. A single supernova headlight flashed behind me. So much for solitude. Another bike broke free of the wilderness and came off the same private road I had been on.

"You fucking kidding me?" I muttered. The satellite radio was playing Kanye's "Stronger." I accelerated and took another turn. The bike's headlight vanished from view only to reappear a second later as the driver took the curve fast trying to catch up. "Okay, asshole, I hope your insurance is paid up."

There was a straightaway, and I twisted the accelerator on the quarter-of-a-million-dollar bike. The speedometer was climbing closer to ninety. The bike was light as hell, and it had a fucking two-hundred-horsepower rocket attached to it. The headlight of the other bike diminished. I slowed to take a steep turn that dipped downward as the road hugged the mountain's edge. The turn came out into a short straightaway and then another turn, opposite of the last. The head-lights were back by the time I cleared the second curb and were clos-ing. Son of a bitch. The driver had taken those turns at close to full speed to catch up.

I gunned the accelerator, and the bike almost popped a wheelie. I was heading into another tight curve. I dipped the bike low to cor-rect for the speed going through the turn. The grindstone of the road flashed inches from my face for a few seconds. Then I was up, loose rocks from the edge of the turn flying as I came out into another straight strip of highway and kept flooring it. The other bike took the turn, I glanced back to see the driver's leg flash out in a spray of gravel, and then the rider was clear and back on my ass. I was pretty sure now that the other bike was the fucking red Ducati from the garage, and that made it pretty clear who the rider was. How the hell he had shaken off the spell, I had no clue.

There was the angry bleat of a car horn, and I snapped my head forward to see a convertible Jag barreling down on me. I had drifted over to the other side of the road; at this speed a split second was too long to get distracted. I swerved at 120 miles an hour and accelerated instead of braking, even though my instincts were screaming to stop. I was about six inches from the car's paint. I managed to keep it on the road. The guy driving the car flipped me off and screamed at me; his voice was lost in the tunnel of velocity.

Another turn coming up at 140. I could feel the Streetfighter bucking like a titanium bronco, fighting against the contact patches on the tires, wanting to leave the pavement, to fly into the sky. As fucked up as this was getting, I felt the same way. I had wished a few minutes ago that I had a drink or two in me to loosen me up, but now I was high on a much stronger drug. I was going to lose this crazy motherfucker, and there was only one way to beat a crazy motherfucker. I looked over at the coast below. The waxing moon was rising, not full, but so large and bright it felt like you could touch it. The sea, the stars, the wind, the speed—I drank it all in, felt it burn in me like no pill or powder, no drink or smoke ever could. The turn was coming up, wide and sharp, dipping lower toward the rocks and sea far below.

I hit the turn at 165, a literal half-second to scan the road below and ahead, then I snapped off the headlight, plunging me into darkness. There was no thinking, no feeling. All that existed was the moment. It was, I was. Act, no time for consequence, no time for weighing choices. My leg shot out from the left peg, and my steel-toed boot caught the guardrail solidly as I used it as a guide. I kicked off the rail and then counter-steered, turning the handlebars left instead of the instinctual right. Everything was rhythm now, the blink of an eye, a single thud of a heartbeat, the throaty growl of the engine. I straightened out the front wheel. There was the dizzy, sick feeling of my stomach settling in my balls as the road vanished under me with a hiss of gravel, the bike going airborne, finally getting its wish to leave the road behind, but only for a second. Impact, I turned into where the road should be. I was still up and still going into the yawning darkness. I had the accelerator jammed forward, trying to make as much time and get as much distance while he was, literally, in the dark as to where I was. I had no idea how much straightaway until the next turn. Time to Obi-Wan it. My third eye, my Ajna, opened wide, and I was driving on pure mystical radar, which contrary to the movies and TV only gets you so far, especially when you're not calm, not ever at fucking peace, and have adrenaline tearing its way through your blood like a freight train.

Far behind me was the rev of the Ducati's powerful engine as it cleared the curve jump too. I saw the bouncing headlight, heard the distant scream of the tires for traction and a whoosh of scattering gravel. He had almost gone over. The man was fucking deranged, clearly. I sensed the straight was about to give to another curve, another drop. I hit the turn, tires and suspension angry, jerking, and wailing in protest at the speed and the angle as I launched off into space again. I didn't need mystic instincts to know I had pushed this game as far as I could.

I snapped on the headlight and saw I was plummeting toward the end of a long straightaway I had just bypassed by going airborne. The bike landed, and I stood up on the pegs as it hit, then dropped and fought to keep it on the road going into the beginning of a new yawning curve, headed to the bottom of the mountain.

My speed had decreased considerably, but I now had a good half a mile or more of curves and road between me and Vigil. I accelerated out of the turn and along the straight line of the coast that was leading me toward the city. I checked behind me several times, but I seemed to have lost the knight. I gave the road behind me the finger, and kept on keeping on.

The streets of Spetses were still crowded with tourists, mostly young, mostly beautiful, and all loaded in more ways than one. This whole place was a playground for the ultra-rich, people who had no clue what it did to a human being to have to sweat the rent or decide if they should buy food for their kid or buy the meds the kid needed. I couldn't help feeling like an intruder on this island as I glided the Streetfighter through the traffic. Most of these folks' biggest concern tonight was which restaurant or club to blow their money in. I didn't belong here, I never had.

I know my own poorer-than-fucking-dirt background informs my opinion on all that. I had known plenty of rich folks sadder than fuck for real, and good reasons, but there was no denying sad and rich beat the shit out of sad and poor any day of the week and twice on Sunday.

I found Caern's neighborhood and parked the bike across the street. Her building was whitewashed with a trim of bright blue. There was a tasteful, wrought-iron fence around the building's grounds that included a courtyard with a few plastic beach chairs and a little round table under a stand of palm trees. There was an electronic lock next to the gate that required a tenant's key card to open. I placed my hand on the box and whispered as I let the charge of power flow from my Manipura chakra, *"Apertus."* The gate clicked open, and I walked through.

Caern's condo was up a short flight of stairs. She had the left side of the building, and someone else lived on the right. The first floor was about a half-dozen smaller apartments. The ward hit me in the face walking down the hall to her door. Fae magic was formidable, but it was so fucking ostentatious, it practically shouted at you. It was like they had to bling the hell out of even the simplest lock and alarm spell. I felt around the edges of the working and then snipped and silenced it with a few words.

I stepped inside Caern Ankou's life and closed the door behind me. The air conditioner hummed, set to keep the place comfortable for no one. The place looked more like a hotel than a teenage girl's home. Nice, cream-colored furniture, muted tones, a rug with no stains from Cheetos crunched underfoot or spilled Cokes. I frowned and walked the spacious rooms. They were silent to me, silent to even my Ajna chakra. There were no traces of any significant emotional imprints on this place. Caern may have slept here, eaten here, watched TV here, but she hadn't *lived* here, in any meaningful way. I found that very sad. Children, teens, usually smear the air with angry, brilliant colors of emotion and experience. I expected a teenage fairy princess to leave me a trail like a bunch of My Little Ponies had puked all over the place, fucking rainbows and glitter. But this . . . it told me a lot about her by how little it told.

I sat down at the edge of her perfectly made bed. I wanted to smoke, but it felt like I was in a museum or something. I'm sure Sir Vigil would be giving me that look, the one I had already seen enough to call it "that look," if I lit up an American Spirit in here.

There was not even a faint charge of sexual energy from the bed, the bedroom. If she'd had raging hormones like most teenagers, she kept them in check like a Trappist monk, at least at this address. Some of this began to make some sense. Daddy set all this up and obliviously paid the bills here. This would be the last place on Earth you'd get any sense of the real girl. I started opening cabinets and rummaging through things as a last, feeble attempt to find anything I could use, or track. I'm sure every gumshoe and private dick before me had done the same.

I found a half-full bag of cat litter, two empty bowls, and some cat toys under the cabinet beneath the kitchen sink, next to the household cleaners, folded paper grocery bags, and packages of yellow rubber gloves. I knelt down and found a few cans of wet cat food specially formulated for kittens near the back of the cabinet. During my rummaging and scrounging, I found something else. It was faint, faded from age and distance, I'd imagine, but there was a trace of some of Caern's Anahata, her heart energy, here. The energy was drifting lazily around the toys, appearing like tiny green fizzy soda bubbles to my perception. She had loved this cat, loved it so much that it still showed years later.

A bit more hunting, and I was able to find a tuft of gray cat fur in the cabinet. I could work with this. I found plastic sandwich bags neatly stored in one of the kitchen drawers, and I carefully placed the fur in one bag and a few of the frayed feathers from the end of a much-abused cat toy in another bag. I sealed them, folded them up, and tucked them in the pocket of my jeans. I also took a small, pink, gnawed-on rubber mouse. I squeezed it, and it squeaked. I stuffed the mouse toy in my pocket too.

I left everything as I had found it, and then switched off the lights on my way out. Waiting for me across the street from the condo, leaning against the red Ducati Desmosedici, was Burris, with his arms crossed, giving me "that look." He stood as I crossed the street toward him and the Streetfighter.

"You know, young man, speed kills," I said. "You're lucky to be ali—" I didn't get to finish my smart-ass remark. Vigil drove a jab into my jaw and followed it up a beat later with a half-knuckle strike to my solar plexus. I fell back onto my ass and couldn't breathe and sure as hell couldn't incant any snappy magical Latin retorts. He took a step toward me and as fluidly as water runs, drew a handgun from a holster located at the small of his back and thumbed back the trigger with a click.

"You ever try that shit again," he said calmly, "and I will put a bullet in your fucking kneecap. You don't need a kneecap to be a drunken piece of shit has-been, still pretending to be a legend."

"Fair . . . enough," I wheezed, as my breath came back to me. He slowly lowered the hammer on the gun, holstered it with one hand, and offered me the other hand to help me up off the street. I took it, and as I rose, and he pulled, I drove a nasty sucker-punch into the side of his face. He staggered back, his lip split, just like mine. We were matchies now.

"That's fair enough too," I said and spit some blood into the cleanest gutter I had ever seen. I pulled my forearms in and kept them up, like my old boxing coach had screamed at me about a million times, and shuffled back. Vigil rubbed his jaw and lip, examined his blood, rubbed it between his fingers and thumb, and then looked up at me.

"You throw a pretty good hook for an old, white drunk," he said. "What finishing school of the mystic arts you learn that at?"

"Million Dollar Boxing Gym," I said, "Hull Street, Richmond, Virginia. The Hogwarts Pugilism Society wouldn't take me 'cause the sorting hat said I was with House Huffle-Puff-Puff-Pass. You?"

"Over-the-Rhine, Cincinnati," he said. "Finals were a bitch."

A Greek cop on a Vespa slowed and looked at the two of us facing off on the sidewalk. He was a cop for the tourists, in a short-sleeved, light blue, button-down shirt with epaulets, dark blue pants, and a cap. For the genteel folk of Spetses, he seemed to have left his riot gear and truncheon at home tonight. He looked more like an airline pilot than a cop, and he was smiling, which was weird. He flashed the beam of a Maglite over us and asked something in Greek. I got the gist of it, which was the polite these-guys-may-be-richer-than-Bill-Gates version of "What the fuck are you two skells doing here?"

Vigil did the talking, keeping his gun out of view. He offered his identification to the cop, and I heard the name "Ankou" tossed out liberally. The cop nodded, still smiling and seeming to apologize. He waved to us and putt-putted away on his little scooter.

"This shit is just surreal," I said. Vigil, standing next to me, nodded.

"You never get used to it if you didn't grow up in it," he said. "Different world for these people, different cops, different laws. We'll always be tourists, hired help."

"You want to get something to eat?" I asked.

"Cool," Vigil said. "Chasing a moron on a two-hundred-thousand-dollar bike down a hill without a perfectly good road, in the dark, always makes me hungry." We both began to climb onto our bikes. Vigil picked up his helmet and adjusted its straps. "I wasn't fooling about the kneecap," he said.

"Yeah," I said, "I kinda got that. How the hell did you shake off the working like that?"

"Oh, I felt it," he said, "but it didn't take. I'm half Fae, on my pop's side, whoever the fuck he was. A lot of magic just doesn't stick to me too well. Comes in handy when dealing with low-life, sucker-punching wizard types."

"You're an Elf," I said. Vigil paused from pulling his helmet over his head and locked eyes with me. He knew that I knew what being an Elf meant in his world.

"You have a problem with that," he said. It wasn't a question, it was a challenge.

"Nah," I said. "Mind if I call you 'Dobby'?"

"Mind if I beat all the red out of your neck?" His bike roared to life.

"I'll take that as a no," I said and started the Streetfighter up. We pulled away from the curb in search of burgers and beers.

FIVE

I woke up around ten and prepared everything I needed for the ritual, pulling items from my old canvas bag. Vigil was up already, of course, out on the deck overlooking the fantastic view of the sea. He was doing tai chi in nothing but a pair of old, torn sweat-pants. He paused after a moment when he sensed me watching him.

"I'm going to start the working," I said. "So leave me the fuck alone."

"This is already turning into a good day," he said and turned back to the ocean. "Remember, kneecap." He settled into his form again, and I flipped him off and walked back inside.

I found an exercise room with a treadmill, some free weights, a rack with big exercise balls, and a wall of mirrors. It was perfect for what I needed. I dropped all the goodies I'd need on the floor, moved the equipment to a far corner of the room, shut the door, and locked it.

I set up a small circle of squat, partially melted silver candles in front of the wall of mirrors. At the center of the circle, I placed a small, ancient, and weathered statue of a cat, made of onyx and gold. I drew a chalk circle on the industrial carpet exactly three feet south from the circle of candles. I drew symbols above the circle for the opening of the *Ma'at,* and below the circle was the hieroglyphic name

of the being I was entreating. I placed the tuft of cat fur, the feathers
from the cat toy, and the small rubber mouse in the smaller circle, and
then I lit the candles of the larger circle. I turned off the fluorescent
overhead lights. The room was dark except for the light from the candles, reflected, jumping, in the mirrored wall.

I sat cross-legged exactly seven feet away from the circle of candles
and four feet from the chalk circle. I spent a few moments clearing
my mind and regulating my breathing. I aligned my energies and
felt the silence and shadow of the room begin to congeal. Time stut-
tered. Silently, I began the prayers, venerable and precise, filled with
formula and geometry that defined the undefinable, named it, gave
shape and dimension where none existed, called out to something
primordial in the deepest recesses of the endless wheel of the *Ma'at*.

الحكمة كما ليلة ،
الصمت كما ليلة ،
حارس الأسرار ،
العارف القلوب ،
أم ل أعنف موجة من قلوب ،
اللحاء ، كين للقطط ،
ساق معي الآن ،
مطاردة معي الآن ،
يؤدي بي إلى بلدي فريسة ،
ل مجدك ،
ل مجدك ،
تشغيل يلة معي.
قادني الى المجد.

The prayer was a silent song in my mind; I continued it and hoped
one of the most capricious of goddesses would oblige me with her
wisdom.

It took a while, I knew it would, but I began to feel her silent approach through the tangled forest of the mind. I opened my eyes and
saw in the reflection of the mirrored wall a shadow, deeper than the

darkness of the room, pad gracefully toward the circle of candles. Her eyes were blazing amber, alien, and devoid of any emotion or motive I would ever understand. She regarded the ritual and me through the reflection, searching for any reason, any flaw to allow her to pounce and devour me. Luckily for me, she found none.

The Mother of Cats didn't deign to speak in human tongue; it was too demeaning for her. She snatched the thoughts from my head as easily as flashing out a paw to catch a mouse. She sifted my thoughts like streams of flowing sand and considered my request and my offerings. After a moment, the shadow with eyes of amber fire shifted, seeming to silently spill over to my side of the mirror. It devoured everything in the small chalk circle, and then, as it retreated to the other side of the mirror, it snuffed the ring of candles out. The room fell to darkness. I felt the goddess's presence striding away, tail swishing. I heard two squeaks of the rubber mouse. This window to the *Ma'at* closed and she was gone.

I stood, switched on the harsh overhead lights, and blinked. The chalk circle was empty save for a tiny silver bell, like you might find on a cat's collar. I picked it up and began to hear a tiny jingle in my mind. As I walked toward the door to the room, the frequency of the jingle increased. She had accepted my offerings and given me what I had asked for.

I grabbed a shower, changed into black, button-down jeans and boots. I walked past Vigil's room and heard his shower going as well. No sense in interrupting. I told one of the house servants downstairs to tell him where I was going before I left. I had a spare kneecap.

I decided to take the bright blue Lamborghini Aventador today. It was a convertible, of course. Halfway down the mountain toward the city, the little bell's silvery tinkle in my head was getting faster and faster. I realized I was really hungry, having skipped breakfast to amuse a cat goddess. The car's stereo was playing "Endless Sleeper" by the Raveonettes, loud.

I had the buzz that came from digging up a strong lead, being back on the hunt, one step closer to getting the answer. People have asked me my whole life why the fuck I get mixed up in shit like this. The simple answer is that it distracts me from my own sorry train wreck. Getting up in other people's business keeps me occupied and out of my own damn skull. So, no noble aspirations here. I'm no hero—far the fuck from it. Just good old-fashioned self-interest. I keep hoping I'll run into some sorry son of a bitch one day more fucked up than me, or at least as badass, to boost my obviously flagging self-esteem and feed my passive-aggressive death wish. To date, no credible challengers.

It took a little over an hour of Tinker Bell in my skull to narrow the search once I hit the city. The ever-increasing ringing led me to a small cluster of waterside apartments and finally to the door of one on the third floor. These places were not as nice, nor as expensive and exclusive as where Caern had lived. The neighborhood and the dwellings made me figure its tenants were mostly townies, the locals who did all the real work around here, to keep the idle rich, well, idle.

No magic spells or locks on the door to apartment 3E. It opened easily enough with a simple working, and I was in. I snapped on the lights and saw, as well as felt, that this was a real home, a place someone had invested some of the energy of living into.

Clothes were scattered over several pieces of furniture. There was an abandoned ring of jeans with panties coiled inside them about three feet from the door, like someone had come home from a rough day and shucked off their clothes right there. Takeout food boxes and cartons littered the coffee table beside a plastic, transparent, rainbow-colored bong; a baggie with weed; and about a dozen empty, or half-empty, diet soda and beer cans. Wandering the small, four-room apartment, there were emotions—love, excitement, sadness, anger, desire, self-doubt—splashed about the air like someone had opened big cans of bright paint and spattered them about randomly.

There was an insistent yowl, and a little gray-and-white cat padded out from the debris. Her paws were much bigger than the rest of her. Her eyes were the color of a stormy sky. She looked at me, and I looked at her. The bell in my skull silenced. This was the cat that had been in Caern's condo. I knelt down to pet her, and she bolted back to her hiding place. I had a way with women.

For a second, I had thought it was going to be this easy, that Caern had changed her name and had been living the normal life of a twentysomething within spitting distance of her old life, but checking through the piles of mail stacked up on the small table by the door dissuaded me of that premise. This girl, Dree Elias, had bills and was behind on several. She had a job and benefits statements from her employer, including several past-due notices on a loan against her 401(k). These kinds of things were chum to any serious hacker or investigator, the kind of bread crumbs that they could track from life A to life B. If Dree Elias had been Caern Ankou, I would never have been summoned by her dad.

A few pictures were framed about the place—most people her age had ditched the notion of paper photos for digital memories. Most of the pictures were family: Mom, Dad, and maybe Grandma. A few of a pretty girl about the right age for either Dree or Caern with brown hair and green eyes, snuggling the cat that had greeted me. One pic of the same girl with maybe a boyfriend on the white sand of one of the beaches.

I was figuring Dree as a friend of Caern's, maybe, or maybe she had picked up Caern's cat at a shelter, or she was just an acquaintance that took the cat in. Doubtful. This skittish little furball was loved. That love was the only connecting tissue between my lost princess and this girl. That didn't feel like a coincidence. From the bathroom, I removed a clump of hair from a hairbrush and tucked it away in case I needed it.

From the mail and an ID badge with a lanyard hung on a key hook near the door, I was able to get the address of where Dree worked, at the local branch of Alpha Bank, one of the massive European banking corporations. I opened a tin of cat food and left it by the cat's bowls. She was immediately out again and noisily letting me know she wanted the food. I gave her a quick rub, which she allowed, because she was already devouring the food from the can. I locked the door on my way out.

The Spetses island branch of Alpha Bank was a two-story build-ing that blended well with the quaint cafes and shops it was nestled alongside in the cove of Ntapia Beach. I found a small place a few doors down and had some fresh seafood and several frosted mugs of beer at a table under an awning, looking out over the waters. I worked on a quick arts-and-crafts project with my linen napkin and Dree's hair from her brush. When it was done, I pocketed it and finished my beer before strolling over to the bank.

I walked into the cool, shaded lobby and saw the girl from the photographs and the ID, Dree, with her long, brown hair pulled back in a ponytail. She was dressed in a cream blouse and dark blue pants. She had a lanyard about her neck, like the spare she had at home. Dree gave me a once-over as I walked in, so did the security guard, a balding older gentleman who did not look as good in his trousers as Dree did. She smiled at me, and I returned the favor.

A gray-haired, very tan and fit gentleman who made me reflex-ively think of George Hamilton approached me. He had the faint scent of soap and Royal Eagle cologne. We shook hands, a good solid, "Hey, let's build a relationship where you give me all of your money, and I charge you to use it" kind of handshake. He did a very good job of not seeming weirded-out by how sketchy I looked.

"Good afternoon, sir," he said in slightly accented English. "How can we help you today?"

"Yeah," I said. "I work for Theo Ankou." I handed him one of the cards Vigil had given me a stack of. The card stating that I, under an assumed name, was a consultant for the Arcadia Group, Ankou's um-brella of legit corporations. I waited to see the name sink in behind the banker's eyes. "Mr. Ankou is considering doing some business with your institution, and I wanted to sit down and discuss that with somebody." The smile was in danger of splitting his face in half as it grew past human limits.

"Of course, sir," he said. "If you'll step into my office here . . ."

"That will be fine," I said, as I stopped him at his own door, "but I want to discuss it with her," and pointed to Dree, who was just finishing up with a customer at her desk.

"Oh, I'm afraid Dree isn't an executive accounts supervisor," he said, like everyone would know what the fuck that was, "but I'll be more than happy to see to Mr. Ankou's—"

"Mr. Ankou said I talk to her, or he'll take his business elsewhere," I said. The smile dimmed a bit, but the guy was good, and he was obviously very adept at dealing with the mad requests of rich douchebags. He nodded and gestured toward Dree, who look confused, but also put on her best customer service smile and walked over, heels clicking.

"Dree," the tanned man said, "Mr. . . ."

"Hammett," I said, "Dashiell Hammett," and shook Dree's hand. She smiled, I smiled, management guy smiled. Somewhere, puppies and children smiled. A tear came to my eye.

"Mr. Hammett wants to discuss some new corporate account business with you."

"Certainly, Mr. Hammett," Dree said, shaking my hand and nodding. She glanced at her boss for a second but stayed cool as she did it. She had obviously learned from the master.

"If you need anything or have any questions, please let me know," the manager said. "Please use my office so you can have some privacy." We entered the manager's office. It was all mahogany wood and leather furniture. Dree closed the door and sat behind the moat of a desk. I sat in one of the comfy chairs before it.

"Thanks," I said. "Okay, first things first. I am working for Theodore Ankou, and I'll make sure he parks some of his wealth in your bank and that you get credit for that, Dree, but I need to have a conversation with you, and I need you to be straight with me. I need to know where Caern Ankou is."

Dree's eyes darkened. "Get the fuck out of here," she said.

I slipped my hand into my pocket and clutched the makeshift doll I had fashioned at lunch and focused the energies of my Manipura chakra, my will, stoked them, and then connected to Dree through the sympathetic connection of her hair. I had sensed her slight attraction toward me when I walked in, and I knew from her apartment she was a very sensual person, so I focused her Svadhisthana chakra, her desire. I knew the initial response would be one of arousal and confusion—why the fuck would she be so turned on by some sketchy old bastard here under false pretenses looking for her friend?

"If you insist," I said and stood, headed for the door.

"Wait," she said, visibly flushed. "Don't go. Please sit down." It worked. Score one for Team Manipulative Bastard. "Why are you looking for her? Is it her father? You said you worked for him."

"Yes," I said and eased up a little on her sacral chakra. It would be hard for her to think of much else if I didn't, and I needed her thinking with her brain, not her glands. "He's worried about her, just wants to know she's safe and happy. I'm not here to drag her home if she doesn't want that. Just checking in."

"I don't believe you," she said. "That sure doesn't sound like old Theo to me."

"Did Caern talk a lot about him? He the reason she took off?"

"Pretty much," Dree said. I could tell her head was clearing, and I could see the nagging doubt struggling in her mind. She was questioning why she was telling me anything. I flexed my will and sent the power of it straight into her Svadhisthana again, through the genetic ace up my sleeve I had with her hair. This was bad fucking shit I was doing, and I knew it, and as usual, I kept right on doing it. "He was so controlling after Caern's mom died, afraid she was going to break like a china doll. She really loved her mom. I wish I had gotten a chance to meet her."

"How did you two meet?" I asked. She was relaxing again, fascinated by me and clueless why.

My dad is a career guy with Alpha," she said. "Years ago, he got the job that Mr. Artino"—she nodded toward the tanned owner of the office—"has now, corporate accounts manager. We moved from the mainland to Spetses when I was nine. I met Caern that summer, when she and her dad came from Britain for holiday. When she moved here a few years later, we started hanging out all the time at my family's place."

"Yeah," I said, "her place seemed pretty cold."

"She loved hanging out, sleeping at our place. I never really understood why," she said. "My parents, my brothers and sisters, everyone shouting and screaming all the time. Greek family, we scream 'I love you' at each other. It was crazy."

"It was family," I said, and I felt another sharp sting of connection to Caern and I felt a lot more like a dirty, evil old bastard for doing what I was doing to this girl. I stopped the working. I knew it would fade in a few minutes, quicker if I pushed her. I didn't care. Dree blinked and straightened in her chair. The suspicion began to slip back behind her eyes.

"She gave you her cat," I said. "She loved that cat a lot."

"Artemis," Dree said, "yeah, she's a moody little thing. Caern got her when she was a kitten, after her mom died. Sometimes it seemed like the two of them could actually talk. It was cute. Caern wanted Artemis to have a good home, so she gave her to me before she left. Theo, everyone from her other life, she didn't tell them about me. I was kind of like her safe place, her escape, y'know?"

"I do, very well. Where did she go, Dree?" I asked. "I swear to you, I won't drag her home to Theo, if she's happy and okay," and I meant it. "I swear. I just want to make sure she's all right. You have to be worried about her, unless, of course, you two keep in touch."

Dree shook her head. She looked close to crying. She looked down at the blotter on Mr. Artino's desk, looking for guidance there. She talked to the blotter, not to me. "Nothing for about five years, then I got a letter back in 2014. She was happy then, said she was getting into films. She'd met some people while she was working a waitress job, and they were going to get her into movies." She looked up at me and saw the frown on my face. "Yeah, I thought the same thing, but there was no return address, no phone number, nothing, no way to find her, to get her help. I'd have gone myself, y'know. I didn't even know where to start. I haven't heard anything since.

"She's my sister, in a lot of ways more than my flesh and blood. She was always so . . . alive, even in her sadness it was like she felt, she experienced everything . . . more. That make any kind of sense?" I nodded. "The thought of someone like that getting all that life stolen away, snuffed out . . . it's obscene."

"The world's a jagged place," I said, "especially for people with too little skin and too many nerves." I saw literally hundreds of faces of the dead, some still walking, most long gone. Killed by this world's apathy, its rapacity. Your choices were to weep or get calloused up.

Dree was crying. She held it together, no sobs, no shaking, just a trickle, like raindrops racing to oblivion, sliding down her cheeks. I dismantled my makeshift voodoo doll in my pocket and handed her the cloth napkin to dab her eyes. She took it.

"She said she was in L.A.," Dree said and sniffed. "In America."

"Thank you," I said, standing. "I'll make sure Ankou sets up some large accounts . . ."

"I don't give a damn," Dree said, also standing. She offered me her hand to shake. I took it. Her red eyes locked with mine. "Just do what you promised. If she's okay, leave her alone. If she's in trouble, you get her out of it."

"I will," I said. She didn't let go of my hand.

"Swear it," she said.

"I promise," I said. She released my hand. I opened the door and walked toward the lobby and the front doors.

I stopped to assure Mr. Artino that Dree had closed the deal. He seemed relieved. I wasn't sure if that was because the deal went down or I was leaving. Probably both. I was almost to the door when I heard Dree's heels click, coming toward me. She had an old Polaroid Instamatic photo in her hand. She handed it to me.

"Here, it's the only picture I have of us. She was weird about getting her picture taken."

The photo was taken in a crowd of people. Dree was on the left with a red plastic Solo cup in her hand, her arm around Caern's shoulder. Caern was on the right. She was small, with blond hair, almost platinum, and bright blue eyes. She had her dad's angular features and high cheekbones. Both girls were laughing, frozen in time.

"This is from a Muse concert in Rome we went to back in 2009," Dree said. "We would both have been about thirteen. It was a few months before she left."

"Thank you, Dree."

"Just . . . be sure to tell her Artemis is okay," Dree said, "and that she misses her."

SIX

The club was called Naos, and it looked like a neon fortress in the city's Old Harbor. I had been drinking at a bunch of small bars and pubs after I left Alpha Bank. The pub crawl had led me here. I moved through the dance floor, hundreds of beautiful bodies swaying under a shower of multicolored lights. "How Many Fucks?" by Erika Jayne pumped through the sound system as rays of greens, blues, reds, and golds swept back and forth across the floor, bathing the crowd in time to the music.

I felt a little bit like Death walking through all the laughing, tanned, drunk faces. I slipped into a gap that opened at the bar and waved down a bartender, a young black guy with a Fu Manchu mustache and Afro, wearing a red mesh T-shirt.

"A bottle of the shittiest tequila you got," I said, sliding him a couple hundred euros. "Plastic bottle, can also be used as oven cleaner."

"Gotcha," the kid said, palming the cash.

"And Budweiser, bottles," I added. "Keep them coming. You know, you bear a slight resemblance to Isaac on *The Love Boat*."

"The who on the what, *malaka*?" he said.

I shook my head. "Forget it."

I did four shots of the nasty tequila in rapid succession and then followed them with my first beer. Isaac kept the beers coming.

I watched the dance floor. The DJ, who was wearing a Guy Fawkes mask, and who occasionally lobbed smoke bombs of different colors into the crowd, shifted the music to tyDi's "Fire & Load." I figured this was as good a place as any to repay my debt to the Mother of Cats. The Egyptians' favorite holiday a long time ago was Bubastis, a festival of dancing, singing, and, above all else, boozing in honor of Bastet—or Bast—whichever you prefer, the goddess of dance, joy, music, families, love, and oh, yeah, cats. I had offered her the well-loved squeaky mouse and a night of my life devoted to drunken revelry in her honor, and you know how much I hate to welsh on an obligation. So I drank, and drank, and tried to enjoy the revelry part vicariously through all the happy, shiny people out on the floor.

Magdalena had loved dancing, so much so that it had become a component of many of her workings. The music syncing with her mind, her body. The movements, the sweat shining on her tattoos. I remembered for a moment the taste of her, her lips, her skin. I remembered her voice, husky, like wine and smoke. I could feel her body heaving against mine. She found so much joy in the simple acts of breathing, of letting the universe work itself through her. She was in love with being alive, and I have to admit that it was intoxicating to be around; a little bit of it had even started to rub off on me. She was as giving in her magic as she had been as a lover, as a friend.

Magdalena was submissive by choice. She was passionate about the experience of power exchange, the sensation of giving yourself freely to the will of another. She was strong enough, confident enough in herself that she didn't need to be in control of every little thing. She thrilled at the novelty, the mystery of being part of another.

She told me, when we first met, that she had once been pulled under the influence of a cruel and manipulative dominant, a mage, like us. This woman had nearly devoured all the light in her, nearly made Magdalena her slave in soul as well as body and mind. Magdalena had gotten away from the toxic relationship, running, hiding, until she healed herself. She shared all this with me the night I told her about her potential, her power. I had promised her that night I would be her friend, that I would never take advantage of her or use her. I told her she could trust me. I drained the last of the bottle of tequila and gestured for Isaac to bring me another one.

One evil, mind-fucking bastard had nearly broken her, and then I had taken my best shot at it. I was proud of Magdalena; she didn't stand for my shit. She told me to get the fuck out. I filled my glass again from the new bottle and drained the shot.

"It can't be all that bad, can it?" the woman said to me as she slid up next to me at the bar. "Give me another old-fashioned, please, Terry," she said to the kid I had been calling Isaac all night. As her drink was being made, she turned to look at me. I returned the favor. She was in her thirties, I'd guess, with ringlets of jet hair falling past her bare, tanned shoulders. She had laugh lines and warm, playful brown eyes. She was very fit with a hint of some lovely curves under her red boho dress. She took a slender cigarette from a clutch purse that I'm pretty sure if sold would go a long way to alleviating Greece's financial problems. She put the cigarette to her lips and waited. I let her wait a second while I weighed the pros and cons of moving ahead here. I finally clicked open my old, dented Zippo and lit her cigarette; the reflection of the flame danced in her dark eyes, then I lit my own.

"It's usually never 'all that bad,'" I said, exhaling smoke. "When it is, it's usually too damn late to do much of anything about it anyway." I tipped my beer toward her. "Laytham."

"Kynthia," she said, taking her drink and tipping Terry about three hundred euros. She clinked her glass to my bottle. "I love your accent. Texas?"

"Close," I said. "West Virginia. You ever been to the States, Kynthia?"

"Shopping trips," she said. "New York City, Los Angeles. My husband and I do well." She watched my eyes when she said "husband" and must have been satisfied with whatever she saw or didn't see there. "It doesn't bother you I'm married. Good."

"Any particular reason it should?" I asked and finished my beer.

The music warped into "California Dreaming" by Benny Benassi. I poured another shot.

"You drink like you want to die," she said. "I lived with one of my university professors in Paris. He drank like that. He was a fascinating drunk. I think you will be as well, Laytham. Tell me, do you want to die?"

"Not at the moment," I said. "So where is the hubby tonight? Let me guess . . ."

"On our yacht with . . . what day is it? Thursday? That would be the blonde tonight. Kristos's got one for every day of the week."

"Poor choice on his part," I said.

"We've an arrangement," she said, "which brings me back to you. Do you do anything but drink and brood?"

"I look good," I said, "and I have fun. Oh, and falling down, I'm good at falling down." She laughed politely, but I could have quoted Urdu poetry and I'm pretty sure she would have laughed. I was pretty sure that I was now part of Kynthia and her husband's "arrangement."

"Dancing," Kynthia said. "Do you dance?"

"Why me?" I asked. "All these young, tanned little stud-muffins unce-unce-ing about. Any of them would give their six-pack abs to get up with a woman like you."

"Eager is boring," she said, smoke streaming from her nostrils. "Those bruises, the scars on your knuckles, that split lip—you look like you were just in a fight. You look dangerous; I'd wager you're the most dangerous man in this club."

"You'd win," I said.

"Have you ever killed anyone?" she said, leaning forward and sipping her drink.

"You just lost points, darlin'," I said.

"I'll take that as a yes," she said. "Dance with me." It was an order. I narrowed my gaze, and we locked eyes.

"You can ask prettier than that, a fancy lady like you." I saw a tiny flash of real fear pass behind her eyes. She hid it well.

"Please," she said, a smile playing at the edges of her lips. I crushed out my cigarette and took her hand, leading her toward the dance floor. I hadn't danced since Magdalena. It felt good. The smoke was rainbow-hued clouds drifting, the bass was thunder, and then came the electronic rain falling on the crowd, on the floor, washing away our minds, our sins, sweating out the poisons, and making us all pure and one. Dancing, at its core, is ecstatic ritual, is magic.

When the two of us couldn't anymore, just couldn't, Kynthia and I fell back to the bar. She drank water that cost as much as a swimming pool and smoked, and I bought some water laced with K from a nice young lady selling it covertly at the fringes of the crowd. I chased it with another beer, and more tequila. By the next song, an extended mix of How to Destroy Angels' cover of "Is Your Love Strong Enough?" I was deep in the K-hole, feeling like I was watching my life from a detached, comfortable distance through a warm, soft gauze of pleasure. I drank some more of the water and kissed Kynthia deeply, enjoying the playful wrestling of our tongues, the taste of the nicotine smoke, the soft, yielding of her lips, the salt of her perspiration. It was all so familiar and so alien, so different than with . . .

My last memory of the club was seeing a woman undulating to "Secret" by Oceanlab. She was swinging two glowing poi, one in each hand, and was wearing an oversized mask on her head, à la deadmau5, but this mask was of a cat. She nodded to me, and I gave her the sign of the horns.

A warm, dry wind embraced my sweat-soaked body outside the club. There was a hint of the moisture of the sea, the slight tang of salt on my lips. Was I kissing Magdal . . . Kynthia . . . Kynthia, or was I kissing the sea?

Her driver was taking us to her home, one of her homes. Time was flipping like still images on pages in a book, one after the other, speed giving the illusion of movement to frozen pictures. Through the tinted windows of the car, I watched the lights stream by us, like trails of burning, neon starlight. I watched the people walking the street, in the dregs of the night, morph and stretch, swell and diminish.

I was a fractured mirror, and the light of the world moved through me, twisted and distorted by my flaws, my broken, jagged paths.

I felt Kynthia's hand slide between my legs; it pulled me back out of my broken shell and to the safe place of observing, of feeling nothing, remembering nothing but sensation. I grabbed her by the hair and pulled her to me, almost kissing her, but then looking into her eyes.

"What are you going to do to me?" she whispered, fear and excitement wrestling behind her eyes.

"You don't know a goddamned thing about me," the broken, flawed thing in me said to her. I clutched her hair tighter, and she hissed a little in pain but also in pleasure. "You have fucking everything you could ever want. People over on the mainland are starving, desperate, shooting poison into themselves to ignore the misery of their lives. Begging, waiting for death to end their suffering, and you actually court suffering." She struggled to reach my lips, they were a breath apart. "You're a spoiled, slumming dilettante, playing at pain, aren't you? Answer me!" I growled. Her driver looked back; he looked confused and worried. I watched his eyes melt along with the dripping silver of the rearview mirror as the ketamine burned through my brain.

"Madame?" the driver said. I was trying to figure out how he could speak with no face.

"It's . . . it's all right, Barry," Kynthia said. Her hand was working frantically below, tugging at the zipper of my jeans. "Please raise the partition." Barry did as he was told, and shadowed glass slid between him and us. I saw our distorted faces in the glass; they didn't sync up with our movements. "You don't give a damn about those whining parasites," Kynthia hissed to me; there was some anger darkening her eyes now too. She still struggled to reach my lips, and her hands were pulling me free of my jeans, frantically. "Just like you don't give a damn about anyone but yourself, about what you want, how unfair life has been to you, you poor little criminal. You think you're better than me? You're just like me, except you can't wash the stink of shit and poverty off you. You think that you're some champion of the working class? You use them, just like you use everyone else. You're a parasite, a fraud, a hustling fraud, you fucking peasant."

She saw she got what she wanted from me in her words. I felt cold cruelty settle over me and with it calm control and disciplined desire. This woman's words were a mirror. "I'm glad," I said as I slid my hand under her dress and between her parting thighs, "we understand each other." I pulled her to my lips and she moaned, almost growled, trying to devour me as much as I was trying to encompass her—an ouroboros—consuming each other, fangs biting.

I pulled her onto my lap, still leading her by her hair. She guided me, put me where she wanted me. I felt her heat, her need, envelop me; she arched, and I pulled her down. We both gasped at the union. She bit my shoulder as I pulled her breast free of her dress and teased her nipple with my teeth. There was no thought; there was action and reaction, risk and reward.

Some gray time later, in her big bed, in her lovely, lonely house on this pretty island of make-believe, after many hours of rough games, of playing at master and servant, of passion, pleasure, and pain, we were making love again, slowly, almost sleepily. I looked into Kynthia's eyes, down into the core of her. She was open and raw and vulnerable. She had given me every part of herself, but it had been for the most selfish of reasons. I understood that perfectly. There was no lying between us in this place, and that was a sort of magic too, far rarer than any alchemy or spell.

"Who . . . who do you need me to be?" she asked. "Tell me, who do you want me to be?"

"Magdalena," I said. "Who do you want me to be?"

"Kristos." She said the name like a prayer.

"Close your eyes," I said. I kept mine open.

That was the last time we made love before we both fell asleep. In a half-aware space, I thought I heard her sobbing. I didn't try to reach for her, to hold her. I would have been no comfort at all, worse than no comfort.

I awoke feeling like I had been in another fight. I had scratch marks and bruises all over me. Kynthia was gone. I wandered the empty house, silently, looked at photos on the walls of ghosts in people suits, and left.

I made it back to the villa in the late afternoon. I found Vigil in a ratty Ohio State T-shirt and sweats sitting at the dining table with one of his pistols disassembled in front of him. He was running a metal rod with a small cleaning cloth attached to the end through the gun's barrel. He didn't even look up at me as I walked in.

"Left or right?" he asked absently.

"Between the ears, if you please," I said. "I feel like someone emptied a dirty ashtray into my skull."

"So how was your . . . investigation?" he asked.

"I got something," I said.

"Go see a doctor," he said.

"You're a real card," I said. "We're headed for L.A." Vigil looked up; he seemed a little impressed, but he hid it well.

"Okay," he said. "You can keep the kneecap. I'm not carrying your ass onto the plane."

SEVEN

LAX was a madhouse on greased wheels, and one of the wheels wobbled the wrong way, like a bad shopping cart. People from all over the world landing in, and getting the hell out of, planet L.A. I began to feel the city's energy, its rhythm, again about twenty minutes before final approach, as we began to pass over the outlying colonies and glittering arms of the great beast squatting at the edges of the desert and the sea. It had been a while since I had been here. I hadn't called it home in almost thirty years. When business pulled me back to L.A. I always got out of town quick, before I ran into an old enemy, or worse, an old friend. As the years ground on, it got harder to keep the distinction straight.

Ankou's private jet landed, and we were escorted by more of the Fae crime boss's soldiers, looking like models for the *Vogue Yakuza* spring fashion edition, to a shit-brown, nondescript-looking, late-model Dodge van with a couple of faded bumper stickers in Spanish and an ancient BABY ON BOARD yellow yield sticker on the hatch-back window. It wasn't exactly caviar in the back of a stretch limo, and that seemed weird for Ankou. All of the security detail were on their toes, acting like we were going to get jumped before we got out of the terminal. I looked over to Vigil and saw he had picked up on the vibe as well. He nodded to me and then accelerated a few steps to walk beside the security detail leader, an ex-military-looking fella.

"What's with all the amped security, Sergeant?" Vigil asked. Sarge kept walking, not even pausing to look at Vigil.

"Nothing that need concern you, short-ear. Just keep walking and watch the wizard." Vigil didn't miss a beat. He stepped in front of the still-walking sergeant and drove the heel of his hand hard under his chin. Vigil's other hand held the back of the man's skull, shoving it forward into the strike. The security guy stopped and jerked back from the force of the strike, sputtering. The inside of his mouth was bloody. He blinked. Vigil had hit him so fast, even watching it made you doubt whether it had actually happened. Vigil's hands were back at his side. He looked into Sarge's watering eyes with the same expression as before the exchange: calm, serene.

"You know how to swear like you're one of them, don't you, you blunt-eared little primate? Do you know my title?" Sarge looked down and said nothing. "Answer me, flyspeck. You know that's what they call you—blunt ears—when you're not around, flyspeck? That's all you'll ever be to them; they blink and you're dust. Don't get no grand motherfucking notions that it ain't so."

Sarge was sullen, and I saw the smoldering rage behind his runny eyes. After a moment, he muttered through bloodstained teeth, "Yes, Sir Burris."

"You and your detachment will address me by my title," Vigil said, "or I'll bathe in the watery blood of every single one of you, and Lord Ankou will give less than a damn if I do. We understand each other?"

"Yes, Sir Burris."

"Good, now take us to our fucking ride," Vigil said. And they did, hustling us into the old Dodge van like we were going to experience sniper fire at any moment. As we entered the van, I felt the web of protective spells and anti-scrying wards dripping off it. It was hard to miss the tripod-mounted, fifty-caliber machine gun in the hatchback section either, or the security man ready to use it, crouched like a door gunner in a tailored suit.

Weaving through the concrete moats of I-405, I leaned over to Vigil and spoke softly. "So what is with all this?"

"My best guess until I can have a proper sit-down with the sergeant is that one of Ankou's rivals must have gotten wind of the operation. Probably looking to collect you to find out the particulars or kill you, to stop whatever it is."

"This is fucking stellar," I said, slipping an American Spirit out and lighting it. "This is exactly why I don't do the whole other-people thing."

"Uh, Mr. Ballard, no smoking, please," the sergeant said. I ignored him.

"I can't drag a whole fucking security detail with me to the places I need to go," I said. "They get one good look at them, or just you, and they are going to think 'cop.'"

"Mr. Ballard, no smoking in the car," the sergeant said. "These windows are made of Chimera lens; they provide plenty of protection, but we can't lower them, so . . ."

I took a deep draw on the cigarette and blew some smoke the sergeant's way. "Funny, I don't hear Sir Burris saying anything about it. 'Course I am at a disadvantage with my tiny little blunt, human ears." Vigil almost smiled, almost.

"Man can smoke," Vigil said.

"Yes, Sir Burris."

The Ankou clan had a modest little compound of three buildings and a dozen guest bungalows on twenty-seven acres in the hyper-exclusive, gated fortress community of North Beverly Park. You couldn't swing a prenup without hitting a multimillionaire actor, musician, or pro athlete in the hood. The Ankous were also not the only high-profile drug dealers hiding out in Beverly Park from the majority of their customer base behind big, safe walls, patrolled by private police. We pulled up into the circular drive about forty minutes after getting clear of LAX. The drive featured a large, splashing, burbling fountain. I could sense a domesticated kelpie, a murderous water spirit, inhabiting the fountain's waters, ready to strike and drown any unwary intruders to the grounds.

The *GQ* goons took our stuff inside. When I walked into the foyer, I was suddenly reminded of Tony Montana's mansion in *Scarface*. The world is fucking yours. I looked all over the place, and then I felt Vigil's gaze on me. I turned to him and cranked my cornpone up to eleven.

"Well, sha-zam! Where do y'all keep your fancy cement pond?" I said. Vigil shook his head and walked past me toward what looked like a study the size of a small Latin American country. I followed him. "Now what?" I asked.

"Now, I check in with Ankou, and you tell me where we're headed." He pulled out a cell phone and slid into a thick leather chair.

"Hold it, chief," I said. "I wasn't kidding in the car. I can find this girl's trail, but I can't do it with the goddamned Bulgarian police department hanging out with me."

"Just me," he said. "I'll be discreet. I'll leave the strappado and thumbscrews at home."

"You can't be this fucking discreet," I said. "These folks are deep, deep background in the Life. They are skittish as hell, and they only talk or deal in front of people they are one hundred percent on."

"And that's you?" Vigil said. I walked over to the full bar and rummaged around, finding a glass, some ice, and a bottle of Tanqueray and made myself a drink.

"It is indeed," I said.

"I doubt you've been a hundred percent on anything in your whole life," Vigil said. My response was to take a long, cool drink of the gin. Vigil dialed his phone, making sure the security encryption was active.

"If you want results, you have got to do this my way," I said. He held up a finger for me to pause.

"It's Burris," he said into the cell. "We are on a semi-secure line. The asset has been delivered to Los Angeles . . ."

"'Asset,' well, you sweet-talker, you," I said, grinning.

Vigil glared at me but continued, unabated. "If I may ask, which of your friends might we expect a visit from while we are here?" He listened for a bit and then made an even sourer face than usual. "Yes, I will give them your regards if our paths cross," he finally said. "One more thing, the asset wishes to freelance his investigation." Vigil paused as he listened to Ankou. "I see, yes. I agree. Very good. Yes, we will notify you of any progress. Good-bye." He put the phone away and pulled himself out of the comfy chair.

"The answer was no," he said, "and I agree with his reasoning. Ankou's agents have learned that House Xana has sent a Carnifex here to kill you."

"Xana, those are the Fae out of Spain, right?"

"Yes," Vigil said. "You know what a Carnifex is, don't you?"

"Yeah, they're mystic hit men for the Fae Houses. Every family has a few on retainer."

"Then you know how dangerous they are," Vigil said, "how much of their lives they devote to death and magic."

"Yeah." I sighed and polished off the drink, poured another, and had it with an American Spirit chaser. "Look, I can handle a button man, even a skilled one. I'm not fresh off the turnip tru—"

Vigil drew his gun fast, faster than he had punched Sarge on the airport tarmac. He fired as it cleared his holster. I was already rolling over the bar before my drink had hit the floor. I heard the whine of the round miss me by less than an inch and rip into the leather bar panels. I pulled the smoldering cigarette from between my clenched lips.

"*Ignis ceram audieritis me hostem feriunt,*" I said, staring at the cigarette. A gout of flame roared from the instantly disintegrated cigarette and covered my hand. I visualized Vigil and the chair he was standing in front of and used my visualization like the sight on a gun. A streamer of flame shot over the bar and flashed toward the Elf.

"Shit!" I heard him mutter, and then I heard the hiss as the bolt struck, the flame crackling hungrily as it devoured the leather chair. I made a gesture like tossing a ball from one hand to the other, and now both hands were wreathed in flame. I popped up, ready to shoot again. Vigil was on the floor on his stomach, in front of the blazing chair. Fire alarms were squealing all over the mansion. Vigil was holding his pistol in both hands. He had me, dead-bang, an easy shot to the head. The fire danced and frolicked between my hands.

"Drop the spell," he said.

"You drop the gun," I said.

"I can kill you, easy, right now."

"And you can enjoy your brief victory with a barbecue," I said. "I ain't dropping shit."

A team of security men, some with guns, others with fire extinguishers, appeared at the archway to the room. Sarge was at the forefront. "Sir Burris?" he asked.

Vigil didn't take his eyes off me. "Well?" he asked.

"After you," I said. Vigil lowered the gun and holstered it as he stood. I dismissed the working. The fire sputtered and was gone.

"Put out the fire," Vigil said to the detail. He walked over to me, he on one side of the bar, I on the other. "That was pretty good," he said. "If I had waited for you to have a few more drinks, I'd have tagged you in the arm like I wanted to."

"But you were in too big a hurry to show me how right you were." I looked over to the smoldering skeleton of the chair that the security detail had sprayed. "I've been handling magical hit men, monsters, and worse my whole life, on my own. I don't need backup; I don't need a fucking babysitter. I don't need you."

"I have my orders," Vigil said. "I'm not any more thrilled by them than you are. I figure from what I've heard of you, you stay alive because of dumb luck and letting everyone around you die so you can live. I have no intention of being your latest victim, but I have a duty and I plan to carry it out. I don't give a damn what you think."

"Swell," I said. "Well, let's get this over with, then."

We went to our rooms to freshen up before heading out. I sat on the edge of my circular bed, still damp from the shower, wrapped in a towel, and called Grinner on the Solarin smartphone.

"Got anything?" I asked.

"Ankou is a serious player," Grinner said over the encrypted line. "Last couple of years, he fought a turf war with the Taliban over some key poppy real estate in Afghanistan and won. He's cozy with the Russian mob and worming his way into controlling key choke points on the Silk Route, the northern distribution route for smack through Central Asia and the Russian Republic. That means the Triads are pissed at him and looking to cut the legs out of his business. His net worth is staggering, man, like GDP-fucking-staggering. Oh, and his enemies tend to just vanish. Keep this guy on your good side."

"I'm working on that," I replied. "Anything on his family, his kid?" I asked as I lit a cigarette.

"Wife died in a car crash in 2000," Grinner said. I thought I heard a baby coo over the line. "Never remarried, never saw anyone else, as far as I can determine."

"Touching," I said. "Are you playing with Turing or something, 'cause I can hear the little future Anonymous member in my ear."

"I'm changing a shitty diaper," Grinner said. "I don't fucking get how a kid that eats such a tiny amount of food can produce so much poo, so often."

"Maybe he's a prodigy," I offered, "and did you just say 'poo'?"

"Hey, go fuck yourself, Ballard," Grinner rumbled. "Christine don't want me fucking swearing so much around the kid, okay, so don't go busting my balls."

"I cannot wait until he starts saying 'shit,'" I said. "Christine is going to fucking murder you."

"Yeah, keep it up, and I won't give you the good stuff," he said. The baby giggled, and I heard a grunt from Grinner that I knew passed for a happy chuckle from him. "Caern Ankou drops off the face of the Earth in 2009; however, since you have employed a fucking data god—"

"Fuck is a swear word," I interjected.

"So it is. Fuck you," Grinner said. I heard the baby make a "fffff" sound. "Shit," Grinner muttered.

"Shit is a swear word."

"Shut the fuck up before you corrupt my kid more!" Grinner bellowed. The baby laughed, and so did I. "What I was trying to tell you, dickhead, is that she has dual citizenship, British and American. I back-traced her passports and nothing, but I got a few hits on some credit card and bank activity with her Social Security number in several different Central American and Mediterranean countries. It was from back in 2010, and it looked like I wasn't the first guy to find it."

"Yeah," I said, sliding on a clean pair of jeans. "Ankou had a ton of investigators and hackers looking for her for years."

"Ah, but he didn't have the best-endowed hacker in the universe and his rummy wizard sidekick on the case back then," Grinner said. "Turns out it was all identity theft issues. That got me thinking . . ."

"Yeah?" I said. I picked a black T-shirt with the Black Keys logo on it from the crumpled pile in my bag. It passed the sniff test, and I slid it on, juggling my smoke and the cell as I did. "Go on. I'm literally on the edge of my seat."

"Those other bozos probably tried to track the guys who used her info," Grinner said. I heard the "tack-tack" of a keyboard, faintly. "I focused on where they got the data from, who put her shit out on the web, and who made bank off it from the jump. That's an information channel most snoopers can't dip too deep into . . ."

". . . But the best-endowed hacker in the universe could," I finished for him.

"Damn straight," Grinner said. "It took cracking some secured files on about a half-dozen servers in about that many countries, but I got you a name. And this trail looks cherry, man."

"Name?"

"Luis Demir," Grinner said. I imagined him reading from a computer screen, his son held to his chest. "Born in Turkey, citizenship in Mexico, the States, U.K., all over. He's the fucking Bill Gates of carders; he sets up huge, multimillion-dollar alliances to bring coders, phishers, and the Mobs, the guys with the money, together. They make bank, and then everybody goes their separate ways until the next caper. Given the places her information ended up on fake debit and credit cards, Demir is your guy. He's the link to all those places."

"Where do I find him?"

"He's in the refugee and human-trafficking business these days," Grinner said. "Splits his time between Greece, Mexico, El Salvador, Honduras, and L.A. He's doing a lot of work for the maras, MS-13, you know, those gang assholes, these days." I heard more clicks. "He's in the city of angels right now." Grinner gave me an address. "Do not start a fucking war with fucking MS-13, Ballard."

Mara Salvatrucha, better known as MS-13, was an organized crime gang with roots here in L.A. The *mara*, Spanish for gang, was a monster; they had juice all over America, Mexico, and Central America. A quasi-military, tattoo-faced brotherhood with the numbers and the firepower to rival an army, they owned a lot of L.A.

"Yeah," I said, crushing out my stub of a cigarette and lighting a new one, "I might need a little muscle, here, someone I can trust. You think you can get ahold of Ichi for me?"

Ichi was a centuries-old Japanese artisan of the gun, a Gun Saint. He was one of the five Bloodhisattvas, enlightened beings who had mastered all forms of death, literal demigods of murder. Ichi had watched my back on several capers. He was the best and his word was beyond reproach.

"Shit," Grinner said, "you ain't paying me enough, asshole. The Gun Saint's in London, hanging out with his daughter and his new grandbaby. You think I'm going to disturb him, you're high. 'Sides, I thought you had backup from Ankou, this Elf knight guy?"

"Don't trust him, he's Ankou's man," I said. "Is Samnang still running the Freakz and Yeakz, out of the northeast part of L.A.?"

Grinner chuckled, and I heard keys tick. "Yeah, still fighting over some of the Tiny Raskuls' turf back in Long Beach too. Why?"

"I need you to send him a message from me," I said.

Vigil drove the CCXR Trevita off the freeway and down Eagle Rock Boulevard. The lights from the shop signs were smeared across the night like neon paint. The Trevita looked kind of like a black-and-silver fighter out of *Star Wars*, only cooler and faster. I had wanted to drive it, but Vigil had refused.

"If that trip down the mountain on Spetses was any indication," he said, "you don't need to drive anything, ever."

"Hey! That's really unfair," I said, blowing cigarette smoke out the open window. "I lived, you lived. Unfair."

The car stereo was pounding "Let it Bang" by A$AP Ferg. Even in a city of mind-boggling excess, we were getting looks in this car, which I have to admit, I liked, but I also kept thinking that somewhere in this city was a highly trained occult hit man sent to kill me. It made me wish a little that we had taken the shit-brown Dodge, but only a little. I mean, who honestly wants to die in a shit-brown Dodge? Maybe Vigil was as sick of me as I was of him, and he wanted to get me whacked. I wished Ichi was available. The old bastard ate Carnifexes for their high fiber content.

Despite my best efforts, I kind of liked Vigil, but I didn't trust him, not to go deep into the shit with me. I had to try to find some local muscle I could count on to watch my back, no matter how this all shook out. I had an idea about that. I'd need Dwayne, but first things first.

"You speak any Khmer?" I asked.

"As in Cambodian?" Vigil said. "No."

"Okay, these guys are Cambodian gangbangers," I said. "So let me talk to them, okay? I speak a little, and I know the boss."

"How did a redneck from West Virginia learn how to speak Khmer?"

"When I was with the Nightwise, I was in L.A. most of my career. Being any kind of cop in this town is like being a fucking UN peacekeeper. You pick up what you can of whatever language that gets thrown at you, helps keep you alive."

"And this Cambodian gang . . ."

"They call themselves the Huntington Freakz and Yeakz," I said. Vigil shook his head.

"Yeah, whatever. So this gang is connected to the Life?"

I nodded.

"You could say that. They split from a Long Beach Cambodian gang back in 1984, a crew called the Tiny Raskuls. I met their leader, a kid named Samnang Bun, my first year on the street out here. Samnang's brother got killed by a Kru, a kind of Cambodian sorcerer. I brought the asshole down. It's hard to do, since they're pretty much indestructible, but I did it, of course."

"Of course." Vigil nodded, the smart-ass leaking out his eye holes.

"Samnang became a gang leader at thirteen, inherited the title from his brother."

"How old were you?" Vigil asked. I shrugged.

"Eighteen," I said, "maybe nineteen."

"Awful young to be a cop, especially a cop that deals with the things the Nightwise do."

"Just kinda happened," I said, looking out the window at the neighborhood we were driving through. Once the hunting grounds of the Hillside Stranglers and the Nightstalker, today Eagle Rock was a hipster's wet dream. We passed vintage vinyl shops, comic book stores, and all manner of upscale mom-and-pop restaurants. I told Vigil to slow as we approached a building on our left across the street from a Jack in the Box. "Here," I said, pointing. "Pull in the parking lot."

"You have got to be kidding me," the knight said. The building's sign, which looked straight out of the seventies, said ALL-STAR LANES. Smaller signs declared DANCING, COCKTAIL LOUNGE, ARCADE, AND BILLIARDS. "You're going to meet an occult Cambodian street gang in a bowling alley?"

"Nope," I said. "I'm meeting them in *the* bowling alley."

We parked the car and walked into All-Star Lanes. The place smelled like most bowling alleys, greasy french fries, foot sweat, stale beer, and floor wax. The decor was every bit as eclectic and seventies as the sign outside. It was a little like stepping onto the set of *The Big Lebowski*. The jukebox, playing "All the Gold in California" by Nick Cave and Warren Ellis, competed for attention over the thunder of balls rolling down wooden lanes, the crash of pins, dozens of televisions chattering, and the rumble of conversation. Vigil was in a charcoal-gray Brioni suit with no tie. He and I walked like we owned the fucking place, side by side. Despite the heat, I had never seen him sweat. I had to admit, Burris carried himself well. He was no hired goon.

"No way in hell am I wearing those nasty shoes," Vigil said as we walked down the lanes. At the last two lanes, next to the wall, were a bunch of Cambodian guys in their teens and twenties. There were about fifteen of them, total. All of them were dressed in the same kind of gear most bangers, rappers, and wannabes wore: expensive baseball caps, the bill, with a sticker still on it, turned at an angle; some wore knit beanies. They almost all wore baggy, sagging jeans. Some wore tight, ribbed tank tops, commonly referred to as "wifebeaters" back where I came from. Others wore plaid shirts, hanging out. They all had lots of gold and silver bling, tattoos, and guns. It was a shame the shitty jewelry wasn't hidden like the weapons. All of them had worked the colors of red and blue into their attire, the colors of the Cambodian national flag.

Samnang Bun was sitting at the scoring table. Samnang was an older man, in his thirties, dressed the same as the others, in a baseball cap, blue-and-red plaid shirt, hanging loose. He had facial tattoos that gave him the look of an Asian-style demonic mask, with tusks and horns. His right eyelid drooped due to an ugly scar that ran down to his eye and then below it. That eye was drained of color, like glass, while the uninjured eye was a deep brown. Samnang stood as he saw Vigil and me approach their lanes. Several of his guys went for their pieces under their shirts, but Samnang stopped them from drawing the weapons with a curt shake of the head.

"Hang back a sec," I said, "let me talk to him." Vigil didn't seem thrilled with this but held back while I walked down to meet Samnang.

"You got old, Ballard," Samnang said in Khmer.

"Look who's talking, punk," I replied in kind. "You own any age-appropriate clothing, or are you going to keep dressing like Wiz Khalifa when you're eighty?"

"Don't intend to live that long, *baulis*," he said with a shrug. I hadn't been called that for a long-ass time.

"I'm not a cop anymore," I said. "I quit."

"Shit, *bangabros*, way I heard it, they canned your ass. Something about you going widdershins, and then you fucked up that thing with that dead girl. You remember that thing with the girl?"

A wet, tumbling nightmare unfolded behind my eyes, crouching in my skull meat, waiting to jump out and drag me back screaming to 1984. I remembered her face, perfect and unmarred, and what had been done to the rest of her. The lonely strip of beach, the gulls, screaming, the only witnesses to the atrocity. "Yeah," I said, "I remember, and I fucking quit." Samnang shrugged again.

"Don't mean nothing to me, either way," Samnang said. "Once a *baulis*, always a *baulis*. Can't wash that shit off you. Why you calling me up after all these years, and how the fuck did you get my fucking cell phone number to text me?"

A thought crossed my mind. Samnang and his boys would be great mercenary muscle to back me up, as long as my check cleared. However, I knew they'd balk when they heard I was going to be squaring off against MS-13. The mara employed Aztec wizards with a penchant for cutting out hearts. Even reckless supernatural brawlers like the Freakz and Yeakz would think twice about crossing MS-13. No, it would have to be Dwayne.

"I looked you up in the 'Who's Who of Cambodian Gangsters,'" I said, "small book. Don't matter how I did it, all you need to know is I can. I need you to do me a solid, Sam. You see the guy that came in with me? I need you to keep him tied up for a bit, you and your crew. Don't kill him. Just give me some time to get out of here, okay?"

"Asshole looks wound way too tight," Samnang said. "He's strapped. What if he decides to start shooting?"

"I don't think he will," I said. Vigil was crossing his arms and leaning against the back wall. He obviously saw us discussing him and didn't like it. The jukebox was playing Coleman Hell's "2 Heads" over the ceiling speakers. "Not unless your boys draw. He's got a code."

"Oh shit, one of them," Sam said, shaking his head. "Fucking honor. Nothing gets you killed faster on the street, man. Hey, remember when I met you? You used to be like that too, huh, Ballard? Only reason you're still breathing is you wised up, *bangabros*."

"You'll do it?" I asked. "You owe me, Sammy."

"Yeah, I sure do," he said. "Okay, we'll keep him occupied."

"Watch yourself," I said. "He's Fae, an Elf. Knight to the House of Ankou."

"You forget who you're talking to?" Samnang said. "Like I said, we'll keep him busy. You just play stupid and scared, and we'll get you out of here quick. Take him out back behind the building. Give me five." We bumped fists, and I headed back up to Vigil, slipping a cigarette between my lips as I did.

"Well?" Burris asked.

"He's got a lead for me," I said, lighting the smoke. "He's meeting me in the alleyway. You stay put. He doesn't like the look of you."

"Can't do that," Burris said, like I was pretty sure he would. "Come on, I'll be charming."

We stepped out a large metal fire door with a sheet of yellowed paper taped to it that said: "Please keep door closed! Back lot is not a bathroom!!!" Behind the bowling alley, there were several large Dumpsters and rows of large plastic garbage cans, all of them overflowing. I saw a rat scuttle into hiding between them at the sound of the fire door clanging open. The night sky above was slate gray, no stars, no moon, only a diffused aura of light pollution that clung to the sky like thick, filthy cobwebs.

By the time I had tossed my cigarette, Samnang and the boys came through the fire door. Sam pointed to Vigil and spoke in Khmer. "Your unlucky day, *phng dar*," he said and gestured to two of his larger men. They moved toward Vigil with arrogant smirks on their faces. Burris looked over to me, and I did my best to look surprised and ready to throw down. I didn't get a chance to gauge his reaction, because the bangers were on top of us by then.

Both of Sam's men came in on Vigil. One went high with a solid right, the other low with a kick that showed he had some Tae Kwon Do training. Vigil jumped straight up, using the guy's incoming fist and arm the way a gymnast might use a vaulting horse. The other gang member's low kick missed, because there was nothing there to connect with, and the first guy's punch never got a chance to find its way to Vigil's face. At the apex of his jump, Vigil snapped both legs out, kicking both of his attackers in the face. Both large men staggered back, crashing into the garbage cans, noses bleeding, lips split, and eyes swelling shut. Vigil came back down, assuming a martial arts stance I didn't recognize. His face was serene, calm. His eyes were dead.

"This is going to end poorly for all of you," he said. "Only warning." Samnang barked a curt order in Khmer, and six more of his men charged at Vigil, joined by the first two injured bangers. They leapt through the air toward Vigil in defiance of gravity like something you'd see in a wire-fu movie, but this was no Hollywood trick. I saw Vigil's stone expression shift ever so slightly in surprise, then he was too busy to do anything but fight.

I once dabbled in aikido when I was maybe fourteen. Surprise, surprise, it didn't take. I didn't have the patience for it. I had studied it in a little shithole dojo in a really bad neighborhood of Washington, D.C. I was trying to learn more about Chi, trying to find my way as a fledgling wizard. Each of us comes to the power a different way, most often by the philosophy of whoever discovered us and brought us into the Life. That would have been my granny; she was a West Virginian Wisdom, a kind of witch-woman, a healer. I was angry, childish, and pigheaded and fought her gentle way of using magic to serve life and protect beauty. Then she died, and I was on my own. I'm a magical mutt; I take and use from any system that works, and at fourteen, I wanted to learn Chi. The sensei gave us a demonstration once, taking on five of his best students. They were standing and surrounded him. He was kneeling with a serene smile of welcome on his face. He tossed all of them around the room like they were rag dolls, letting them do a lot of the work of taking themselves out. I now realized that one of the forms Vigil was trained in was aikido.

Vigil struck one of the gang as he began to land from his flight, driving the heel of his palm into the man's temple, stunning him. He grabbed the stunned man's forearm and swung him in a semicircle, smashing him into three of his fellow bangers as they too landed. With half of his opponents tied up in a tangle, Vigil shifted styles and went to work on the other four using tight, vicious close strikes. The knight was never where they tried to land a punch, already moving. Vigil still wasn't sweating.

A hand grabbed my shoulder. It was one of Sam's men. He smiled at me and winked. "Going up," he said in Khmer. I saw Burris trying to reach me, but a few of the gangsters he had played bowling pin with were back in the fight and made a violent curtain between him and me. He took out two of them before he had to turn to deal with the ones at his six.

Samnang sent in his last five men to reinforce the five still standing. He shouted out in Khmer, "Let's show this Fae bastard what he's stirred up!" Sam and the others all began to change, to melt and shift from their human guises to their true forms, their true natures.

The name of the gang, Freakz and Yeakz, is actually a warning to anyone up on their Cambodian mythology. The Yeakz are Cambodian boogeymen, monsters like ogres or trolls. They show up in all kinds of tall tales and stories as shapeshifters with monstrous tusks, bulging, burning eyes, and superhuman strength. They always reminded me a little of the troll under the bridge in the old story of the *Three Billy Goats Gruff* that my granny used to tell me.

To join Samnang's merry band, a Cambodian had to demonstrate that they were either pureblood yeak from the old country or still had enough nonhuman blood in their veins to shift. Vigil now found himself surrounded by eight-foot-tall, drooling, shaggy monsters. Vigil had the strangest look cross his face as he saw the gang transform. He looked . . . happy. It came to me then that this was a good fight for him now, a challenge. I could get that.

The guy grabbing me was getting his yeak on too. The giant monster tensed his leg muscles and launched skyward, holding me. Oh, yeah, they can fly too. I think I forgot to mention that. We landed on a building about half a block away from the fight. The yeak let me go and looked back at the rear of All-Star Lanes. His monstrous face, a cross between an Oni demon from Japanese myth and the faces of the dragons that were in Chinatown parades, looked shocked. His big-old bugging eyes obviously worked better than mine. "Oh shit," he rumbled, "I gotta get back and help them!"

"Tell Samnang thanks," I said to the yeak's tattoo-covered back. He threw me a gang sign and launched off into the flushed, hazy L.A. demi-night. In a second, I lost sight of him.

I listened to the jangled murmur of traffic on the freeway—all day, all night—it was the constant rhythm of this city. Sirens punctuated by horns, the bone-vibrating thud of bass from car radios below me. L.A. was a champagne call girl with a razor blade hidden between her knuckles. I hated this fucking city, and I had missed her like a junkie misses what his veins scream for. I lit a cigarette, tipped it to the glittering sprawl, and got to work finding Caern Ankou.

EIGHT

Wilcox Avenue's in Hollywood, right off the boulevard, where reality and dream began to get fuzzy. It's the part of L.A. most people think of when they think of the city. It's a little like what you see on TV, but they hose the less colorful and more fragrant street people off the sidewalks before the cameras roll.

I walked past the Sayers Club, where celebs, studio execs, reality TV stars whose names have *K*s in them, music moguls, and their collective drug dealers chilled out like regular folk. I passed the lines of the faithful in their skintight, glittering vestments, their silicone stigmata, hoping to be allowed past heaven's bouncers to get inside and become real by hanging with people who are mostly illusion.

"Hey, hey!" a voice, salami thick with a Jersey accent, called out. "Ballard! Laytham Ballard! Holy shit!" I paused and turned. A guy with greased-back hair, his chest fur spilling out of the V of his black silk shirt, sprinted up to me from the paparazzi lines behind the velvet ropes. He was clutching a camera. His sudden rush to me had gotten the attention of some of his peers.

"Do I know you?" I asked, flicking away my cigarette.

"Sonny," he said and laughed; it sounded like an asthmatic weasel having a stroke. "Sonny Brozo? I did the paperback about the

Westerland murders, *Gotta Kill 'Em All*? Remember your old buddy Sonny, now?"

"Yeah," I said, "I sure do."

There's this game app where you run around in real time, in real space, hunting cute little animated Japanese monsters. You might have heard of it since it's been downloaded more times than porn. A Japanese wizard, a rather nasty one, a *Jaakuna hakkāu~izādo*, created a computer-virus-spell that ended up on the cell phone of a twelve-year-old kid from Lansing, Michigan, named David Westerland.

David ended up possessed by the app. He used it to track down and kill twenty-seven people, sacrificing each victim to the avatar of the respective Oni, Japanese demons, that were hiding behind the adorable little animated critters on his phone. I stopped David and the other kids who had been possessed by the virus. All of them died in the process—big surprise there. A guy I know who works his magic through cell phones, a twittermancer, helped me. He tracked the app back to the psychopath who had created it before it could go out of "beta testing" and be transmitted across the world. Scumbag died too; that didn't make any of it better.

In the aftermath of this shitstorm, it was all chalked up to the usual culprits, by the usual assholes: gaming, poor parenting, fluoride in the water, and, of course, a lack of family values. The press had a circle jerk with this sweet kid, a Boy Scout for chrissakes, murdering strangers and dismembering their bodies in an occult ritual.

My old buddy Sonny, here, had been working for some tabloid TV show at the time. He got pictures of me at the Westerlands' home trying to say . . . something, anything that might comfort David's mom and dad, that they hadn't raised a monster, they had raised a sweet kid who got fucked over by fate, by God, whatever you wanted to call the rigged, cosmic lottery. Sonny made me the hero of his literary work, calling me an "occult hustler" in the book and tossing around some of the more well-known and nasty public stories about me. He dredged up every speck of dirt he could find to kick on the

Westerlands and their boy too. David's parents are dead souls now walking around in slowly rotting skin, waiting for time to put them out of their misery.

Now, in the hot L.A. night, I thought of Joey, the shooter from the school, of the parents of all his victims. I wondered how many Sonnys were camped outside their doors, waiting to lap up their tears. Let's get this straight, right now—I am a very evil man. I have done wrong to so many people, damaged so many lives for my own selfish purposes. It may be hypocrisy of the highest order to judge a man like Sonny Brozo, but hey, like I said, I'm a bad guy.

"Small fucking world, huh?" Sonny said. "I'm with TMZ now! What you doing, man, you checking out the club? Meeting someone? Got another caper going? You still dating that fetish model? Stepping out on her? What?"

"Aren't there leash laws in this town?" I said, smiling and patting Sonny on the shoulder, palming a few greasy hairs in the process, and kept walking. I lit a fresh cigarette and muttered under my breath, *"Si me imago, novissima erit umquam,"* burning the hairs in the fire of my Zippo as I wove the working, a good, old-fashioned curse; it didn't need much juice other than my animus.

Sonny's pack had caught up to him. I heard the chirp of digital cameras, the panting of excited scavengers at my back.

"What's up! What's up! What you got Sonny-boy!"

"This guy get some hits? Who's he sleeping with? Gay? Straight?"

"I think he was in some band, wasn't he? He looks like he was in a band somebody OD'ed in!"

"Name's Laytham Ballard," Sonny said, "some kind of occult asshole. He's good copy; shit follows him everywhere!" I slowed and began to turn.

"I'm ready for my close-up," I said. Cameras beeped, clicked, and whirred; my face, in their viewfinder, on their camera screen, was the last thing any of them would ever see. The screams began. Sonny pulled his face away from the camera. Thick, ugly calluses of skin had grown over both of his eyes. The calluses leaked blood from painful, inflamed cracks in the thick skin. The other paparazzi who had taken pictures of me had the same deformity.

"Shit!" Sonny screamed, one voice in a chorus of terrified shouts from his companions. He clutched at his face, dropping his very expensive camera on the sidewalk. "I'm blind—my eyes, my fucking eyes! Somebody help me!" Other paparazzi who hadn't shot me or had stayed back by the club entrance now descended on the chaos and began to shoot pictures of Sonny and the others, surrounding them. I kept walking, pleased with myself for blinding these men for life. The sounds of the feeding frenzy diminished behind me.

A few blocks down from the Sayers was another Hollywood institution, but it was a much more exclusive club than the Sayers. The building looked like a generic warehouse; an office section jutted out of the front with two black-tinted glass doors and a large two-story featureless structure beyond. A shiny, stainless-steel plaque was affixed next to the doors with two words stamped into it: HARD LIMIT. There was a driveway beside the building with a ramp descending into the underground parking deck. I pushed open the black glass doors and stepped in. "Acquainted" by the Weeknd was pulsing through the speakers hanging high on the walls. I could hear the music echoing through the building. The "office" was an entry foyer. The furniture was all black leather and chromed steel. The walls were dull steel scratched and scoured by steel wool. A lovely young lady, looking like an executive office manager, approached me as soon as the doors shut. She had blond hair swept back and flesh-colored lipstick.

"Good evening, sir," she began. "Welcome. Is this your first time with us?" She glanced over to a large, muscle-bound Asian gentleman in a Valentino suit who stood with his massive arms behind his back, his hands clasped. I hadn't noticed him there, mistaking him for one of the walls. He scanned me and did a threat assessment. I looked more like a street person than their usual clientele, but they had to be sure before they threw my ass out that I wasn't some shabbily dressed billionaire.

"Actually, no," I said, "I was kind of a charter member. I'm here to see Lady Anna, or maybe Dragon, if she's still here." The attendant looked surprised, and maybe a tiny bit offended, like holy words were coming out of the mouth of an infidel.

"Sir, *Mistress* Anna does not accept clients, and I would have no idea who 'Dragon' is. Good evening. Malcolm can see you out."

Before the wall could put a hurting on me, I lifted my shirt and pointed to a mark on my left flank. It was a brand, a ragged circle of raised flesh, once seared with three scars like claw tracks intersecting it. "You recognize this?" I said. The girl gasped, and I lowered my shirt and lit a cigarette. "I'm here to see Anna and Dragon. Now where the fuck are they?"

"What?" Malcolm asked the attendant, stepping toward me, unlimbering his arms.

"He has an owner's mark," the girl said, "like the ones *they* have."

"Where are they?" I asked again.

"Mistress Anna is in the Akari room," the attendant said, then added an uncertain ". . . sir." I nodded to the girl and walked past her, pushing aside gray drapes covering the doorway.

"I'll find my way," I said.

I walked down a claustrophobic hallway of cracked mirrors of every imaginable style, age, and shape. "Acquainted" shifted, mixed, and became "Way Down We Go" by Kaleo. The hallway opened into a great cavernous room, dark, with walls of stone like some ancient castle. The illumination came from blue low-watt bulbs, covered by industrial cage fixtures. There were more leather couches, mostly occupied by beautiful, wealthy people; some wore masks, others didn't. There was a bar of surgical steel, edged in fluorescent tubing. Behind it, bartenders in leather pants and harnesses served more masked patrons.

The main attraction in the room was a large, vertical, radiating spiderweb of chains mounted on a steel ring bolted to the floor. A young man with dyed blue hair and an older woman with a bright green Mohawk were restrained, splayed on either side of the web, the man's head was near the floor and the woman's legs, spread-eagle, were pointed toward the floor. They were both nude save for their tattoos and masks.

A house dom in black boots, black T-shirt, and black military-style pants was kneeling on one knee, tracing the edge of a very sharp, very large hunting knife over the man's skin. He was currently teasing his nipples with the tip of the knife. Fine, red lines crisscrossed the man's chest, back, and legs. With each new slice, the man convulsed. His erection was fierce.

A house domme, dressed like her male counterpart, was working the other side of the web on the woman, striking her breasts and stomach with a flogger made of thin leather strips. The woman's skin was bright red and her nipples hard. Tears found their way out from under the leather mask, but she was smiling, laughing after the wince of each new blow. The domme leaned toward her captive. She brutally pinched one of her nipples as they kissed, as if the domme were tasting the scream of pain and pleasure that escaped the restrained woman's lips as she shuddered in release.

I moved on, heading up a marble staircase to the second floor. A velvet rope blocked the top of the stairs, and a well-dressed Latino clone of Malcolm was the rope's guardian. He was talking to someone on his cell as he looked me over and obviously didn't see me as much of a threat by the dismissive look he gave me. He nodded, muttered a good-bye, and ended the call, tucking the phone away in his jacket. He reached for the rope and unhooked it, stepping aside.

"Mistress Anna is in the third room on the left," he said with a heavy Spanish accent. "She is expecting you, sir."

I walked down the corridor; this level was all exposed wooden beams among the stonework, giving it the feeling of a great Viking hall. I wondered for a second if Grendel was lurking behind one of the heavy wooden doors, covered in leather, ready to devour me like Hrothgar's kin. Then I remembered I had already dealt with the scaly bastard and his harpy of a mom in Sweden, sixteen years ago with Boj and Harrel by my side. Still, it did remind me that it took a dragon to bring Beowulf down, and at least one of them was still lurking around here somewhere.

I opened the third door on the left without knocking. The room smelled of Nag Champa incense and a faint musk of sweat. The light was low, coming from a small circular brazier full of hot coals. A good-looking athletic man in his forties was strapped to an X-shaped St. Anthony's cross. He was nude and panting like an animal, his eyes were rolled up in his head, and his body was covered in a sheen of sweat. Anna was standing before him.

Anna. There are a rare few who move through this shadow box with so much genuine life and love in them, or so much pain and anger, or so much control and care that they echo, that they impress a mark of their passing through this time and place, indelible, on every life they intersect with. Anna was one of them.

She looked as young and beautiful as she had almost thirty years ago. I see the world through many lenses, many windows of perception, but nostalgia isn't one of them. If she had noticeably aged, I couldn't tell. Maybe a little thinner, her beautiful features a little more angular. Her hair was still russet silk; it fell below her shoulders when she wore it down, but tonight was business, so it was coiled in a long, tight french twist braid and pulled back severely from her face. Her eyes were sapphire stars, quizzical, intelligent, with equal parts innocence and trespass warring in them. Right now, the trespass had ascendancy as she regarded her charge.

She wore a leather catsuit the color of dried blood and stiletto-heeled boots that ended at her thighs. Her lipstick was the only makeup she wore, and it matched the color of the catsuit. Anna seldom wore makeup; she didn't need it. The lipstick was a prop for her sub. The suit's zipper was fastened all the way up. The large metal ring hanging from the zipper rested at her throat and reminded me of days when she wore a collar with two such rings. The only skin exposed was her slender, delicate hands. They were strong hands too, marked with the passage of hard work, a life of struggle. Her whole demeanor spoke of wiry strength. Her build was slight, but she possessed enticing curves and I burned inside remembering the way her body moved. The suit hid ivory skin and a lithe body. I remembered how her skin felt; it was intoxicating. Touching her could get you high. She had been mine once, and I considered myself very fortunate to have had that time. In a lifetime of damnation, pettiness, anger, fear, and a hundred other hollow heartbeats, my time with Anna had felt like a brush with a kind of divinity.

Anna saw me, and her eyes widened a little and became a lighter shade of blue, then she was back in character. She raised a finger with a nail that matched her lipstick and suit in color. She traced it along her sub's chest, pausing to toy with his nipple. The sub came out of his stupor and was looking at me too. Anna slapped his cheek, hard. The stinging crack of the blow made him jump, and his cheek was red and flushed from the force of it.

"Eyes forward," Anna said. Her voice was not harsh; it was precise. No emotion leaked into it. It did not rise or betray an iota of stress. It was the voice of someone in complete control of her environment and everything in it. It occurred to me that it might be how God's voice might sound. The sub's eyes glazed over with pleasure. His sex stirred.

"Yes, mistress," he muttered. Anna cupped his face now, caressing the skin she had just struck.

"I am your focus," she said, "I am your universe. Do you understand?"

"Yes, mistress," he said. His voice was getting hoarse, and his erection was brushing Anna's thigh now. She ran her hand from his cheek down his toned chest to rest for just a moment on his hardness. Her touch was light and fluttering, and he moaned a little, and then her touch was gone. She turned her back on her sub, facing me. I leaned against a wide wooden beam and enjoyed the show.

"Confess to me," she said. "Tell me what you've done since we were last together. Tell me your sins."

And he did. I stood there and listened to a litany of the things this guy was doing in his life he wasn't proud of. By my standards, it was pretty benign—cheating on his wife by doing this and other things, petty theft at work, lying, some drug use—but to this guy it was grade-A, straight-to-hell, evil. It made me almost laugh, but a quick glance from Anna told me doing that would get my ass kicked, so I didn't.

"Is that everything?" Anna asked, keeping her voice even and authoritative. There was no judgment, no approval in her tone. It was masterful, no pun intended.

"Yes, mistress . . . I think," he said, eyes locked on her.

"You sound uncertain," Anna said and stepped over to a table where various tools and implements were laid out in meticulous order. "Let me help you obtain . . . clarity." She selected some nipple clamps. She lowered her face to his chest and teased his nipples to hardness with her lips and tongue. He moaned a little but tried to maintain his composure; he hadn't been given permission to enjoy this. Anna applied the clamps and tightened them to her satisfaction. Her sub paled a little as he struggled in the throes of pain and ecstasy. Next, she applied a Velcro band with a small black plastic box to the base of his hard penis and made sure it was snug against his balls. I spotted two squat metal fangs inside the strap, like the terminal leads on a Taser or stun gun. Once it was fitted to her liking, Anna picked up a small black box and pulled open a telescoping antennae from it. The sub looked apprehensive. Anna stood in front of him again.

"I want you to meditate on your transgressions," she said. "Make sure every corner of your mind is free of uncertainty and doubt. We will scour your mind until it's pristine, won't we?"

"Yes, mistress," he croaked. His voice was raspy with ache, desire, and fear. Anna pushed a button on the small box in her hand, and there was an electrical snap as a current went through the collar. The sub's eyes rolled again as they had when I had first entered, and his mouth went slack as current burned through his most sensitive places.

"Good boy," she said, releasing the button. Her sub slumped, jerking mildly. Anna adjusted the power of the shock by a dial on the box and then switched it on to a lower, continuous charge. The sub grunted and thrashed a little, but he remained quiet, obedient. "Meditate. I'll come back, and we can discuss what you have found within yourself and what you have cast away."

Anna walked to another door in the room next to a large black-silvered mirror fitted into the stonework of the wall. She walked through the door, and I followed, closing it behind me. The room we were in was like any small office you'd find behind the scenes at a business. A computer on the desk, stacks of papers, a whiteboard with scribbled notes by employees needing days off or to switch shifts, and a fucking OSHA safety poster. The mirror was two-way, like an interrogation room, so Anna could keep an eye on her charge as he wrestled with his karmic dilemmas as his junk crackled. Anna rested on the edge of the desk and crossed her arms as she looked at me.

"Still the sin-eater, I see," I said. "It's good to see you, Anna. You look great."

"Damn it, Laytham," she said in a very low voice. Anna's voice got lower the more serious, the more emotional the subject. It was another beautiful thing about her. "Did you just decide that enough time had passed, that we had worked our way through enough of the pain you left us with, that it was time to come back and inflict some more?" I could tell she wanted to say more, but she didn't. We locked eyes, and I looked away. "What do you want?"

"I'm on a job," I began. I saw the shields of understanding crash down behind those beautiful, open eyes. "I need Dragon's help."

"Of course," she said, nodding. Her voice remained calm, even, but I could hear the sharp barbs of pain and anger come into her inflection. "That makes perfect sense to you, doesn't it? You need, you want, so of course that makes coming here okay, logical even. She's a resource to you. We both are. Another asset to use and then forget until the next time you need us."

"Look," I said, finding a cigarette and slipping it between my lips, "you want me to say I'm sorry, I will, but you and I both know that doesn't change a goddamned thing. I was spiraling down here, and if I had stayed, I would have dragged you two with me. I didn't want to go, but I needed to. At least I had a long enough binge of clarity to see that, to do something about it."

"So that was you being noble?" Anna said. "That was you taking a hit for us? Laytham, you are so full of shit. I have never met anyone as afraid of letting someone inside them, of pain, of loss. You are selfish, and you're scared, and that's why you invent ways to keep everyone who loves you away. It wasn't about us, it was about you. It's always about you. You hide from everyone, and you lie to everyone, yourself most of all." I raised my lighter and prepared to flick it. "You light up that cigarette in here," she said, "and I will put it out in your eye." I put the lighter and the cigarette away.

"Where's Lauren, Anna?" I asked. Anna sighed and shook her head.

"Do you know how long it took her to get over you?" she said. "Her kind feel everything more intensely; they don't have the bull-shit filters we humans build up from birth. Every day for her is the first day: every emotion is the first emotion, the only emotion. She defended you when everyone else thought you had lost your mind, had gone dirty, she never once considered that. And you never even had the courage, the decency, to say good-bye."

"Where, Anna? Please, I'm trying to—"

"I'm sure whatever it is it will sound terribly noble," she interrupted. "But that's not you anymore. That hasn't been you in a very long time." I waited, and I took it, every word, let them burn me like brands, let them unchain every ugly monster in my head, because I deserved it, I deserved a lot worse. Finally, she said, "The roof, she's on the roof."

"Thank you, Anna," I said. "You may not remember this, but I did try to warn you, both of you. I told you what I am from the beginning. I'm sorry I hurt you and Lauren, I truly am."

"I believe you, Laytham," Anna said, walking past me, reaching for the door back to her sub. "I just didn't believe you back then. I had faith in you. Please don't hurt her again." She walked through the door and closed it behind her.

The cargo elevator to the roof had been refurbished like the rest of the Hard Limit, so now it was more like a moving parlor with a love seat and shaded lamps in the elevator. They hadn't changed my code from the days when I lived here with Anna and Dragon. I punched it into the keypad, and the elevator obeyed and carried me past the private living quarters and up to the observation deck on the roof. I stepped out of the cool interior into the heat of the L.A. night. The darkness was sticky, like hot tar, and all the dying animal noises of the city shouted at me as I left the womb of the elevator. Dragon was there, one hand and one booted foot propped on the observation deck's rail. She didn't turn; she just kept looking out into the gray haze of the counterfeit day the city brandished to keep shadows at bay.

"You're getting old," Dragon said. "I could hear the dust creaking in your joints as you came up in the elevator, and you reek of those cigarettes, that poison you enjoy so much. I could smell you coming from a mile away."

"You, of all people, are not going to jump my ass about smoking," I said, sliding my cigarette from earlier back to my lips.

That dry noise in the back of her throat, which passed for a chuckle. "Still have your sense of humor, I see," she said. A jet of brilliant orange flame lanced out from the shadows that clung to Dragon and lit the tip of my smoke.

"Thanks," I said.

Lauren Hawthorne regarded me as ash-gray smoke trailed from her thin lips and nostrils. She exhaled it, but she had no cigarette in hand. She was five-ten and had a light build that had always made me think of tumblers or jugglers and Robert Plant in the seventies with no shirt, strutting across the stage. Rock and cock, baby, rock and cock. She always had been thin, as long as I had known her, which was over thirty years.

Her hair was dark brown with some gray, thick and straight, falling to the middle of her back and covering her trim breasts. She had a scar on her upper lip, which made her look like she had perhaps been born with a cleft palate. That was the usual story Lauren gave for the scar, but the truth was, as best as Lauren could recollect, it was a memento of a tussle back in the tenth century with an enchanted blade that almost took her face off.

Her eyes were brown and could be warm, overflowing with love and compassion, or darken when full of wrath and fury. Few got to see past those eyes to the secret country that existed within, and fewer still had ever seen those brown eyes suddenly vein with burning gold, as Lauren shook off her mortal guise. She wore a faded T-shirt with the logo of the band Clutch, a well-worn pair of jeans, slightly flared at the feet, and Dr. Martens boots. On the streets, in the Life, they called her Dragon, and she had a fearsome rep, every bit as dangerous as mine. We had been a deadly pairing, she and I. She had been my partner, my lover, and my best friend. Now I was given access to none of it; the brown eyes were a wall, the wall reserved for strangers and skells.

"I figured you'd turn up when you heard," she said. I had no idea what she was talking about, but I played it straight. Never give anyone a solid idea of what you know or don't know. "Have you seen Anna?" she asked, walking away from the edge of the roof, striding toward me. "You hurt her terribly, you know. She wasn't used to how much of a bastard you really are, not like me. It surprised her, wounded her. She didn't know you had it in you."

"I did see her," I said. "I know I hurt . . . her. I told her I was sorry." Dragon smiled. It wasn't a thing of pleasure; it was the opening volley in an assault. I had seen that smile enough times to know.

"Well, I'm sure she's already halfway to forgiving you," she said. Her hand flashed out as she punched me hard in the side of the face. The force of the punch almost knocked me out cold. I flew across the deck, hit the rail, and flipped over it, landing with a crunch on the tar and gravel of the unfinished roof, near a grimy skylight. If she had hit me with all her might, my head would have popped like a

Rice Krispy, but she didn't want to kill me. I oddly counted that as a win.

I groaned and pulled myself up to my feet. My jaw was numb. I spit some blood and slipped under the rail back onto the deck. "That the beginning of the healing process?" I asked. Lauren shook her head.

"That's a long time coming," she said, "and it's a damn sight gentler than you deserve, Ballard."

"Agreed," I said. "I need your help, Lauren." There were couches and chairs and a few love seats set up around the deck, and Dragon sat in one of the larger chairs. She tucked her legs up under herself and pushed her hair out of her eyes.

"Nice to see some things never change," she said. "I figured sooner or later, one of the more recent ones would leak, and I'd have you sniffing around my city and my case again."

"Dragon, what are you talking about?" I said, and I saw something shift behind her eyes.

"Why are you here, Laytham?" she asked.

"I'm tracking a runaway," I said. "Fae nobility. It's a cold case, and the last lead I could stir up says she came to L.A." Lauren looked genuinely troubled. "Now, your turn," I said. "What the hell are you talking about?"

"The girl," Dragon said, "the little Jane Doe from 1984, the case that got Nico killed. And then the second one . . ."

"In 1989," I said. My hands were shaking a little as I pulled the cigarette away from my lips and let the smoke stream from my mouth. Dragon nodded.

"The one that got you dismissed . . ."

"I quit," I said. "What are you telling me, Lauren. I fucking deserve to know, more than goddamn anyone." I felt my control slipping, a rainbow of chakra energy spilling out of me like I was a novice. The power swirling about me, vomiting out of me, was enough to level this city, turn the desert to a sea of liquid glass.

"Laytham," Dragon said, her eyes widening as she perceived what was happening. "Get your fucking shit together!"

"You . . . tell . . . me," I growled, and I saw genuine fear on the face of one of the most powerful beings I know. "There were more? More fucking murders?"

"Yes!" she said. "Goddamn it, yes! Now get it under control, before you kill everyone for miles with your goddamn temper tantrum!"

I blinked and realized that I was at the center of a maelstrom of me. All the hype, all the ego and legends and bullshit aside, I *am* that powerful. I *can* move mountains with faith, faith in me, in my power. It was what my granny saw in me when she tried to put my feet on the path to become a Wisdom, like her. It's what had terrified, enticed, or threatened most of my teachers over the years. It was the hungry, horny, angry god at the fractured core of me, and I tried to keep it in check, not out of some selfless lie, not to protect others, but because it scared the hell out of me too, scared me to think what I could do if I ever completely let go of it, scared I would lose my comfortable, mortal self in all that mindless power. And as much as I fucking hate me, at the end of the day, I'm all I have.

Breathing, it was the key to everything. It was the first lesson and the last. It's remarkable how much we control, focus, increase, and diminish through the keyhole of breath alone. Breathing is the music of life; it is the throttle to our power and our health. If one does not breathe well, one does not live well, and a wizard who cannot control his breath cannot control his magic. Primary lessons, first principles. I fell back on them, and I let go of the self, as much as a selfish S.O.B. like me is capable. I let the meat and the bone, the blood and the breath drive. The mind slipped back and away, and slowly, slowly, I felt the jagged edges of the storm-tossed sea that was my power. I let the thinnest sliver of my consciousness enter the awareness and I, with aching care, spread my will over the raging force of my aura, like oil on water. The energy smoothed, calmed, and then finally retreated back to the recesses of my mortal shell.

I was back on the deck, back on the roof, back in my body. I was shaking, like the aftermath of an adrenal high. My hands clutched the rail I had tumbled over a few moments ago when Dragon had punched me. I looked down at my hands; the knuckles were white from my grip. Steam was curling up from the metal of the deck around my hands. My vision refocused, and I saw the millions of lights burning across the city. I had almost snuffed them all out. I exhaled carefully, an even stream of air. My heartbeat was even, I was even.

"How many?" I asked. My voice sounded weird to me, small and fake. "How many dead the same as the other two?"

"Seven," Dragon said. "Jesus, Ballard, it's like before—you lose your shit too much over this."

"So nine total," I said, ignoring her. "Including my two girls. When was the last one, Dragon?"

"A month ago," Dragon said, "before that 2013."

"All killed the same as my girls?" I asked. My old partner nodded.

"All young and pretty, all Jane Doe, all tortured and drugged, sexually assaulted, violated," she said.

"All mutilated horribly except for their heads, their faces. Those parts of the body were all pristine." I didn't need her to verify it, I knew it. "And the symbol, the brand? They all have it, don't they?"

"At different places on their body, but yes, all marked the same," she said.

"And the other part," I said, bitterness and anger seeping into my voice, "the other part was the same too, wasn't it, Dragon? Otherwise the fucking Nightwise wouldn't give any of these murders a second fucking look, would they?"

"Ballard," Dragon said, "I know you bled for this case. I know how much Nico meant to you. I know he was the one who brought you up, but . . ."

"It's a simple fucking question, Lauren," I said. "Were they all the same as the two I worked, as my two girls?"

"Yes," Dragon said. "All the victims had their souls ripped out of them."

NINE

It was after one in the morning when I left Dragon at the Hard Limit. The excuse I'd given myself for seeing Lauren and Anna again was that if anyone in this city would know where I could find Dwayne and could give me an idea of where MS-13 would have Luis Demir stashed, it would be Dragon. It was a lie and a thin one. The real reason I came to see them was because I missed them and I was too damn close geographically, and too fucking sober, to get my own humanity to shut the hell up. Once upon a time the three of us had loved one another, had shared everything. Anna and Dragon had given me a sense of love and belonging I never had as a kid, except when I was with Torri Lyn.

I loved them, but I had never told them that. Mages knew words carry power, power over yourself, power over others, and over the world. "I love you" was a pact, stronger than any you could make with a demon, more potent than any hex, any curse. It was higher order magic and it left the powerful and mighty helpless in its thrall. I never told them, even when I walked away.

As a compromise to my inner bastard, I had tried to hustle Lauren into helping me and that worked. It was an awful feeling to emotionally manipulate someone you loved and who trusted you in spite of yourself. However, you do it enough and you can distance yourself from the shame and the guilt. I could teach a class on how to do it.

She had agreed to help me and to try to keep the Nightwise out of it as much as she could. She had even promised to give me more info on the murdered girls, but I was pushing her on that one, because even if it was a cold case and technically *my* cold case, it was still in the jurisdiction of the Nightwise and I wasn't one of them anymore. Dragon was at heart a creature of order. I often wondered if all of her kind were like that. Lauren was born to be a cop, and being a cop, being Nightwise, was at the core of who she was. It made her a steadfast friend, a loyal lover, but it also made her a pain in the ass when it came to circumventing the rules, so that left her out of my direct involvement in picking a fight with one of the largest and most dangerous street gangs in L.A. I was going to need muscle to get next to Demir, the *mica* maker that had acquired Caern Ankou's identity data, somehow. He was cozied up next to MS-13, and I had ditched my bodyguard-nanny, left his untrustworthy ass playing slap and tickle with a bunch of flying Cambodian ogres. I was going to need Dwayne. Dragon told me she had no idea where he was these days, so I started looking.

The number of homeless in L.A. fluctuates, but it's been going up the last few years. Between the city and the county, there are over fifty thousand people living on the streets. Dwayne was one of them. If you get off the freeways, like the 110 that's a major artery through downtown, you'll find makeshift communities of people living close to the highways, along the overpasses, in the islands between the lanes as you leave the exits. I started looking in these cities and towns that don't appear on any maps. I had wandered so much since leaving L.A. that, despite all the years I'd spent here, maybe some tourist had crept back in, but I felt an odd sense of juxtaposition between the gleaming towers of light and the clusters of shacks made of wood and plastic tarp in their shadow, the tattered Walmart tents reflected in the tinted glass windows of the stretch limos that glided by. L.A. is bipolar and on all the wrong meds.

An old black guy, skinny, wearing a clean denim work shirt that said TERRY over its pocket nodded when I asked if he knew Dwayne. I held a hundred dollar bill between my fingers just out of his reach but well within his sight.

"'Pends on the Du-Wayne you lookin' for," he said, puffing on a stub of a Swisher Sweets cigarillo. His eyes were clear and wise with old pain. "You lookin' for tranny Du-Wayne, the crack dealer? You lookin' for three sweaters Du-Wayne? You lookin' for crazy Du-Wayne with the dog?"

"Crazy," I said, "with the dog." The old man man's face slid, just a notch. Most wouldn't notice. I did. He nodded again and tossed away the stub of his smoke. He looked at the money and then looked kinda sad.

"Oh," he said. "You not no cop, I can see that, but you ain't gonna hurt him, are you? He's a good man. I had a woman, she was real sick with the AIDS; she's passed now, no more pain, praise the Lord, Jesus, but Du-Wayne, he helped her, put her pain in an old mayonnaise jar for a time. He brought her some herb to help when his hoodoo couldn't hold it no more. Made her passin' easier for her and for me." He moved his body a few inches away from the lure of the money. He looked away from me and out to the river of car lights below us. "I like crazy Du-Wayne."

"I swear, I ain't intending him no harm," I said. I almost called him sir, but that would have lost me points, I just knew it. "I just need his help, and he knows me. He helped me way back. I need his help again." The old man looked me over like he was weighing my sin against the weight of a feather. He sighed and took the money.

"He's flopping these days over in Skid Row," he said. "Near where he and his mamma lived when he was growin' up, God rest her soul. You might try that bar where they play all that hoochie-coochie music, the Satellite, I think it is. He likes that hoochie-coochie music."

"I'm a fan myself," I said, digging my American Spirits out of my pocket.

"The last place I can think for you to check is over at Dogtown. He likes to surf over there with the kids."

Dogtown was a nickname for a neighborhood near Venice Beach, and the "kids" Terry was talking about Dwayne surfing with were numerous gangs, Latino, Mexican, Crips, Skinheads, and whatever localist surfing crew assholes were claiming the rights to the water these days. The gang turf in this city extended to the waves on the beaches. You didn't just wander down to the water, slide into the lineup, and enjoy the tasty waves. You'd get your ass kicked. I'm pretty sure if Frankie Avalon and Gidget had a beach blanket party today, they'd get a train pulled on them.

All these gangs, all these certified badasses were afraid of Dwayne. He gave them respect and they all stayed the fuck out of his way. "Du-Wayne" walked and surfed wherever the fuck he wanted in this town. That was one of the reasons I needed him.

"Thanks," I said. I handed old Terry the hundred and the rest of my pack of smokes. He had set my foot on the path, and I was grateful. I started looking for a cab to take me to the House of Hoochie-Coochie.

Satellite was on Silverlake Boulevard, a squat gray-and-white build-ing, with very little parking, except what was on the street. People didn't come here to admire the architecture, or for valet parking, they came for the sound. Satellite was one of the places in this town to listen to music you hadn't heard a million fucking times on the radio, to be surprised.

It was almost two when the cab slowed and dropped me off. The cabbie had put me together with some cocaine. It had been a long day: hurt ex-lovers, a cold case—no, *the* cold case fucking with me—and it was still far the hell away from being done. My head was full of humming warm brass after the coke, and a hammer made of light pounded in 4/4 time on my heart. I felt good and it was kind of weird to feel that way again. I knew I'd get over it.

Inside, it was wall-to-wall people, hot, noisy, your organs shaking from the walls of speakers beside the stage. A band called Nympho

Punch was on stage, and I could see random body parts thrashing about near the edge of the stage while the sea of flesh near the back, closer to the bar, swayed or headbanged to the thunderous beat and the unrelenting advance of the guitars. They were good. They had a female lead singer with hair dyed Joy Division black and a septum ring. Her voice was a dove frantically trying to stay aloft above an ocean of musical pain. They were good enough for me to stay and listen for a spell. Maybe it was the drugs. I ordered a shot of tequila and a Budweiser for last call. I asked the bartender if he knew Dwayne, and he said of course. I asked if he had been in tonight and he said no. Hadn't seen him for a few weeks. Then the bartender got an odd look on his face and seemed to really look at me for the first time.

"Hey, man," he said as he slid my empty shot glass toward him, "are you Laytham Ballard by any chance?"

"Yeah," I said. Now I knew it was definitely the drugs working on me.

"Holy fuck," he said. "Wow, hey man, I loved you guys. I had all your albums." I started laughing and shook my head. Jesus Christ, this city. "Hey, you doing anything now, you know, solo projects, producing?"

"Solo stuff, mostly," I said, nodding to the empty shot glass. What good is celebrity if you don't use it, right? The barkeep refilled my shot and slid a second next to it. "I'm not much into groups anymore."

"Well you guys thrashed, man," he said. "I listened to you back in high school; a buddy got me bootleg tapes of your shows. I wasn't old enough to go."

"High school," I said, "damn," and drained the shots fast, chased them with the rest of the beer, offering the empty bottle to him with raised eyebrows. He replaced it with a fresh cold one.

The band was finishing up, and I saw some folks drifting out the doors, guided by the bouncers. Nobody was in a big hurry to leave just yet, and that was fine by me. I loved places like this; I loved the ebb and flow of people, the energy, being part of it, and at a distance. I sensed a blossom of energy, like someone had just kicked on a floodlight in the middle of the crowd. I couldn't see who it was; I thought perhaps it was Dwayne, but whoever it was they were more powerful than I recall him being; of course it was a while back and people change, wizards grow.

The lead singer of Nympho Punch was back at the mike. "Hey everybody," she began and a bunch of folks clapped and hooted, figuring the band was going to do an encore. "Hey everybody, we got a surprise tonight. There's somebody in here that you might know. He was the lead singer and guitarist of a band you might have heard of . . . Leaving Season!" The crowd erupted with cheers, hoots, a few shrieks as memory kicked in, and more than a few calls of "who?" The singer smiled and nodded at the bar's reaction.

For a second I felt coiled power, disciplined, trained, close to me, then it was gone. Probably someone in the Life headed out the door. I dismissed it, still wanting to get a look at who was throwing off all that juice in the crowd. The tequila was warm in my chest and I felt loose and relaxed. Most of the folks around me now were clapping and cheering. A random hand offered me an unlit joint and I took it and tucked it in my pocket. I felt the bartender patting me on the back.

"I bet if we give him a little encouragement, we can get him up here to do a little something," the lead singer said. The place went apeshit, and I have to admit I missed all this. It was as powerful as any drug you care to name, and it burned you out faster than any of them. But what a fucking way to go. I stood up and the cheering grew, people made way for me through the crowd, and I found my way to the stage stairs. At least from up here, I could see where all that mystic power was coming from.

The members of Nympho Punch shook my hand and hugged me. The lead guitarist had a threadbare Leaving Season concert shirt. When I saw it, he grinned and we fist-bumped. I huddled with them for a moment, and then one of their roadies handed me a guitar. I slipped the strap over my neck and shoulder and walked to the microphone at the edge of the stage. I was picking at the strings, making sure it was tuned, adjusting the fret pegs on the neck. People were

pouring back inside the club, and the crowd was primed. I could feel
their energy, their almost sexual excitement roaring through my sacral
chakra as it built.

"How y'all doing tonight?" I asked, my West Virginia drawl falling
out. The crowd surged, whooped, cheered, whistled. I saw a bunch of
Bic lighters come out in salute. I couldn't help but notice the white
ones. I suddenly remembered the energy again. I was tripping right
now, between the drugs, and the booze, and most of all the ego-
stroking. Svadhisthana energy always got me kinda high, especially
when it comes at me fast and in large doses. "Y'all not ready to go
home yet?" The crowd howled.

I looked toward that section of the crowd where the torrent of energy was centered and saw the source. Magdalena was sitting there at
a small table, a look of amusement on her face. She wore a black tank
top, black jeans, and boots. Her hair was jet, long and straight, with
thick bangs falling just above her warm brown eyes. She was small,
about half a foot shorter than me, but when she carried herself like a
queen, she always seemed much taller. Almost every inch of her olive-
complected skin showed ink. She had a phrase in Italian tattooed in
thin, elegant cursive running along her left shoulder and collarbone,
partly obscured by the straps of her top. She had more tattoos hidden
from view and she had gotten more during our time together. Some of
the tats on my body matched the ones on hers, now. If it was possible,
she had gotten more beautiful. It was hard to guess where she was from,
maybe Greek, maybe the Middle East, maybe Italian. She spoke with a
lilting accent that also hinted at many places but always sounded French
to me. I had met her years ago and had broken every single promise
I ever made to her since then. I winked at her, and she shook her head,
a smile tugging at her full lips. She raised her plastic cup in salute.

I looked over to the lead singer; she had told me her name was
Effy when she hugged me.

"You guys know any Pat DiNizio?" I asked the kid.

She nodded eagerly. "Hell, yeah," she said.

"Fuckin' A," the bassist agreed, "old school. I saw 'em in Chicago."

"All right," I said to the crowd and the band, but my eyes were on Magdalena. "In the immortal words of Joey Ramone, one, two, three, four!"

I kicked into "Behind the Wall of Sleep" by the Smithereens like busting down a door, and the band followed me in. It was beautiful, like kissing an old love again after too, too, too fucking long and thinking, why did you ever stop? My fingers found their way over the neck of the beat-to-shit Fender Telecaster, and my body dropped back into that practiced, arrogant stance. I made out with the crowd, teasing them, pulling them close only to push them away again, make them ache for a little more, a little further. It was like I never left.

We followed it up with "Burnin' for You" by Blue Oyster Cult. They gave me everything they had and I took it. Back in the old days, I would have stroked more than just my ego. I used to skim the power, the energy the crowds gave us when we were a band. Emotion, adoration, desire, they are all power, and I took it in to work some seriously fucked-up ritual. Most times I just took enough of them to make them feel high and tired in a good way after the show. Some nights, I took every drop they begged me to take, and I left them exhausted and me humming with divinity. And back then, some nights I gave them every last drop of me I had. I emptied myself on the canvas of their desire. Some nights they were the sacrifice, other nights I was. Most nights, it was them.

Tonight, I dealt in surfaces, no workings, no coaxing out mystical energy, only the natural emotional storm of the crowd and the band, ebbing and flowing like tides. Even this was a magic of a sort, and I loved it, and so did they. I gave some back tonight, but I didn't give them everything. I didn't do that shit anymore for anyone. They were screaming for me to do "War Engine," one of Leaving Season's songs that did pretty well on the charts, but it wouldn't have been the same without the band, so we did a twenty-minute jam of Tool's "Forty Six & 2" and called it a night.

It was after three, and I ended up signing cocktail napkins and the guitarist from Nympho Punch's shirt. I also got lots of phone numbers on scraps of paper, a few demo tapes, and some questionable drugs. At a quarter to four, the band and most of the bar's patrons and staff were out the door, on to the next party. I got invites for more places to go, and I was politely vague about my arrival. Magdalena remained at her table as the crowd thinned and dispersed. I sat down across from her with a cold Budweiser, given to me by my new best friend, the bartender.

"You should have kept making music," she said. "You love it. It makes you happy. I saw it in your eyes. It was nice to see. You make music like you build a working or make love. Passion, but there is technique behind it, barely hanging on."

"What are you doing here?" I asked. "In L.A.?"

"Working," she said. She slipped a cigarette between her lips and I lit it. She hadn't smoked when we met; she used to make fun of me and my "hipster smokes." The Surgeon General has determined that knowing me is hazardous to your health.

"You have a shoot? Didgeri with you?"

"No," she said, sounding irritated as she blew the smoke out her nostrils, "not that kind of work, *your* kind of work. Messy, ugly, probably violent. And I don't need Didgeri Doo running after me to make sure I don't fall down and bust my ass. I can handle this myself, Laytham. She's not my mother, and you sure as hell are not."

"Okay," I said, "just making conversation." I sipped my beer. "You want to tell me what this caper is about?"

"No," she said. "I can deal with it." She paused for a second. "That's exactly how that feels, by the way, for all the times you ran off on your own. Enjoy it. What are you doing out here, other than re-kindling your rock and roll career?"

"Skip trace," I said. "A Fae noble lost his daughter, so I'm out here looking for her."

"Fae," Magdalena said, "so, Torri's involved in this. You're doing it for her?"

"No," I lied. Magdalena shook her head.

"You know how I can always tell when you're lying, Laytham?"

I made a low groaning sound and rubbed my face. "Your lips are moving. Of course it has to do with her; most things that get you motivated in your life have to do with your ego or your kinda dead girlfriend."

"Hey," I said, "I was with you. I tried, I really fucking tried. I stopped drinking, I cut back on the smoking. I even kept you as far away from the fucking Satan thing as I could. I tried, okay?"

"I know you did," she said. "I did too. It was just . . . bad, we were just bad. I tried to give you what I thought you wanted and needed but were too stubborn to let yourself have. I tried to love you, and you kept pushing me away. Banging your head against that wall, Laytham, it wears you out."

I heard an echo of Anna's words earlier. "I know," I said. "I'm a selfish son of a bitch. It wasn't you. You gave me every scrap of you, freely, with love, with really good fucking love. I just . . . fucked it up."

Magdalena watched her cigarette burn toward entropy. "I finally figured out why you're still mooning over Torri," she said.

"Don't," I said.

"No, Laytham, you need to hear it," she said. "Because she's the perfect woman for you, she's unobtainable, unreachable; you can stay faithful to her because any trespass is forgiven. You have memory and grief instead of messy living, clumsy, uncertain love. A dead woman is the perfect partner for a man who doesn't want life to touch him." I stayed silent. There was nothing I could say to any of that. Magdalena reached out and touched my hand. "I was angry and hurt when we parted. I thought you had presented a lie to me about who you are. But you did tell me the truth, you did warn me. I just lied to myself."

"What are you working on?" I asked. "It sounds dangerous."

"And now we run as fast as we can away from the real danger," she said, smiling, "the ugly truth." She crushed out the cigarette in the glass tray on the table and then stole a sip of my beer. She made a face, and for a second, she was the old Magdalena again. "It's about . . . her," she said. Magdalena never said her name if she could help it, as if the act alone might summon her, and it actually might.

"The domme witch that messed with you before we met," I said.

"You said she was in the Life and she tried to make you her slave, not just her sub. Why the hell would you poke into anything dealing with her?"

"I had met a girl on Fetlife, Jeannie," she said. "It was a tantric group. She was starting to develop some abilities, it sounded like she might be like you, and Didgeri, and me. Then this woman, this domme was suddenly in her life. This bitch sounded a lot like . . . my old bitch. I tried to warn her and get some more information, and then Jeannie stopped answering me. Grinner tracked her for me, and here I am. I'm going to find her, and I'm going to help her, the way I wish someone had helped me when she had her claws in me."

"Magdalena, you told me this psycho is building up a paramilitary cult with her as the goddess. You have no idea how powerful she might be, what kind of firepower."

"And she has no idea how strong I've become," she said. I could see something cold and beautiful set behind her dark eyes. "I'm not running away, and I'm not leaving a good person to twist on the end of that monster's little finger."

"When do we start?"

"'We' don't," she said. "I'm doing this myself, Laytham. I figured you, of all people, would understand that."

"I do, it's just . . . Does Didgeri know you're up to all this? Does she . . ."

"Approve? No, she doesn't," Magdalena said, her eyes darkening. I knew the look; she was getting pissed. I was pretty sure our mutual friend, and her teacher, Didgeri Doo had already had this conversation several times. "I don't need anyone's permission to do this, any more than you do. The power is all the permission I need."

It could have been me saying the words. I had said them or something damn close many times in my life. I suddenly felt very sorry for all the people I had said them to. They had only been trying to help me, protect me. You live long enough, you time travel, you run back into yourself. I nodded. "You're right," I said. "You're free to do what you want. You've been trained; you know how to use your powers and how to defend yourself. Just . . . my granny tried once a long time ago to warn me off a path I was on. I didn't listen, darlin', and that's part of the reason I'm the way I am now. It wasn't anyone's fault but mine, but you wander far enough down some roads, and you can't make your way back again. I don't want that for you, neither does Geri. Please, just try to remember who you are, and who you're not."

She stood, still holding my hand. I rose with her, and we looked into each other's eyes. Our arms and bodies fell into instinctual positions. We hadn't been so long apart yet that we had forgotten them, forgotten how our skin felt together. I was holding her and she was against me, holding me. She looked up, and I saw the intent forming behind her eyes and then almost on her lips. She almost said it, but then she remembered she had promised herself she wouldn't. I was proud of her for that, and more than a little sad, that I had made this sweet, open human being become just a little more guarded with her heart. I didn't deserve to hear those words again. She kissed my cheek and hugged me fiercely, then she let me go, and I let her go.

"Be careful," I called out as Magdalena reached the door. "You're not alone out there, you know." She nodded, and smiled with her eyes. She was so beautiful she made my chest ache.

"Neither are you," she said. "Don't you forget that. Ghosts are terrible backup, old man."

She was through the door and out onto the street. Lives intersect, we circle, we knot, we untangle, we part. The bartender waited a few minutes and then came over. "Hey man," he said, "you need anything else? I'm headed out."

I paid him three hundred bucks to slip me a bottle of Herradura tequila, his half a pack of shitty Marlboro reds, and a baggie of fet. Now armed with my own backup, I headed out of the empty bar and onto the blissfully uncaring streets.

TEN

It was after four in the morning, and I still had no idea where Dwayne was. I bumped some of the speed I had picked up off the barkeep in the back of a cab and chased the pills with the Herradura. The cabbie didn't give a shit. My kinda guy. I felt like fine grit had settled in me. I was tired but amped, drunk but wired. I was walking in a low-resolution dream, grainy and as flat and colorless as 4 A.M.

Enough fucking around. I wasn't going to spend the rest of the night hitting homeless camps or wandering down to Venice Beach to have to deal with gang assholes. Louie would know where Dwayne was, if I could get Louie's attention, which was sometimes easier said than done. I decided to try to check with one of the best-connected street operators I knew in L.A. "Take me to a rooftop," I said. "Make it a high one." That got a raised eyebrow in the rearview.

I snagged a chintzy ring from a bubblegum machine at a Circle K. I had the cabbie stop there to get more smokes, buy a cheap-ass prepaid cell phone, and take a piss. The ring was fake gold metal that bent like tinfoil, and it had a little bright-red, fake plastic transparent "jewel" in a shitty pronged setting on the front. It was perfect, Louie would love it.

The cab dropped me off at the ziggurat of City Hall. There's an observation deck set up for folks to gawk on the twenty-seventh floor. It was, of course, closed at five in the morning, but I made my way up there through a combination of black-belt-level bullshit and some subtle use and abuse of the Ajna chakra to fuck with folks' nervous systems to make them simply not look where I was, at any given moment. In ten minutes, I went from curb to rooftop. Suck it, Gandalf.

It was a hell of a view. I liked having it all to myself, but I didn't have long to enjoy it. I was running out of time to make shit happen. Dawn was our best shot to hit the gangbangers sheltering Demir, and that wasn't far off. I placed the toy ring on the edge of the deck, smoked, drank, and waited.

Twenty minutes later, a section of night tore free from the graying sky. It glided down, great black wings fluttering, dropping and landing with a loud "caw."

"Niiiiicccce," the crow said, examining the ring with quick pivots of his head. His voice was a warm baritone, rich and deeper than you'd expect.

"Hey, Louie," I said. "How you been?"

"Well, well, well, it's my favorite hillbilly," Louie replied, making quick hops toward me on the ledge. "How you been, Ballard? I hear you were busy up in Michigan a while back. Something about a corrupted water elemental?"

"Yeah," I said. "They fucked up the water there really bad, and the thing kind of went berserk. It was killing sewer workers, started coming aboveground to kill people. I took care of it."

"Good for you, good for you," Louie said. "So, ahh, I heard you were the Devil's bitch these days too."

"How can a guy with no visible ears hear so much shit?" I asked. "I've more or less wrapped that bad business up," I said. "How about you, old bird, how you been?"

"Ah, don't even get me going!" the crow said. "These youngsters in the murder, I swear to Bran, they're killing me. I hope I didn't do all that to my clutch warden when I was a young punk."

"I suspect you did worse," I said, "knowing you."

"Yeah, well, you're not exactly the guy to be bringing up past behavior, now, are you, Mr. 'tried to fool around with one of the Corvus noble ladies when he was just a lowly crow'?" Louie made a sound like a toy machine gun; it passed for laughter from him.

"Hey," I said. "All that class shit aside, she was totally into me."

I had met Louie years ago, back in my Nightwise days. Sometimes the souls of dead humans are taken in by crows and allowed to be reborn as the birds. Lou was one of these "ghost-born" crows. He had the life span, the brain, and the voice of a man but could interact with either society. Given his unique talents, Lou had become an invaluable agent of both the Nightwise and what passed for nobility in a society full of thieving, practical joking smart-asses, the Corvus Court. I had to become a crow for a time to help a transplanted human soul solve his own murder, and Louie had been a good partner and a good friend during all that. Come to think of it now, looking back, I have more in common with crows than I do people.

"Hey, the Maven know you're in town?" Lou asked.

"I don't work for that asshole anymore," I said. "I don't have to fucking report in to her. I quit, remember?"

"Fired," Lou said. "Well, I'm still Nightwise, so she'll pretty much know soon, my boy."

"You'd rat me out?"

"Now you're just being insulting," Lou said. "I'd crow you out. Hey, the lady has some really good sparklies, and she appreciates my info." He looked over to the ring still sitting on the ledge. "Unlike some people."

"You'll get it eventually," I said. "How's the radio gig going?" Lou was the midnight-to-six DJ on KROQ. He'd been doing it for years under various assumed names and with the help of a line of eventually-irritated-beyond-reason human assistants. Not many people outside the Life knew the voice talking to them in between sets of alternative music in the night was not human.

"Meh," he said. "It's a living for a bird. I don't know how the hell the humans who do it get by. It's all a pain in my ass feathers! I got to renew my FCC license, and that's a load of bullshit! I got this new kid helping me. He's a total meat wagon—big, muscled-up, blond surfer. Sexy as fuck, but he's dumb as a fucking turkey at an NRA convention."

"Speaking of cute surfers," I said, "I'm looking for Dwayne, and I'm running out of time . . ."

"When aren't you?" Lou said. "I figured you were looking for someone tonight, the way you've been blundering all over town."

"Well, if you were keeping such good tabs on me, then I'm sure you know exactly where he's at right now," I said.

"Oh, sure," Lou said, turning his head sideways to admire the toy ring, then looking back up at me.

"It's yours," I said and then dropped my hand down over the ring a second before the crow could grab it with his beak. "Once you tell me where to find Dwayne."

Lou made the machine gun laugh again. "Okay, okay! He's over on West Sixty-Ninth."

"South L.A.," I said, "over by Figueroa? What the fuck is he doing there?"

"That," Lou said, "will cost you another pretty." He gave me the address. I headed for the door to the observation deck, already pulling out the cell phone to call Dragon.

"Thanks, Lou," I said. "Enjoy the shiny. I may have some more of those for you soon. I'm looking for a missing person."

"You picked a good city to do that in," he said. "We've got plenty to choose from." He started to pick up the ring with his beak, but then he paused. "Hey, Ballard, one more thing . . ."

"Yeah," I said looking back through the open door. I saw a mischievous glint in the crow's eyes.

"Oh, nothing!" he said. "You'll figure it out. Tell Dwayne I said hi."

"Yeah, you tell the Maven I said fuck off." Again the machine gun laugh and then a quick "caw, caw" of excitement over the new treasure;

then Lou was airborne with the ring. He flew away from the brooding, still-hidden sun.

I called Dragon in the cab headed to West Sixty-Ninth. I told her the address. "That's 6-Pacc territory," she said. "A bunch of different gangs have carved that area up, Ballard. You're walking into the E/S 62 Crips' house. If any of their buddies want to join in killing your ass, you could have half a dozen gangs on you. You want me to meet you there?"

"No," I replied. "You get everything set up, and get our final destination locked down. We'll meet you there."

"You sure you don't want me to at least contact some other members of the order to . . ."

"No fucking Nightwise," I said, sharper than I had intended. I rubbed my face, felt the scruff of my beard shadow, and felt very old and very tired. All of my cheats were coming undone. I fumbled around to see if I still had any more drugs from my fans, eschewing the weed in my present condition, or another hit of speed from the bartender. Nope. I was tapped out, not even a fucking cigarette. "The last fucking thing I need is the goddamned Maven or some of her robots up my ass about getting out of her fucking town."

Dragon chuckled. "It's hard to believe you used to be her golden boy."

"Fuck her," I said. "'Her fucking town', bullshit. It's my fucking town."

"I'll be sure to bring a tape measure," Dragon said. "If she shows, you two can have a pissing contest, and I'll see who gets greater distance." She hung up. I groaned a little and laid my head back; it was starting to throb.

It was a quarter to six when the cab dropped me off a half-block from the address and took off like a bat out of hell. I walked, hell, weaved a bit down the sidewalk. There was a flare again; my venerable, damaged, cranky, unresponsive nervous system couldn't ignore the presence of power, real power close by, too close. I spun and tried to think of some kind of a defensive charm, something simple, but my brain was flat. There was nothing there, and the power I had felt was gone, just like in the bar. I tried to convince myself I was getting paranoid. I kept swearing off coke and speed, and this was one of the myriad reasons why. But the never-sleeping, rat-brained bastard in me knew better. That was not a paranoid shiver; that was someone in the fucking Life messing with me. I quickened my pace and headed for the address Lou had given me for Dwayne.

There were about a dozen expensive cars parked on the street and in the narrow drive around the shitty-looking house on Sixty-Ninth. Urban ghosts, men standing around on street corners, huddled, all sporting Crips blue, eyed me as I walked up to the door. I had their attention. They started to come up but then they whispered to each other and glided back into the darkness. I looked around to see what had chased them off, and that was when I noticed the bloody streaks of fingerprints, of a partial handprint on the slightly ajar door.

I tried to clear my skull of all the shit I had poured in there and managed to push out some of my fatigue and the fuzz of the drugs and booze. I pushed the door open and found a severed hand greeting me on the floor in a pool of fresh blood. I stepped around it. There was a dead man on the stairwell that went to the second floor. He had a pistol in the one hand he still had attached. I smelled no cordite; I didn't think he had gotten a chance to get a round off.

To my right was a large room that may have been designed as a living room. If it was, then some serious cosmic irony was on display. Dead men were everywhere, at least a dozen. Unfired guns, thousands of dollars in loose bills, and cooling bodies carpeted the floor. Overturned card tables and broken laptop computers were scattered around the room; one laptop still showed a spreadsheet program on its blood-smeared screen. There was a dead man impaled to the smashed plasterboard wall with a folded metal chair. Next to him was a whiteboard that was sectioned off into a grid with names and odds. Painted over the grid in blood were the words, "Second warning, next I get SRS." The impaled man had a loaded Uzi machine gun lying at his feet. No spent shells on the floor anywhere, no stray bullet holes this kind of firepower produced. I heard a scraping noise farther back in the house, and I moved over the dead toward the sound.

The next room back was a dining room. It was adjacent to a kitchen. The room smelled the way I imagined Hell would smell. A musty, wet-animal scent, the stink of loosed bowel mixed with blood and fear-piss. There were more dead here, a lot—bodies stacked on bodies. More impotent guns, more cash discarded as casually as the lives had been. At the center of the room was a makeshift arena, made up of doors turned sideways and connected to hinges so they could be folded up. There were two dogs, a chocolate pit bull and a reddish-brown Rottweiler mix, in the center of the arena. The Rottweiler was dead, his throat torn out. His body was crisscrossed with old scars. The pit was struggling to keep breathing, his eyes crazy with fear and pain. His wounds all came from fighting the other dog. I knelt by the pit and ran my hands over his sleek, muscled flank. A tiny whine came from the dog. The anger in me washed away the need for sleep; the soft wall of the drugs was torn down to let all of this pour in.

"I already tried to help him, Ballard," a familiar voice called out from another part of the house. "He's too far gone, brah, too close to the dark."

As if in response to the stimulus of the voice, one of the men in the pile of bodies moaned; a bubble of blood popped from his open mouth. His one remaining eye opened and moved about lazily. He said something in Spanish I couldn't make out, but it was the human equivalent of the sound the dog had made, a last feeble groan for help, for life.

I wasn't thinking, I wasn't casting a spell, I was pulling up all the wires and conduits that the universe had seen fit to give me access to; this wasn't magic, it was rage. And to be honest, the two, at their core, had always felt very pure and similar to me. I clutched my hand, clawlike, on the wounded man's face and kept my other hand gently against the dying pit's side. The man's energy was still vital, was still strong; he could live with immediate medical care. I reached down into this anonymous man's soul, his life force, the well of all he was, and I tore it out in big, ugly hunks. There was no care for the fragility of it, no concern for the fact I was taking every single thing this person had ever been from the time his soul gelled in his body, until this instant—good, bad, saintly, evil—every scrap of his contribution to the human condition. I pulped it, stealing it from the great wheel of karma, from his final judgment with his creator, from the Godhead, take your pick of whatever flavor you subscribe to. I was God in this bloody arena of doors, and I had judged.

The man's soul shattered and fragmented like a snowflake made of spun sugar and light. I took the raw, undefined life force, the ineffable spark that changes a living, animate, aware being into a pile of rotting meat, and I pumped every iota of it into the dying dog. I felt the fading flame in the pit jump and sputter at the infusion of raw life. The dog's life force struggled, fought, and finally fortified.

The pit lay on his side. His breathing was strong, his eyes closed, and he slept. I patted his flank gently and stood up, trembling from the anger and the effort, a little high and feeling indestructible after the stolen life energy had channeled through me. I noticed a wedding ring on the finger of the soulless man. For a second, I thought of going through his pockets, taking a look at the life of the person I had just erased. The cherry coals of my anger hissed *fuck him*, and I did none of it. I climbed out of the arena and headed toward the voice, headed toward Dwayne.

I found him in one of the two bedrooms on the ground floor. The walls were covered in dripping spray paint gang tags, and the air was thick with the smell of dog shit and death. There were steel wire pet crates, about half a dozen in this room, stacked on top of each other. Half the dogs in them were dead. The others, four fierce, muscular, scarred veterans of the arena, were quiet; they didn't bark at my entrance. They didn't growl or flinch in fear. They were surrounding a man sitting cross-legged on the filthy floor. He was rubbing and loving on the dogs, and they were eating up the first genuine affection most of them had ever received in their lives, licking and nuzzling the man.

"Hey, Ballard," Dwayne said. Dwayne Perez-Walker Li was beautiful. I've yet to meet anyone living who disagreed with that statement. He was the best parts of several different ethnicities: African-American, Mexican, Chinese, Japanese, and Pacific Islander. His long, thick, black hair was clumped in dreadlocks, and he wore a fringe of a black beard and mustache. He was a shade over six feet and built as solid and muscular as these fighting dogs. His eyes were hazel, and he wore a frayed gray hoodie, baggy black shorts that fell to his knees, and leather sandals. Resting next to him was his badge of office, a length of steel rebar, wrapped in strips of colorful but weathered duct tape. A Barbie doll head was mounted on the top of the staff, colored in various hues of ancient, faded Sharpie and covered in glitter. The hair on the doll's head was half shaved off. Radiating from the base of the doll head were small chains, like those used in toilet tanks. They hung with various charms on them: seashells, bottle caps, pigeon feathers, and old bus tokens.

"Hey, Dwayne," I said. "You busy?"

"Not anymore, brah," he said. There was no malice, no harsh edge to his voice. He sounded for all the world like a stoner surfer, innocent, at peace, even though he had just single-handedly slaughtered close to fifty people in this house without anyone getting off a shot. A large black dog with white paws, a German shepherd–pit bull mix, stood behind Dwayne. The dog was uninjured, clean, and not half-starving. She had been with Dwayne as long I could recall.

"Hi, Gretchen," I said to the dog. Gretchen narrowed her eyes and growled lowly at me.

"She still fucking hates me," I said. "Even after all these years, your dog hates me, Dwayne."

"Hate's harsh, man," Dwayne said. "She just knows when you

show up, we tend to get put into some ugly predicaments, Ballard." Gretchen made a sound like "glomph" in agreement. "So tell me, brah, is she wrong this time?"

"No," I said, "she's an excellent judge of character. I need your help, Dwayne."

"No, shit, man," Dwayne said, continuing to rub and stroke the abused animals. I could feel the power shifting between his fingers, like invisible sand, as he was gently healing and soothing these dogs' pain as best he could. "You definitely need some help. I felt what you did in there, Ballard, and that was majorly uncool. That's unnatural, man! You're gonna end up junking up what little bit of soul you got left."

"Yeah," I said, "thanks. I'm not really looking for a morality lesson from a guy who worships the expressway toll plaza."

"Hey, brah, everything has a spirit," Dwayne said. "There's voices in the concrete, whispering, burning rain in the power grid. The lotto is the numerological oracle, and the traffic jam is the great serpent uncoiling across the land. Life finds its way, brah, anywhere, everywhere. The city is every bit as alive as the forest, the ocean, or the desert, and this city has a heartbeat. She's good and loyal to those who love her back and treat her right, who listen. I was just born with better ears than most. She's beautiful, you know that, Ballard, you used to love her true. What you just did in there, it's against life, against nature, against the cycle. You know that, man, you feel it. You act like you don't care, but I know your heart, man, and you do."

"The asshole was betting blood sport on innocent animals," I said. "To hell with him, Dwayne."

"Your people find out you did that, and they are going fuck you up, brah," he said.

"Look," I said, "I need a sit-down with this guy who does business with MS-13. Dragon is on board to get me in, but I could really use your help, Dwayne. What do you say?"

Dwayne looked to Gretchen. The German pit made a sound like "Mmph."

"Gretchen says I should shine you on, man."

"Oh cut the shit, Gretchen," I said. I tossed the accumulated loose weed, Thai sticks, and joints I had scored from my fans at Satellite earlier tonight at Dwayne's feet. "This guy can help me find a runaway, lost out here. She's a kid, scared, desperate on your streets, Dwayne. You know better than anyone the kind of two-legged predators hunting out there."

Dwayne gave the fighting dogs a final skritch and looked to Gretchen as he stood, gathering up the drugs. "Find me a cell phone off one of these losers to call the shelter and the cops, Gretch," he said. Gretchen padded out of the room, giving me an indignant sniff as she passed me. I gave the finger to her back as she headed down the hall. "I'm pretty sure about eighty percent of what you just told me was bullshit," he continued. "But if you're even doing twenty percent good, that's better than your usual average, and your ass needs all the karma you can get, brah, so okay, we'll help."

"Thanks," I said. "We need to get moving. Hitting those MS-13 assholes at dawn was probably the best way to do this."

"Yeah," Dwayne said, as Gretchen returned with a smartphone in her mouth. Wayne took it and petted her. "We'll try to do this all quiet and cool, Ballard, but we might want to get our hands on boku hardware in case it goes sideways. Some of those MS-13 guys are Nahualli—Aztec sorcerers—and trust me, brah, you do not want to piss with them or their creepy-ass gods." He swiped the screen of the phone and began to dial a number.

"Dwayne," I said, "man, there must be like fifty guns or more lying around this house. All loaded, never fired, only dropped once, remember?"

"Oh, yeah," the man responsible for all the carnage said, nodding as he put the phone to his ear. "I kinda forgot, I don't do hardware unless I gotta . . . uh, hello? Hi! I wanted to, like, report some nasty-ass illegal dog fighting and, oh yeah, a bunch of like, dead assholes." He pulled the phone away from his face. "Yeah, we're going to need a trash bag, or maybe a laundry basket to put the hardware in . . ."

There was a tiny voice speaking on the phone. Wayne put the phone back to his ear. ". . . wha? No, man," Dwayne said, as casually as if he were ordering a pizza. "Sorry, I wasn't talking to you . . . no, I said dog fighting, *then* murders . . . get it straight, man."

I looked at Gretchen and she cocked her head at me. I shrugged and started gathering up guns, as the sky outside crept closer to dawn.

ELEVEN

Sherman Oaks was west of Studio City and decapitated by the 101. Located in the San Fernando Valley, it was a quiet little oasis of suburban calm in the pretentious smog of hipster pollution and the staccato machine-pistol frenzy of gangbang chaos. It was the kind of strip-mall, chain restaurant, P.T.A. place to which you'd flee to raise a family. So, naturally, it was the perfect place for the particular strain of MS-13 I was hunting to hang out. The mara had bought a ranch compound on about an acre of land, just off Round Valley Drive.

On the way over in a cab, I texted Dragon the address of the gang safe house. "Me and Dwayne are on our way there now to pry Luis Demir away from some MS-13 mouth-breathers," I typed. "We'll need evac, most likely a garbage run. Our ETA is about twenty minutes." Three minutes later I got a curt text reply from Lauren:

"Asshole."

I looked over to Dwayne as I put the secure smartphone away. "We're golden," I said.

It was about an hour after dawn when Dwayne, Gretchen, and I knocked on the front door of their house.

A young man, maybe twenty, opened the door. His face was tattooed with various slogans in Spanish and large stylized letters: MS.

He had shaved his head, presumably to have more canvas space. He wore no shirt and had the black eagle off the Tecate beer logo, wings spread and talons dripping blood covering his muscular chest. I thought to mention misappropriation of intellectual property to the gentleman, but somehow I managed to hold my tongue. The kid had the butt of a pistol jutting out of the sagging waistband of his baggy jeans. He looked pretty much how I looked, like he had been hitting it hard all night and now just wanted to crash, equally as hard. He reeked of weed.

"What the fuck?" he said in Spanish. "How'd you assholes get past the fucking gate?"

"Hey, brah," Dwayne said, replying in Spanish. He was holding Gretchen's chain leash and the German pit was sitting quietly by his leg. "My name's Dwayne. I'm here to see Nester."

"Nester's in the fucking hospital with a machine breathing for him," the kid said. "He got hit. Took two in the chest."

"Shit, man, I'm sorry to hear that," Dwayne said, and he meant it. The kid grunted and narrowed his eyes.

"I don't give a fuck," he said, his face stone, "stupid motherfucker too fucking slow to not get his ass shot, don't mean shit to me."

"Well, maybe I can talk to you," Dwayne offered. The kid was having none of it. Somewhere down the hall, past Mr. Compassion, I heard male voices shouting back and forth to each other. Something about where the fuck was the milk for the Cocoa Puffs. Music started up down the hall, "Wake Up" by Immortal Technique.

"Who the fuck are you, you dog-walkin', blasian motherfucker, come up to my house, jump my fence, don't know you from shit! Got some junkie-looking, *vieja perra blanca* with you . . ."

"We actually wanted to share the good news of Jesus Christ with you, if you have a few moments," I said in English. "Are your mommy and daddy home?"

"Shiiiit," Dwayne said, his unflappable cool slipping for a second. "Ballard, shut the fuck up, man!"

"What did you just say, you *maricón?*" the kid sputtered, reaching for his gun. I drove a knuckle into his Adam's apple. He gagged and gasped, grabbing instinctively for his throat. I took his gun away from him, cocked it, and aimed it at his lowered head. There was a chorus of oiled "snikts," and we now had a half-dozen guns pointed at our heads, from a half-dozen dead-eyed, tattooed faces.

"No disrespect intended," Dwayne said in Spanish, still sounding pretty cool. "We wanted to discuss some business with Nester." The kid stood, glaring at me. I handed him the cocked gun back, butt first.

"Sorry," I said in Spanish. "He dropped it, and I was just giving it back to him. I'm old; I have spasms."

"Chinga usted!" the kid said as he aimed the gun at my face. A tattooed hand flashed out behind him and smacked his head, hard. The kid winced and looked back.

"You fucking stupid?" the older mara member said. "You know who the fuck this is you talking to? That's Dwayne, *pendejo*. He's a fucking bruja, boy, like Francisco!" The older banger looked at all his brothers. "Put those the fuck away, Dwayne's the one that healed Nester's mama when she was in the hospital and the insurance gave out on her, and he got Lonzo's sister, Aleta, back from those coyotes that were going to sell her. He's good."

The name Francisco set off a little screaming fire alarm in my skull. Shit. Dwayne caught the shadow of recognition cross my face, but he played it cool. Guns were put away and most of the bangers drifted back inside, questing for milk for the cereal again. The kid I hit was still pissed and he wanted payback, bad. The older mara member and Dwayne gripped in a complex handshake and then embraced, slapping backs.

"Good to see you, Fabian," Dwayne said. Fabian smiled and nodded.

"You should call first, man," Fabian said, gesturing us inside. "Who's your friend?" he asked as we walked down the hall; Gretchen stayed by Dwayne's side. I could hear the silent "cop" in Fabian's question.

"Ballard, Fabian; Fabian, Ballard," Dwayne said. "Ballard's cool. He needs to talk to one of your guys—no beef—just trying to reach some understanding. That's why we came by. I'm sorry to hear about Nester, brah."

Fabian gave me a curt nod and led us into an open and airy living room with high, wide windows giving a view of the sparsely wooded hills and canyons in the compound's backyard. Besides the MS-13s who greeted us at the doors, there was another group in here, close to twenty in all. These guys all looked like they were on the last legs of a night of partying. Empty liquor bottles, bongs, rolling paper, and flavored cigar wrappers were everywhere. There was enough coke and marijuana residue on the faux stone Aztec coffee tables to make the DEA's bust quota for a month.

"You guys move out here to the 'burbs for the better schools?" I asked. Fabian gave me a sidelong look.

"Who you need to see?" he asked, ducking the question. He sat down on a couch and offered us a pair of stuffed chairs.

"Luis," I said. "Luis Demir. He's a Blackhat identity thief. He works for your mara, among others." Fabian nodded.

"Yeah, he's here, got into town a few days ago. He's got a workroom upstairs. Let me see what I can do." Fabian stood and headed upstairs.

"This is going to go to shit," I muttered to Dwayne. "Get ready. You too, Dragon," I whispered to her, knowing she was listening in through the "scrywire," the mystic equivalent of a surveillance wire, a henna tattoo that I had Dragon draw and incant on my chest.

"You're being all kinds of negative, brah," Dwayne said, lowering his voice. "It's going to be fine. Fabian is righteous. Don't lose your shit." Two of the MS-13 members near us yawned and passed the dregs of a bottle of Jack back and forth. I wished for the millionth time this morning that I hadn't been such a fuckup last night.

"Listen," I hissed, "I know this Francisco they're talking about. He's one of those damn Nahualli you were talking about earlier, an Aztec sorcerer. He is nowhere near righteous."

"Aw, shit, brah, really?" Dwayne said. Gretchen made a nervous "mmrph" sound, and Dwayne stroked her head to calm her. "You guys good? We wouldn't get that lucky."

"I nearly fried his ass a few times back when I was Nightwise," I said, "what the fuck do you think?"

"Well . . . that's disappointing," Dwayne said matter-of-factly. "I was really hoping we'd get through this without any harshness."

I looked around at the groggy street soldiers, at all the guns. "Yeah, me too," I said. "Dragon—Lauren—darling, get ready to crash the party. I'll give you the word."

"Can we at least try to not hurt Fabian?" Dwayne said. I nodded.

"You hear that, Lauren? Try to not hurt this Fabian guy. Everyone else, hurt the hell out of."

Fabian descended the open staircase to the upper floor of the ranch. Following him was Francisco. He had changed in over thirty years, the long black hair was now gray, he was still slender, a little too thin, and there were shadows under his eyes, which were still merciless wells of pitch. I stood as he walked down the stairs, locking eyes with me. I already felt some of his power playing through his eyes at the edges of my awareness, a subtle testing. I returned the favor, but I felt brittle and off my game.

"Laytham Ballard," Francisco said. "The years have worked you over, Holmes, rough. You still got those balls, though, I see, walking into my house asking favors of me. You get Alzheimer's or something, Nightwise?"

"Still like the junk, Francisco?" I said. "That shit will eat your soul, put you off your game."

"Shit, this coming from someone who gave away more of his soul than his mamma gave away hand jobs." Several of the mara bangers laughed at this. I felt ice crack inside me.

"Now, don't go bringing family into this, Frankie," I said. "Otherwise I might have to mention how your brother screamed like a little bitch when I cooked him from the inside out. You recall that, don't you, 'Holmes'?" I didn't blink; my eyes were empty and evil, just like his. I felt the tiniest flutter of his pain, and I licked it up like a cat with cream.

"Look," Dwayne said, getting to his feet. Gretchen stood as well. "We don't want no war. We're just here to do some business. History is bad for everyone's money, you all know that. No future if we close each other's eyes over someone else's beef." The MS-13 guys were up and aware shit might start flying, hands drifting to their pistols, shotguns, machine pistols. The Amazon Alexa near the bar was playing "Hard Time" by Proper Dos; even the air was getting ready for this. "Ballard just wants a sit-down with your *mica* maker; that's it, and he's willing to make it worth your time."

"Is that so?" Francisco said, stepping off the stairs. Fabian and Dwayne exchanged quick glances. Dwayne shrugged. "What's in it for us?" I already knew he wasn't going for it, and he knew I knew. Everyone in the room knew.

"Well," I said, lining up and opening my plexuses of power. I felt him doing the same, shields and wards dropping from that initial testing push. I left my defenses down and focused on building energy, taking the ragged scraps of spiritual energy in the room, and the raw electromagnetic power of the universe. The room got colder. My breath trailed behind my words, "You all get to live. You too, Frankie. I got no cause to end any of you. You're just a means to an end."

I felt something old gather around Francisco, its power emanating from hot stone, bitter pulque, and stained obsidian. He was summoning help from outside. The air around him got hotter, and you could smell the metallic tang of fresh blood. Several of the hardened gangsters whispered prayers or crossed themselves. I glanced at Dwayne. His eyes told me he was ready. I was less than ten feet from Francisco.

"I've missed this, Francisco," I said in Spanish. He nodded. I nodded back. "Let's war."

The kid I fucked with at the door drew the pistol I took away from him, stepped toward me, aiming to blow my head off. He turned into screaming hot ash as he was caught in the first exchange between me and Francisco. Dwayne squeezed a tiny pin cable release on Gretchen's leash and the chain disconnected from her collar. The dog launched herself at the throat of an MS-13 banger who was about to spray both Dwayne and me with a MP UMP machine gun. The kid gurgled and screamed as he fell over, struggling with the German pit opening his neck. Dwayne snapped the leash chain in his hand like a whip and cracked the temple of one of the mara killers. The chain bounced off the now-dead man's skull with a flick of the urban shaman's wrist and blinded the shooter next to him, pulping one of his eyes. Dwayne cleared the distance between them and crushed his windpipe even as he was screaming about the lost eye. The banger's hand convulsed on his pistol's trigger and Dwayne grabbed and aimed his rapidly drooping arm to shoot two more of the MS guys dead.

"*Iyolo tlahtec nian cuaz,*" Francisco commanded, his hand out-stretched. I felt a horrible pain in my chest, like it was splitting. I flexed my Manipura chakra, as I anchored myself with my Muladhara, and the pain decreased, but it had given me pause. Francisco pressed his attack. The otherworldly force he had entreated hovered over him, ready to spike my spells back, but I had an idea about that.

"*Coatl cocoliztli izqu cocoa,*" he spat. My blood felt like it was beginning to burn in my veins, and I felt sick, like I was going to vomit. He had tried to turn my blood into venom. I closed the gap between us. I was close enough now to drive a right hook into his face. Francisco managed to block part of the punch but not all of it. His head snapped to the side, and he grunted out a spell.

"*Fenestra aperta est. Et omnes leges ejus. Intrate, grata,*" I said as I punched Francisco again, this time in the stomach. It was getting hard to see straight; the poisoned blood had done a number on me, but I needed to push through. No time to fall back.

There were shouts from upstairs, the clatter and dull thuds of automatic weapons and grenade launchers as something crashed through the compound gates. Dragon had arrived. I wish I could have seen the look on the faces of the tired, drunk, stoned mara members as an armor-plated, thirty-two-short-ton garbage truck blasted through, Lauren at the wheel.

Dwayne and Gretchen tore through the MS-13 soldiers like a buzz saw. Bodies and parts flew everywhere. The man and the dog moved in seamless coordination. More bangers were pouring down the stairs into the living room. Several of them fired on Dwayne as they descended, but he spun his body, twisting and snapping the chain. Impossibly, the chain was everywhere a bullet was supposed to be, knocking them off their path toward him. Dwayne launched himself up the stairs, plowing into the stunned mass of gunmen. Gretchen had Dwayne's back, finishing off the last of the gang standing in the living room, ripping at their shins and wrists, maiming them and disarming them.

Francisco shoved me back, trying to get enough space to cast. He barked out a quick, dirty spell, *"Totonqui xochitl tlaxilia,"* and flowers of black fire spilled from his free hand, engulfing me in ebony flames. I felt my clothes begin to catch and smelled crisping hair, but I had to hold. I charged at him, low, with a roar and felt my arms wrap around his legs in a football-style tackle. We both went down, and he began to burn too.

"Coyonia," I began, speaking in the ancient Nahuatl, the language of Francisco's gods, *"talaih tlamanalli . . ."*

"No!" Francisco shouted. The awareness of what I was doing fell on him. I had torn down his pacts and wards with his own patrons. He was just another piece of sacrificial meat to his vengeful gods now, like the rest of us. I was offering him up, along with myself, if I died. Bloodthirsty gods hated getting played by mortal wizards, and they really couldn't pass up a twofer.

". . . *otechompahpaquilti,"* I finished as I began to feel my skin redden and blister from the black fire. I grabbed a pistol off the floor, discarded by a now-dead banger. Francisco struggled with me, panic giving him strength. I jammed a thumb into one of his wide eyes, and he screamed and let loose of the gun long enough for me to double-tap two rounds into his chest. I rolled off him, both of us burning, me hacking and tossing the gun. *"Aquam mergit et lenire flamma ignis,"* I gasped, and the wizard fire was gone. I was smoking, and soaking wet. My burns stung, but they felt better, a temporary magical remedy. I leaned back and watched Francisco burn, as a proper sacrifice should.

"Good to see you again, Francisco," I wheezed.

There was a loud boom, and the house shook. I was pretty sure that was our ride backing up to the front door. I struggled to my feet, pausing on my knees to puke. My blood still had more than your daily recommended requirement of magic venom. I knew the spell would unravel and fade now that Francisco was past tense, but in the meantime I felt like ass.

I looked around at all the bodies and recalled why I had wanted Dwayne with me. He had already worked his way upstairs, and I noticed that it seemed pretty quiet in the house. I stumbled against the walls, like a pinball, until I reached the front door, unbarred it, and opened it. The garbage truck's interior, usually filled with garbage, was on the other side of the door. The compartment was clean and had benches for passengers. The walls of the chamber were packed with bulletproof blankets. I heard an intercom speaker hiss as the mike in the cab was keyed. "You got him?" Dragon asked.

"Not yet," I said. "I ran into Francisco, you remember that asshole?"

"Yeah," Dragon replied with a hiss and click. "You give him my love?" I looked back at the still-burning remains.

"Yeah," I said, "I did."

"Okay we got incoming, LAPD and sheriff's department, in about four minutes," she said. "Get your answers and let's go!" I struggled up the stairs, pausing until a dizzy spell passed, and reached the second floor. More bodies, and Dwayne and Gretchen leading a man in a Thom Browne suit and tie out into the hallway. He looked Middle Eastern. His haircut was short and professional and he carried a dull silver armored case. He looked more pissed than scared.

"I was just bringing him down to you," Dwayne said. "This guy gave me like twenty different names, but he was packing up and deleting computer stuff in there, and the computer told me his real name is Luis Demir."

"You looked him up using his computer?" I asked. Dwayne shook his head.

"No, brah, the computer's shot. The spirit in the computer actually told me; it's got a voice, man, we've discussed this."

"I don't know what sitcom you two fell out of," Demir said in flawless, unaccented English. Gretchen growled at him, showing bloodstained teeth.

"Three," I corrected. "She's touchy about that."

"But you have no idea how big the people are you just fucked wi—"

"Let me save you some time," I interrupted Demir. "I don't care about you or your business associates. You acquired identity data from a girl some years back. Her name was Caern Ankou. She was in Greece at the time. You traded her identity for a fake one, and you got her off of Spetses. I need all the info on that identity you cooked for her and where you last saw her."

Demir shook his head. "You set all this shit up for *that*? Are you fucking mental? You have any idea how many paper spoofs I do in any given month, a year? How many identities I farm or buy from paper farmers? You really expect me to remember one name out of hundreds of thousands, out of dozens of countries?"

I slipped the photo of Caern out of the dry inside of my wallet. It was the one Dree had given me of them. I slammed Demir's head hard against the wall behind him. I was beginning to hear sirens, and I felt another wave of nausea churn inside of me. I shoved the photo into his face.

"Okay, I'll make this easy for you, since you're such a busy man. One of the girls in this picture is the girl you helped out. One of the girls in this picture has a father with enough juice he makes you and your business associates look like fly shit, and who will personally oversee your vivisection if you don't help him and us, his humble representatives, find his daughter." I smashed his head against the wall again. "Is this thing on? Is this working? Anything coming back to you?"

"Okay! Okay! Shit!" Demir said. The sirens were louder now, closer. I nodded for Dwayne and Gretchen to head on downstairs. They did. Demir knelt and opened the case at his feet. Inside nestled in cut foam cradles were hundreds of small, black, cylindrical, encrypted USB drives, each with a tiny numeric keypad on their face. Demir ran a finger along the rows and finally pulled one loose. He handed it to me. "The key is," he closed his eyes, recalling, "2621985045."

"Ballard! Cops, brah!" Dwayne yelled from the front door.

"I remember her," Demir said with a grin. "Sweet young thing, running away from something, burning down her old life, so she sold it to me. Gave something else to me too on the boat. She was my little cabin pet for the whole trip. She fought for a little bit. I was her first. By the time we reached Portugal, she was broken in just fine."

A cold snake of bile and anger thrashed in my guts. Part of it was the poison, but most of it was Demir. "You left her in Portugal?" I said coolly. I was looking around the hall. Demir nodded.

"Yeah, but she told me she was coming here. I toyed with the idea of selling her or keeping her for myself, she was a sweet little piece, but she bolted as soon as we were off the boat. End of story. You going to get me out of here now, or what?"

The sirens were on top of us. "Yeah," I said gesturing toward the stairs, "go on, get to the truck."

I was thirteen in an eighteen-wheeler at a rest stop off I-64, just over the Kentucky line. He had picked me up, fed me, let me sleep in the warm cab when it was so cold outside. He put something in my food, and I couldn't move, couldn't think while he touched me and made my body respond to his dirty thick fingers all over it. He tore me as he entered me from behind; it felt like fire, like broken glass pushed by stone, like my insides were going to crush up into my heart, my lungs. I couldn't breathe. It hurt so bad and I was so ashamed.

I had the power of the stars and the planets, the whole universe, turning inside me, like a secret clock, and only I had the key to turn it, to make it spin, to slow, to stop, or to break the whole fucking thing. I was a young god, and I could do nothing while he stole the last shreds of me not dipped in pain, and loss, and fear. Adult me knelt in the hallway as Demir descended the stairs and the sirens heralded consequence. I stood.

"Hey," I said. Demir turned to look back. He saw the pistol in my hand, aimed at him. "She was thirteen." I shot him in the head, and his face folded in as it disappeared; a dark mist sprayed out the back of his skull. He tumbled down the stairs and was still. I dropped the gun and headed down the steps. I almost fell. I was dizzy and sick. Everything seemed like a dream, and I had nothing left. I reached the bottom and started to turn toward the short hall, the front door, and the garbage truck. I sensed something was wrong and turned.

The death hex sizzled the air as it bore into me. I reacted with nothing but animal instinct, trying to deflect it with raw power—no spell, no focus, no finesse—just my life screaming "No!" If I hadn't stolen that tiny dram of life force in the transfer when I saved the dog's life, I'd be dead, courtesy of a spell designed especially for me. The blast took me off my feet, knocked me back into a wall. Everything in my chest felt broken and jagged inside, as I slid down the wall and coughed, choking on my own blood. I heard Dwayne shouting and Gretchen barking. The sirens were a chorus of demons, singing hallelujah as they opened the gates of Hell for me.

There was a man, dressed in black, wearing gloves and boots. A hood hid most of his face. His skin was black and had pockmarks on the chin from a bad bout of acne. He wore a black nylon combat harness with various holsters, sheaths, and pouches all over it. Behind him, one of the large windows that gave a view of the mountains and canyons was melted. He seemed impressed I was still alive. He casually fired a blast down the hallway from the completely, magically, silent machine pistol in his hand. I thought I heard Dwayne shout and dive back for cover. The assassin was standing in front of me, bringing the machine pistol up to my head. The gun was covered in arcane runes, and I was pretty sure the bullets in it were too, built special to deal with folks like me. Some part of my brain that hadn't already shut down knew this had to be the Carnifex, the hit man that Ankou's rivals had sent. I looked up and could see his eyes under the hood; they were yellow, the color of strong piss. There was no gloating, no smart-ass lines. He was just going to pull the trigger and that would be that.

"You can't cast a death hex for shit," I muttered, blood spilling out with my last words.

Another of the windows behind us exploded as a figure flew into the room, wreathed in a million tiny slivers of glass, all reflecting the morning sun. It was Vigil, and he had a pistol in either hand. A bullet from one of them had shattered the window; he pumped three bullets into the assassin's back with the gun in his other hand as he hit the floor and tumbled behind one of the couches.

The Carnifex had defensive magics, bullet wards, and the like, but I was certain Vigil's guns were enchanted too. In a war of magic weapons, the side with the most money usually won. A hot spray of the Carnifex's blood hit my face and chest, even as he dove for cover behind a steel-and-glass entertainment center. My vision was narrowing, but I saw the Carnifex touch a rune on the machine pistol, and the rune glowed for a moment. The hit man whispered something to the warm metal of his gun. He held his arm out, straight up, and pulled the trigger, letting slip a burst of silent fire and a swarm of bullets. The bullets zipped skyward, then twisted in midair and headed for the other side of Burris's couch. There was a series of dull thuds as they hit behind the couch. Everything was silent.

I lost awareness for a second, but when it came back, I saw the Carnifex carefully peer out of his cover, stand, and begin to advance. Vigil popped up a second later, behind the couch, holding the corpse of an MS-13 solider in one hand, like a shield, and his pistol in the other. His suit's upper chest was stained with blood from a hit. Burris fired again, and again, advancing on the killer. Vigil's initial volley of bullets ripped into the side of the Carnifex's face and his collarbone. The magical assassin grunted in pain but didn't drop.

The Carnifex stopped the Elf knight's advance with a withering blast of machine gun fire that forced Vigil to dive for cover behind one of the stone Aztec coffee tables. The silent blast of bullets sent drug and booze debris flying everywhere. There was a rattle and a crack as a chain shot out from the corner of the hall and snapped the machine pistol out of the Carnifex's hand. It fell to the floor, out of the hit man's reach, and I heard Gretchen's triumphant bark as Dwayne ducked back behind cover, a second before that whole area was blasted full of bullet holes from the Carnifex's backup pistol, which he had drawn with his still-functioning hand even before his machine pistol had hit the floor.

Burris took the second the assassin was firing at Dwayne to pop up from cover and put another rune-covered bullet into the trigger man's upper back. The Carnifex's defensive wards were losing their effectiveness and he hissed and staggered at the hit. Vigil dropped back behind cover.

"Enough of this," the Carnifex rumbled. *"Chak zam nan sal sa a monte ak touye motherfucker sa a, kounye a!"* Every loose gun in the room floated into the air; bolts and slides clicked and moved into place of their own accord. The animated guns all aimed at Vigil from every direction. He was dead.

I tried to stay aware, but it was so hard, and I was really cold. Someone was shouting on a bullhorn, and the sirens were the wail of a heart monitor flatlining. The pain was far away, but so was my body. I made myself feel it, fought the slipping away, fought the warm comfort of the big sleep. I wiped my face, made a fist full of blood—the assassin's blood—and aimed it at the Carnifex's exposed back, just as he was hissing out the final syllables of his spell to fire the hovering guns. I spit out all the malice I had left in me. After this night, I was pretty much running on empty, so I pushed the thimbleful of hate with the last burning embers of my life force; I gave it up, burned it like nitrous. The hex hit the assassin, and he gasped and fell to his knees. Every floating weapon fell with him. I felt him die as my will, my life broke his. The Carnifex slumped face-first.

After a night of drugs, drink, rock and roll, old pain, old enemies, being burnt, shredding souls, human sacrifices, and getting death hexed, I was done. Not a bad last night as bar stories go, I thought with the last sputter of my awareness. Not bad at all.

"That," I said, "is how you throw a death hex, motherfucker."

And then the party was over, and someone shut off all the lights. No encore, no sea of trembling lighter flames, only the gray hum of an unplugged amp, then silence. I was thankful for the peace and quiet.

TWELVE

§ *May 1, 1984* §

The ride out from L.A. had taken about three hours, so the sun was just starting to climb behind us as we neared the beach. "Panama" by Van Halen was playing on the tape deck in Nico's 300ZX. You couldn't find a decent radio station out here, and he had been playing the album to death since it had come out at the beginning of the year.

Nico had picked me up at my apartment after we caught the call at around three. My partner looked pissed, but then he usually did. Nico Flores was half-Cuban, half-Mexican, and all badass. He was thirty-eight, gaunt, with thinning black hair he kept slicked straight back. Ever-widening gaps of scalp showing through the combed-back hair often reminded me of rows in a garden. Nico had a mustache that was Magnum P.I. meets Ron Jeremy. He wore a rumpled, Hawaiian shirt that was so bright it could keep you from getting shot in the woods by hunters. Around his neck were several short beaded necklaces, Ilekes, Santeria charms of protection and power made from different colored eleke beads, to represent different Orisha. He had a cigarette dangling at the corner of his dour mouth. I knew how much Nico hated working these late night cases now that Doris was so far along. In spite of his often public and vocal bitching about his family, I knew how much he cherished them, and that he was with the Nightwise in large part because he wanted to keep the monsters of the world away from his beloved wife, little girls, and soon-to-be-born baby boy. This close to the birth, he wanted to be there for his wife and the girls, but most of the things the order needed us for only came out at night. I had offered to go out on the call alone when he picked me up, but he had just grunted. "Get the hell in the car," he said, and that was pretty much that when it came to Nico.

As we were leaving the city, headed out to the 111, Nico began to tell me about the girl. "Imperial County sheriff's department found her a little after two," he said. He pulled out a pack of unfiltered Chesterfields, lit one up, and offered them to me.

"How long you going to keep doing that?" I said. "I don't smoke anymore, okay?" Nico laughed and put them away.

"Right, right," he said. "You fucking jog now, right?"

I shook my head as he laughed again.

"I run. Those things are going to kill you, man," I said.

"When Charles Bronson fucking quits, I'll quit," Nico said, invoking his patron saint. "Okay, so this girl, she's a Jane Doe at this point. Basket Cayce gave the Maven the tip that the death was our kind of case." "Basket Cayce" was a very powerful divinator, a homeless man who wandered the streets of L.A. living off garbage and handouts. He had foreseen otherworldly threats to the world that no one else would have ever seen coming, and he had saved the world more times than you could count. The prevailing theory was that his mind was a fulcrum point, a prism upon which countless alternate realities balanced and tipped. He was hopelessly insane from living with that, but at his core was a decent, selfless person who fought the madness to help the Nightwise. I saw him as a noble figure. Nico pitied him and had told me he wondered why the poor, suffering bastard hadn't offed himself a long time ago. Nico saw the world in such dark tones, it often worried me, but I knew the man under all that scar tissue, and he was a good man, an honorable man, one of the best I'd ever known.

"Your girlfriend wants us to check out the crime scene," Nico continued. "It's a section of Bombay Beach, hard as hell to get to, apparently."

"I wish you wouldn't call the Maven that," I said. "It's disrespectful." Nico laughed. It was a rare, raucous sound, but it was infectious. "You jerk," I added.

"Hey, she practically creamed herself when you agreed to join the order," he said, checking the notes he'd taken as to the exact location of the section of beach. He reached back behind the seat and pulled out a large ADC map book and dropped it in my lap. I clicked on the dome light and flipped pages. "All the rumors and shit about you, kid." Nico raised his voice to a falsetto in a feeble attempt to sound like the Maven. "Ballard raised the dead, Ballard saved a family from the Goatman of Beltsville, Ballard sealed the gate to Hell in the house of four hundred demons in Iowa . . . Ballard actually made me feel sensation below my waist for the first time since 1963 . . ." He guffawed.

"Watch your mouth," I said. "The Maven's a great lady and a hell of a wizard. She hear you saying any of that, and she's liable to spot-weld your mouth shut. You know most of that stuff about me is crap anyway." I told Nico to slow and pull off the road about three hundred yards up. Nico grunted an affirmative. I clicked off the overhead light and put the map book away.

The Maven was named Gida Templeton, and she was one of the most powerful mages in the world. She commanded the resources and agents of the Order of Nightwise for the entire western seaboard of the U.S. She had met me during some bad business in San Francisco back in 1982 and had finally convinced me to join the order last year. She was a beautiful woman, and I had fantasized about being with her many times since I met her, but I couldn't imagine that ever happening. She was completely out of my league and about twenty years my senior.

"Laytham," he said, "at the end of the day, the Maven is just like the rest of us, a human being. She gets paid just like we do, by the Builders, to do a job. Wash away all the fancy titles and reputation and stories, and she's a cop, like you and me."

"Maybe like me," I said with a grin. Nico muttered something nasty in Spanish and casually flipped me off. We pulled off the road, gravel crunching, as we parked beside the guard rail. This strip of 111 was dark. You could hear the waves crashing far below. The spring sky and the Beltane moon were masked by clouds. Nico kept the Z's headlights on, and we climbed out. We walked down to the exact spot the Maven had given Nico, making sure to scan the ground with our flashlights for any evidence that might help. On the other side of the guardrail was a steep, hilly, rocky slope that led down to a narrow scar of equally rocky beach.

"How did they get her down there?" I asked. "Throw her from up here?"

Nico shook his head.

"No," he said. "The body was placed ritually. It wasn't just pull over and toss her down. Plus, no tire tracks or footprints up here. The sheriff's department's crime scene guys worked the scene. Nothing like that."

"Obscurement spell?" I offered. I reached out with my senses and felt the fabric of this place, trying to sense any trace of it recently being altered with magic. I extended my perception farther down the cliff over the narrow beach. I sensed nothing. "Scene's clean, no magic."

"That was one nasty-ass crude-as-hell bit of magic you just did," Nico said, flicking his cigarette butt over the cliff. "Boy, you can't just get by on muscle. You have got to start working on refinement, visualizations, mantra, something."

"Why?" I asked. I've always been able to get done what I want to get done with just power. Workings are a waste of time." I looked over at the dark, choppy ocean; the waves looked angry. "Bottom line, if it ain't broke don't try to fix it. They didn't do anything that left a trace here."

Nico shook his head. "I guarantee every time you've done anything tricky, anything that took some finesse, or some serious heavy lifting, you did some kind of working. I'd put money on it. You're a mutt, Laytham. You didn't get brought up in one style or philosophy. Your granny started you on her path, as a Wisdom, but you've learned as you've gone, and you'll keep doing that until you find the things, the ways, that work best for you." Nico raised one of his bead necklaces to his lips and kissed it. He then whispered what I knew was a prayer to the Orisha it represented. He stood at the edge of the rail and began his spell: *"Bendita madre, padre bendito, levantar las escamas de mis ojos. Mostrarme todo lo que está oculto, me habla en el lenguaje del silencio y secretos."* I was still learning Spanish, but I had to admit there was a poetry to the working. Nico kissed his beads and turned back to me. "They brought her here by boat," he said. "There is a little magical residue from the ritual. It was done down there. It wasn't a summoning. I fucking hate climbing. I'm too old for that shit." As he walked by me, wearing an insufferable grin on his face, he slapped my cheek good-naturedly. "A sledgehammer won't do shit for you if you need a microscope, boy wonder."

We walked back to the car. A delivery truck rolled by us on 111. It was daylight now. The sky above the slate waves was flint. We got back in the Z. Nico yawned and lit a cigarette. He riffled through his case of cassette tapes, popping out Van Halen and replacing it in the case before slipping a new cassette into the deck.

"If it wasn't a summoning, what was it?" I asked.

"It was faint magic, subtle," Nico said. "Its lattice is already crumbling, and it's only been about six hours. I think the magic was a means, not an end."

I rubbed my face and watched the sky beyond the water. A flock of seagulls glided and dove toward the water. Their voices were taunting.

"To what end?" I asked. Nico shrugged.

We pulled away from the side of the road in a spray of gravel. "Saved by Zero" by the Fixx began to play through the speakers.

"I got us rooms at a little no-tell motel a little ways down the road. In a few hours we meet up with Rosaleen over at the county coroner's and take a look at the body."

"Rosaleen," I said. "Good, she's the best." Nico gave me a side-long glance, nodded, and laughed around the cigarette. "What?" I said.

"Nothing," Nico said. "She's here with us tonight at the motel. Maybe you two could go out, have a drink."

"We're working a homicide, Nico," I said, shaking my head. "For god's sake, don't try to match-make; it's disturbing."

"Nothing like looking at death to remind you why life beats the hell out of it," Nico said. "You're too fucking young to be this up-tight, kid." He paused for a second and winced like he had been wounded. "Young, shit, I forgot. Sorry, man. How was your birthday, Beltane boy?"

"It was good," I lied.

"You do anything special? Get drunk, get high, pick someone up?"

"I ran the beach," I said. "Pushed a couple of extra miles out. And I got a few chapters read in that book I was telling you about, *The Hevajra Tantra*."

"On your eighteenth birthday? You read a book and you jogged?"

"Ran, and yeah," I said. "Can we drop this and go back to the dead person, please?"

"Son, you have got to learn how to live, while you got some living left in you," Nico said. "Right now is the perfect time to be wild, to have fun, and make bad choices."

"So you want me to tone down my magic and blow up my private life," I said. "Got it. Thanks for the life advice. You're like the dad on *Family Ties*."

"Ain't adulthood fucking great?" Nico said.

"Don't worry," I said. "I've made enough bad choices already to last a lifetime."

We checked into the rooms at the motel about ten miles down 111 from Bombay Beach and then drove into Niland. Niland was the closest town, about twenty miles from the ghost town that was the beach. Compared to the minuscule population of Bombay, Niland was a thriving metropolis with around a thousand souls living in the community. We found a coffee shop to have breakfast and wait for the coroner's office to open. Nico had a huge plate of scrambled eggs with peppers and onions, bacon, home fries, and coffee. I had coffee.

"You do all that jogging, you should be able to eat like you got some hair on your balls," Nico said around a mouthful of food.

"Because that's a life goal," I said. The waitress walked up. Her name tag said PATTY. She refilled our coffee.

"Go on, ask her," Nico said. Patty smiled and looked at me, a little confused.

"Were you this annoying to your other partners?" I asked.

"They came to appreciate me like a fine wine," he said, "or a stinky cheese. Speaking of wine, go on, you haven't tried here before."

"Um, ma'am," I said, my West Virginia showing, "do y'all carry Cheerwine?" Patty looked puzzled, like she was trying to decipher the language I was speaking. I got this a lot in L.A. My country would slip out no matter how hard I tried to blend in. Nico loved to give me crap about it, and he loved my never-ending quest for my favorite soda.

"Is that soda, hun?" Patty asked. "'Cause, like, we can't carry any wine or beer here, y'know . . ."

"It's soda," I said and sighed. "Thanks anyway." Patty gave me a smile with perhaps a little pity in it. She placed the check on the table and went on her way.

"Another county heard from," Nico said. "You sure they don't make that shit in a still?"

"I'm glad I amuse you so much," I said.

"Me too," Nico said, grabbing the check. "God knows, I need a little laughter in my life."

The Imperial County Coroner's Office was, like most coroner's offices, in the basement of the government building. When Nico and I arrived a little after nine, Rosaleen was waiting for us, sitting on a long, wooden bench in the hallway outside the office door, sipping coffee from a Styrofoam cup. Rosaleen Goossens-Main was five foot three and slight. She had a youthful appearance that made it hard to peg her age, but I figured her for being in her late twenties. She wore her long, thick, brown hair straight, in defiance of the trend of "big hair," and it fell almost to her hips. Her ears were prominent, and she tucked her hair behind them. She dressed a bit like a hippie, in a tie-dyed T-shirt and bell-bottoms that hugged her body in a way that was hard to ignore. An old, brown, suede coat over her shirt completed the image of someone wandering the Haight circa 1972. Her brown eyes peeked out behind wire-rimmed glasses. She stood and pushed her glasses back on her nose as we approached.

"Hiya Rosie," Nico said, and shook her hand. She smiled; her teeth were a little bucked but were white, and her smile made her look more like a mischievous Elf than a forensic savant. She tried not to smile much at work, but it was hard not to smile around Nico.

"Mr. Flores, Mr. Ballard," Rosaleen said in her clipped Australian accent. She had come to the States to work for the Maven. She was supposedly related to an infamous Australian witch and a disgraced English composer who was into the occult. "Good morning. I trust your examination of the crime scene was productive?"

Nico shrugged.

"A little," he said. "We're the right folks to be looking into this. So who are we today, Rosie?"

Rosaleen removed a slim leather ID case from her jacket. "Feds," she replied. I found my badge wallet in my jeans pocket that identified me as F.B.I. Special Agent Laytham Ballard. Nico didn't bother digging his out. He had the role down to a science. "Part of an occult crime taskforce," she added.

"Trendy," I said. Rosaleen smiled.

We walked into the office like we owned it. The coroner's assistant was a gangly man with tufts of white hair on a liver-spotted pate. His rubbery lips were an odd color that made me think of squid tentacles. We caught him in mid breakfast, egg biscuit and coffee, so we already had him off balance. Nico did most of the talking, big surprise there. After a few phone calls to check our bona fides, the assistant took us down to the cold room and we got to meet our Jane Doe.

Rosaleen had her kit with her, a large, square, forensic field kit slung over her shoulder. The kit had all the standard stuff and few things most forensic scientists wouldn't carry. The tech clicked on the lights in the lab and pulled the victim out of her steel drawer, an impersonal filing cabinet of loss. She was covered by a sheet with an unzipped black plastic body bag under her. He rolled her over to the examination table, and then he and Rosaleen slid her over onto the table.

About this time, the county coroner arrived. He was a stocky man in a suit straight out of JCPenney. He had steel-gray hair in a high and tight, and he talked and acted more like a politician than a doctor. He wanted to chat us up and make sure we knew he and his office had cooperated. Nico gave him the right amount of glad-handing and then shooed him and the assistant off with a bunch of talk about reports, deadlines, and bosses chewing up his ass. They laughed and left us alone with the girl. Rosaleen slid back the sheet, and I was introduced, face to face, with "Jane Doe." I audibly gasped. I thought I was more jaded, tougher than that. I wasn't. Nico whispered, *"Santa Madre,"* crossed himself, and then kissed his beads.

Jane was about seventeen, maybe eighteen, my age. Her hair was shoulder-length, sandy blond, and layered around her bangs and face. It had been curled and cut professionally not too long ago. Her face was narrow, and she was beautiful. She looked a little cocaine-thin in her features and the rest of her body, but her face was flawless, not a scratch, not a bruise to mar her features.

The rest of her body was a nightmare. Her skin was mottled with bruises of blue, black, green, yellow, and purple, like a savage topographical map of alien continents. She had been cut, narrow incisions with razors and scalpels and deep, ugly gashes with heavy, cruder blades. Some of the wounds were fresh, others days, weeks old. Scar echoes, souvenirs of distant pain, crisscrossed her body. She had track marks, also of different ages, chronicling her use. The oldest spots were in her arms, newer ones were in her feet and between her toes. The exceptions were a few ugly, bruised marks on her inner forearms near the junction of veins in the wrist. She'd had IVs in both of her arms recently. The slender wrists had some of the oldest scars—white, pale crossroads of choices made when it felt like there were no more options. They mirrored my own wrists.

She had been whipped, brutally and recently. Her back, buttocks, and breasts were dull red ribbons of split flesh. Again, raised scar tissue spoke that this was not a new experience for Jane. There were signs of trauma and traces of seminal fluid in the wounds where her nipples had been before they were torn off. Her genitals and rectum were also savaged, torn, cut, bitten, and penetrated. She had been burned with brands, most likely a fireplace poker, and with electricity. An odd-shaped brand appeared on her left thigh. It was an old wound.

The perfect, almost angelic head resting on the desecrated altar of her body somehow made it all the more obscene, all the more mad.

Rosaleen spoke evenly and professionally into a small handheld cassette tape recorder as she documented the minutia of each atrocity. She took photographs, Polaroids, 35 mm, and videotaped the examination. Only once did I see her resolve falter for just a second. There was a catch in her voice, and I saw her eyes flutter; I thought she might cry, but she didn't, and she continued through all the physical examinations, all the tests and the analysis, undaunted. I could never do the job Rosaleen does.

Six hours later, she clicked off the recorder, pulled off her stained rubber gloves, and rested against an empty steel table. She look haggard. I handed Rosaleen a Pepsi Nico and I had retrieved from a row of machines near the elevators. She took it and I saw gratitude in her eyes for the simple act, behind the weariness. "She's had multiple children and several abortions," she said. "She shows signs of long-term alcohol and opiate abuse among other drugs and physical abuse stretching back a long time, badly healed broken bones, radial fractures. It's all evil, but nothing specifically occult or ritual in the manner of her death," she said. "How about in the placement of her body at the scene?"

Nico and I had been reviewing the photos the sheriff's department had taken last night and reading their reports. "Her body was placed in a Y shape," Nico said. "The sea to her left hand, the land to her right. Rocks were placed around her feet, which were facing east. It feels ritualistic, but I have no clue what mystic tradition."

"It could be a psychopath," Rosaleen said, "an offender with his own internal cosmology and mythology, acting it out on the victim."

"Then he's a magical psychopath," Nico said. "The real stuff was flying around at the scene. It wasn't a spell to call anything over, but it was legit magic."

I looked at the grainy, black-and-white photo of Jane's body on the beach. Her arms were raised above her head; even her fingers were each meticulously spread like . . . I sorted through the pile of pictures until I came to the one of her feet, the rocks piled around them and over them . . . over them as if her feet had been . . .

"Okay, let's see if she can help us any on this," Nico said to Rosaleen. "You good with that, Rosie?"

"Of course," Rosaleen said, but I heard the ice crack, the hesitation

slip into her voice. I was walking over to Jane's body. I felt the frag-
ments of memory shift and slip.

"Laytham, get the door . . . Laytham?" Nico's voice. I was looking
at the deep, savage wounds on Jane's body. The placing. They began
at her throat . . . Then next was a hole where her heart used to be.
The next was at her solar plexus; it bordered between the floor of her
lungs and the top of her intestines.

I heard the door click and lock. Nico adjusted the blinds on the
glass of the door to obscure the room. He stood near the door to
guard it. He was giving me an odd look but said nothing. Rosaleen
removed several bones from her forensic bag. Each was wrapped in a
different color of silk cloth. The cloths were embroidered with complex symbols around a circle. The first bone she removed was a human
skull. She placed the cloth it was wrapped in on the steel table, on
the circle side up above Jane's head, and then carefully placed the skull
on the cloth. She repeated the process. Each bone was human and
placed at specific spots around Jane's body. Long bones for arms and
legs and then small spinal vertebrae opposite the skull, at the feet,
completing the circuit of marrow around the dead girl. Rosaleen
stepped around me as I stood looking at wounds.

"Laytham," she asked, "is everything okay?"

"I think I know why she's mutilated the way she is," I said, "at
least in part. These big, serious wounds, here and here, all the way
down her body."

"Yes?" Rosaleen said, standing beside me. Nico was listening,
arms crossed, still guarding the door.

"These wounds correspond pretty accurately to the traditional
locations on the body of the chakras," I said.

"That New Age bullshit?" Nico grunted.

"Look," I said, "you are always talking about me visualizing,
focusing; well, I've been playing around with using chakras for visualizing workings. And that book I was telling you about, the one I'm
reading? It's talking about this, plexuses of power running through

the body. What if the killer wanted to, I don't know, take her power away?"

"You think she was one of us, a magic worker?" Nico said.

I shrugged.

"Not a clue, supposedly every human has chakras, and they are connected to our mental, physical, and spiritual health. This guy may just want to . . . deface them in her for some reason."

"It's a valid theory," Rosaleen said. "I've read some works equating the chakra system to the Kabbalic Tree of Life, so Laytham may be onto something here, Nico."

Nico sighed and made the raspberry sound in frustration as he did.

"'Cept that there are supposed to be two chakras on the head, right? One at the crown and another at the forehead. He left her head alone, kept it perfect, not a bruise, not a mark. Shit, even her hair is not messed up too bad. Why?"

"I don't know," I said.

"Well, let's see if you can wake her up, Rosie, and we'll see if she was killed by Maharishi Mahesh Yogi," Nico said. I stepped away from Jane's body and let Rosaleen begin her working. Besides a formal and impressive education in the forensic sciences and criminalistics, Rosaleen had discovered early in her life that she had an affinity for the dead. She was one of the most powerful and prominent necromancers and necropaths in the world. I watched and tried to keep up. Rosaleen took wide, squat black candles out of her case, placed them meticulously around Jane, and lit them with a lighter. She also took a small glass vial from her case; it almost looked like a cocaine grinder. Rosaleen uttered something in Arabic, standing at the head of the table, gesturing over the skull and the candle behind it.

تأتي من الخروج من الظلام و الغبار. ترك القاعات التي لا نهاية لها من "
ذوي القربى الجديد الخاص بك. يأتي الى النور أقدم لكم. التحدث مع
". اللسان البارد بك في فمي, ورأيي. التحدث معي, الظل

She sniffed from the vial as she repeated the incantation. I was pretty certain it was grave dust. I felt the power build around her, move through her like she was a breathing window. The temperature dropped in the already cool room, and all the metal drawers of the morgue cabinets began to shudder, as if they were being pushed against from within. Rosaleen, her eyes closed, cocked her head quizzically and motioned with her hands as if she were coaxing some unseen force up and out of Jane's still form.

إذا كنت لن تأتي بحرية, وأنا آمرك, أطالب تتكلم, وإعطاء اسمه الحقيقي كا"
"ل لي. هل هذا الآن

The candles' flames shot up, and the room was now arctic, yet Jane remained still and silent. After a few moments of her power surging and crashing against the walls between worlds, Rosaleen's hands swept out, and all the candles snuffed out. The pall began to depart the room. Rosaleen opened her eyes. She looked confused and perhaps a bit frightened.

"Rosie, you okay?" Nico asked, stepping toward the necromancer. Rosaleen waved him off.

"Fine, I'm fine," she said. She looked at both Nico and me and shook her head in disbelief. "Gone, she's completely gone."

"Gone?" I said.

"Her life force, her soul," Rosaleen said, "every single thing she was, or ever might be again, is gone, devoured. The bastard ate her soul, Laytham."

We found the one place to drink and eat at Bombay Beach; it was a dive called the Ski Inn. The food smelled good, but none of us was much in the mood to eat. The beer was cold, and the shots weren't watered. I tossed back my second shot of tequila. Rosaleen and Nico kept pace with me. The smoky heat of the drink swirled in my chest.

"How is it even possible?" I asked. We all looked at each other; we all knew the answer. Someone in the Life, someone with real power could mess up a soul, tear it, break it, but to completely remove every trace of a human soul, that took a degree of power and malice that it was almost impossible for me to comprehend.

"We're looking for a seriously twisted fuck," Nico said, and raised his beer. "Doubtful it's a Satanist, or those Elder God freaks; those guys send the power down a hole. The crime scene doesn't show any signs of that." He drained his beer and ordered another round of shots.

"I really shouldn't," Rosaleen said. "I have to drive back to L.A. tomorrow."

"Me too," I said. "I'm running the beach in the morning." Nico laughed and lit a cigarette.

"Okay, kids. One more each and then you two can go back to the flop, brush your teeth, put on your jammies, and hop in bed. Me, I plan on having trouble sleeping tonight."

"So where did her energy go?" Rosaleen asked. "If it had been destroyed, it would have bled over into the scene. It didn't. A healthy, whole human soul can't just be snuffed out without leaving some residue, like those shadows of the people who were atomized at Hiroshima."

"A whole, healthy soul," I said, and drained the shot Nico put in front of me. "She had been tortured, drugged, raped over a long period of time. What if . . . what if he kept her . . . and slowly . . . wore her down, degraded her, corrupted her? What if he rotted out her soul before the son of a bitch killed her and pulled it out like a bad tooth?" Everyone at the table was silent. Nico had a look I rarely saw; he looked afraid. He buried it quickly.

"That is one of the sickest things I've ever fucking heard," Nico said, and downed his shot. I nodded and motioned for the waitress to bring me another. Rosaleen slid her drink to me.

"I thought you were done, Laytham?" she said. I said nothing but downed her tequila. "If your theory is correct," she continued, "that would mean our suspect spent years working on her, ritually degrading her, tormenting her. The human soul is a paradox; it's fragile, but it's enduring."

"Not enduring enough for what Jane went through," I said as the waitress placed another drink in front of me. "I'm going to find him. I'm going to make him pay for Jane."

"We will," Nico said. We tapped shot glasses and drained them. I was flush with anger, with booze. "Something you have to be ready for, though, kid, is that it may be a very long haul. Riddle me this, what kind of sick-ass fuck can do something like this to a person day in and day out for years: focus their attention on a single human being, provide drugs, provide everything it takes to keep themselves and this other person alive, not just alive, but to live in a way that this kind of abuse is never reported, never comes back to karmically bitch-slap him? Tell me who owns a boat to leave his handiwork lying on a beach?"

"Someone rich," I said. Rosaleen was looking at me; she moved her eyes back to Nico when I looked at her.

"And powerful often ass-drags along after rich," Nico said. "I've worked enough of these, Laytham. They break your fucking heart. They'll make you weep like a little child, because most times there is no end to it, no resolution, and the fucking skell gets away with it."

"That's a terribly bleak way to see the world, Nico," Rosaleen said.

"Yeah, Rosie," Nico said, "it is. I'm just trying to get him ready for it, if it happens on this one."

"Not this time," I said. "I'm going to find this fucking monster, and I'm going to stop him."

"And that is what keeps us in the game, kid," he said. "Gets us up out of the bed and keeps us out of the fucking loony bin. 'Not this time.' It's why we took up the Brilliant Badge."

We drank a final, quiet round.

It was four in the morning when the knock came at my motel room door. I had passed out with a mangled copy of a Spenser novel by

Robert B. Parker on my chest. I rolled over, jumped up, almost fell on my face as the tequila and the gravity conspired against me. I opened the door expecting to see Nico, to hear there was another body. It was Rosaleen. She was in an oversized and faded *Star Wars* T-shirt, and she wore knee socks. Her face was freshly scrubbed, and her eyes were red.

"May I come in for a moment?" she asked. "I'm sorry if I woke you."

"Please," I said and opened the door wider. She walked in, and I closed the door. "You didn't wake me. I was pretty zoned out from the drinks."

"Nico was snoring so loudly he was rattling the door to his room," she said. "I . . . I'm sorry to trouble you. I've been thinking about your theory and . . . it's horrible, Laytham, just horrible, for someone to do that to another person, to ruin them and then just snuff them out. You'd think dealing with the dead every day, learning the craft I've learned, would somehow . . . callous me, but it hasn't. Death is . . . natural, organic, if that makes any sense? It's part of the universal cycle of learning and unlearning, of growth and closure. This poor girl, what was done to her is the most unnatural thing I've ever seen. It's monstrous." She blinked, and I saw her eyes glisten. "That poor girl."

I pulled her to me and let her sob into my chest. Her hair smelled good, and she was warm and soft against me. I felt my body responding in spite of myself. "We'll get him, darlin'," I said. Something angry and proud tightened in me. "I'll get him." She looked up at me, behind her glasses.

"It won't bring her back; it won't renew her soul," Rosaleen said. "Part of the cycle of creation was murdered with that girl, Ballard. The . . . thing . . . that did that to her didn't just kill a human being, he killed part of . . . everything."

I cupped her chin. Our eyes searched, trying to look past, look inside. I felt her body shift around mine, molding to me. She lifted up on tiptoe, and we kissed. At first it was gentle. I tasted her tears on her lips. Time became blurry at the edges. We kissed for a long time, then it became hungry, urgent, tongues finding each other, moans. We bumped into the bed and fell onto it as we surrendered to the relentless need, as we tried to devour one another. I removed her glasses and placed them on the nightstand next to the clock radio I had left on when I passed out. It was softly playing "Relax" by Frankie Goes to Hollywood from some far-off, ghostly, static-filled station.

I pulled her nightshirt off and she fumbled, reaching into my running shorts, as we scooted farther back onto my bed. Her breasts were apple-sized, and I ran my fingers over her nipples, softly. She gasped and pulled my shorts down and off. I was immutable diamond and yielding silk, and she explored me, cupping and caressing. She climbed on top of me, and her hair fell down like a curtain, hiding our faces as we kissed again. I kissed the tears away from her eyes. She came up, and we both murmured in pleasure as we fell into a rhythm, my hands on her hips, hers on my chest.

"Wait," I said. "Stop, we have to stop. I have to stop. I'm sorry." My hands stilled her hips, and her eyes opened. She looked down, concerned.

"What is it?" she asked. "What's wrong?"

"Me," I said. "I'm wrong. I'm sorry, Rosaleen, I shouldn't be doing this." She rolled over next to me in the bed and kissed my cheek. We were both breathless. Our eyes met again.

"I . . ." I tried to find the right words. "I'm in love with someone, still in love with someone, and I shouldn't be with you or anyone else, until I get my head straight. It's unfair to you, it's unfair to me, and in my head, it's unfair to her."

"This the girl you were with before you came out here six months ago?" she asked me. I nodded.

"Yeah. Her name's Torri, Torri Lyn, and the last time I saw her, I said terrible things to her. I don't know if I'll ever be able to be with her, but . . . I'm still with her." I turned onto my side, still facing her. "I've wanted you since the first time I saw you," I said.

"I wanted you too," she said. "I hope you know it wasn't my intention for all this. I just couldn't sleep and I was so sad, and I needed to talk. I wanted to talk to you. You've always seemed to understand, to empathize with the plight of the victim. They're not just 'DBs'—dead bodies—to you. I think your compassion, your passion, those things are your strength. That's where all that power in you comes from."

"I did bad when I was young," I said. "I ruined the life, the soul, of someone who was the world to me, who believed in me when no one else did." I told her what happened with Granny, how I damned her, how I destroyed her soul and every wonderful, shining, brilliant part of her, forever. Rosaleen held me tight and listened. She brushed the hair out of my eyes.

"So the legend is true," she said. "Laytham, you were a child. You didn't know what you were doing, the implications. You can't blame yourself for that."

"I did it," I said. "Exactly what this bastard did to Jane. I'm the same as him, at my core. I'm selfish and careless, weak . . . evil, and guilty."

"No," Rosaleen said, "far from it, darling boy."

"I've been reading a lot about the samurai," I said, "their code, their self-discipline. For them, it was better to be dead than to live without honor. Joining the Nightwise is my chance to master myself, master all that hateful tar deep down in me, to change before it's too late. To prove I can be good, can do good; I can make it right."

She kissed me very lightly on the cheek. Rosaleen pulled the covers around herself and around me. Alphaville's "Forever Young" was whispering through the fog of static on the radio. "You thought it wouldn't be honorable to be with me with another woman in your heart and your head," she said. "You had the integrity to stop even though things had gotten as far as they had. You are a good man, Laytham Ballard, an honorable man. You could have used me to ease your own loneliness, and later I would have been hurt and confused by why you were acting cold and guilty. You didn't. Thank you, and thank you for telling me why."

"You deserved that," I said.

"Do you mind if I stay here, with you?" she asked. "Just to sleep, to not be alone?"

"Please," I said, "please stay."

I turned off the lights, and we held each other tightly, listening to the tinny music on the radio until we slept. My last thoughts before sleep swallowed me were of Jane Doe, lost in all but memory, and only a dim shade there, and the promise I made to her.

THIRTEEN

hrashing through an opiate fever dream, infection, pain, through hot, black, claustrophobic oblivion, the darkness like a coffin too close all around me, my breath bumping against it. The cold, silver bite of needles pinching at my elbow joint, in my forearm, on the back of my hand. Brief flutters of awareness. I was in a bed, in a room, not a hospital, not a prison infirmary.

Painful daylight stabbing my eyes, making me want to retch. Shadowed night, too cramped, out of sync with the humming cadence of the living world. The dead visit me. Dusan Slorzack crouched beside me, his breath smelled of shit and cum; his body was covered in safety-pinned wounds. He tells me he's waiting for me in the ceramic room with no doors, the sound of cockroach legs scratching on filthy tile engulfs me. I think I manage to flip him off. August Hyde was there too, pale and bloated from the water, his skin splitting, gasses leaking from him, telling me he forgave me for what I did to him. I was a kid and I didn't understand. I'm positive I flipped him off, too.

"Well, there's a sign of improvement," a man's voice said. I knew it; it resided in one of the uncoupled rail cars of my mind, hidden behind pain and drugs.

"He's fighting." A woman's voice, also familiar, also lost to me in the wash of dying.

"He's losing," a third woman's voice added. It was Dragon's voice, and I knew she was telling the truth.

It ends in fire, sweet, acrid, sizzling fire, numbing my lips and razor-scraping my throat. I am a speck hanging before the great crimson jewel, the thudding sun full of ancient blood. It burns the petty mortal pain away with transcendent agony; it makes me whole by annihilating every tattered, ragged edge in me, filling up all my festering wounds, inside and out. The red is too old, too endless, and too merciless to leave anything alone. Tight, semi-aware darkness again. The taste of metal in my mouth. Time passes, but I've lost all reference to it.

My eyes opened; I was awake. It felt wrong, uneven, to be so aware.

I sat up in the bed. It was night, and Vigil was across the room from me, so still in his chair, in the shadows that I thought he might be asleep.

"You set me up," he said.

"You know the story," I said. "'I'm a snake, what did you expect me to do?'"

"It was a good scam, a good fight," he said. "I put some of your Cambodian buddies in the hospital."

"I'm only chummy with one of them. You never drew your guns with them, did you?"

"No," he said, and I heard the pride in his voice. "Tempted, but no. Some of them may not heal up as good as they were. That bother you any?"

"Serves them right for trusting me," I said, searching my body for bandages, still-healing wounds. I appeared to be whole.

"True," Vigil said.

"Where am I?"

"The Hard Limit. Dragon insisted we bring you here."

"When did you pick up my trail?"

"At that club. You put on a hell of a show, by the way, real low-key.

The Carnifex had already made you, so I hung back and tailed him loose. So he followed your unobservant ass, and I very carefully followed his. Lost you two a few times, but I caught up."

"How long was I out?" I asked as I rubbed my face and discovered an unkempt beard there.

"Two weeks," he said. "They were pretty sure you were going to die. That death spell you did at the end, it did some serious damage inside of you, especially spiritually."

"Yeah," I said. I looked at Vigil, started to say something but held my tongue.

"Don't get all teary," Vigil said. "You're the job, that's why. You gave me the slip. If I let you get dead as well, I've failed my house."

"Understandable," I said. "You got hit. You okay?"

"Do us both a favor, and don't act like you give a shit," he said. "After a few days of you not getting better, I called in the best street doc Ankou's money could buy. He took care of me, but you were still too far gone. Those rune bullets are a bitch if they have your number on them."

"Even if they don't," I said. "I feel weird, like I should have drains and tubes running out of me. I feel strangely okay."

"Dragon," Vigil said. "When you didn't get better after the doc, she called in some of her Nightwise contacts."

"Shit," I said. "The last fucking thing in the world I need are those jag-offs getting up in my business." Vigil paused and looked at me; he rested his steepled fingers against his slightly smiling lips, and finally he shook his head.

"Yeah, I know how much it sucks to have all these people fighting to save your life," he said. "Pain in the ass, man. Well, you'll be happy to know the panaceas they tried didn't take too well. You had too much spiritual damage for the healing magics to do you much good. As shocking as this might seem, they said inside you are pretty much a big empty.

"Anyway, Dragon sent everyone out, and she did . . . something, and you screamed. Never heard a man scream like that. We heard you all the way down the hall, but you started to get better after whatever she did."

My mind was clear, clearer than it should be, and while I did have bullet scars, they were fully healed. I began to tumble in my mind what I thought Dragon had done to me, and it made no fucking sense at all.

"I can tell you're gushing with appreciation," Vigil said. He held up the USB drive Demir had given me just before the Carnifex showed up. "I had this looked over while you were getting your beauty sleep, and none of Ankou's people could break the encryption. Even the best Emerald Tablet Hermetic Hackers in the Life came back with nothing. Perhaps your friend Grinner could take a crack at it."

I sat up in the bed. "Excuse me? You and your creepy-ass boss stay the fuck away from him, or I will burn what little bit of a soul I got left dropping both of you! He's no friend of mine. He's business, and he's a fucking asshole! Leave him out of this!"

Vigil cocked his head, like he heard a noise I couldn't hear or had suddenly seen something that confused him. He raised a palm and shook his head. "He's here. We didn't reach out to him. He came about a week ago on his own. He refused to look at the drive until he talked to you. He said he was under contract. He was very insistent on that point." I tried not to laugh.

"I kind of keep him on retainer. He's the best . . . but he is an asshole."

"You two must get along famously. He must be something to get that initial reaction out of you," Vigil said. "For a second there, I thought you actually gave a damn about someone other than yourself."

I was sitting on the edge of the bed when Dragon came to visit. She was dressed in an old flannel shirt and bell-bottom jeans. She wore no shoes, and she smelled of wood smoke and wildflowers. She sat down in a chair and folded her long legs up into the chair, close to her knees, and sat kind of sideways.

"You look like you're feeling better," she said, smiling, but I could tell it was her false smile. When she really smiled, she was like a happy kid, unaware and uncaring of how she came off. This was a practiced, polite smile. I liked it best when she smiled with her eyes, when genuine joy overcame her, surprised her. "The Maven wishes to see you. She said to come by her office when you were up and about."

"Swell," I said. "Did Her Majesty happen to say what about?"

"I'd hazard a guess that it's the same reason she usually calls you in."

"Hmm, well, that's changed with time," I said. "First, she thought I was her best cop, then she wanted to fuck me but didn't want any of her 'people' to know, and then I was her greatest disappointment, and she wanted to lecture me on how I'd fallen."

"I'd put my money on C," Dragon said. "You were in town for a few days, and you stirred up the Freakz and Yeakz, pissed all over MS-13's turf, and left her with a lot of dead bodies to sweep under the rug, including a gangland bruja and a Fae Carnifex."

"Tell her I'll be by eventually, when I get around to it."

"Suit yourself," Dragon said, "poke the bear." She looked tired and a little too pale.

"Why did you do it?" I asked. "Do you understand what it means for you? What it could do to you?"

"Hello pot, meet kettle," she said, the fake smile slipping a little. "In case you forgot, I do whatever I damn well please, and you, least of all people, shouldn't say anything to me but thank you. That was some Mickey Mage bullshit you pulled with MS-13. You lied to me, kept me out of the loop until you needed me to pull your ass out of the fire. Did you even care what would happen to Dwayne and Gretchen, to you, if I couldn't, or wouldn't play your stupid game?" I ignored her question.

"You gave me your blood," I said, "a transfusion. Lauren, you only have a finite amount. You don't keep making more like humans do, and every drop you lose takes a little bit of you away, forever."

"I just gave you enough to let the healing magics kick in, enough to keep those heart-seeker rune bullets from finishing you off. It's not like it's the first time I've ever shed blood, Laytham. Your blood was mostly magic toxin, by the way, did you know that? And your soul is so hacked and hewn, there's hardly enough left to call it that. A soul, a human soul, is infinite, enduring, or at least it's supposed to be, with regular care and feeding. Laytham, what have you done to yourself, and why?"

"Stupid shit, for stupid reasons. You shouldn't have done it," I said, standing. "You're . . . unique, the last."

"I don't know that, and neither do you," she said.

"Regardless," I continued, "you're like a walking museum of unnatural history. The world loses you, it loses part of its . . . magic. I'm . . . dogshit compared to you. A broken-down old man with a lifetime of horrible decisions behind him and nothing much of a future. I've squandered my life, my gift. If I had died in that firefight . . . shit, there's already someone out there younger, more powerful, with a lot less cosmic baggage, and a damn sight more common sense."

"Doubtful. You forget your power echoed through this city a few weeks ago when you were agitated. You've done good; perhaps not as much as you've done ill, but that is not for me to judge. Why have I always been the only one you show this side to?" she said. "To everyone else you are the cool, swaggering, egotistical rock star. You piss magic potions and eat monsters for lunch, but not to me."

"You've seen me fall, you've seen me royally fuck up, but you've never judged me once, even when I deserved it. You still love me, even after I hurt you, after I hurt Anna. You've never stopped loving me, having my back. You were the only Nightwise to stand with me when all the bad shit I had been doing started to blow up. The Life will devour you if you blink. You know that. I'm too fucking scared to be this way with anyone else but you, Lauren. I'm a fucking coward at heart."

"The bravest people I've met usually were," she said. "We're partners. That never changes, no matter how dirty we do each other, no matter how much you've hurt me. I wish I could love and hate like your kind do, Laytham, but I can't. Your emotions are all too cramped. Mine are like storms on Jupiter. You and Anna are the only people that love me, even the completely terrifying bat-fuck alien parts of me, the parts I can't explain to you, or to her. You love me blind, and you deserve that coming back to you. You deserved a little blood."

"Does Anna know you did it?" I asked, looking for some clothes other than the pair of sweatpants I was in. "She couldn't have been happy about it."

"She was with me when I did it," Dragon said. "She loves you too. She just hates to see me hurt."

"And I did that a lot," I said.

"You did," she said. "But not nearly as much as you hurt yourself. Tell me, do you think you are enacting some kind of penance upon yourself for the things you've done?"

"For fuck's sake," I said, finally getting angry. "You're a goddamned ancient, city destroying, mythical-ass dragon, and you're going to try to sit there and make fucking psycho-babble excuses for me, for how I fucking use and hurt people? Maybe I'm just an immature fuck-up, Lauren. Did you ever consider that? Did you ever consider that I'm no more deep or complex than a fucking con man who swindles old folks out of their life savings or the fucking skell that kills a family for the thrill of it?

"I was a dirty cop, I almost dragged you down with me, and I might as well have put a gun in Nico's mouth." Silence passed between us, hardening like ice. "I'm one of my favorite topics. I've made a lifetime out of getting to know me, and I can assure you that there is no noble heart hidden under that moth-eaten soul. I tried to be that, and I failed, I kept on failing. You were there, you know better than most."

"As long as you are alive, you can change," this ancient, powerful being said to me softly. "It takes will and it is easily as painful as the decaying orbit of self-destruction you are on now. You have more will than any human being I've ever met, and your capacity for pain is

seemingly endless." She unfolded herself from the chair. "In my estimation, you were worth saving, worth a few drops of my life. I guess
we'll see which one of us is right and which is a fool."

"I'll give you a hundred bucks on the fool," I said. "Where are my
cigarettes?"

I got a shower, passed on shaving the two-week beard, and dressed. I
found a green-and-black paisley button-down shirt, a pair of well-
worn jeans, and my boots, still with a few old flecks of dried blood,
in the closet of the room. I figured Vigil had brought them from the
mansion. I tied my hair off in a ponytail and went out to meet up with
Grinner.

I found Robert Shelton, aka Grinner, in the galley-style kitchen
that was a nexus for this floor of the Hard Limit, which included
Dragon's and Anna's suites and an arm of guest rooms, like mine.
Grinner was sitting at a small table, a tea nook that Anna often
haunted, sipping from a bottle of water and reading a dog-eared paperback copy of Gibson's *Mona Lisa Overdrive*.

Grinner was tall, well over six feet, and stocky; his midnight-black
dye-job hair had grown out to a lazy military-cut length, no longer
high or tight, but close. He was sporting matte black plugs in his ears
these days, and I thought I caught a flash of new ink on his thick,
muscular forearms. He was clean-shaven except for a black soul patch
on his wide face. He wore baggy gray cargo shorts that fell to just
below his knees. The pants had more pockets and pouches than
Batman's utility belt and most likely a very similar content. He wore
ripped-up black Chuck Taylors that had a three-teardrop yin-yang
symbol on the sides, as well as a black Motörhead T-shirt that he had
owned since I first met him more than twenty years ago. Grinner
had an earbud in one ear, connected to his smartphone on the table.

"What the fuck are you doing here, Mr. Robot?" I asked as I
opened the fridge and fished out a cold can of energy drink.

"Waiting for your lazy ass to wake up so I can get back to work,"

Grinner said, putting down the book and slipping the earbud free. "How you doing, man?"

"I'm good," I said. "Ready to get back on this. Oh and what's this shit about 'being on retainer'? Does that make you my faithful man-servant?"

"That makes you a fuck lump," he rumbled. "Don't push it. You contracted me for intel, and I'm doing that job. That makes you a client until we settle up, so it would have been a conflict of interest to take another job."

I laughed and sat down at the small table.

"'Conflict of interest'? When did you get a morals transplant?" I said. "Besides, I paid you up front."

"For what I already got for you. So now you're paying me more. That makes you still my client. Oh, and I'm adding a little more to the tab since you questioned my business ethics."

"Thanks, man," I said. "If you'd cracked that drive for Ankou, I've got a feeling I would have woken up back in a Dumpster."

"A 'thank you' from you, Ballard, is about as sincere as a kiss from a whore," he said. "And don't be so sure. Ankou may be a smeghead, but his man, Vigil, he seems pretty solid. He treated me square."

"I don't trust him," I said, "that whole samurai, honor, thing."

Grinner laughed.

"Shit, man. He's you back in the day, when you still gave a shit, still believed in something."

"No wonder I don't like him."

"Didgeri sends her love," he said. "She was going to meet me out here when I got the word you were laid out, but she had a last-minute consult with some cops in Texas about some red-skinned, tentacled Aussie critter called a Tara-ma-yha-who. Apparently they got one out there eating people. She's worried about you and about Magdalena, but she felt she had to go help them stop this thing."

I nodded. "Yeah, they're part of the Dreamtime and can be a bitch to dislodge from the material world. Give her my love back. I saw Magdalena. Tell her she's . . . she's okay."

"Mmhm," Grinner said. "I wish she had never crossed your path, pal. You fucked her up bad."

"Yeah," I said. I didn't know what else to say. I slipped the USB drive out of my jeans pocket and handed it to Grinner. "We cool to talk business in here?" Grinner examined his smartphone and made a few swipes at the screen.

"We are now," he said. "Dragon and Anna have some kick-ass security in this place. They like to keep their clients protected. I just did an extra sweep, and we're good." He examined the thumb drive, and then it disappeared into one of the pockets of his utility shorts.

"Somewhere in that data is the identity Caern Ankou slipped into back in 2009. It's the next path stone on the road. I need it quick. The trail is ice cold. She may have already ditched this ID and moved on."

"If she did, I'll pick up the trail," he said. "Give me a few hours."

"Vigil said the Emerald Tablet Hermetics struck out trying to crack the encryption," I said. Grinner gave me a faux expression of gasping fear.

"Oh no!" he said. "If those fucking, wand-waving script kiddies can't hack it, then what chance could I, a mere mortal, have?"

Grinner was in the Life, of the Life, but he was no wizard. All his voodoo was pure talent. He was a savant, seeing code the same way Mozart or Bach had seen music. He once told me that magic was nothing more than another type of coding, universal source code.

"Give me an hour, chief," he said.

I spent that hour ordering some food from a Thai place Anna, Dragon, and I used to eat at all the time. I ordered way too much food, but ended up devouring all of it. Dwayne and Gretchen came by to visit since they had heard I was back on my feet.

"I owe you, Dwayne," I said. Dwayne shrugged.

"I'd say pay it forward, brah, but I know better. I'd get out of town if you can, Ballard. MS-13 is pissed about what went down at their crib and you whacking Francisco and Demir. You got every fucking mara in L.A. looking for you. Those guys were a valuable commodity in their business. If they get a whiff of you, they will rain down on you hard."

"Thanks," I said. "I'm hoping I can finish this bit of business up quick and be on my merry way."

"May not be that easy," Dwayne said. "She's missed you and she wants to keep you here as long as she can."

"Who?" I asked.

"The city," he said. "She thinks you two belong together. She wants to hook back up with you like in the old days, wants to finish what you two started. Says you owe her something. Watch yourself, man. She's crushing hard."

I knew what this bitch of a town wanted from me, and I was half-tempted to give it to her. We had made promises to each other, vows, and I had broken mine—big surprise there. Who knows, before this was over, maybe I'd make good on my word and give L.A. what I owed her. Dwayne said he'd give me a heads-up if he heard of any badness headed my way on the gang, or citygeist, front. I tried to pet Gretchen good-bye; she growled, snorted, and padded away.

It was two hours before Grinner found me downstairs at the bar. I was on my third whiskey and "A Sorta Fairytale" by Tori Amos was playing over the hum of the client hive. Anna kept me company for a time.

"I recall when you first came here," Anna said, her elbow on the bar, watching me drink. It should be an Olympic sport. "You got so frustrated you couldn't find that silly drink anywhere."

"Cheerwine," I said, sipping my drink, "and it's still hard as hell to find in some places. Besides, it's not silly, it is a powerful elixir of all things good and pure."

"No wonder it's hard to find," she said. We were quiet for a moment, letting the music and the conversations around us fill the gap. Most of the men and women in the room were watching Anna, wanting her, or wishing they were her. I knew she felt the attention. She was one of the most hyper-aware people I'd ever met; she could read the energies in a room without any supernatural abilities. She also presented as very comfortable in her own skin, and, for the most part, that was true. Anna had fought more demons than I, all in her head, and had conquered many of them and made strict bargains with the ones that she couldn't. Just being near her, she radiated wellness, life.

"You used to drink a lot less," she said. "Up until things got bad, near the end. You ever think about quitting it?"

"Yeah," I said, gesturing to one of the bartenders to hit me again. "I do pretty good for a while, then I run into something that shakes me up, reminds me of what a fuck-up I am, and I fall down. No big."

"Do you remember when we used to meditate together? The yoga? That could help."

"Why do you care?" I asked.

"You know why I do personally," she said, standing. "I love you, no matter how hard you make it to do that. I also hate to see potential go to waste. It offends me."

"That should be my epitaph," I said. She sighed and looked at me with those bright soul-stones she called eyes.

"I have an appointment," she said. "Some music industry mogul that needs his ass minced into hamburger meat. To be continued." Anna walked away and the whole world watched her, me included. The music had shifted to "Cold Desert" by Kings of Leon by the time Grinner took Anna's seat and ordered a club soda. He'd had his blue AA chip for several years now.

"I found her," he said.

"I thought you said an hour," I said with a grin.

"Fuck you," he said. "The attack took forty-eight minutes to crack that ugly bitch. The rest of the time was gift wrap for your sorry, ungrateful ass. I put training wheels on this, so even you can't screw this up. Cheers, asshole."

We clinked glasses and drank. Grinner nodded toward the elevator. "Come on."

Upstairs, in an empty office Anna had instructed Grinner to use, he sat down behind the most heavily modded laptop on the planet. I stood behind him. "Here she is," he said and clicked the mouse. An image appeared on the screen of a beautiful young woman, a few years older than the photo Dree had given me, with longer platinum-blond hair, blue eyes that seemed to burn out of the screen, and a wistful, sad expression that was eons away from the girl laughing beside her best friend at a concert.

"She's using the name Karen Anew," Grinner said. He clicked on a file icon, and an MP5 clip began to play. It was a clip from a porn movie called, in a flash of cinematic brilliance, *Myth-Bust-Hers.* The star of this tale of four guys trying in a very unconventional way to pay for their pizza was Caern, or "Karen," if you prefer, in a pair of thigh-high, rainbow-striped socks and nothing else. "Her stage name is Crystal Myth," he added.

I sighed. That minuscule, gnawed-on section of my insides that hadn't turned to oily, black water had hoped the trail wouldn't end up here. The majority of me that swam in that oily water knew better, knew it would. "Well, shit," I said. Grinner closed the video clip.

"Yeah," he said, "It's a goddamned shame. 'Crystal Myth' has been huge in the adult entertainment biz for almost five years out here. She's been in over four hundred films, been nominated for a ton of industry awards, if you can believe it."

"Sadly, I can," I said. "A faerie princess doing porn. I'm sure that's a draw."

"Well, at least you know she's still in L.A., and now you know where to start looking for her," Grinner said.

"Yeah," I said, "unfortunately, I do."

FOURTEEN

Most of my connections in the porn industry had faded, gone legit, or died, but I was pleasantly surprised to discover that Meat abided. "Meat" was born Christian Norlender. He was six foot seven, around two hundred pounds, blond with blue eyes like a Viking surfer, and endowed with one of the most infamous penises in the shadowy history of the industry.

Meat had worked with everyone in the biz. He was just coming up when I had met him in the nineties; by the end of the decade, he was a certified porn legend and one of the most recognized male talents around. Everyone in porn had a Meat story or two to tell, and Meat knew everyone else's stories too.

Only a select few knew that Meat's "endowment" was truly divine in more ways than one. He was the offspring of Priapus, a C-list, country-fried, slumming Greek fertility god who had been summoned up in L.A. during the Summer of Love by some hippie wannabe tantric magi. Priapus was the closest thing the Greeks had to a god of pornography, and there are still small, secret cults connected to the adult entertainment industry that practice rites to him in New York, L.A., Mexico City, Eastern Europe, and a few other places. His shrines are the peep-show booths with sticky floors.

We all know how great Greek gods were at keeping it in their pants, right? Well old Priapus literally couldn't; there weren't pants stretchy enough. In true Dirk Diggler fashion, the god was cursed with impotence, but the advent of cocaine injections and later, little blue pills from mortal medicine helped him enough with his problem to work in the adult entertainment field for decades under the cunning alias, Dick Knight. Mankind's chemical magic also provided an opportunity for the god to impregnate Meat's mom, a corn-fed USC undergrad by way of Kansas who was paying for college by stripping and the occasional porn shoot.

Old Priapus disappeared around the time AIDS started decimating the porn industry, perhaps no longer getting what he needed to stay corporeal. Some say Dickie Knight is still around and is a leather-skinned, dirty-Hawaiian-shirt-wearing old man who produces porn in Florida these days. The skin trade has as much mythology to it as *Bullfinch*.

Meat grew up in L.A. in as good a middle-class lifestyle as his dear mom could provide. Given his looks, his endowment, and his pedigree, he eventually was pulled into the gravity of the very insular porn world, where things like legacy can give you the keys to the kingdom. Meat did his first movie at sixteen, which was almost as big a secret as his divine blood.

These days, Meat's income came from being a 'Roid Warrior, a dealer in all manner of anabolic cocktails to the wealthy and vain gym rats of greater Los Angeles. He still dabbled in the adult entertainment industry as a sometimes-producer, and on rare occasions, talent.

Vigil was now my official rock-faced shadow. I drove the Trevita toward the gym where, according to Dwayne and Dragon, he was conducting most of his business these days.

"If I get jumped by a gang of leprechauns dressed like droogs, or something of that ilk," Vigil said, "I'm shooting you in the face first thing."

"Then by all means let's avoid Hollywood and Vine," I said. "I'm too pretty to die."

"Clearly," he said.

We caught up to Meat on his sales route. This stop was at a chain gym on Hollywood Boulevard that I recalled having a really sketchy reputation. Meat was doing dumbbell curls with a gentleman who wore numerous gold chains in spite of having no discernible neck. The walking man-wedge possessed a torso that was the size of a frozen side of beef and a small, pinched, red face under the awning of a salt-and-pepper crew cut.

"Okay, Dutch, give me three more, come on, bro-mato!" Meat bellowed inches from the face of the human tunnel support. The guy's face was twisted up in struggle and anger. It reminded me of a clenched fist. "Dutch," or "bro-mato," if you prefer, roared as he struggled through the last three reps of the set and dropped the dumbbells with a loud crash, making sure everyone else in the gym was made fully aware of his accomplishment. I thought of golf-clapping, but when I saw the slow head-shake of disgust coming from Vigil at the atrocious gym etiquette, I let it go.

"Meat," I said over the rumble of testosterone thunder, "hey man." Meat's eyes widened with recognition and he lumbered over to me, scooping me up off the floor and giving me a big bear hug. The parts of me that were still a little ouchy protested, but I told them to shut the hell up.

"Ballard!" Meat shouted in my ear. "Ho-ly shit, man! How are you?" I patted his back and hugged him back as best I could. For a moment, I felt like Bugs Bunny in that old cartoon with the abominable snowman. Meat sat me down, and I nodded to Vigil.

"Meat, this is Burris; he's cool. Sorry to barge in on y'all during business hours, but I could use your help." Meat and Vigil fist-bumped, and Meat gave a thumbs-up to Dutch. Dutch nodded.

"See you next week, bro," Dutch rumbled. Meat scooped up his gym bag and slid his dark blue Vans hoodie on over his tank top. I saw the flash of a small pistol butt in Meat's hoodie pocket, and I knew Vigil had too, adding it to the violent equations he had running constantly in his skull. We followed Meat through the maze of free-weight stations and machines, weaving between beautiful people in five-hundred-dollar workout clothes with perfect hair and makeup, and old-school gym rats in tattered boxing trunks and cutoff T-shirts soaked in sweat. The music thudding through the gym's sound system, "Pray to God," by Calvin Harris and Haim, was at a volume so loud you couldn't hear yourself sweat. Meat stopped several times to hug someone or to take a quick order whispered in his ear. The blond giant would nod, smile, and keep moving. Once we hit the doors and made our way to the parking lot behind the gym, Meat glanced back at me.

"You don't look like a total loss, Ballard," Meat said, inspecting me. "Looking pretty good. You still work out?"

Vigil gave me an odd look and then replied, "He's kept up on his forty-ounce curls." Meat laughed.

"Not in a while," I said, giving Vigil a mock silent laugh. "Life tends to give me plenty of cardio."

We reached Meat's car, a fire-engine-red 2016 Mustang with white stripes. His nickname was proudly proclaimed on the tags. He put the gym bag in the trunk and then turned and leaned on the back of his ride. "What you need, Ballard? I owe you big, man."

"We're looking for someone in the biz," I said. "She works under the name Crystal Myth. You know her?"

Meat nodded as soon as I said the name. "Yeah, yeah, Crystal, yeah, I've heard of her. That's the only name I think anyone knows her by, though."

"We know who she really is," Vigil said. "We're trying to find her."

"I know folks who've worked with her," Meat said. "She was working everywhere, for everyone, up until a few years ago, then she, y'know, kinda faded . . . the way a lot of folks do in the business. But she dropped off the ride at, like, the top of her game. She was making serious bank, man."

"Who for?" I asked.

"Far as I know, she never had an agent," Meat said. "She had a boyfriend, some producer that was looking out for her. I'm trying to remember the guy's name—"

"It's important," Vigil said, interrupting. "We can make it worth your while." Meat looked at Vigil with the demeanor of a deer in headlights, mashed up with the suspicious scan reserved for street predators and undercover cops. He glanced over to me for confirmation again that this guy was cool. I nodded.

"It's okay, Meat," I said. "Do me a solid and ask around a bit; see if you can shake loose some names for me. There is a finder's fee involved. I'd like you to get it, man."

"Yeah, sure, Ballard," Meat said. "I can tell you this: Crystal wasn't just working the teenybopper circuit. Before she dropped, she was doing the sick shit—gonzo, shaky-cam, semi legal stuff—simulated snuff and rape, extreme fetish—even grotto. She swam out to the deep end, bro."

"Wait," Vigil said. "Grotto? Porn with actual supernatural beings in it? That's a real thing? I thought that was all bullshit." Again, Meat gave him an incredulous look and shook his head.

"Yeah, right," Meat said. "First time in the big city?" He looked back to me. "I know she worked one of the Weathermen's parties a couple of years back. They might be able to help you."

"Fat chance, but I'll look them up anyway. Is the Iron Cauldron still in business?" I asked. Meat nodded and grinned.

"Yeah, it's in Westmont right now, a couple of blocks west of Century and Vermont. You fucking owls are still trying to shut it down. You can't catch what you can't find."

"Owls?" Vigil asked.

"The Nightwise," I said. I was getting a little irritated with him now. "Dirty Fifi still run the Cauldron?" Meat shook his head.

"Naw, they did the 'saw a man in half' trick with Fifi back a few years ago, but they didn't bother to put him back together. It's Roland Blue's place now."

"Shit," I said. Meat nodded.

"Yeah," he said, "your favorite soul-challenged L.A. Mobster. I hear you and Dragon gave him hell back when he was coming up, working muscle for the Golem Father."

"Son of a bitch is crazy, and that's coming from me," I said. "He enjoyed his work for Saul a little too much. But I'm pretty sure he'd rather rip me off for information than kill me."

"Hope is a beautiful thing, Ballard," Meat said, slapping me on the shoulder. "Dare to dream, but watch your ass and the officer's here too, man." Vigil bristled at the remark but said nothing. "I'll put out some feelers and see what I can dig up on Crystal for you." I gave him my number and like any professional street criminal he didn't need to put it in his phone or keep it on paper. Meat snapped his fingers as he was opening the door to his Mustang. "Oh, shit!" he said as he slid into the car's seat, "I just remembered, Elextra used to be Crystal's roommate!"

"Elextra?" I asked.

"Elextra Dare," Meat said. "Talent. She's on her way up these days. She's not in the Life, but Lexie and Crystal were besties back before Crystal took off. She's one of George Wilde's girls." Meat named a few clubs where we could probably find Elextra and her manager partying. I slid him several hundred dollars as he clasped my hand. "Talk soon, man. Good to see you, Ballard."

We walked back to the Trevita. I glared at Vigil, and he looked back at me.

"What?" he asked.

"That," I said, jerking my thumb in the direction of the gym, "is why I need to do this alone. You were freaking him out back there. He almost bailed on us a couple of times because of you."

"Look," Vigil said, "first of all, the last time you went out on your own, I had to jump in to save your drugged-up, drunken, arrogant ass because you don't think, you react, and second, I do not read like a cop, okay?" He stood on one side of the sports car and I on the other. We each leaned on the roof, regarding the other. "It's not my fault that your sketch-ass contact got hinky."

"Of course he fucking did!" I said. "He *is* sketch! You read like someone who doesn't hang out with sketch-ass people." I pulled out a cigarette and lit it. "You are a damn knight of the houses of the

Shining Lands. You don't normally traffic with pornographers, low-lifes, and drug dealers, except for your boss, of course. You come off like a tourist, a cop, or the hand of wrath for some angry Mafia god, and it shows."

"Good!" he said. "I worked damn hard for a very long time to wash the stink of that life off of me." He gestured toward my cigarette. I handed it to him across the roof and he took a long drag on it. He savored the smoke in his lungs like a fine wine, exhaled it, and passed it back to me. "I tossed out the code of the street, all that bullshit from the bangers, the junkies, the players, the whores. I built something for me, something that didn't make me want to eat a gun or drink myself into a coma every night. I'm never going to apologize for being who I am. "

I nodded and took a long pull on the smoke. "Look, right now, we're heading into the deepest parts of the pits you dragged yourself out of," I said. "I am a hustler, a player, and probably the biggest whore you'll ever meet. This is my backyard we're walking through, not yours, not anymore. Ankou knew that. He knew he'd need a scumbag to find his little girl. You send someone like me down into the sewer, because it's my home. Let me do my job. It's a pretty awful job, but I'm the best at it. Let me do it."

I offered Vigil the cigarette again. He considered it for a long moment and then shook his head, curtly. "You know exactly what Ankou and his needle-eared country club buddies see when they look at me." Vigil's voice was cold slate. "Product—a commodity, a resource—a half-breed, trap-house thug his people recruited straight out of prison. You know what being a 'short ear' means in their society, their world. It's the same shit I dealt with before I even knew what the fuck the Fae were—being invisible in broad daylight, or the center of fucking attention, like you're going to jump someone or steal something every second. Being disposable, anonymous, to being feared and mistrusted. Getting told silently every goddamned day that it's not your world, not your home. You feel that acid eat away at your insides, day after day, year after year, until you're empty, hollow, but still walking around. Hell, the color of my skin barely lowered me another rung in their estimation once they found out I was half-Fae.

"I owe Ankou a debt, do you understand that?" I nodded. "I didn't give a damn about myself or anyone else, and it locked me up so tight I couldn't feel a scrap of daylight, couldn't feel the sun warm on my skin. I rebuilt myself one promise at a time, one unbreakable line at a time. That's the power of discipline, of a code. It's your armor, no one can take it from you but you. I made an oath to keep you alive, to find Caern, and make sure she's safe. I made that oath not just to a man I owe a debt of honor to, I made it to myself. If you don't got a code, you have nothing."

"Codes won't save you," I said. "Honor won't save you. I'm the ghost of Christmas-yet-to-come. You cling too tight to that shit, when it fails you—and it will fail you—you go under fast and you go under deep."

"So what *does* save you from yourself?" he asked.

"Let me get back to you on that," I said.

Vigil sighed and shook his head.

"Look, my job is to be the shield," he said, "even if that means protecting you from you. I kill people; I lay the mighty low. It's the only thing I've ever been good at—killing—since I was thirteen. I gave my word—that's all life has left me—so you let me do *my* job and keep you alive."

It was quiet for a time, the traffic of the boulevard muffled by the buildings. In the ruins of a life full of lies and violence, failures, and terrible mistakes, we'd each navigated the rubble by the guttering light of our better selves. Vigil and I locked eyes. I nodded. Vigil nodded back. "Okay," I said.

"Okay," he said. "Where to next?"

Tucked away at 7734 Santa Monica Boulevard is a secret shrine, a monument to lives and souls hacked and hewn upon gilded beds. It is a haunted place of fallen street saints, chewed up and spit out by Moloch, by Hollywood's honeyed lies, devoured by you and by me. It is a temple that holds testament to the loss of the dearest of commodities, and it is home to a hidden goddess.

Vigil and I parked on the street and walked back. It was close to midnight. The theater was partially hidden behind a large Moreton Bay fig tree. The marquee declared STUDS THEATRE. When I had lived in L.A., it had been called the Pussycat. This old porn movie palace was the site of the skin-trade's version of the Hollywood Walk of Fame. The handprints, footprints, and signatures of the stars and starlets of porn's "Golden Age" were arrayed along the sidewalk in front of Studs.

I walked up to the ticket window. "Two tickets for the main screen," I said.

"What are you doing?" Vigil asked.

"Taking you to the movies," I said. "You buy the popcorn."

There was a stale smell in the dark theater. The feature currently playing was a classic piece of cinema called *Rude Boyz 3*. Vigil and I stood by the lobby doors, and I began to count rows and seats silently.

"What are we doing here?" Vigil whispered. There were about a dozen shadows occupying seats in the theater. I carefully counted down four rows from the back and then counted over eight seats over from the far right wall.

"Ritual," I said. "I learned about it from a pornomancer who owed me five ounces of cocaine, blessed by the Antimatter Buddha. Fucker turned out to be full of shit, but he taught me this in trade."

"Why would you even need blessed . . ." Vigil dismissed the troubling thought with a wave of his hand. "What does this ritual do?"

"I'm consulting a local expert on our missing princess." I spotted the seat I needed and moved down the aisle toward it. The seat was occupied by a man who looked like a guilty suburban husband. I sat down in the row behind him and Vigil sat a few seats down from me. "Hi," I whispered to the man. He practically jumped straight in the air. "I really need your seat. It's kind of got sentimental value for me. It's where Dad proposed to Mom after she got out of prison." I dangled a hundred-dollar bill beside his face. The man snapped the hundred out of my hand, got up, and left the theater without a word. I moved to the now-vacant seat, and Vigil sat down next to me.

"Okay," he said, "you got the seat you had to have, now what?"

"Now," I said, "I masturbate."

"I'll see you in the lobby," Vigil said, standing back up. "Someone tries to kill you, you got my number if you can't bludgeon them to death." I couldn't help but laugh softly.

"Hey, you're the one who insisted on coming along," I said. He gave another dismissive wave.

"Who the fuck you trying to contact?" the Elf muttered as he exited the theatre. "Pee-wee Herman?"

The room settled down after Vigil departed, and I felt the raw Svadhisthana force permeate the room, and I was physically at its center. I opened my senses, viewing it like a swirling orange fog, billowing out of every patron in the room. I opened my sacral lens wide and felt the lust, the wordless need, strum my nerves like a harp. I began my tantric breathing, my focus, as the power flowed through me, an invisible river of silent aching, so sweet and so demanding, all at once. Desire makes crack look like Skittles.

I felt myself become aroused. I stoked that fire inside me, almost oblivious to the shabby, counterfeit lust playing out a dingy fantasy on the movie screen. While the intent of many of the patrons may have been unsavory, wrapped in chains of guilt, violence, and repression, their energy was as pure as sunlight. I was acutely aware of myself, of my body and the root power churning around me. My hands clutched the arms of my seat, but slowly my fingers loosened and my hands came free to clasp each other, palm in palm, facing skyward, thumbs in opposition, acknowledging the dominance of the water element at work in this place. I began to shape and carve the energy around me, in me, of me, using very precise hand movements, mudras, as my sculpting tools. To a casual observer, I was

moving my hands quickly in my lap in a dark porn theater, nothing
to see here.

I felt the sweet pressure build in my loins, and I denied myself the
release, raising the desire to even greater levels, build and deny again
and again like climbing a mountain built of ache. In a timeless place,
my body and mind were aware only of the subtext of my reality, not
the trappings. Because of the nature of what I am, my building energy began to flicker at the edges of the other patrons' auras. I felt
several of the men in the room ejaculate, pushed past the threshold of
self-control, or casting that control away willingly. To my perceptions, each release was an explosion, a bloom of salamander fire. I
almost came too from the flood of sexual energy but my training won
out, and I rode the swell of power, greedily hoarding my own sexual
energy, using it and theirs to send my call out through the jagged
walkways to the other places, the other spheres, lands where energy
and intent replaced words and coin. This Svadhisthana power, harvested this way, it was her language, and I used it to barter with her.
I felt her near, always near to her city, to her unknowing worshipers
and sacrifices, to her sacred places. She was outside, waiting for me.

The movie, the men fucking on the screen, the patrons, many
of their faces still locked in a grimace of ecstasy, all slowed to exist in
the silence between two heartbeats. The shuddering stream of light
from the projection booth was now a solid beam. An orange fog rolled
all around me, and the shadows seemed to congeal. I stood, adjusted
my jeans to accommodate my tumescence, and headed up the aisle.
Best not to keep a goddess waiting.

Vigil was in the lobby, sitting in an old chair with duct tape covering rips in the faux leather upholstery. The chair was next to a sun-
faded plastic fern in a pot. He had his cell phone to his ear, engaged
in a conversation. The orange fog swirled everywhere, making him
move very slowly as it cheated time. His Fae physiology was resisting
the spell I had just cast, but the power behind the spell was powerful
enough to slow even him down until I got my answers. I walked past
Vigil, the recognition and surprise just beginning to spread across his

face in slow motion, and waved as I pushed open the lobby doors and stepped out onto the street.

The streetlights and the now-muted glare of the marquee were all pale hues of tangerine. Everything seemed grainy, slightly scratched and jumpy, like an old celluloid film from the seventies. I walked down the rows of hand- and footprints of the old porn stars, carefully avoiding some as I had been told to do, and stepping on others in the correct sequence. It reminded me of playing hopscotch, and "step on a crack, break your mother's back." My trip down the sidewalk ended at a young woman who hadn't been there a moment ago.

She had blond hair falling to the base of her neck and shoulders, styled in a fashion that reminded me a bit of Farrah Fawcett from the zenith of the seventies. Her eyes were large and brown and gave her the semblance of wide-eyed innocence. If you looked closer, weren't distracted by her youthful body, by those legs, you'd catch the haunted, frightened look that surfaced, fighting against practiced, drugged apathy, and you'd see the real her.

She was dressed in a costume, a caricature of a Dallas cheerleader with white mini-shorts, white cowboy boots, and a blue shirt, open to reveal her cleavage and tied and knotted up to expose her midriff. She held a white cowboy hat in her hands, clutching it tightly. Looking at me, she smiled; it was sweet and very sad, like she was glad to see me, but she bore awful news. Her true name had never been known, but the name she took during her brief time in the porn industry, when she had been alive and mortal, was Bambi Woods.

"Hi," she said. Her voice was childlike, lilting, almost musical with a raised, halting inflection, like she was reading every word she said off a cue card she had never seen before, like maybe she was a little high. There was a very faint northern New York accent in her voice.

"Hey," I said. "I'm sorry to trouble you. Thanks for responding."

"Sure," she said. "Wow, I'm surprised anyone still knows how to get in touch with me like this. People, y'know, forget."

Bambi had disappeared after becoming an overnight porn superstar. There were more rumors, urban myths, and speculation about her fate than actual porn films she had starred in. Legend had it that "Bambi" had been ritually murdered in a drug-and-sex-fueled ritual in L.A., back in the early eighties. Another myth was that she was now a plump and happy housewife and grandma in the heartland of America and just wanted to forget her porn star years. Even I didn't know the full story behind what had actually happened to the real, flesh-and-blood woman behind the sex symbol. I knew a few of the touchstones to the myth, however. She had been drug-addicted, sad, and frightened. She got caught up in the belly of the beast to pay off a drug debt. Was any of it true, was all of it? In this town, what was real and what was fake shifted like sand in the wind. I had learned that the image, the idea of Bambi Woods, had become a separate entity, the Madonna, the holy mother, of the skin trade, an archetype that had little basis in fact, fed and fueled by lust, greed, and fantasy. Bambi had become the Marilyn Monroe of the sex industry, of this dark corner of Hollywood. Bambi died for their sins and for ours.

Ideas fed power often take off on their own, become boilerplate in this shared hallucination we call reality. Bambi was hardwired into the universe of porn now, into the growling, humming nexus of the meat-grinder that took in people and spit out husks. She was the Pornoracle, and she saw it all, all the time.

"I'm looking for someone," I said. She nodded.

"Yeah," she said. "You've been looking for her for a really long time."

"Actually, not that long. Her working name is Crystal Myth. What can you tell me about her, where she is, if she's alive?"

"Yeah," Bambi said, taking a step closer to me. "She's alive, but she won't be for much longer. That's sad. And Crystal Myth, that's only one of her names. You've been looking for her for a real long time, Laytham, as far back as when you used to jerk off to those videos and think of Rosaleen just before you came."

"Wait, what are you saying? Rosaleen . . . how?"

"I could see you on my side of the screen," she said and giggled a little. It was practiced and fake. "I'm on the other side of all the screens, watching.

"Y'know Rosaleen, that necromancer you were so hot for? You've been looking for Crystal, for all of them, since back when you still used to cry. She's got lots of names, lots of faces, always a pretty face, never torn up. You've searched for every one of them."

"What are you trying to say?" I asked. "Are you telling me the asshole who's been killing women since the eighties, been destroying their souls, is hunting Crystal now?"

"Yeah," Bambi said, nodding, a shadow of a smile at the edges of her face, her eyes full of wisdom, fraught with pain. "They are, but they didn't start in the eighties. They've been at it for a real long time, honey."

"They?" I said. "Who, please, Bambi, tell me who's been doing this to these girls? Why are they after Crystal now?"

"A lot of it's outside, y'know, my field of vision," she said. "They have lots of names. They're real old. 'Dog'-something? They wear like . . . hats? I don't know, sorry. But they've been here, in the city, for as long as the movies have been made, and they've been killing, destroying, all that time . . . ten to the hundred and nineteenth power . . . plucking petals off a flower . . . so many petals you can never see an end . . . but each one diminishes the flower. They do all this . . .'cause they like, y'know, get off on it, the annihilation." Bambi cocked her head and looked directly at me, into me. "They're . . . kinda . . . like you."

"No," I said. "They're not."

"You guys have a bunch of stuff in common, y'know? That's sad too. I thought you were a nice guy."

"I am nothing like the sick bastards who did this!"

"She's the last," Bambi said. "Crystal, she's gonna be the last petal that gets plucked."

"Where is she, Bambi? I need to know, I've got to get to her; I've got to stop them!"

The Pornoracle looked at me so wistfully, like she knew the saddest secret in the whole wide world.

"Try to remember, okay, Laytham? I know it gets hard with all the little cuts that you get moving through life, but please try to remember how you were a long time ago. Bye, the movie's over. I'll see ya around."

The streetlights all went dark for a breath, and when they came back up they were their normal color again. Time had caught up to me, and Bambi was gone. Vigil burst through the lobby doors. I think he expected me to be long gone.

"How the hell did you get past me?" I shrugged. "We good?" he asked, his hand moving away from his gun under his jacket.

"Jury's out," I said. "But I'm done here. Come on, let's go."

FIFTEEN

We took Dragon's jeep the following night to go find Elextra Dare, Caern's old porn-star roommate. After a few hours of dead ends and cold leads, Vigil, Dragon, and I finally found the porn diva and her producer boyfriend in downtown L.A. at the Vault, a nightclub and lounge located in what used to be a bank.

Grinner had wanted to ride along too, but I'd said no. "I need you," I said, "to watch a lot of porn for me. Anything and everything with Crystal Myth in it. I want to know who she's worked with in the industry, what companies, what producers, directors, talent. I want as much intel as you can gather on all of them too."

"Affirmative," Grinner said. I handed him a cardboard document box. "What's all this?"

"LAPD homicide files," I said, "plus everything the Nightwise had on the same cases. Nine women over the last thirty-four years, all Jane Does, all cold cases."

"What the hell does this have to do with your missing fairy princess?" Grinner asked.

"Can you use these photos of the victims and see if you can locate them online, make some IDs?"

"Yeah," Grinner said, taking the box. He opened the cardboard lid and leafed through the folders inside. "I can mash up some military and intelligence facial recognition software with an AI program they've been developing to scan photos online . . . see if we can get some hits. You didn't answer my question. What's this got to do with what you're working?"

"Nothing, I hope."

The music, a cover of "Sweet Dreams" by JX Riders and Skylar Stecker, boomed as we moved through the line at the bar and skirted the edges of the dance floor. People knew on an instinctual level of self-preservation to give Dragon space and clear a path for her, despite her seemingly innocuous demeanor. She was dressed in a gold-and-black, leopard-print blouse, a black, leather coat that fell just above her knees, black leggings, and Dr. Martens. Her long hair was up, held aloft by two solid jade hairpins, both carved to look like Chinese dragons. I had given them to her a long time ago. Vigil was in a charcoal-gray Desmond Merrion suit, looking like he just fell off a *GQ* cover, and yours truly was slumming in a black-and-silver paisley button-up, black leather pants, and boots. I'd tripped over a razor and finally managed to shave too. I let my hair fall to my shoulders. Who says a country boy can't dress up all dapper in the big city?

"You look amazing," I said in Dragon's ear as we searched the crowd.

"I do," she said. "You look like you paid someone in the kitchen a fifty to let you sneak in."

"Charmer," I said. She laughed. It was a magical sound.

Elextra was in the actual vault from the old bank, redesigned as a cozy little V.I.P. section with bottle service. It wasn't all that hard to suss out that the majority of the folks in the vault section were in porn. A bouncer gave us a hard look as we walked up to Elextra's table. Dragon made him get preoccupied with something else with a glance of her own.

Elextra Dare was a giggling, jiggling temple to surgery and drugs. Her face had been narrowed, her chin tightened. Her lips, puffed up with collagen injections, looked like deployed airbags. The skin around her glassy, unfocused green eyes was drum-tight and dead from Bo-tox. Her age was difficult to determine due to the butchery, but I put her in her late twenties. Her boob-job made it impossible for her to have any idea what her feet looked like, but in the event of a water landing, they would act as a flotation device. She was in a too-tight, pink-and-silver-sequined minidress that left little to the imagination and matching shoes with skyscraper-like stiletto heels. Her hair was auburn, straight, and falling to mid-shoulder and breast. I saw at least one tat on her upper bicep, a variation on barbed wire with roses and thorns. The ink looked a little faded. She looked up at me and seemed to be trying to focus.

"I'm sho shurry," Elextra slurred. "No autographsh right now."

The guy Elextra was curled around in the booth, who was pawing her, was squinting at me with dark eyes glazed with simmering anger and numerous chemical libations. His body language told me he had no patience and thought himself the baddest cat in the jungle.

"Let me guess," I said, snapping my fingers and pointing at the man, "George Wilde, right?"

"Auditions are Wednesday and Thursday at the fucking office," he growled, "now fuck off." George was in his late sixties, with his gray hair close-cropped to his thick face. He wore an expensive silk shirt, halfway open with a gold chain adorned with golden razor blade visible among the ash-colored chest hair. The Italian loafers he wore with no socks could pay the rent for a family in Encino for six months. Despite his expensive clothing, there was a cheapness to his demeanor. George had invested everything he was into this facade, and the paint was peeling. He had been hard once, maybe a middleweight boxer; given his career choice he was surely a little mobbed up, but you could see that soft had crept in at the edges, like flood water seeping under a door. To the average tonic-water-swilling haircut in this club, he was dangerous. To me, he was an old lion who hadn't realized yet how many teeth he had lost.

"I need to speak with Elextra, George," I said. "It's about her old roommate, Crystal."

"Oh shhit, Cshtal," Elextra exclaimed as the name penetrated her drowning awareness. "How ish she?" George squeezed Elextra's arm tightly, and the porn actress squeaked in pain and shut up.

"You don't get shit but dead unless the three of ya get the fuck outta here right now," George said, putting the best dangerous mobster look he could on his spray-tanned face.

"We got no beef, George," I said, "but we need to talk to the lady. You hurt her like that in front of me again and we will have a problem. This won't take long. We'll be on our way before your little blue pill kicks in, promise."

"Always did have a way with interviews," Dragon muttered.

Wilde had been on a low boil before we even came into his world; now he was hot. He started to rise, his hand slipping into his baggy pants pocket. Vigil took two steps and clasped George's wrist while still in the pocket. Vigil's other hand rested under his jacket.

"You pull that .38 out, George, and I'll have to shoot you in the gut, so don't. Ease off the grip and take your hand out nice and slow." George's anger guttered a little, but not much. He removed his empty hand from his pocket and sat down, glaring. Vigil released his wrist and stepped back.

"He's good," Dragon said to me. I sat down opposite the porn producer, Dragon and Vigil at my back.

"I don't know who you fucks think you are," George began, "but you're diggin' your own fucking graves here. You're not LAPD, I fucking know every one a' the swinging dicks on the Pussy Patrol, so you're not vice. Did Gregor send you? You tell that Vladimir-Putin-looking sonofabitch he'll get his goddamned cut! I got production overhead! I got fucking Vegas up my ass for their cut too!"

"We're not vice or with the Russians," I said. "All we want is to know what Elextra can tell us about Crystal Myth. That's it, then we're gone."

George sat and looked over to his girlfriend. Elextra was so out of it, I wasn't sure she had comprehended the conversation going on around her. I placed a finger on her tumbler of scotch, smeared with her lipstick, and uttered a single word.

"*Sobrii,*" I said. The glass was now empty, and Elextra blinked several times and then winced as if she had been struck.

"Ow, fuck!" she said. "My fucking head! I think I'm gonna puke! It's so fucking loud in here, Georgie!"

"What is this shit?" Wilde said, backing up a little. "You one of those gonzo freaks, those Satanists, whadda they call that shit, 'grotto,' or somethin'? You part of Blue's crew? Buncha weird-ass fucks."

Dragon leaned down to my ear. "Why the hell haven't *you* ever used that to sober up?"

"Why the fuck would I?" I said and then leaned forward to Elextra. "Okay, Elextra, we're looking for Crystal. We think she might be in a lot of trouble. Can you tell me anything about where she might have gone to, who she could be with?" Dare's eyes were clear now, focused. She reached for a glass of water and nodded as she drank.

"Yeah, Crystal, Crissie, yeah. We were roommates back when I first came to L.A.," she said. "She introduced me to Georgie."

"Spooky fucking little bitch," George said, nodding. "I worked with her for a while, but she thought she was fuckin' Meryl Streep . . . shit, like I couldn't buy twenty pieces of ass just as good, better even—"

"Georgie," Dragon said, interrupting the pornographer, "shut up." Wilde began to say something to Dragon, but she let a tiny sliver of her mask slip, and George paled, even through his orange tan. "Go, Elextra," she said.

"Yeah, well, she was kinda . . . different, sad a lot of times, like she didn't belong here, or anywhere. She was a good friend. One time this guy, he hurt me real bad, and Crissie, Crystal, she did some kinda witch stuff and she made me feel all better. Not just made the hurtin' stop, she made me feel, I don't know, special, safe, like when you're a little kid, sleeping in the backseat of the car, y'know, and you just know everything is gonna be okay. You know what I'm talkin' about?"

"Yeah," I said.

"That loony cooz was into all kinds of witchcraft and shit. Thought she was too fuckin' good to spread her legs and—"

"George," Dragon said. "You're doing that thing again that makes me want to nail your head to the table. Close your gassy trap. Go on, Elextra."

"Well, she was into some weird shit. She told me she was like, not human, like a fairy or something. Oh, and Crystal wasn't her real name . . ."

"We had our suspicions about that," Dragon said looking at me and raising an eyebrow. "Go on."

"Yeah, well, she kinda gravitated into the gonzo porn, y'know, all the weird kink stuff. It pays better, but I always kind of got the idea it wasn't about the money for her."

"What was it about?" I asked.

"I think she kinda wanted to die," Elextra said, her eyes falling to the table. "I don't think she had any family, nobody, y'know, real. If you ain't got some kind of anchor, something real, away from all this . . . it will eat you up."

"Oh, look who's suddenly a P-H fuckin' D," Wilde said. "What the fuck would you know about anything, tits for brains? You don't get paid to think."

"Vigil," I said. "Would you please take Georgie outside and try to come up with a good reason not to shoot him?"

"At last, a real challenge," Burris said as he pulled Wilde to his feet, his other hand once again on his gun under his jacket, and walked him out from behind the table. Dragon stepped over and grabbed a clump of George's chest hair. The old man gasped.

"No, please, allow me," Dragon said. "I'll keep him company out front." George looked like he was face-to-face with a cobra, and, truth be told, he'd have been better off if he was.

"Hey, l-look, I don't want no trouble, okay?" George said. Vigil smiled and nodded to Dragon, gesturing toward the entrance to the bank vault. The knight and Nightwise escorted George away, and it was just Elextra and me.

"I miss him already," I said. "He really brightens a room."

"They won't hurt him, will they?" Elextra asked. "He can be a jerk, but he's really sweet sometimes and he takes good care of me. He spent a ton on surgery to make me prettier."

"Did you think you needed it?" I asked. She shrugged.

"It's a tough business," she said, "always someone with firmer tits or a nicer ass. Someone younger. Georgie, he's just trying to help me keep up, y'know?"

"I think I do," I said. I realized in that moment I could spend the rest of my days trying to save Elextra Dare and a legion of others just like her. I washed my hands of it and hoped that the old bastard said something to Dragon that got him eaten. "You were saying about Crystal?"

"Yeah, she was like a fairy, like Tinker Bell or something; she tried to explain it to me a few times when she was really drunk and high."

"Didn't that freak you out?" It was obvious that Elextra and George were not part of the Life, and her aplomb surprised me.

"Honey, I've had Guatemalan little people shit on me while I was dressed up like Lady Gaga, gettin' fucked by the Easter Bunny. You think I'm gonna lose it over someone telling me they're a fairy? Anyway, she said she couldn't go home no more, she didn't have a home no more. She had that 'girl next door' thing going on, and that got her lots of good gigs in the business. Nobody wants to watch a whore screw, but they will line up with their dicks in one hand and their cash in the other to see Little Mary Sunshine fuck. So she had plenty of jobs, but she started going down the slide, y'know?"

"How so?"

"You ride this train too long, sweetie, and it runs you over, one way or another, unless you got something real in your life, like I said. Some people in the business spend all their cash like they're real fucking movie stars, others it's booze or blow, or some other drug.

Then there's people like Crystal, who go further and further out into the gonzo shit, the kink, the real meatball bullshit. You work without a net in this business and sooner or later you just . . . disappear. I think that's what might have happened to her. She was working more and more of that grotto stuff. Y'know grotto?"

"Yeah," I said, "I do. She working for anyone in particular? Roland Blue?" Elextra nodded.

"Yeah, he pretty much owns the grotto scene in L.A.," she said. "Georgie figured you and your crew for some of Blue's guys. You got that whole *Army of Darkness* vibe goin' and that weird way you sobered me up."

"We don't work for Blue," I said. "I'm working a private investigation."

"Ohh," Elextra said with mock awe. "A shamus, a gumshoe . . . a private dick. Those are rare in my line of work."

"Shamus?" I said. "Nice. So Crystal was getting into the real extreme end of the weird shit? Started taking bigger risks?" Elextra nodded. "For Roland Blue?"

"Yeah, mostly. I think Brett tried real hard to get her back into mainstream stuff, but she was pretty determined. It was like she was on a mission to destroy herself, to let herself be degraded, 'til there was nothing left of her."

"Brett, who's Brett?"

"Oh, Brett Glide, he's a producer, director. Real sweet guy, even for this sewer of a town. He was one of Crystal's regular employers when she got started out here in the business. Brett's got a real good eye for finding talent that's different. That's how he made his money. Anyway, he and Crystal went out for a long time. I think he might have ended up being her one real thing, y'know, her anchor, if she had just let him. She up and left me holding the bag for rent and utilities when she moved in with Brett, didn't even come back for her stuff. That was probably the last time I saw her, about two years ago, except at a few industry parties and stuff. We just hugged and said hi, said we'd hook up. We never did. She and Brett were pretty serious, but I heard she dumped him, maybe six months after she moved out, about a year and a half ago."

"You don't seem too pissed she left you holding the bag," I said. Elextra smiled; it was pretty and genuine, and I wanted to take a crowbar to George Wilde for convincing her she needed to mutilate herself for him.

"Yeah, well, she was always sweet to me, kinda lost. I could see how she might not be from this world. I'm a sucker for love stories. I hoped she got a happy ending."

I looked at Elextra Dare, a train wreck, a caricature of a porn queen, and I wanted so much to take her the fuck out of this fun house mirror of a city, get her back to where she had been before all this. Someplace safe and free, somewhere that George Wilde or any of a hundred other scumbag jackals just like him couldn't find her, couldn't hurt her, couldn't destroy her soul a tiny slice at a time. The moment passed, and the ice water of reality hit me, reminding me of how things work—predators and eager, stupid prey.

"You're like her," she said.

"What?"

"Sad. You hide it good; she did too, especially for the cameras. Like you ain't got a home to go to no more, no anchor."

"Anchors can pull you under," I said, "drown you." Elextra smiled a sad, almost pitying smile at me.

"You're already under, aren't you, sweetie?" She touched my hand briefly, squeezed it. "It takes one to know one." We didn't say anything for a minute. Just listened to the music and the crowd.

"You said she left her stuff with you," I said. "You know what happened to it?"

"Yeah, I kept a lot in storage," she said. "I had to, y'know, sell some of it to make the rent, but all of her personal stuff, it's in boxes in me and Georgie's storage. I could get it for you tomorrow if you think it would help?"

"That would be terrific," I said, "and could you tell me how to get in touch with Brett Glide?"

"Sure!" Elextra said. "Y'know, I was up for a legit part when I first got here. It was like a plucky college girl detective pilot for a TV show. I didn't score it, obviously. I always wanted to be a plucky girl detective."

"Okay, Nancy Drew," I said, "you got your first case. Find me Crystal's old stuff and think up anyone else who might have an idea where she is now."

I walked Elextra out of the club, and she gave me the name of Glide's production company and her and Georgie's address out in Laurel Canyon. I found Vigil outside on the phone. He finished his call, hung up, and walked over.

"Where's Georgie and Dragon?" I asked. Vigil smiled.

"She took him around the corner for a heart-to-heart," the knight said. "I heard an 'eek.'"

"A what?" I said, beginning to walk toward the corner, a little afraid of what I'd find.

"An 'eek,'" Vigil said, "the sound, a terrified 'eek.'"

"Oh, that'd be Georgie," Elextra said. "He 'eeks' sometimes when he's scared."

As I was about to round the corner, Dragon walked into view, a look on her face I knew all too well.

"All done?" my former partner said. "Great! Let's be on our way then."

"Where's George?" I asked. "What did you do?"

"Nothing," Lauren said, still grinning at her own secret joke. She handed a wallet and car keys to Elextra. "Here you go, dear. George said he'd meet you back at the house. Here's his wallet and the keys to the Porsche. He said he wanted to walk and reflect on a few things. He's a very deep guy."

"Georgie?" Elextra asked. "He hit his head or something? He takes the car to pick up the newspaper at the end of the drive." She turned to me and hugged me. She smelled of honey and menthol cigarettes. "Nice to meet you and your angels, Charlie," she said. I laughed. "I'll see you tomorrow night, and I'll have anything that will help together for you."

"Thanks, Elextra," I said.

"Peggy," she said, "my name is really Peggy. It sounds weird to say it after so long."

"It's a real pretty name, Peggy," I said. "I like it. Thank you."

"See ya!" she said, smiling and waving bye to all of us. She walked half a block down, got into her car, and drove away. I turned back to Dragon, standing with her arms crossed.

"Okay, fess up. What did you do with George?" She smiled wider, showing some teeth, but said nothing. "Oh, man! Tell me you didn't . . ."

"Eat him?" Dragon said. "Of course not! You know I hardly ever eat meat anymore, Ballard. I'm very careful about what I put into my body, unlike some people, thank you very much! Who knows where that filthy old degenerate has been?"

"A vegetarian dragon?" Vigil said. "Yeah, this is Cali."

"So where is he?" I asked.

"Probably trying to find a clean pair of pants on his walk back to the canyon," she said. "I just had a little chat with Georgie in private, told him to rethink some of his attitudes and behaviors, especially when it comes to . . . Peggy. I may have allowed him to get a glimpse of me, the real me, when I was doing that, and I may have sort of implied that I was . . . the Devil."

"The Devil?" I said. "Really?"

"Don't get that tone with me, Laytham Ballard," Dragon said. "If there is any person on this planet that should not give me attitude about the Prince of Darkness, it would be you."

"Point taken," I said. "Okay, Roland Blue is mixed up in this somehow, so we need to put him on our itinerary, and now we've got a lead on Caern's old boyfriend and employer. I think I should pay him a visit tomorrow."

"*We* should," Vigil said. Dragon nodded.

"Oh, for fuck's sake," I said.

"As far as I'm concerned," Dragon interjected, "this is now a Nightwise investigation into our old cold case. "If Roland may be involved, he's my beat, and I got you those homicide files you gave to Grinner. So I'm in it now too, like it or not, Ballard."

"Fabulous," I said, walking to the jeep. "We're a fucking TV show, the Bastard Squad."

"I know a guy who knows a guy at a studio," Dragon said. She fell into step beside me. "You should pitch it." I shook my head.

Vigil was now on my other side. "Midseason replacement," he said to Dragon, "at best."

SIXTEEN

Brett Glide's adult entertainment empire had its global HQ in a warehouse on Del Sur Street in the San Fernando Valley. The warehouses in San Fernando were once the major production studios for most of the pornography produced in Los Angeles. It gave rise to the nickname, Porn Valley, or, if you prefer, the San Pornando Valley.

The porn industry's refusal to use condoms, apparently due to the disharmonious aesthetics of screwing on-camera with a rubber on, combined with new city and county ordinances requiring the use of condoms for any adult film shot in their jurisdictions, had most of the film production companies pulling up stakes and moving to other locales. Prop. 60, a statewide attempt to require condom use in the industry, got shot down, but Nevada and Florida were still both popular spots for shooting movies. A large portion of the industry still had offices, casting, distribution, and post-production facilities in Porn Valley. Brett Glide's Red Hat Productions was no exception.

A little digging online by Grinner bore out that Glide was pretty successful and a fairly mainstream twenty-first-century pornographer. He owned numerous pay-to-view porn websites, each catering to a different fantasy or genre, but nothing too over the edge, as well as a legion of webcam performer sites. He owned sex clubs in Nevada and as far away as New Hampshire, a smattering of restaurants, bars, and nightclubs, mostly with partners. Each adult enterprise had premium subscription content, pay-per-view events, and even fucking T-shirts and mugs you could buy. Glide paid his taxes and gave a living wage to his employees too.

"This guy gives smut peddlers a bad name," I said as Grinner had given us an overview of his holdings.

"Hey, adult entertainment is big business," Grinner said. "Legit business; it's everywhere, and the stuff Glide finances is very, very mainstream. No mob connections I could find. Guy looks like he was born well-off, attended Harvard, picked up his MBA, and decided he wanted to make his own fortune off of people screwing. He's done very well for himself with that."

"Ah, the American Dream," Anna said from a corner of the office, curled up with Dragon in a chair they were sharing.

"Ab-so-fuckin'-lutely." Grinner nodded.

At Red Hat Productions, an office manager named Jennifer explained that Mr. Glide was on location for a shoot in Death Valley. Jennifer said she had been told to expect us to be coming by and that Mr. Glide could talk to us out there.

"How did Mr. Glide know to expect us?" Vigil asked.

Jennifer smiled.

"I'm not entirely sure," she said. "I spoke to Mr. Glide this morning, and he told me then. I guess you can ask him when you see him." She gave us the GPS coordinates, and we gassed up Dragon's jeep and headed northeast for about four and a half hours into the desert park.

Dragon's radio was playing a cover of "Stripped" by Shiny Toy Guns as the city slid away and was replaced by wilderness, mountains, painful blue sky, and then eventually pristine wasteland, occasionally marred by roadside gas stations, fireworks, and souvenir shops. Lots of plastic rattlesnake skulls, leering with fangs, to be had with your Slurpee.

"Reminds me of where I first woke up," Dragon said. She had on her round sunglasses with the green-tinted lenses. Her long hair was tucked under a floppy campaign hat that snapped and jumped in the wind. She wore a tan, military-style tank top, ripped and worn jeans, and her boots.

"I heard the stories about you," Vigil said. It was a rare occasion; he was dressed in a yellow body-armor tee that complimented his build and black basketball shorts that fell below his knees. He wore a pair of black-and-yellow Air Jordan 5 Low athletic shoes that cost more than Dragon's old jeep. His eyes were hidden by a pair of very expensive sunglasses. "I think everyone in the Life has," he continued. "I just didn't think they were true. Are they?" Dragon smiled and nodded.

"Yeah," she said. "A few of them anyway. Everything you hear in the Life has a slight seasoning of bullshit."

Vigil glanced at me. I was slightly hungover, my old seventies cop-style sunglasses shading my bloodshot eyes, a burning cigarette dangling at the edge of my lips. I was in a wrinkled old black Pixies T-shirt I'd found at the bottom of my bag, faded jeans, and boots. My hair was tied back in a ponytail to keep it out of my face in the high wind of the interstate and now the desert. "So I have come to discover," he said as he looked at me and then turned back to my old partner. "So you really are a . . . you know . . ."

"The D word?" Dragon said, enjoying this. "That word works about as well as any other. My natural form is big and reptilian, with wings and claws. I breathe fire. But the specific detail of what I look like seems to be based on the observer. I doubt you and Ballard would experience me the same way."

"And you're the last of your kind?" Vigil asked. I could feel Dragon stiffen a bit even though she gave no indication the question bothered her at all. "I'm sorry," the knight said. I kept forgetting how good Vigil was at reading people. "I didn't mean to offend."

"You didn't," she said. "I'm not sure if I'm the last or not. I woke up in the deserts outside L.A. in 1946. I had a good sense of who and what I was but little memory of where I came from and how I had ended up here. I recall voices, two men, calling to me, some kind of spell or working, and a single word . . . 'Babylon,' but nothing else. I've never met another of my kind in all my years living among humans, but I like to think that I'm not the only one hiding in plain sight."

"You're not," Vigil said, nodding. "The world sees what it wants to see and pretends the other inconvenient things away. It doesn't make those unseen things any less real. I'm sure you're not alone, Dragon."

"Lauren," she said. "I chose the name Lauren."

"Pretty name," he said. "It suits you." Dragon smiled, and the sun came out from behind a cloud. We drove along for a long time to the sound of the radio and the desert wind.

It was late afternoon when we arrived at the filming location at the edges of Death Valley National Park. A motley collection of cars and trucks parked off the shabby secondary road we had followed for almost an hour told me we had arrived in the right spot. There were about a dozen crew and talent mostly hiding out under tent stands or coming in and out of an air-conditioned RV, busying themselves touching up makeup and tending to equipment while Brett Glide directed his performers, camera, and sound technicians. We waited near the sidelines while they got the shots they needed. Glide looked younger than me, but he may have just been living better. He shaved his head down to a fine black shadow, which included long side-burns. He wore a black goatee and mustache and looked to be in his thirties. He was lanky and tall, dressed in an old Tibetan Freedom Concert T-shirt and cutoff jeans shorts. He looked like he should be running a health food store instead of being a porn mogul. One of Glide's assistants pointed us out to him, and he smiled warmly and waved to us as he walked up the rocky dune to meet us.

"Hey!" Glide said shaking our hands, still smiling, "I'm Brett. It's really great to meet you guys. You have a good trip out? C'mon, let's get you guys out of this sun." He led us back to one of the pavilion tents. A twentysomething production assistant with a trucker cap and a truly majestic hipster beard handed Glide a small bucket full of ice and bottled water. We joined Glide in folding director chairs in the shade. Glide offered us each a water, and I took one from him, careful to hold it near the neck and cap as I sipped it. Glide leaned forward in his chair, clasped his hands, and looked earnestly from one of us to the other. "So, you guys want to know about Crystal, right?"

"Yeah," I said. "How did you know to expect us?"

"Lexi," he said, "Elextra. She texted me last night that you were like P.I.s or something, looking for Karen, Crystal. I'll help all I can. I've often wondered what happened to her. I didn't figure she would ever go home, so I kinda thought it was something worse. Nature of the business and the town."

"Why would she never consider heading back home?" I asked. I felt an odd shiver in my Ajna, my third eye. I glanced to my old partner, and Dragon nodded slightly to me. I narrowed my eyes and studied Glide as he took a swig of water and then replied.

"Your accent's cool, man. What is that, North Carolina? Y'know you could totally get work out here just on your voice."

"West Virginia," I said. "I'll keep that in mind. Why would Karen never want to go home?"

"Her mom was dead, and her dad was an asshole," Glide said. "I know that sounds way judgmental, but he was always busy with work, and it got worse after her mother passed on. I think he may have tried to . . . y'know, abuse her somehow." I looked to Vigil and saw the knight's jaw set, his eyes darken. "She didn't want to talk much about her life before L.A. I'd be really shocked if she had gone home. You guys, you aren't working for her old man, are you?"

"No," I said, and I could tell Glide sniffed the lie on me, but he nodded and kept smiling. Far out, man.

"How much did you know about what she was getting into?" Dragon asked.

"You mean the gonzo work?" Glide said. "The grotto stuff? Yeah, I knew. That was near the end of the time we were together. I tried to get her to take more healthy gigs . . ."

"Healthy?" Vigil broke his silence. "You think any part of this business is healthy for a kid who may have gone through the ordeal she suffered?" I saw a flash of something hard in Glide's eyes, just for a second. It read like anger. I shut up for a change and watched.

"Tell me, friend, what's your name again?"

"I didn't give it to you," Vigil said, "and you are not my friend." Glide nodded and held up his palms.

"Okay, okay, it's cool. I know this is a messed-up business. I've been in it since I was a kid. It does chew you up, and it changes you. But, hey, isn't that life? I'll bet if you took away all the pain and the struggle from your life, you wouldn't be the man you are now. You like the man you are, right?" Vigil was silent and Glide continued. "The folks who stay, who survive and thrive in my world, they make it by being professionals, by doing the job, getting the check, and putting most of it in the bank. That wasn't Crystal. I think she saw this as some kind of ordeal, a trial. That if she could handle the worst the beast could give her, be broken down by it and still endure, still survive, she would be . . . purified . . . reborn?"

' "That's a real poetic way to describe using damaged people to make yourself rich," Vigil said. "There's nothing noble in suffering; ask anyone who's really done it. You don't learn from it; you learn in spite of it. I think you, your 'industry,' and all your buddies are a bunch of parasites."

"The parasite has its place in nature too," Glide said. "Look, I won't try to defend our business. I can't. All the freedom of speech and expression arguments aside, this is a high-stress, high-risk industry, and it does tend to attract damaged people. I do what I can to help the people who come into my orbit, and I even end up loving a few of them. I loved Karen. I wanted to help her. Some people don't want to be helped." He turned his sincere gaze from Vigil's sunglasses to me. "Wouldn't you agree, Mr. . . ."

"Ballard," I said, "Laytham Ballard." I saw the surprise and recognition dart across Glide's face and then quickly vanish. "I'd agree with you that there are a lot of folks in this world who are more than happy to show you their throats. It doesn't make it right to open them up. Tell me, how much do you know about grotto porn, Mr. Glide, and the Life?"

Glide leaned back and rubbed the bridge of his nose. "Enough to try to stay the hell away from it," he said. "Roland Blue has extremely bad karma, right? He saw Karen at some industry thing, a party, whatever, and wanted her. Son of a bitch practically licked his chops. By then, Karen was already using way too much—molly, blow, lots of booze, lots of weed—and Blue got her onto smack. Like I said, this business isn't full of Sunday school teachers, but some of us have a line we don't cross, and that's one of them for me. He recognized that Karen was . . . special, you know all that, right? I've heard of you, Mr. Ballard, and you have the same kind of reputation as Blue, not very savory. Blue recognized Karen's potential for grotto, the kind of clients and audience she could attract. I mean how much would you pay to watch a faerie princess get busy, right? Blue runs a freak show, a carnival of occult sexual oddities—"

"Not 'freaks,'" Dragon interrupted, "just different, still thinking, feeling, beings, locked up in a world too dogmatic and frightened to even try to understand them, let alone accept them."

"Right, right," Glide said nodding, "of course, I'm sorry. I didn't mean to bring that big old judgmental hammer down. That's not my scene at all! I'm just trying to say that if you want to know what finally became of Crystal Myth, my best guess would be to ask Roland Blue."

Glide stood, and a few of his production people barraged him immediately with questions and clipboards. He politely stepped through them to shake our hands again. Vigil refused, and Glide steepled his fingers and bowed slightly to the knight, seemingly not disturbed in the slightest by the snub. "If I can be of any additional help to you, please, reach out," Glide said as he accompanied us to the edge of the pavilion. "If you find her, please give her my love."

"We'll be in touch," I said. "Thanks for your time. Have a nice day." Glide ignored my smart-ass remark. He looked past me out to the landscape behind me, as barren as an alien world. The sun was beginning to dip, and the shadows lengthened across the land, cut and shaped by the rocks into skeletal fingers reaching, grasping.

"I love it out here," Glide said, talking less to us and more to himself. "My grandfather found great spiritual enlightenment in this place. He used to race dune buggies out here when he was young. It's so pure, so . . . beautiful in its annihilation, and yet life clings to death, almost like a parasite, thrives at the edges, in the cool shadows. The place fills up your soul even as it tries to destroy it." Then he looked back to me, his eyes focusing again. "Safe journey back, Mr. Ballard. I hope you find your answers."

The sun died in majestic 3D IMAX as we headed back for L.A., bleeding out across the horizon in currant, orchid, and fire. The Red Hot Chili Peppers' "Californication" was playing on the radio. Dragon was the first to speak.

"What do you make of him? Glide?" she asked.

"He's covered in more slime than a Nickelodeon game show, but he thinks he's Gandhi," Vigil said. "Smug, self-righteous, believes because he does yoga, drinks fair-trade coffee, and contributes a little of his blood money to benefits for the Dalai Lama, he's clean."

"Not an unfair assessment," I said. "He may also be a wizard of some stripe or other. I felt a little current coming from him."

"Really?" Vigil said. Dragon kept her eyes on the road, but she nodded.

"I got a little sizzle off him too," she said. "It could just be he's a dabbler in mysticism who's got some natural aptitude. I've run into my fair share of those out here."

"Could be," I said. "He knows more about the Life and grotto than he's letting on, though."

"He hates Roland Blue," Vigil said. "That much was pretty obvious."

"Lots of people do," I said, "for all kinds of reasons, but in Brett's case, maybe he's the one who fed Crystal to Blue, once he realized how valuable she could be for Blue's business."

"Maybe things got out of hand with Blue, and Glide's pissed he lost his meal ticket," Vigil said.

"An old-school motive," Dragon said. "Greed. How novel. Usually, these cases involve sacrifices to elder gods, ancient Armageddon-causing artifacts, or reincarnated lost loves, that sort of thing. I think I understand why cops like simple answers." I said nothing. "You obviously are not a fan of simple answers," she said, glancing at me in the rearview mirror, "you never were."

"Just a feeling." I held up the plastic water bottle, still holding it by the neck. "Let's swing by Elextra's place and see what she's got for us. Then I want Grinner to run Glide's prints off of this and see if anything interesting pops up."

I tried calling Elextra Dare, aka Peggy, several times on the scrambled phone Ankou had given me. No answer. Finally, she responded to one of my texts around nine, saying that she and George were home and to come on over. She misspelled a few words, used abbreviations, and ended her text with a little smiley face and a heart emoticon. She signed the text "Nancy Drew." I couldn't help but smile and shake my head. We made it back into town around nine-thirty and pulled into the drive of the porn diva's ranch home close to ten. The headlights of Dragon's jeep caught the back of George's dark green Porsche coupe, including his vanity tag HRNDAWG. Classy. We parked and headed up the walkway to the front door of this normal home in this very quiet, very upper-class neighborhood. About five feet from the door, I almost puked as I felt a wave of stabbing agony and nausea hit me hard. It felt like someone had poured hot grease into my skull.

"Shit," I said, and raised a hand for everyone to stop. I held it together, pushing the sickening sensations down deep, and looked to Dragon. Her eyes were veined in burning gold. Vigil's pistols were in his hands.

"What?" he asked softly.

"Something . . . not from here," Dragon said, "a predator, a big one."

"Come on," I said, running to the door. "It's inside!"

"Ballard, wait!" Vigil shouted, charging up behind me. I kicked the door at the knob plate and felt it give, smashing open beneath my boot. My breathing was tight, angry, and not proper or healthy—I didn't give a fuck—I threw open my Manipura chakra wide and gathered pure, annihilating force around me, like a cloak made of screaming suns. Vigil was beside me, covering me as best he could, the guns arcing, his senses tracking every mote of dust in the air. Dragon appeared at my other side. I could feel the heat roiling off her, streamers of ash smoke wreathing her face, her molten, alien eyes cutting through.

The smell hit me almost at once. Anyone who's ever dealt with gut wounds knows it, fresh blood and opened bowel. There was music playing on the sound system in the den off to my left. It took me a second to recognize it. It was the Velvet Underground's "Venus in Furs." Vigil tried to get in front of me to sweep and clear, but I'd have none of it. I stepped into the doorway of the den.

"Peggy!" I yelled.

"Damn it, Ballard," Vigil muttered, coming in right behind me.

The moment my boot touched the carpet, it squished. I looked down to see bright, fresh blood pouring out of the saturated carpet. The den looked like it had been decorated by a couple of grandparents from Miami Beach. There were photos from vacations, a nautical themed compass-clock, a stuffed swordfish, a wide-screen TV that was on, but muted, showing what looked like some kind of celebrity dancing contest. A wide static shot, like something out of a Stanley Kubrick film: George Wilde sat on his plastic-wrapped sofa, both of his eyes ripped out of their sockets, leaving ragged, dark holes. His legs splayed stupidly, his checkered golf pants slowly soaking up the blood on the floor, the stains up to the level of his socks. His eyeballs were speared on little plastic cocktail swords, one in each of the large martini glasses on the table in front of the couch, clouds of diffused crimson swirling in the gin and vermouth.

Peggy, Elextra Dare, sweet, funny, honest, comical Peggy, was cut into dozens of pieces, chunks actually, scattered across the floor. Her intestines and organs were partly pureed and sprayed everywhere, as were blood-splattered scraps of paper. I knelt by one of her severed hands. It clutched a stained black-and-white still of Caern Ankou, Crystal Myth, captured from one of her films. I took the photo out of Peggy's lonely, orphan hand. Something in the picture startled me, jarred a memory loose. I crumpled it up and stuffed it in my jeans pocket, almost without thinking. *Of course,* some part of me whispered.

"I'm sorry, Peggy," I said. "I'm damn sorry, Nancy Drew."

"It looks like they shredded the boxes of Caern's effects too," Dragon said, picking up part of a torn cardboard box. Shredded photos and notebook paper tumbled out, scattering pieces of Crystal across the floor to mingle with Elextra's torn flesh and cooling blood. I heard a squeaking sound, like the rubber wheels on a shopping cart. My head snapped in the direction of the noise, toward an open door and a corridor just outside the den. An odd, boxy-shaped shadow shrunk as its source disappeared down the hall.

"Son of a bitch!" I cried and dove toward the open door. Vigil and Dragon shouted and cursed after me. I spun around the corner, almost slipping on the blood-wet floor, ready to hurl all my seething power, guided by my anger and guilt. I felt more than saw the space at the far end of the hallways twist and fold like origami as something that looked nothing like a human slipped between the folds of what was and wasn't, and then it was gone. Dragon was beside me.

"What was it?" she asked.

"I have a notion, but it seems impossible," I said. "They aren't supposed to exist anymore."

"One of the Hungry?" she said. "From the outside?"

"No," I said. "It came from inside."

There was a shout from the den, Vigil and some other voices.

Dragon and I moved back to see what was going on. A man and a woman, the man in a work shirt and Harley-Davidson T-shirt, and the woman in a black pantsuit and white blouse, stood by the broken front door. Vigil was covering both of them with a gun.

"Stand down," the woman said.

"Not going to happen," Vigil said, his gaze as unswerving as his hands. A glowing, golden light shimmered into being around the left hands of both the man and the woman. Vigil began to squeeze his triggers.

"Vigil, wait!" I said. The knight held his fire as the glow diminished. A swirling, three-dimensional five-pointed star—a pentacle—hovered silently above the two strangers' hands. I recognized it, it was the Brilliant Badge. Vigil recognized it too.

"Nightwise!" the man said. "By order of the powers that bind and protect, stand down." Vigil holstered his guns, and looked to me and Dragon.

"Bridgette, Luke, what are you two doing here?" Dragon asked.

"Got orders, Lauren," the woman, Bridgette, said. "We were told to find Ballard and bring him in, now. Didn't realize we were going to be walking into a goddamned slaughterhouse, but then again, that is Ballard's reputation."

"Bring me in," I said, "for fucking what?"

"Just conversation," the man, Luke, said. "The Maven wants a word with you."

SEVENTEEN

S ections of Chinatown are a little run-down, not the kind of places a tourist would, or should, go. You'd drive by the brick, three-story warehouse on North Spring Street that was the home of AAA Distribution without giving it a second glance, never realizing one of the most powerful sorceresses in the world worked there.

The two Nightwise goons, Luke and Bridgette, parked their Range Rover on the street and led me inside the warehouse. It was close to midnight by then. AAA received all kinds of cheap goods manufactured in China, stuff like menus, fortune cookies, those wooden chopsticks in red paper envelopes for American Chinese restaurants, flimsy folding Chinese fans and parasols made of paper, and small smiling Buddhas carved from red teak or fake jade, the kind of tourist-chow sold a few blocks over in souvenir shops. We walked past crates and plastic-wrapped pallets of that stuff on our way to the venerable, closet-sized elevator that led up to the business offices of AAA. It was like stepping back in time, the sawdust and ginger smell of the place, the dim metal-cage-covered lights hanging from the exposed steel beams of the ceiling. Even the stiff, formal way my chaperones were on guard around me. Ah, it was like I'd never left the order.

There had almost been a throw-down when Bridgette had explained that my invite to see the Maven was for me only. Vigil had been adamant in his refusal to let me out of his sight, and I thought the situation was about to get very Tarantino very quickly, but between Dragon and myself reassuring him that no harm would befall me, he finally relented to search the crime scene with my ex-partner and then head back to the Hard Limit.

My shadows and I crowded into the elevator. There was a little less than a foot of open space with all three of us in the car. The old, dented, and scarred door slid shut and the elevator groaned and lurched as it lifted us. I looked over at Luke. He was watching me, but his eyes darted away from my gaze. I smiled.

"I don't bite, rookie," I said. His complexion darkened.

"You try it, and I bust your teeth in, Ballard," he said tersely, but he knew behind the cop-talk I saw his nervousness.

"How'd you get partnered up with a fire hazard like old Bridgette, here?" I asked, looking over to his partner. She had been with the order for a few years about the time I had left L.A. Bridgette narrowed her eyes at me, not bothering to disguise her revulsion.

"Behave yourself, Ballard. Don't let this broken-down old skell rattle you, Luke. He's not worth spit anymore."

"Very true," I said.

"What's it like to be the biggest fuck-up in the Life?" she asked. "The order's greatest mistake?"

"It's sort of like this," I began. I drove my knee into Luke's balls as I crunched my elbow into Bridgette's face, hard, driving her head back into the wall of the car. As she slid to the floor, leaving a red smear from the back of her head, I gave Luke, who had instinctively bent forward in the crowded car, an uppercut that lifted him straight off his feet. He slid down on the opposite side of the car from his partner. The door opened on the third floor with a feeble ding, and I stepped out, letting the sprawling bodies of the two Nightwise slump over and jam the door open.

I walked down the hall past the door labeled ACCOUNTING and

the one that said DISTRIBUTION AND SALES to the inconspicuous door at the end of the hall labeled only PRIVATE. I opened it without knocking.

The office was cramped and looked like it belonged perfectly in this dingy warehouse. There was a whiteboard on the back wall, covered with obscure alchemical formulas. The desk looked like something picked up at an old city school surplus sale. There were two folding metal chairs in front of the desk and a several-years-old PC and monitor on it along with a corded, multi-line telephone. Two dented, gray file cabinets rested side by side in the corner opposite the door. There was a window on the left wall. The old, tattered metal blinds were pulled up to accommodate a decades-old air-conditioning unit that was almost more duct tape than plastic.

"Nice to see you redecorated," I said to the woman behind the desk. "That new tape on the AC?" The woman was in her mid-sixties, with a body still hard from a daily regimen of swimming, racquetball, and kickboxing. Her hair was silver more than gray and worn high, always up at the office, but I suspected it still fell to her shoulders when she allowed it to come down. Her features were noble, almost haughty, in their proportions and beauty. She had the face of someone who commanded obedience and was used to getting it. There was nothing soft about her, including those piercing, blue, intelligent eyes. Looking at her brought back up some of the feelings I'd had for her over thirty years ago. She was powerful, beautiful, terrible like a storm, and I still felt the power of her pull. Her name was Gida Templeton, and she was the High Maven of the Nightwise.

"What did you do to them?" She sighed, closing the file in front of her.

"They're napping in the elevator," I said, sitting down in one of the folding chairs before her desk.

"I warned them," she said, "but you can come off so . . . unassuming. You look terrible, Laytham. Are you taking care of yourself?"

"As quickly as I can," I said, smiling as I rummaged for a cigarette, "but I keep putting up a fight. What do you want, Gida?"

"I want to know why you're crashing about my city, stirring up elements of the Life and the gangs, leaving chaos and dead bodies in your wake, like you never left. Why?"

"I'm working a job," I said. "Missing person. Nothing to do with you."

"Rubbish," Gida said. "You have been leaving big, muddy boot prints all over since you arrived back in Los Angeles. In roughly a month, you've managed to infuriate MS-13 by assassinating one of their in-house brujas, rile up a Cambodian Yeak gang, bring a Fae Carnifex to my doorstep, and get two civilians murdered, one of them turned into bloody compost, all on my watch. So please, Laytham, spare me your innocent lamb routine. It only played well when you really were one, a million years ago."

"In my defense," I said, "I was in a near-death coma for at least two of those weeks." Gida opened a drawer of her desk and removed a bottle of 1926 Macallan whiskey, her favorite, and two tumblers. She poured me a glass and slid it across the table to me, then poured herself a glass.

"Well, let's hear it for effective time management," she said. "Three times the cock-ups in half the time." She raised her glass and I did the same. "I am glad you're not dead, Laytham. Cheers." We both drank. "So tell me about your missing person."

"Daughter of Fae nobility, the Ankou clan, went missing in 2009. Dad may want her back for some kind of political marriage or a Mob alliance. I told him I'd look into it. If the girl doesn't want to be found, I intend to let her fade away again. It looks like she may have been mixed up in Roland Blue's grotto trade."

"Blue, eh?" Gida said. "Nasty business there. You have a picture of the girl?" I handed her the photo that Dree had given me of the two of them at the concert, and then a printed still of her face from her last porn film, courtesy of Grinner. I kept the crumpled, torn photo I recovered from Elextra's bloody den my little secret for now. The Maven studied them for a moment and then slid them across the table back to me and sipped her expensive whiskey. "And what is your percentage in this mess?"

"The dad owes me a favor," I said. "A sizable one."

"Favors," Gida said as she casually scanned me with her bright, cold, diamond eyes, "the only currency any wizard worth his salt gives a damn about. That's adorable by the way."

"What?"

"The way you honestly think if you find her that you'll just nobly let her stay hidden if she doesn't care for a family reunion. You still want to be the samurai so badly, don't you, Laytham?"

"That's the plan," I said and took another long sip of the whiskey. "No way in hell I'm dragging her back kicking and screaming to this guy if she doesn't want that."

"Oh, of course not," she said. "You will convince the poor child it's her own idea. As great a wizard as you are, and you truly are brilliant in the craft, you're a savant in emotional manipulation. At that you are unmatched . . . except for me, of course."

"Of course," I said.

"You possess the aptitude to talk the knickers off a nun, dear boy."

"I recall talking yours off a time or two," I said. Gida smiled.

"You did indeed," she said, "just like I wanted you to."

"Okay," I said. "It's been a slice of peach pie catching up, but I'll be on my way now."

"Yes," she said, "you will. I want you out of L.A. by tomorrow."

"I want Salma Hayek's digits," I said. "We don't always get what we want, Gida."

"I usually do," she said. "You were a . . . rare exception. I expected too much from you and you fell, hard. To call you a mercenary now is to be generously blinded by nostalgia and my past affection for you, Laytham. You are not one of us anymore, you really never were. I took a feral thing and tried to domesticate it. I failed. To put it in the vulgar but accurate parlance of the street, you're dirty, and I don't need a dirty ex-Nightwise—the *only* ex-Nightwise—wandering my town causing trouble and poking into our cold cases."

"This is about the murders," I said. "Just like it was back then. They are the real reason you pushed me until I left, back when there were only two of them; now you've got what, nine? Great progress, Maven."

I saw Gida's face shift slightly. If you didn't know her as well as I did, you'd never see it, but I had spent countless hours kissing those lips, watching ecstasy and weakness, cruelty and joy shift behind those blue eyes. Now I saw anger, cold and sharp, but always controlled.

"You're no better than Roland Blue," she said, "a street-hustling criminal, a predator, a user. The only difference between you two is that Blue is honest enough with himself to admit what he is. You, Laytham, you cling to the delusion that you are a good man, a just man. You hang onto it like a drowning man clings to a life preserver. You failed as a samurai; you failed as a rōnin, even. You have no code, no honor. You do as you please and try to justify it later, and you have the audacity to sometimes call it doing good. Tell me, Laytham, can you still summon it? Can you?"

I said nothing. I looked at my empty glass. I knew what she was talking about. There is a working taught to each prospective Nightwise. A simple exercise for one trained in magic, to summon a three-dimensional symbol made of light and will—a five-pointed star, a pentacle of protection—the symbol of warding from the forces, agents, powers, and principalities of the darkness. We . . . they call it the Brilliant Badge. It is a secret ritual, taught only to those who wish to be Nightwise. To summon it you must believe, truly believe in the cause of the order, in protecting the weak and the innocent, to selflessly stand between the blind world and the things that would devour it. It is an act of ultimate self-sacrifice, of self-discipline, of faith. You can't lie to the Brilliant Badge; the spell's far too simple, too beautifully direct to counterfeit. You either believe or you don't. It's part of what keeps the Nightwise honest, above reproach. In the Life, it's a powerful currency. You live or die by your reputation.

"You show me that you want justice for those murdered girls because it's an affront to your sense of decency, to your desire for justice, not because it's a challenge to you, to catch the killer, to win to soothe your own rapacious ego. Do what you enjoy doing so much, Laytham, prove me wrong. Summon it."

I raised my palm. I focused my energies, the lenses of my chakra opened. They were the visualization I had settled on as my primary focus for my power. They couldn't help me here. This was rote magic, a specific visualization exercise, which tapped into your mental state, your belief systems. It was, in a way, like a Rorschach test for wizards. You had the qualities the spell sought to unlock its tumblers and activate, or you didn't. I tried to focus my thoughts on Jane Doe, on all the Jane Does, on the horrible things that had been done to them, to the ultimate affront of having all that they were torn from them and just . . . ripped apart, lost, gone, forever.

Unbidden, my thoughts went to the man at the dogfighting house, the one I had casually reaped of his soul. I felt the current of his life force burn through me, and the high, the almost godlike purity and power it gave me. I had done the same thing the killer had done, almost without a thought, and it was far from my first time doing it. The Brilliant Badge flared for a moment, then sparked feebly in my hand and collapsed. The light failed, and my palm was empty. Gida said nothing for a time. She slid the bottle across the table to me.

"Take it with you," she said. "Twenty-four hours. Be out of my city, Laytham. You should never have come back here." I stood and took the bottle.

"I know why he's doing it," I said. "It's a drug, a rush. He cultivates these girls, carefully, slowly degrades them, makes them fall a few inches at a time. It probably takes years—that's why the time between the kills—and then he . . ."

Gida stood, her face still a placid frozen lake, but there was a sharp edge in her voice, no mercy, no compromise. She was done listening. It was the Maven of the Nightwise speaking now. "Twenty-four hours, and then I order all of my people, including your ex-partner, to hunt you down and drag you out of L.A., dead or alive, Laytham. It's over."

". . . and then he fucking harvests them like goddamned crops!"

I said and drove my fist down on her desk. Luke and Bridgette came through the door, eldritch power dancing at their fingertips. Both looked a little worse for wear from our time in the elevator, and both looked more than ready to open up on me. Gida raised a hand for them to hold. "He fucking smokes their soul like really good weed, and he gets off on it. It makes him feel like a god. Maybe he even keeps a little of their energy to supplement his own! He's in the fucking Life, Gida, goddamn it, are you fucking blind? I know him! I understand him!"

"Yes," she said. "You do. And that, Laytham, that is your problem. Good-bye." She looked to her two loyal agents. "Mr. Ballard is leaving. Make sure he finds his way out unmolested."

"Yes, Maven," they intoned. I pushed past them, the bottle in my hand.

"I know my way out," I said. "Fuck you, Gida."

I wandered through the streets of Chinatown, multicolored lanterns and lurking dragons my companions. It was late, but clusters of drunk tourists still weaved along the streets of light, avoiding the shadows I had walked out of. The whiskey bottle was my companion too, and I remembered its sweet, smoky voice offering forgiveness, understanding, comfort. I chuckled to myself, Southern comfort.

I smashed the bottle in the gutter, scaring a flock of tourists and making them hustle to the other side of the street. I watched thousands of dollars' worth of golden absolution drain into the gutter. I hailed a cab and headed back to Elextra's house.

The way a Nightwise investigation worked was like this: my elevator-buddies, Bridgette and Luke, had contacts with LAPD, detectives who either were in the order or knew the score. This would be investigated as a homicide by the daylight cops, and the Nightwise who caught the case, in this instance, most likely Bridgette and

Luke, would run a parallel shadow investigation into any and all connections to the Life and its denizens. A lot of so-called occult crime had nothing to do with the Life or anything even remotely occult. It was often the mentally ill or posers who had read the paperback of the Necronomicon and thought they were John Constantine now. That wasn't the case with what had killed poor Elextra, and not-so-poor George. I had a hunch what it was, but it seemed that my hunch was impossible. I wanted to go over the crime scene, and I was pretty sure that the LAPD wouldn't "discover" the scene for at least another day or so. I also knew that Luke and Bridgette were patching themselves up and cursing my name right now, so I didn't have a lot of time to dick around.

The mystic seals they had placed on the house were tougher to crack than the ones on Caern's apartment back in Greece, but I was up to it. I had been taught how to bypass protective enchantments by one of the best thieves in the Life. I hadn't seen her since she had been part of my caper to rip off Joey Dross in 1999, relieving him of the philosopher's stone. She was a hell of thief, and I had paid attention. The wards folded like a bad poker hand and I was in.

The place reeked even worse of marinated blood and feces. The lights were on, just as they had been when we had arrived, and I took a moment before I reentered the slaughterhouse of the den. I wished for the tenth time I hadn't chucked the bottle. It was now almost two in the morning. This scene had been gone over by Dragon and Vigil, but I needed to feel like I was doing something and I had ways to suss things out of a scene that neither of them could. I started out standing at the doorway to the den, trying to make order out of the blood-spattered chaos. I noticed that the cardboard file boxes that had contained Caern's possessions were gone. I assumed that Dragon and Vigil had spirited them away, even though they had been shredded by the thing that killed Elextra and George.

The killer spent virtually no time on George. Plucking out his eyes was an afterthought, a sick joke for whoever found this scene. The killer had gone out of its way to annihilate Elextra and even more out of its way to shred the boxes of Crystal Myth's life. It was sent with specific mission parameters, like a good little kill-bot. So this was a hit to keep Elextra from talking any more about Crystal and from helping us find her. I had found a pigeon feather resting on a bench in a bus stop shelter. I held it up now and directed my will and power through it. *"Surge Sursus,"* I said. Everything in the room drifted upward, ignoring gravity's demand. Each drop of blood, each chunk of Elextra's body, the furniture, it all rose. A tiny scrap of white drifted downward as the leather recliner in the room drifted up. It had been stuck under the chair, and I walked over and plucked it from the air where it now hovered under its hiding place. It was part of a doctor's prescription pad. The full name of the doctor and the practice's phone number were not on this scrap, but it was enough to start looking. I pocketed it next to the crumpled photo of Crystal I had recovered from the room earlier. I had almost slammed it down on Gida's desk in my anger, but I was glad I hadn't. It gave me an edge, knowledge she didn't have, and I'd have to worry about her and the Nightwise soon enough if I wasn't smart enough to heed her deadline. I let everything drift back to its place on the ground.

After another of hour of poking about, both physically and metaphysically, I had zip. If Dragon or Vigil had turned something up in the room, they took it with them. I walked to the hallway beside the den and felt the shiver of the still-bruised space that had been torn for the killer to escape. The house was stunted in its silence. I once again reached out my perceptions and sought to feel my way along the slowly healing wound in the world. My awareness didn't get as far this time as it had when the thing was running away, but I reached the same conclusion. The killer had not fled into the outer worlds; it had fled inside this world, inside someone's mind.

I rubbed my face and wished I weren't out of cigarettes. I considered making myself a drink at the bar in the corner of the den, but I saw Elextra's face in my head, and I suddenly wasn't thirsty anymore. I took out the scrambled satellite cell phone Vigil had given me. I dialed a number I had committed to memory. I pulled the crumpled photo of Crystal Myth out of my pocket and unfolded it as I held the phone in the crook of my neck, waiting for the connection. I knew that the phone call was bouncing across the world and perhaps through several others, in an act of electronic and mystic legerdemain that would make Grinner's head spin. There was an electronic beep, a pause, then a second beep, and then a click as the call was answered at a quiet little farm tucked away in Harrisonburg, Virginia. A woman's voice answered. "Hello?" she said, sounding a little wary.

"Pam, it's Laytham Ballard," I said. "How are you? Sorry if I woke y'all."

"No," Pam English said. "You didn't wake me. We're on farm time, remember? I'm on watch with a foal that's got a bad case of colic. I imagine you want to talk to Wayne?"

"Yes, please," I said.

"Now him, you're waking up," she said. Pam was the gatekeeper for her husband, Wayne. The couple had already lost a son to Wayne's decades-old connection to the Life, and Pam had no intention of losing her husband as well. She was very protective of Wayne, which was understandable. Wayne English was one of a kind, the last of the Acidmancers, a prodigy, a Man in the Gray Flannel Suit for IBM, back at the dawn of the information technology age. Wayne had found the world-changing power inherent in the computer revolution to liberate and ennoble the human soul being turned into another gimmick, another marketing tool, another way to chain and control, tabulate and sort mankind. In his search for truth and freedom, he began to wander down some very unconventional rabbit holes. He worked with the military and intelligence boys on projects like Grill Flame and Stargate. Eventually, the twisting pathways led him to the White Rabbit himself, Timothy Leary. Wayne became one of Leary's Acidmancers, psychedelic knights of the Summer of Love, the first psychonauts. Using LSD and computers, Wayne achieved a heightened state of awareness and could actually "hack" the Akashic record, the collective unconsciousness of the human race.

I had met Wayne a few years back when I was tracking a Serbian war criminal who had struck out at the demigod game. Wayne and Pam had opened their home to me and my squad and given me a rare taste of hearth and family. I liked them, and I hated having to push my corrosive presence back into their world, but I had no other option if I was correct. All Wayne's brothers-in-arms, and even his Merlin—Leary, himself—were gone now. I needed Wayne's unique expertise to help me learn the truth about the creature that slaughtered Elextra.

I heard Pam pass the phone, her hand over the receiver muffling whatever she was saying. A groggy voice, an older man, picked up the phone on his end. "Laytham? Wayne, here. How can I help you, son?"

"I'm sorry as hell to trouble you, sir, but I need your help to track down and bag a critter that killed two civilians during an investigation I'm into out here in L.A. Your line's secure, right?" I heard an odd digital tone, like a MIDI with hiccups, and then Wayne's voice again.

"It is, and so is yours, just to make sure," Wayne said. "Tell me everything."

So I did. In a strange way, it felt like a confession to a priest. If I managed to stay alive long enough, maybe one day, I'd grow up to be Wayne English. It was doubtful I'd live that long, and I'd given up on the notion of someone beside me to love, a child, a home like Wayne or Grinner had. I'd pissed away every opportunity the universe had tried to give me to be happy. I'd die alone, no love, no nothing, like a meteor that flares to ash in the sky, a bright second of beautiful destruction, then gone, forgotten. It was a fair fate. I had my chances, but my ego, and my ambition, and my fear always made sure I passed them by. Life is choices and trades, you gain and you lose. It was too late in the game to whine about it now, especially when you had cheated as much as I had.

Wayne was one of the few people on earth with the power and the experiences to get me sometimes, and I was thankful for him being in this world. I was thankful enough to try to stay far away from him and Pam but like I said, he was the only one who could tell me if

I was right or not about what I was dealing with. I described in very esoteric terms the resonance of the creature's departure and how it had retreated not to an outside realm, but to the interior of the mindscape, the Akashic, Wayne's turf.

"Oh," Wayne said. "That's not good."

"Yeah," I said, and I described the type of shredding that had been done to Elextra, to the room as I slipped the picture of Crystal back in my pocket.

"Damn," Wayne said. "That sounds exactly like Crash Cart or Rib Spreader; did you get a look at it, did it look metallic? Surgical? Did it have wheels instead of legs?"

"I'm not sure, Wayne," I said. "Its shadow didn't look human at all. You sound pretty certain it's one of them. It is, isn't it? I thought you and the other Acidmancers destroyed all of them in the Helter Skelter War?"

"I thought we did," Wayne said. I felt ice, and perhaps fear, settle in his voice. "I truly thought we did. I lost so many dear friends fighting them, purging them from the zeitgeist, from the Akashic record. I'm sorry, son, I agree with you. I wish I didn't. It sounds like one of the Nightmare tulpa."

I felt fear shrink my balls too. These things were legendary, powerful, evil given form. "There's only supposed to be one man who could call them up, build them in his bug-house-crazy skull," I said.

"Yes," Wayne said grimly, "Manson."

EIGHTEEN

I've spent enough time in prisons, on both sides of the cage, to understand that when you walk through those seemingly normal doors, past offices and break rooms, checkpoints and metal detectors, you are stepping into a parallel universe. You pass beyond the veneer of the civilized, normal, safe world into a realm beyond sunlight and mercy, into the forge. The greatest thing to fear on the inside, guard or con, is yourself, what you will do, what you're capable of just to breathe another day, to survive until you make it back to that other soft world or die trying.

Most of the people in prison are there because they fucked up, not out of some great inherent moral failing, more like a sick comedy of errors. They were just tired, drunk, angry, bitter, or broke at the wrong place at the wrong time. They fucked up, usually in a split second. They made a choice, and it was usually the wrong one. Then there are the folks who are inside due to no fault of their own, but because the gatekeepers fucked up. Innocent people fall through the cracks in a clattering, overloaded system that struggles to maintain a facade of safety and order, a system made up of fallible mortals who are overworked, underpaid, stressed, jaded, distrusting, and, sometimes, racist.

Then you have the smallest percentage of the population inside, the ones that you hope never get out, never breathe free air, the monsters. I was meeting an old monster today.

Wayne English had been unable to make it out to L.A. in the rapidly dwindling time I now had to wrap up this caper before my former associates in the "august body" of the Nightwise came for me and kicked my ass out of town. He had tag-teamed with Grinner to produce an airtight cover for me as some kind of shadowy federal agent from some nebulous organization. I think Grinner insisted the acronym for the make-believe agency be "A.S.S." So, now, here I was, in the bowels of Corcoran State Prison, clean shaven, hair slicked back and in a tight ponytail, wearing a charcoal-gray Fioravanti suit with a pale purple Turnbull & Asser tie. I looked good, James Bond good. That's me, Laytham Ballard, international cracker of mystery, the Man from A.S.S.

English had also done me one final solid. I tucked it away in case I needed it later.

I had all the proper credentials, all the necessary emails and verification. For the next twelve hours, this identity was golden. The two best hackers in the universe had even managed to get me a private interview, a whole thirty minutes. It wouldn't take that long to find out everything I needed to know from the old monster, if he was chatty today.

The interview room I was led into by the old monster's keepers—a cadre of guards, the warden, and a prison psychologist—looked like any other corporate conference room, except for the heavy steel door with the narrow sliver of a window made of steel mesh–reinforced glass.

"Mr. Blanke," the psychologist said, frowning as she read my fake last name off my clip-on visitor badge. "Are you sure you want to be in here without at least some prison staff present? I'd be willing to stay if you would feel more comfortable. He can be a bit of an overpowering personality, even given his failing physical health."

"I'll be fine, Doctor," I said. "I'm kinda used to big personalities, and please call me Melvin."

She smiled, arched her eyebrow, and nodded. "Very well, good luck. He'll be brought in shortly." Everyone left. I saw a few guards waiting outside the door.

The room was quiet, except for the hum of the AC. A few minutes passed, and I spent the time breathing, slowing my pulse. While the old monster was no threat physically, he was still formidable in the realm of power. I had felt his madness, like a hot, angry wind as soon as I had entered the prison. I should have my defenses up and ready for him. The part of me that whispered I'd be more loose and ready for him if I had had that drink this morning told me I needed to know, to see how I fared bare-knuckle against him. Sober me told me I listened to that asshole way too much.

There was an electronic click and buzz, and the steel door swung open. Charles Manson entered the room. He had steel-gray hair, shaved up on the sides in a brush cut, and a gray goatee. He was hunched over, his hands close in cuffs, connected to a body chain and then leg restraints, a shuffling old hippie. He looked at me. A little smile played at his lips, and I felt his presence scrape and claw at the edges of my power, looking for cracks to seep in through. The swastika scar was there, above eyes as black and devoid of life as the death between stars.

I had heard he had been very sick, and I saw in him that he wasn't much longer for this world. A horrible thought occurred to me then: would death be enough? Would death erase his stain from the world? Manson nodded and grunted at me as the guards sat him down and locked him to a chair opposite me at the conference table. "Who the hell are you?" he said. I had been interrogated enough times to know that I'd make him wait. Charlie decided not to play my game. "You're witchy. I can feel it coming off of you like stink off a whore. Ain't no agent man, though, no Eff-Bee-Eye, are you, witchy-man?"

"Cut the shit, Charlie," one of the guards said under his breath.

"Behave. Answer the nice man's questions and don't make us come back in here until he's done. Got it?" Manson bobbed his head rapidly a few times, looked up with hooded eyes, and smiled at me. It was the famous Manson smile, the Manson eyes, and I have to admit, it had power to it. My stomach curled, and I felt his energy prying at the tiny crack in my armor his demeanor had created. The guard who had admonished Manson explained to me that they would be right outside if I needed anything. They departed without another word. There was a loud clank as the heavy door closed and locked, and I was alone with the self-proclaimed Devil. Having met them both, I have to say, Charlie was scarier.

"I could kill you right now," he said. "Be across that table before anybody could do shit."

"Take your shot," I said. "I can drop your nasty, decrepit ass before you haul yourself over that table." Manson glared at me and then broke into laughter.

"Shit, man, you're all right," Charlie said. "I kill you, I don't get Pop-Tarts. I like Pop-Tarts more'n pussy these days. Why you here? What's your handle?" I pointed to my name badge. Charlie squinted and then made a face. "Melvin Blanke? Shit, that's the Bugs Bunny guy. What's your real name, the one you call yourself in the dark? That's the only one that matters."

"Laytham Ballard," I said. "Mel Blanke sounded like as good a name as any to deal with Looney Tunes Charlie."

Manson leaned back, a smug expression crossing his weathered face. "Ballard, yeah. They said you might come visit, said I shouldn't say shit to you. They think you're dangerous." Charlie gave me the once-over, nodded. "You are. You got it in the eyes all right, just like me."

"Who's 'they,' Charlie? Who said not to tell me?" Manson seemed to be doing the calculus of betrayal in his head. I sweetened the pot by holding up a pack of American Spirits. He grinned. His teeth were small and yellow, like a rat's. He reached out for the smokes, and I withdrew them. He became irritated. "Spill," I said.

"Shit, why the hell not, man," he said. "Not like they can dream up something to get me in here, as long as I got my guardian angels. No one can touch me in here. I'm a god, and this is my temple."

"Who?" I asked again, trying to keep the irritation out of my voice. I was painfully aware of how sober I was. Manson's energies were frantic, constant, like a dog scratching at the door. He could tell he was getting to me. It was remarkable. Charles Mansion was no wizard, nothing special, but he was a charisma savant. He had raw presence that gave him power over the weak, the young, the scared, the gullible, and the damaged. For all my training, all my godlike ability, at my core, I was a broken human being, and Manson was masterful at worming his way in, spotting your flaws, and crawling inside you. I centered myself and waited, cigarettes in hand.

"The Process," he said, clutching the air with his manacled hands and nodding toward the smokes. I handed him the pack. He fumbled to open it.

"The Process . . . the Process Church of the Final Judgment, the cult?"

Charlie bobbed his head and popped a cigarette between his lips. He murmured in the affirmative.

"Yeah," he said. "That's one of their names. It's what they called themselves when I met them."

"I thought they folded up shop in the seventies," I said.

"Changed their name," he said. "Changed their face, put the old one in a jar by the door. They been around a long, long time. They call themselves different now. They still own this city, just like they did back then, pretty much have for a long time. They like it here. L.A. matches their, y'know, vibe."

I leaned back in my chair and rubbed my face. This could all be the famous Manson rambling bullshit, but there were still rumors in the Life that the idea for Manson's race-war apocalypse, Helter Skelter, was borrowed in part from the doctrine of the Process Church.

"You mean to say that people from the Process came to you recently to warn you about me, specifically, Charlie? Are you jerking me around?"

"You'll see," Manson said. "You got a light?"

"Yeah," I said, "I do." I didn't move or make any attempt to give the little dirtbag anything. "Charlie, what would the Process want from you, after all this time? It have anything to do with the tulpa?"

"My head-babies," Manson said. "Yeah, that's why you're here, ain't it?"

"A thing that may have been one of yours tore a very nice lady and her asshole boyfriend to shreds last night. How is that even possible, Charlie? I thought all those things were destroyed by the Acidmancers."

"You mean Timmy's little helpers?" Manson sneered. "Hell, man, they tried, but I had lots of time in here to figure out a go-around. They don't exist in the fancy, snobby, think-you're-better-than-me collective unconscious anymore, yeah, but I made my own one a' those in here. And then I put them back together in my mind and birthed them right in the jailhouse, just like the jailhouse was my mother."

I tried hard to not show this lunatic how impressed I was by what he was telling me. When Wayne and the other Acidmancers sealed Manson nightmare creations off from the collective thought-stream of mankind, Charlie had created his own new collective thought gestalt, using the isolated, emotional minds of all those locked away in the prisons of the world. His own private mass-mind of fear, anger, and brutal awareness. An untapped Jungian jungle. It would take decades of isolated meditation to build such an occult construct and then populate it with the worst nightmares and most horrific fantasies of those on the inside. Charlie had the deranged focus to do it, and we had given him the quiet, the silence, and the time.

"Yeah," Manson said, "you got it. It's beautiful, isn't it, man? Something you wished you'd thought up yourself. Something you could've. You're jealous you didn't, I can see that in those shitty marbles your soul peeks out of."

"It's impressive," I said.

"Then give me a fucking light for my cancer-stick," Charlie said, gesturing with the cigarette as best he could with the manacles. I remained still.

"You're no miracle man, Charlie," I said. "If you were, you wouldn't be locked up in here still." Manson laughed again.

"Look at who's so enlightened, so blind. These walls, they're glass, they're mirrors. What's in here is all of you on the outside. We're just not as good at faking we're good people, that we're civilized like you pretend. You're the prisoners, not me. I dreamed all of your world up. In here, in my world, that's the only thing that's real. You're all ghosts, living in a god's dream, my dream." I tried to let his words move through me without tainting my insides. Told myself it was the rantings of a narcissistic psychopath. Manson nodded, looking almost grim. "Ask what you came to ask, ghost man, then go back to your haunted world."

"Why did you call up the tulpa to kill Elextra and George? Who told you to?"

"I don't know who the fuck you're talking about. I didn't wake any of my children up . . ." An awareness crossed Manson's face, like he just got the punch line of a joke. He looked surprised and a bit smug. "Oh, okay. Yeah, yeah, right on! He did it!"

"Who did it?" I leaned closer. "Who did it Charlie, if it wasn't you?"

"My boy," he said, "my son. They said they were gonna teach him the way they taught me."

"The Process," I said. "They're gone, Charlie, scorched earth. I need to know who really killed Elextra, and why?"

"People always got to go and try to put labels on things," Manson said. "Things don't change what they're made of 'cause their form changes. You call a glass of water a river, tell me it isn't really. You call death a cigarette. What they are stays the same, regardless if you call them the Process or something else. They're not hung up on names. Blinders to what's real."

"And what are they, Charlie? What's real?"

Manson showed me the cigarette and smiled. "They looking to

move on, to move up, get that enlightenment jones a-goin'. 'Cept they got it right, not like all those bible-thumpers and prissy-ass Satanists. They get you can't know light unless you know the dark, and after a while spent in either, you go blind, and the dark wins out anyway."

It was my turn to get it.

"They're seeking out enlightenment by courting the dark, embracing it," I said. Charlie nodded.

"Yeah, it's beautiful, baby." His eyes were looking into places I couldn't see. "They put my feet on the path a looooong time ago. I was walking it and didn't even know it, 'til they showed me. They taught me the real meaning of family. Children, man, they are the harbingers of our own end and the gateway to immortality. I'm gonna live forever. My seed is in all the blood of mankind now, just like theirs. Everything I foretold is coming to pass right now—the race riots, the hate and anger, the end of the of wagging tongues, the dawn of the raising of fists, the whites and the blacks going to war. I'm a prophet and that will be borne out by history. They sent me out as their prophet, showed me all of it." Manson cocked his head and gave me an almost pitying look. "They'll show you too. They like you, Ballard, that's why they haven't killed you yet."

"Okay, Charlie," I said, leaning closer. "This one is for a light for that cigarette and a carton of smokes. I want you to explain something to me, and I want every detail." And he did.

It's a cult," I said to Grinner, Anna, and Vigil, "a cult of Buddhist mystics. The murder of Jane, of all the girls, they're ritual sacrifices for them, designed to provide empowerment and further their messed-up take on enlightenment. It all makes sense now." We were in the office at the Hard Limit, and daylight was burning. I had spent the morning with Manson, and I now had much less than twenty-four hours to get out of Dodge.

Gida had ordered Dragon out of town on an assignment shortly after we had our little chat. Dragon was to go back to Bombay Beach, where Jane's body had been dumped in 1984, to follow up on local interviews. Dragon and I both knew it was bullshit, a way to keep her from helping me and compromising herself to the Nightwise. I had urged her to go. I didn't want to cause her any more grief than I already had. Gida was making her take Luke along, supposedly as a partner, but really to keep an eye on her, make sure she was nowhere near me.

"Whoa, whoa, whoa, hold the phone," Grinner said. "We're talking freakin' Buddhists here. No attachment, right? Y'know, letting go of aggression and resentment. The Mr. Rogers of religions, right? This sounds nuts, Ballard. I think you and Manson shared too many magic toadstools, man."

"Not a lot of people in the West realize it, but there are different sects and opposing philosophies and traditions in Buddhism," Anna said, sipping her mint tea. "It's not monolithic, any more than any other faith. They've had their internal struggles over doctrine and their versions of reformations and heresies."

I nodded in agreement.

"Exactly," I said. "I remember hearing about this particular heresy at the night schools of Shambhala, when I was studying in the Tian Shan mountains. They're called the Dugpa, or Dögpa, but that's a really loose and inaccurate translation. 'Dugpa' is kind of like calling all Southerners 'klan' or all Muslims 'terrorists.' The West doesn't have an accurate word to describe what they are. None of my teachers wanted to discuss them very much, it was forbidden, so, of course, I was all over it."

"Natch," Grinner said, tipping his coffee mug in my direction.

"They're practitioners of Black Tantra," I continued. "Selfish, greedy, ruthless sorcerers. Their view of Buddhism is ass-backwards from everyone else's. They believe that cultivating negative emotions and thoughts leads to enlightenment. Attachment, possession, in all its extreme tangible and metaphysical forms is to be embraced."

"Okay." Grinner nodded. "So, Sith Buddhists, got it."

"Nothing is considered sacred to them," I continued. "The very notion of sacredness is a joke. They embrace experience in all its per-mutations and perversions, and they gain mystical power through self-destruction and the corruption of others." Anna, Vigil, and Grinner all looked at each other, and I felt an uncomfortable understanding pass between them. "What?" I asked.

"It's nothing, Laytham," Anna said. "Go on."

"The Dugpa were briefly associated with the Kagyu sects, but not for long. Many of the oldest and most prominent Buddhist sects, like the Kagyu, got painted with the same racist broad-brush by Madame Blavatsky and some other western occultists because of the Dugpa. She lumped these assholes in with all the different Kagyu and two other very old and reputable branches of Buddhism. It's something the Red Hat sects have been trying to clear up ever since with west-erners."

"Wait a second," Vigil said, "Brett Glide's production company is called 'Red Hat.'"

"Yeah," I said. "It's one of the western names for the Dugpa. I should have picked that up when we were out in the desert, but I was too hungover, I guess, just not thinking straight. Glide's in this somehow. He registered to me and Dragon like someone with some magical training. I should have known."

"I ran his prints off the water bottle like you asked, and they com-pletely fucked up the Fed's NGI identification system I ran them through," Grinner said.

"Just like mine would do," I said. "He's got some serious magic working."

"No shit," Grinner said. "So I've put him under a microscope, and you're right, Mr. Crunchy Granola is up to his tits in your and Drag-on's cold case. I was able to use facial recognition software matched up to a massive porn image search program to determine that every woman murdered had been active in the adult film industry here in L.A., either online or in films, clubs, chat rooms, or all of the above. They were all working in adult entertainment and I just found another major correlation between them in the wee hours of last night while you were out playing footsie with your old girlfriend. Every woman killed, all the way back to the first you found in 1984. They had one thing in common: they had all worked for Red Hat Productions at some point in their careers."

"It's a small community, relatively speaking," Anna said. "Could just be a coincidence."

"If we didn't know that Glide was connected to the life," Vigil said, "and that his company is named after these Dugpa. It stretches coincidence pretty far."

"Crystal Myth worked for Red Hat too, didn't she?" I said, already knowing the answer.

"Yeah," Grinner said.

"And that breaks coincidence," Anna nodded.

"How did you know?" Vigil asked me. "That she was connected to your old case?" I took out the crumpled still from one of Crystal's movies I had found at Elextra's murder scene. I laid the blood-flecked, wrinkled print out on the desk between us. I pointed to a scar on her hip, an ornate brand made up of lines and whorls with sharp, pointed swoops on the ends of the pattern.

"Is that what I think it is?" Dragon asked. I nodded.

"That," I said. "All the victims had it somewhere on their bodies. Sometimes it was fresh, a few weeks old, other times it had been there for a while, probably years, but always the same symbol. No one in the Nightwise, LAPD, FBI, even Langley's code-breakers, could ever figure out what it meant, until this morning, until I found out we're dealing with Dugpa."

"What is it?" Anna asked.

"Looks like fucking Klingon," Grinner offered.

"It's from the Tibetan alphabet," I said. "The symbols have been packed together and then reversed like a mirror image. It says, '*mchod pa.*' It means 'offering.'"

"Of course it does," Grinner muttered, looking at the old photo.

"Shit. You think your lost girl, this Caern, Crystal Myth, you're looking for is dead?" Vigil searched my face. His jaw was tight.

"I don't think so," I said. "Not yet, anyway. Every victim's body was dropped someplace they would be discovered pretty quickly, like the killers were showing off what they did. The Dugpa corrupt by weakening the resolve, challenging belief. Nothing like a brutal, senseless torture-murder to shake up your faith in a just and ordered universe, right? Each one of these nine murders gave them mystical fuel. That's why the heads were left pristine on each woman, to allow them to feed off the suffering and death pouring through their perfect Ajna and their Sahasrara chakras, the seats of awareness and enlightenment. It's sick as hell, but it makes perfect sense."

"So they degraded these women, over years," Anna said, "wore them down, ruined their lives, destroyed their hope, and then, when they had nothing left to lose, tortured them, killed them and . . ."

"Ate their souls," I said, "like it was caviar. By that point the women were probably thankful for the utter negation of their life force. They wouldn't just want to die, they'd wish they had never been born, and never be reborn. They'd beg the Dugpa for annihilation. It's . . . bad . . . it's fucked up on a different level, even for me."

"We have got to stop these evil things," Anna said. I nodded.

"They're not monsters, darlin', just human beings, that's all they need to be. I've got ten hours to find them and punch their ticket."

"And find the Lady Ankou," Vigil said. "If she's not dead, she is in danger from this cult."

"Agreed," I said, "but we've very little time before I have the fucking mojo po-po up my ass."

"We can't deal with the assembled might of the Nightwise," Vigil said.

"Yeah," I said, "that would suck, especially since that would include Dragon too."

"Damn it, Laytham, you can't put her in that position," Anna said. "All she has is the Nightwise. She believes in what the order is about, even if you don't anymore."

"I know," I said, rubbing my face. I felt so tired, and I was painfully aware of every hour, every minute, every second it had been since I'd had a drink. "I'll figure something out, Anna. I won't hurt her, I won't make her choose. I promise."

"Don't promise," Anna said, "I know what that's worth. Just do it, okay? Please."

"I poked a little deeper into Red Hat," Grinner said, coming to the rescue. "It's weird. That company is older than Brett Glide. It's been creeping around under different names but same holding companies since at least the 1970s, probably further back than that. The electron trail gets cold past a certain date."

"Manson claims the Process is part of this too, that they were his patrons here in L.A. That fits with the seventies."

"It does," Grinner said.

"The Process?" Vigil asked.

"The Process Church of the Final Judgment," Grinner said. "A cult, started by a couple of nut-burgers in England. They went international for a while in the mid sixties."

"Their doctrine was often mistaken for Satanism because they worshiped three forces, including Christ and Satan, but it's actually closer to Dugpa philosophy, embracing the negative to become a fully self-actualized human being. They folded tents under the Process name in the seventies."

"Just in time for Red Hat Productions to open its doors here as the latest incarnation of whatever this fucked-up mess is," Grinner said. "Nice."

"God, Laytham," Anna said, "is it possible something this awful could be operating here in L.A. for generations, shifting around like some dummy corporation or tax shelter, and the Nightwise never even had a clue?"

"They can be a clueless lot," I said. "Cops like easy, neat solutions." I didn't know what else to say. That seemed off to me too.

"So what's our play?" Vigil asked. Everyone looked at me, and I really needed a drink. I hoped it didn't show.

"You and I have a date at the Iron Cauldron with Roland Blue, tonight," I said to the knight. "It was pretty clear Glide and Blue don't get along, so I'm hoping I can use that to shake something loose."

"Unless Glide was lying to you," Anna said. "Roland Blue wants you dead, Laytham."

"Feeling's mutual," I said. "But I have an unlimited checkbook on legs with uncanny fashion sense and serious ass-kicking skills going in there with me."

Vigil shook his head. "Don't remind me."

"I'll keep trying to pry loose whatever I can on Red Hat Productions and Glide," Grinner said. "And I'll pack up to get the hell out of Dodge too."

"I have an idea," Anna said, reaching for her leather coat. "Give me that piece of a prescription pad you found at Elextra's murder scene." I handed her the torn slip of paper as she slid her on her coat and slung her messenger bag. "I'll get back to you on this," she said, examining the scrap.

"You be care—" I began. Anna silenced me with a finger over my lips.

"Shh," she said. She kissed me. Her kisses tasted like sunshine flashing, brilliant, through cool rain. "You were about to say something stupid."

NINETEEN

Westmont was in a stranglehold between Inglewood and Watts in South Central L.A. It was mostly Crips turf, which I never thought I'd be glad of, but MS-13 was nowhere to been seen around here, and that was good, because I can only deal with so many assholes at once. The Iron Cauldron was an institution of the Life in the city of angels. The Cauldron had been started as part of Roland Blue's fledgling empire built on grotto. Roland pioneered grotto, the fusion of the supernatural with the sex industry. If gonzo porn was the extreme and dangerous edge of mainstream smut, then grotto was the Life's version of gonzo, turned up to eleven.

The Trevita purred like a big cat on the hunt as we glided up Van Ness Avenue. The radio was playing Bishop Briggs's "River." I had less than three hours before I was supposed to be on a plane, or Gida was going to sic the most powerful, feared, and disciplined wizards in the world on my ass. I was driving, and Vigil was watching the streets slip by us, hungry faces, staring, washed in neon and ink.

"It never really changes," Vigil said.

"Just the names on the jerseys," I said, flicking away my third cigarette of the trip. "You good? You and Dwayne coordinated?"

Vigil nodded.

"Yeah. He's got us covered outside. Man's got his act together. Do I know him from somewhere? He famous or something?"

"He was huge in the MMA when he was younger, was going to be a world champion. Then this city started talking to him and he chucked it all to become a shaman. He's the best hand-to-hand man I've ever seen."

We pulled up on the street before the slumbering shadow of the Cauldron. The reason the Nightwise had never been able to shut it down was that Roland's best friend and the Cauldron's original owner, Dirty Fifi, had worked a powerful magic over the old warehouse. Besides being all TARDIS-y, bigger on the inside than on the outside, it also just vanished and reappeared at random around the city, usually when the Nightwise were close to finding it again. The club sensed your intent, took your measure—kind of an anti–Brilliant Badge. A man like Vigil would never have found his way to the Iron Cauldron in a million years, or been allowed inside alone. Welcome to my sewer.

"You are going to see some sick, next-level shit in here," I said, lighting another smoke. "I'm not talking about a bunch of Silicon Valley execs puking their unresolved traumas out over a hot cup of ayahuasca. This can get bad, and bad quick. It's the place the jaded and the bored and the truly disturbed go to be surprised, so I need you to be cool, okay?" Vigil said nothing.

You couldn't hear the music until you were up on the two fire doors around the back of the warehouse that acted as the Cauldron's main entrance. The doors were flanked by seven-foot-tall bouncers. The two giants had skin like dried and cracking gray plaster. Tiny, intricate, Hebrew kabbalic cipher-symbols were painstakingly carved into their flesh in lines. They both wore do-rags that covered the prominent symbol on their foreheads, and they were dressed in dark Vivienne Westwood track suits, the hoods up, shrouding their faces. They didn't carry weapons; they had no need for them. "Hey, Bartel, Adir!" I said as Vigil and I walked up on them. "Good to see you guys found work after Sal passed, god rest his soul."

"What do you want, Ballard?" Adir asked. His voice was strangely melodic and well-modulated, not harsh at all, almost beautiful.

"Seems odd you'd be working for the guy that whacked your old boss, though," I said, "Sal being your creator and all."

"How about I rip your ugly head off your shoulders," Bartel said, "shut that redneck mouth of yours once and for all?" Adir raised his hand, placed it on his brother's chest.

"Don't let him bait you, Bart," Adir said. "What, Ballard?"

"Here to see the man," I said. "No trouble, just conversation and spend a little money."

Both Vigil and I allowed Adir to frisk us. We had no weapons on us.

"You bring trouble with you," Adir said. "But Mr. Blue said you might show up, though, and he told us to let you in. Don't give us a reason to break you and your friend, scumbag."

I smiled my best Sunday-school-teacher smile. "You, ah, going to get the door for us?" Bartel almost came at me, but Adir calmed him and opened the doors for us.

"Here's your tip," I said. "Invest in Spackle, you're looking a little crumbly." We walked in, and I didn't look back. The doors closed, and I could almost imagine Dwayne and Gretchen moving out of the darkness, closing on the two golems. I felt sorry for the stone men.

The music was like hitting an invisible wall. The DJ was on a nest-like stage of sorts overlooking the main floor. I recognized him. He went by the handle DJ Tamure and he was the reincarnation of a Polynesian sorcerer. I think I owed him money for some hash oil. He was playing a dance mix cover of Devo's "Going Under." We descended the winding staircase to the main floor below, and Tamure waved when he saw me and then gestured with his fingers to the side of his head for me to call him. I heard the undercurrent of conversation all aimed at me and saw the looks, from excitement, like they had just seen an A-lister, to heads shaking and worried looks at me just being here. It's always good to have a diverse fan base.

"Well, another subtle entrance," Vigil said, taking a few steps ahead of me and opening a wedge for us through the crowd.

"Look, everyone in here's in the Life," I said. "Supernatural beings, magicians, entourages, tourists, or wannabes. I'm, you know, kinda famous with this demographic. What can I do?"

"Don't tempt me to answer that," Vigil grumbled. I saw more familiar faces at a corner booth. I had been wanting to chat them up since Meat had mentioned they might have some information about Crystal. I diverted toward them. The Weathermen were holding court and it was, as always, a beautiful thing.

Okay, a quick test: name for me one TV weatherman that isn't a little . . . odd. Every weatherman I've ever known has had some sort of quirk, some kink, some weird-ass hobby, and, oh, they all love the booze and the drugs, all of them. You party with a weatherman, you best be at fighting weight or you'll find yourself in a hospital ER, an adrenaline needle in you and having your stomach pumped. I guess if your life was all about standing in front of a green screen and pretending to be moving cold fronts around, you'd hit the sauce and the party favors pretty regular too.

One night at a very insane party, four L.A. weathermen discovered over a case of bourbon and a kilo of Peruvian flake that they had something in common besides a love of soothing baritone voices, a perverse sex act called a "monkey face," and El Niño; they could do magic together. I'm talking real, powerful, high-order magic, and they could do this miracle as easily as cutting a ribbon at the opening of a new Dollar Tree. Thus, one of the Life's oddest cabals was born. Oh, and don't mention Ron Burgundy around them; they are really sensitive about that shit.

I hung at the fringes of the crowd surrounding the Weathermen's table. They had groupies, and their parties were legendary, so they attracted lots of lampreys. Stan Sweetenburg, the oldest of the Weathermen and the reigning U.S. quick-draw pistol champion, was telling a story about literally running into his idol, Johnny Carson, in the middle of an LSD-fueled daisy chain at a swingers party in

Burbank, circa 1979. Most of the kids in the crowd had no idea who the fuck Johnny Carson was, but Stan didn't let that get in the way of a good story.

"So there I was," Stan said in his best broadcasting voice, "with the king of late-night television's balls right in my . . . Sweet Mary! Laytham Ballard, you old salty dog! Get over here! Guys, it's Ballard!" I waved at Stan and his fellow Weathermen and moved through the parting crowd to embrace the snow-white-pompadoured gunslinger.

"Still getting mileage out of Carson's junk, I see, Stan," I said as I hugged him. "How you guys doing? This is Vigil Burris." Vigil nodded but kept scanning the crowd. Stan laid his palm out to give Vigil five, but the knight frowned and left the old man hanging. The seventy-five-year-old reddened and refocused on me.

"How long you in for this time? We're having a little camping trip set up for this weekend, and Clive found some primo mescaline. We're going to trip balls, open a gate to the Chinvat Bridge, and do a little limbo dancing. It will be cra-cra, man!"

"It's good blue cap, Ballard," the wooden ventriloquist dummy on the lap of a redheaded, bushy-mustached man said. The dummy was dressed like and had the same hair and mustache as the redhead. The ventriloquist's name was Chet Webley, KTLA Action News Team chief meteorologist, who always did his broadcast with the help of his constant companion and wooden doppelganger, Clive Owen. Chet insisted that he had given Clive his name long before that johnny-come-lately actor showed up and saw no reason to change it.

"I wish I could, guys, but I'm on a clock," I said as I sat at their table. Vigil remained standing and kept scanning. "I wanted to ask you a question about one of your parties."

"Fire away, Laytham," Red Blazer said. Red was big, balding, and black, the only one of the cabal that wasn't painfully white. Red, of course, was wearing his trademark fire-engine-red sports coat. He was a Gulf War vet and his thing was Mongolian throat singing.

"You had an industry girl at one of your do's a few years back," I said. "She goes by Crystal Myth. I'm looking for her. I'd owe you guys a solid if you could help me out."

"Oh, yeah!" the final member of the cabal, Gustav "Gus" Gilwaski, said. "I remember her. Sweet little PYT. She was Fae, one of Roland's party girls, just breathtaking. You guys remember her! It was at Juan's speculum and fondue party."

The other three Weathermen and Clive Owen all said, "oh, yeah." Gus smiled and gave me a thumbs-up. Gus was unhealthily skinny and had a thick mop of prematurely gray hair and equally thick, shaggy, black eyebrows. Gus was the closest thing the cabal had to a leader. He was well known locally for his inexhaustible repertoire of card tricks and his devotion to animal rights causes. He was equally well known in the Life for being the most powerful tyromancer on the planet.

"She was dating some porn producer as I recall," Gus said. "Smarmy son of a bitch."

"Glide," I said, "Brett Glide." Gus and the others nodded.

"Yeah, sounds right," Gus said. "I remember them because of the big dust-up. It kind of dimmed the otherwise festive mood."

"What happened?" I asked.

"She came out of a room with a party guest," Stan said, picking up the story, "and she was crying. I saw her try to get to the head, but there was a line, and she got sick, really badly, all over the carpet."

"I helped her outside," Red said. "She got sick again. She was really upset and scared. She said she thought she was pregnant again."

"Again?" Vigil interjected.

Red nodded. "That's what she said. Then she got hysterical. Asked to use my phone, so I let her, and she apparently called a ride. She really didn't want company, especially after I told her shooting up with a bun in the oven was awful."

"Shooting up heroin?" Vigil said. I gave him a dirty look; he gave me one back.

"She said it didn't matter," Red said, "then she told me to fuck off and I did."

"Anybody see who picked her up?" I asked. Gus drained his absinthe before he replied.

"For like two seconds," he said. "There was drama out on the porch. Her boyfriend, Glide, was grabbing at her, and he seemed pissed, but still really chill. It was weird. This kid pulled up in his car and tried to get her away from the boyfriend. He ended up pushing Glide back and pointing a gun at him. Crystal looked like she was nodding pretty hard by this point. She went with the kid and they peeled out. End of amusing anecdote."

"Gus, you remember what the kid looked like, his car? A tag?" The Weathermen laughed as a collective.

"Ballard, this was just before our GHB period," Clive Owen said, speaking for Chet. "You're lucky they made enough of an impression to still be clinging in our cerebral cortexes."

The waitress brought another round. Stan had ordered me his favorite, a Dark and Stormy, and I wanted it so fucking bad. I held the cold glass, licked my dry lips, and set it down. I wanted to scream and punch a fucking wall. "Thanks guys, but I'm working. Like I said, tick-tock. Anything you can give me would be a huge help."

"I could do some divination," Gus said. "See what I can pull up. I got some fresh Gouda bubbling in a cooler in my basement. I'll need time, some dark, and quiet." I gave Gus my number. I also asked Red if he'd mind if Grinner tried to track that number Crystal had called from his phone records.

"Sure," Red said, scribbling down his old cell number on a napkin, "but that was like three phones and two phone companies ago, but go for it, man."

"Incoming," Vigil said. I glanced over my shoulder. Two of Blue's pit bosses and four of his muscle, all dressed fashionably in Vigil's hand-me-downs, were moving through the ring of Weathermen groupies.

"Thanks, guys. I owe you," I said and stood.

"Fight the power, Ballard," Stan said. Chet raised Clive Owen's tiny fist in solidarity. Red tipped his scotch in salute, and Gus gave me his trademark thumbs-up. Vigil and I turned to face our welcome wagon.

"Mr. Blue's been expecting you, Ballard," said one of Blue's old crew chiefs, a greasy guy with bad skin who I vaguely recalled was a were-rat named Joyce. "This way."

TWENTY

T he music in the club was In This Moment's "Blood" as we made our way toward an old cage-style elevator hidden in the smoke and shadow at the edge of the main floor. Vigil and I were surrounded by our escorts in the cage. The elevator jerked and rose as we headed past the antique tin ceiling tiles of the main floor. Where we were headed was by invitation only. I gave Vigil a quick look, trying to convey *"Be cool."* As usual, he was sphinxlike.

The second floor was less elegant, more functional. There were rising bleachers upholstered in leather, ringing a round stage encircled by an ornate wrought-iron cage. Directly at eye level for the stage were large Gothic Baroque high-backed chairs, for the clients who didn't want to miss a single nuance of the performance and could pay for that. The bleachers held about a hundred people and were pretty full; the chairs in the front were sold out. The crowd looked rich and bored; that's why they came to Roland Blue, for the things money couldn't buy. There was no music up here. The stage was miked so every sound, every utterance was audible to the crowd. Staircases led to the rafters, where our "guides" were taking us, and I counted at least four men on the catwalk above us with AK-47's slung. I was pretty sure there were more, and I knew Vigil had scoped out every single one.

"C'mon," Joyce muttered as he led us to the stairs. The lights dimmed, and the crowd grew still. "The twelve-fifteen show is starting. Keep quiet."

There was a creaking of the stage floor as a man in a leather zippered "gimp" mask led an animal onto the stage. At first I thought it was a horse; then I heard the gasp slip from Vigil's pursed lips, and I knew, and even my stomach turned a little. The unicorn's hide was dingy. Once pearlescent, it was now mottled with gray patches, scratches, stripes from whips, brand marks, and dirt. The iron collar covered with runes of binding and negation had rubbed a raw spot on its neck. The creature's alicorn was almost three feet long and still shimmered like it wasn't entirely real, not trapped in this world like its owner.

The unicorn looked over to the stairway and seemed to look straight at me. They could sense power, and besides it, I was the most powerful thing in the room. The eyes weren't pleading, weren't beaten, just full of pain and a deep sadness like it was very disappointed. The unicorn's gaze was an indictment of the human race. I wanted to look away, but I didn't. It didn't send a telepathic message to me asking for help. I wondered if it couldn't because of the collar, its sickly condition, or if it just knew it would fall on deaf ears. I kept walking up the stairs. Vigil remained, looking down into the light, matching the unicorn's stare. "What is wrong with these people?" he asked. His hands clutching the stair's rail, the knight looked to me, almost pleading. I shouldn't have brought him here. This was sick shit, and he was a good man. He had no business being this deep in Hell.

A second gate opened on the side of the stage, and a being entered that looked like a young woman with teal skin and long, tangled hair the color of dark seaweed. She wore a leather corset and fishnets with garters. It was a sea nymph, and she was collared as well. Her shoulders slumped, and she shuffled instead of walking. She didn't look up, and she almost cried when she looked at the unicorn and moved toward it, but I was pretty sure the sea maiden had no tears left in her. I glanced over to Joyce, his face bland contempt. "A fucking Tijuana donkey show? Really? Class."

"Watch your fucking mouth, has-been," Blue's right-hand man said, pointing up the stairs. "You and your boyfriend can have a good cry after you see Mr. Blue. Move it."

I looked back to Vigil as the crowd began to whoop and whistle. I had shaken hands with what I saw in his eyes many, many times in my life; he was close to a dangerous edge. "Vigil," I said as calmly as I could. "C'mon, man. We got an appointment." Burris began to climb the steps, his jaw tight, his muscles coiled.

We were ushered into Roland Blue's office suite. The window behind his desk looked down into the arena where the nymph and the unicorn were beginning their performance. Blue stood as we entered with his men. The office was decorated in early-contemporary-street-thug-makes-good. Too much gilt, too much flash. The kind of tacky, expensive shit that someone who grew up on the street and got paid would pick out, someone so scary that no one would tell them their taste sucked. In keeping with his name, and his trademark attire, most of the room was done in shades of blue, with gold too, just to remind you he had it.

Roland himself hadn't changed much since we'd last tussled. A few more lines around his eyes, which were always the color of whomever he was talking to, or an unnerving polychromatic if he was addressing more than one person. His hair was long and dirty blond, but the gray was catching up fast. He was dressed in a cobalt Kiton suit with a black dress shirt. The shirt had wing-tip collar blades. He wore a cerulean tie. Roland's patron, a long-forgotten Persian demon, existed anywhere that the color cerulean was present. It was the reason for his street name, the only name he had left since he had undertaken a ritual to blot out his true name with innocent blood.

"Laytham Ballard," Blue said, that too-wide, too-toothy grin spreading across his face. He said my name as "Balhard," his voice pure Baws-ton. "You got a lot of fuckin' balls to come beggin' at my door. I could tell my boys to kill you right now."

"You'd lose a lot of men, asshole," I said, taking a chair in front of his Florence Knoll Table Desk topped with gold-veined black marble, "and you'd fucking die, too." Blue's men chuckled a little, nervously.

"You want we should take this bum outside and teach him some manners, Mr. Blue?" Joyce asked, his eyes red pinpricks of light. Blue waved him off.

"Allaya get the fuck outta here. I got old business with this skid, private business. Screw."

Vigil, standing by my side, looked to me. "It's cool," I said. "They give you any shit, you do what you gotta do."

"Gladly," Vigil said, looking at Blue.

Vigil, Joyce, and the rest of Blue's soldiers took it outside and closed the door. Blue walked over to his bar, dropped globes of ice from a bucket into a pair of short glasses and poured us each a finger of Jameson Rarest. "Nice, huh? I classed the joint up after I gave old Fifi the heave-ho."

"Fifi was your best friend," I said. "The way I hear it, you punched his ticket without so much as a sit-down."

"Yeah," Blue said. "Fuckin' A, and look who gets a sit-down? Life's a mystery, eh, Laytham? What the fuck you doin' here? You outta your fuckin' skull coming back to L.A.?"

"I came for a missing person's job, Rolly," I said, taking the offered drink. I sat it down on the edge of the desk. It seemed a million light-years away from my mouth. I could smell the whiskey, and I licked my dry lips. "It ended up complicated."

"Yeah, no shit, I got ears," Blue said, returning to his seat and sipping his drink. "You pissed on the maras, the fuckin' Cambodians, even your own crew, the owls. They're all gunnin' for you, and I sure as hell ain't gonna give you sanctuary. This ain't no fuckin' church, and I ain't no fuckin' priest."

"Not looking, not asking," I said.

"Good," Blue said. "You still hate me. I can see it. You should. I know I still hate your cracker ass."

"I think you had Nico killed," I said, "cut in half with a fucking twelve-gauge in front of his wife and kids. I came for you the night he died. You ever hear that? You can thank the Maven and Dragon for saving your life, Rolly."

"The Maven." Blue laughed. "Well ain't that a pisser! Let me en-lighten you about that, Ballard. First off the jump, don't think you're still fuckin Gandalf. Your ass is old and used up. Most of what made you so fucking powerful, such a big-fuckin-shot, you've flushed it away. I could take you then and I sure as hell could take you now. If old Gida saved anyone's life that night, it was yours, and that was because you were fuckin' her.

"And two, I liked Nico. There was no bullshitting in him. He was a good cop, he knew when to take, and when to look the other way. He had a line, you fucked with him and he'd fuck you back, hard. His dying was bad for everyone's business, especially mine. Why kill cops when you can rent 'em? Nico was all right, but you, Ballard, you I hated the first time I laid eyes on your shit-kickin' smart-ass. You wanna know who got Nico killed? You look in the fuckin' mirror, if you haven't already hocked your reflection."

"I want to know about Brett Glide, and about Crystal Myth."

Blue laughed and then drained his drink. I saw the ice shift in my full glass. It was goddamned obscene to let smooth-as-silk whiskey just sit there and get watered down, sacrilege. I flicked my eyes back to Blue's; they were my eyes. "The light fuckin' dawns!" He saluted me with his empty glass. "How many years you been sniffin' around that shit, and you finally got a fuckin' clue. Good for you!"

"I don't take you for a Dugpa, Rolly," I said. "So I figure you for being their pimp. How's it work, exactly? Glide aims women that have potential as sacrifices toward you and then you tag-team them to drag them down into the sewer, something like that?"

"Close enough," Blue said, rising and refilling his drink. "You, ah, you need anything, Ballard, while I'm up?" I shook my head curtly, tried not to look at the drink on the desk. "Y'know, you're looking in the fuckin' bag, awful rough, awful old. You need to do better by you. Life's too fuckin' short."

"Your concern is touching, Rolly, really. All I'm looking for is the girl, Crystal. My client can make it worth your while. I'm going to shut the Dugpa down, but you don't have to be part of that if you help me." Blue returned back to his desk with a fresh drink. Mine was sitting there, sweating and getting nastier by the second. It was bad manners. I was being a bad guest.

"Your client?" Blue said. "You mean, Theo Ankou, her pops, right?" I kept my gaze even, tried to not give him anything. Blue nodded, "Yeah, her old man. The Ankous, they got some juice, but I hope you're not plannin' on getting paid, Ballard, I already barked up that tree."

"What the hell are you talking about?" I asked.

"That fuckin' piece o' shit, Glide," Blue said. "He discovered her, Crystal, whateva' her fuckin' name was, and eventually he aimed her at me. We both knew she wasn't human, that she was Fae, and oh man, let me tell you what a sweet piece a' ass she was too. You ever bite into a ripe piece of fruit and have it dribble down your chin—fuckin' sick, man.

"So, the way this little bitch talks and acts, all lace curtain, I figure her for slummin' and I figure that mumzie and dadzie will pay big not to see their little princess taking a pipe on YouTube, so I start diggin' and I find out she's the fucking Thin White Duke, Theodore Ankou's, fuckin' daughter. Holy shit, right? Like hitting the fuckin' Powerball, you'd think."

"You telling me you reached out to Ankou about his daughter?" I leaned forward. My nerves were screaming. I couldn't tell if it was what Blue was saying or my aching thirst for that drink, but I felt jumpy as hell.

"Nah, I never got the chance," he said. "Crystal took off on me, on Glide, on everybody. I was going to rescue her from Glide and the Dugpa and get her old man to give me a nice retirement reward so I could head for warmer, safer climes."

"'Rescue'?" I said. Blue shrugged and sipped his whiskey. Behind and below him, the crowd howled as the performance on the stage reached some new hallmark of depravity. "You seriously going to give up L.A., Rolly? All that power you've been scraping for your whole miserable life? That doesn't sound like you."

"I cross the Dugpa over the girl, I can't stay here," he said. "They'd already given Crystal the sacrificial mark. You know about that, right? Yeah, I figured, you're a fucking professor, Ballard. I fuck them over for Ankou, I'd end up as one of their sick fucking psychological experiments, end up offing myself, or somethin', or they'd send old Crash Cart out for me. No thanks."

"You saying you couldn't handle the heat from a bunch of pervy Buddhists, Rolly?" My nerves felt like they were being plucked by talons of ice. I was breathing heavier, sweating a little. I wasn't sure why. Maybe it was fighting off the urge to drink. "How the mighty have fallen."

"You joke all you want, Laytham," Blue said. "Those fuckers been creeping around this city a long time before you and me were swimmin' in our pops' balls, as far back as there have been people comin' here with dreams. That's power, baby, hard-core, hardwired power. They own L.A., shit, they own me, and a lot more than me. They used to own you too, and you were too fucking stupid to know it. Why you think I'm being so goddamned accommodating to you, telling you all this shit? They told me you were coming, told me to expect you, told me that you'd spoken with that psycho, Manson. They told me you weren't to be harmed unless you got unreasonable. They got plans for you, Ballard."

"Who runs the cult, Rolly?" I asked. "Who's in charge? Is it Glide?"

Blue snorted. "Brett Glide, shit. Little pissant, he don't wipe his ass without clearing it with . . ." He shut up. He was scared of them, really scared of them, and that scared me. Something was trying to get my attention, something was wrong on a basic, subatomic level, some metaphysical fire alarm was screaming. I was close to what I needed. I focused on Blue. "Look, I don't know no names 'cept Glide's. Period, end of fuckin' sentence."

"Right," I said. "Well, here's another name you might be familiar with." I said the name; it was a common, northern, blue-collar, American name, nothing special, except to the person who gave it and the person it belonged to. Roland Blue visibly paled when I said it.

"How the hell did you get that?" He stood. The blood returned to his face and his wide smile was gone. He was furious, afraid, and panicking. "How?!"

"I guess I hocked my reflection for it," I said. "Sit the fuck down, Rolly. Have another drink. We got business."

Wayne English had done me one more solid, an ace in the hole. He had hacked into the Akashic record, the sum total of all human knowledge, past, present, and future, and found a long-hidden name for me, Roland Blue's true name. That simple identifier gave me direct access into the man's soul, into the very core of him. The Akashic was tricky to navigate, and English was the only wizard still alive that I knew who wasn't afraid to go in there. Complex questions with complex answers could take weeks, or longer, to be answered, but a single name, obscured by pact magic with nickel-and-dime entities that the Acidmancer could dig up in the short time I had given him.

"You son of a bitch," Blue said. "I should have known you wouldn't show your ass to me unless you had a fucking ringer. You've always been a sneaky piece o' shit, Ballard. You remember Logan Goddard?"

"Yeah," I said. "You guys were tight, went way back."

"You remember killin' him? Hittin' him with a cheap-as-fuck spell from behind?"

"Vaguely," I said. "I was pretty high at the time. I killed him because he was your friend, Rolly. I thought you should know that."

"You fuckin' mouth-breathin' redneck bastard," he said. I felt him marshaling his power, drawing on his rage to build an invisible murder machine.

"You think I'd go to the trouble of digging up your true name and walk in here unless I had something special to lay you out with?" I said. "Drop that working, or you die right now."

Blue released it. It fluttered angry and hot between us for an instant, then it was gone. I smiled. Blue glared at me across the desk.

"You're going to tell me who yanks Brett Glide's chain," I said, "or I will give your true name to every second-rate demon, back alley spirit, and negative entity you've hustled or shook down over your illustrious career. They won't find a body. They won't even find a grease spot of the great Roland Blue." A dry, rasping chuckle seemed to emanate from inside the cerulean-colored tie.

"But first, the warm-up round. Crystal Myth," I said, "Ankou's daughter. You said she split. You and the Dugpa must have looked for her. They had too much invested in her, and you saw her as too good a meal ticket to just let slip away." Blue nodded, his gangster cool shattered. He was pale and sweaty now, just like me.

"You feelin' that?" he said, rubbing his face. "Like someone crappin' inside me, like catching the flu on the fuckin' wind. What the fuck is that?"

"The girl, Rolly," I said. He nodded, wiped his head, and rubbed the sweat onto his pants leg. I was feeling claustrophobic, like I needed to throw up, to run.

"Yeah, yeah, we turned the city up as much as we could looking for her," he said. "Buses, trains, airport—zip. We thought we might have her when she went to the doc they sent all the girls to, but she never showed."

"Doctor?" I said. I could feel it now, the pressure on my Ajna chakra, like a psychic sinus headache. "She needed a doctor?"

"She was in, y'know, a family way." I remembered what the Weathermen had told me about Caern getting sick at the party and saying she was pregnant to Red. "The Dugpa had me send all their girls that got knocked up to this one doctor. She never showed up, though." All my instincts were in fight-or-flight mode, and I honestly couldn't figure out why. Blue's office's defenses were fine; something was wrong but I had no clue from where. It was time to wrap this up and get the hell out of here.

"Now for the grand prize," I said. "I forget your true name, and we never had this chat. Who runs the Dugpa, Rolly, who's Glide's boss, and how do I find him?"

Something was shitting itself into our world, our space-time, right on top of us, a tumor made of infected emotion. Shadows deepened, stretched, grasped at the edge of the room, as the linkages to our world shivered and warped. "Rolly." I stood, knocking my chair to the floor. Blue stood as well, feeling its arrival, realizing as I did that the ill feelings we had both been experiencing were our world fighting off the infection of this invader. I felt Blue's defenses rise around him, and I snapped mine up too. It was here, tearing through the membrane of the real, born out of nothing, spewing malice as afterbirth.

The thing creaked on three rubber wheels instead of legs and feet; one of the wheels was palsied, like a broken shopping cart's. It sped out of the darkness it brought with it and came directly at Roland. Its face was crumpled metal married to savaged flesh, partly hidden by a blood-soaked surgical mask. Blue spit out a curt spell and gestured with his hand toward the thing. There was an arc of purple electricity from the gangster to the creature, but it didn't even slow it down. I brought my hands together like a funnel and sent directed Ajna force from my third eye into the thing, a spear made of pure thought. That got its attention a little; I thought it might. It had six arms, three on each side of its boxy, metal torso, all of them like flexible steel cables, smeared in blood and oil. The arms were growing blades, like petals opening on a flower. Two of the arms shot toward me, growing, stretching at dizzying speed. I dove for cover under the heavy marble table. The table shattered, taking the hit for me from one of the tentacles, the other sliced into my back, and I screamed as multiple knives stabbed me and then spun in the wounds.

I looked up to see Roland Blue being run through, torn, and shredded by the spinning bladed arms. He screamed as long as he had the functioning equipment to do that, then he just sagged and jerked. Some of his blood splashed on my face, more of it, and soupy parts of him splattered on the stainless steel tray of rusted surgical instruments that was bolted to Crash Cart's torso. I reached back and tugged at the alien, unyielding arm that was tearing apart my back and headed toward my spine. It was too strong, too slippery with fluids. The arm that had shattered the marble desk was headed for my face, its blades whirring. I heard the "pop, pop, pop" of small arms fire and the chatter of machine-gun fire as the office door crashed open. I knew none of it would do any good, any more than any spell, any effort. Crash Cart was a mental projection, imagination given form and power. There was only one way to stop it. I knew what I had to do and I had to do it now, no hesitation, not a grain of doubt in my mind, no fuzzy thinking, no distraction. The blades came at my face, the pain in my back was burning, twisting, humming agony.

I closed my eyes, stayed crouched under the ruined desk and began the earth mudras with my hands and fingers, willing them to not tremble. I tried to remember what Wayne English had taught me, so briefly, about his own war with these nightmares given substance, so long ago. I had to calm my mind. There was no Crash Cart, there was no pain, no wounds, there was only the clean, bright, endless intellect. I was anchored to the world and it was anchored to me. There was no second before impact, no second before my spinal cord was severed; there was no time, it was a shade, a trick, a lie of possession, of attachment. There was nothing. It was all a sick dream, and I gave it no power over me. In this I was infinite, not a single atom of my being doubted, flinched. It. Was. Nothing.

I opened my eyes. The pain in my back was gone, my spine was intact. No blades had touched my face. Roland Blue's body, his bloody, hewn face, was a few inches from me on the floor. His eyes, my eyes even to the last second of life, could no longer see me. His lips formed a word, summoning a bubble of blood to his mouth. The dark bubble popped, and he died, the life leaving my reflected eyes. Then the eyes themselves faded, leaving only bloody, empty sockets. I glanced over to see my spilled whiskey glass, the amber liquid pooling on the floor with melting ice.

Crash Cart was still manifested, ripping into Blue's men now. Vigil, with twin pistols he'd acquired from some of Roland's dead soldiers, was blasting away, making a valiant charge at the creature. He'd die. I stumbled to my feet and tackled him in mid-charge, driving both of us, crashing, through Blue's office window and plummeting down to the stage below in a rain of bloody glass. We both hit hard, and the crowd gasped and then shouted angrily. Vigil and I helped each other to our feet, and he fired off a round into the air; the crowd's anger at us ruining the show was replaced with squeals of fear and lemming-like running for the exits.

"What the hell was that for?" he asked, brushing glass off himself and scanning the panicking crowd for Blue's security.

"The only way to not get killed by that thing is to be absolutely certain it's not real," I said. "It would have done to you what it did to Roland and was trying to do to me." Above us, from the shattered office window there was the burp of automatic weapons fire, screams, and then silence. "We need to get the fuck out of here. It was sent to shut Blue up, but I'm pretty sure it will be happy to slaughter every single person in this building."

As if to punctuate my point there was more screaming and the squeak of rubber wheels from up on the catwalk. I saw some of Blue's pit security headed our way, fighting against the stream of fleeing customers. I headed for one of the stage exits but looked back to see Vigil walking toward the unicorn. "We don't have time for this shit!" I shouted.

Vigil stuffed a pistol in his waistband and leveled the other 9mm in the direction of the oncoming gunmen. A beautiful knife with an ornately engraved silver hilt and a blue, glowing, crystal blade about a foot long sizzled into being in Vigil's free hand.

"You have a soul-bound knife?" I said, shaking glass out of my scalp. "Where the fuck did you get that from?" A soul-bound weapon was tricky, high-order magic. It was knitted into the very essence of the wielder. Very few mages were adept enough to even try it, and few people had the focus and discipline to endure having the weapon tattooed onto their soul.

"Shut up," Vigil said. The hissing blade sliced through the mythical beast's enchanted collar. The warding symbols on the steel flared red-hot for an instant then faded as the smoking metal hit the stained floor of the stage. "I know people too." The unicorn met Vigil's gaze, snorted, and pawed the stage. It lowered its head, touching the tip of its horn to the knight's shoulder. Then it reared up, its hooves pawing the air, and faded away in a soft white light into nothingness.

I helped the naked, traumatized sea nymph to her feet. Vigil sliced off her collar as well, and she gave him a slight sigh as she became seawater, soaking us and the stage floor. A few of Blue's men, who hadn't realized yet they were out of a job, were stepping onto the stage through one of the gate entrances. Vigil aimed the gun at them, thumbed back the hammer, and placed his finger on the trigger. "You looking for this?" he asked calmly. What they saw in his eyes made them slowly retreat. Vigil lowered the gun and looked around at the stage. "Now," he said, releasing the hilt of the cracking, sputtering soul knife so that it evaporated back into nothing, "we can go."

TWENTY-ONE

We made our way through the tide of panicked patrons at the Iron Cauldron, scrambling to the exits ahead of the sounds of screams and gunfire. I looked over to the Weathermen's booth to give them the signal to cut out, but they were already long gone. Outside, we met up with Dwayne and Gretchen and started down the street toward the car. I didn't see the golems.

"What a mess," the urban shaman said, looking back. "Shouldn't we do something to help?"

"We are," I said, "we're getting the fuck out of the way. We already unlocked our compassion achievement for the night." Vigil gave me a dirty look. "That thing will run out of steam if the remaining security are smart enough to leave it alone." There was a rumble of automatic weapons, which got the fleeing crowd shrieking again. "Roland always hired cut-rate help," I said.

Back at the Trevita, the secure satellite phone Vigil had given me chirped. I looked at the screen and noticed I had missed three other calls, all from the same number. "Yeah," I said.

"It's Anna. I got a lead on your girl, Crystal. Can you meet me now?"

* * *

I convinced Vigil and Dwayne to head back to the Hard Limit. Strangely, Vigil didn't give me any shit. He seemed lost in his own head. Some of the revelations from the Weathermen about Caern's drug use and pregnancy had hit him harder than it had me. I also think the exposure to in-your-face grotto had created a toxic waste dump in his skull that he was still trying to decontaminate. Vigil was chasing the ideal of Caern Ankou, the princess, the little girl lost. He still believed in a just world. I just wanted to inspect the wreckage of the real world, and see what, if anything, could be salvaged. One of the few advantages to being a monster was that life seldom disappointed you anymore. This was going to get harder on Vigil before it got easier.

I met Anna and another woman at a coffee shop called Cafe Spot on West Sixth. It was three in the morning, and the place had only a few patrons. I was now officially at my deadline time to be out of L.A. I managed to bury my panic with a yawn. One of the local jazz radio stations was playing softly on the ceiling speakers. I slid into a seat and ordered a Cheerwine, got my usual response, and ordered a large coffee, black, and lit a cigarette. Anna's friend tried to hide her disgust. I knew there was no smoking in here, hell most of L.A. was no smoking. I'm kinda an arch-villain like that. I seldom return library books in a timely fashion either.

"This is a . . . friend of mine," Anna said to me. "Dr. Alexis Matos. I think she might be able to help you. Alex, this is Laytham Ballard." It dawned on me that Dr. Matos, who was perhaps of Hispanic descent, bore a striking resemblance to Anna in build, hairstyle, color, and even her delicate features. The doc's eyes were a warm brown as opposed to Anna's blue, and her skin tone was darker than Anna's. Still, I was pretty sure "friend" meant "client," and the notion of the two of them together was a pleasant one. "Tell him what you and I discussed, please. You can trust his discretion."

I looked like a street bum who'd been run over by a taxi. My hands shook with the beginning of the DTs as I sipped my coffee, and I was puffing away, killing random faceless hipsters with my secondhand smoke. Dr. Matos looked at Anna skeptically.

"Anna, I—"

"What did you just call me?" Anna said quietly, almost politely.

"Mistress," the doctor corrected, her eyes darkening in fear, possibly arousal. "Are you sure he's . . ."

"Tell him what I instructed you to tell him, Alexis," Anna said, her voice still even, conversational, not a hint of threat or malice in it.

"Yes," Dr. Matos swallowed hard, "mistress." She looked to me and managed to get her composure back quickly. "You're looking for a young woman who was working in adult entertainment out here. I'm a plastic surgeon. My practice is in Beverly Hills, and I do a lot of work for that particular industry, most of it through production companies, or agents. Your 'Crystal Myth' wasn't one of my clients, but I have heard the name from some of my patients."

"Do you know who Red Hat Productions used as doctors for their talent?" I asked.

"I've met Brett Glide at numerous social functions," Matos said. "He's charming, well-educated, compassionate—he donated over half a million personally last year to local charities that help children, not what you'd expect from a pornographer."

"Yeah," I said, "he's a prince. The Albert Schweitzer of the money shot." Matos made the stank face again, glanced to Anna, and then resumed.

"Glenn Thobias," she said. "He's an ob-gyn, a really good one, has a lot of A-list celebrity patients. He is also the go-to resource for all the latest infertility treatment therapies. He's given superstars megababies when everyone else said they'd never conceive. He's a miracle worker. I've also heard he has patients from Glide, from Red Hat. He doesn't advertise that, obviously. Why on earth a man as talented and well-off as he is would do that kind of work . . . I heard that Glenn performed abortion procedures for some of the performers. I also heard that he acted as physician for several of the porn actresses that carried their children to term. He's very active with many private adoption services, placing children."

A sick feeling slithered through my guts like an oily snake. I asked Anna for the scrap of prescription pad I'd found. "You ever hear of Crystal Myth being one of his patients? Have you ever heard anything about Glide or this Dr. Thobias having anything to do with a guy named Roland Blue?"

"Some of my patients said Crystal had been to see Dr. Thobias numerous times over her career," Matos said, "after she started working for and dating Brett. I'm afraid I've never heard of a 'Roland Blue' before."

"Yeah, you won't be hearing anything about him either," I said.

Anna handed the torn prescription pad to Matos. "This look like it might belong to anyone you know?"

"No," Matos said. "Do you have any idea how many doctors, public, private, shadow, and street there are in the greater Los Angeles area? You have part of a number and a bit of a name. I'm sorry I can't help you with that, Mr. Ballard."

"It's okay." I took back the prescription scrap. "You've helped. Could you do me one last favor, Doc? If you know them, give me the names of the adoption agencies Thobias has helped out in the past."

I excused myself from the table. I didn't offer to shake Matos's hand, and she didn't offer it. Anna walked with me to the door and just outside the coffee shop. It had started to rain, and the tires of the cars running up Sixth whooshed as they drove by.

"Did that help? Really?" Anna asked. I nodded.

"Yes, thank you. I know you like to keep your business your business, but that filled in a few more pieces for me. If this is what I think it is, it's ugly, Anna. I can't walk away from any of this."

"You're out of time," she said. "Dragon will have to bring you in if she sees you. Don't do that to her, Laytham. This whole mess, you, it's brought up so many bad memories and emotions for her."

"And for you," I said. "I wish there was some way I could tell you how sorry I am for what I've done. There isn't. I can try to keep you two out of the rest of this as best I can. It's all I can do. I'll make sure me and my crew are out of the Limit tonight."

"Take care of yourself, Laytham," she said, and caressed my cheek as gently as the rain. "We still love you, and you're still our family, always."

I wanted to kiss her, but I knew it would just tangle her up inside. If I'd had a few drinks in me, I would have done it anyway. Another pro to drinking, kissing more beautiful women. I smiled and shuffled off down the street to find a cab.

"Ballard!" Anna called after me. I stopped and turned, looking a bit like junk-tripping John Travolta in *Pulp Fiction*. "We believe in you, even if you don't anymore." The thought of that kept me warm until a cabbie, a broad-shouldered Samoan, took pity on my drowned ass and picked me up.

"Where to?" the driver asked. I handed him a hundred.

"I have no fucking clue," I said. "Drive me around for a bit and let me see what I can scrounge up." The cabbie grunted and pulled out into the sporadic four A.M. traffic. I called Grinner on the secure cell.

"I need you to do a little more digging," I said.

"Do you actually comprehend the meaning of 'get the hell out of Dodge'?" he asked. "I am packing. I am going to the airport, I am lying to all the nice TSA people about . . . well, everything, and I am getting out of this cluster fuck of a town. I do have some more intel cooking for you about Glide, but just for yucks, what you need?"

I told Grinner what had happened at the Iron Cauldron, what Blue had told me before Crash Cart had turned him into salsa, and what I had gleaned from Dr. Matos. It would have been funny watching the cabbie's face in the mirror as I laid it all out, but the cold rain had gotten into my bones, and I was having trouble not shuddering like a sick old dog. My blood was freezing acid, and it screamed for a drink, a line of coke, a hit of speed, a benzo, anything to stop the ugly burden of me. I gave it a cigarette and told it to shut up.

"Hey, you can't smoke in here, man," the driver began as I blew my first lungful of smoke out the open rear window. I handed him another hundred with a rapidly steadying hand, and he acquiesced.

"So what you thinking?" Grinner asked. "The Dugpa are doing something with the babies of the sacrificial victims?"

"Maybe. It's sick as fuck to even comprehend," I said. "Manson said something to me about children being the way to immortality, to control the future. To bake a successful Dugpa, you'd have to start indoctrinating them young. You can't get much younger than right out of the oven."

"Especially when you own the bakery. That is fucked up," Grinner said. "Okay, you want me to dig into this Dr. Thobias and those adoption agencies and see if I find any trace of your girl in there?"

"Any of our victims," I said, "not just Crystal. See what you can dig up. This is important."

"Isn't it always," he said. "Meet me in parking at LAX about eleven this morning. I can give you whatever I got by then. My flight leaves at noon."

He hung up.

I drove around in the predawn rain, feeding the cabbie money occasionally. I think I slept for a little bit. I had discovered over a lifetime of wandering that the back of cabs was one of my few safe places. I had an old sliver of a memory in my skull, in the places I seldom visited, never dwelled in. It was of Mom and Pa.

It was my last solid memory of life with my pa. He was driving us somewhere in that baby-shit-brown '73 Buick Riviera. It was raining, like it was now, and I was stretched out in the backseat, mostly asleep. They were talking softly. Charlie Rich's "The Most Beautiful Girl in the World" was playing on the hissing AM radio, quietly competing with the rain on the roof and the hypnotic creak of the rushing wipers to be heard. They sang along, and I could hear, feel, the love between them.

I could smell Pa's tobacco, sweet and musky. His death was not far

away, out there just past the headlights in the onrushing future. It is
my last memory of normal, of childhood, I retained, and it often tiptoed out of the ramshackle haunted house of my mind when I sat
exhausted, safe in the backseat. What Elextra, Peggy, had said to me
about feeling safe in the backseat of a car came back to me too.
Normal people had scrapbooks; maybe broken people had the backseat of cars.

My phone buzzed and shocked me awake. I figured it would be
Grinner, but it was a local number I didn't immediately recognize.
I answered. It was Gus Gilwaski, the erstwhile leader of the
Weathermen.

"I'm sorry if I woke you, Laytham," he said. I could hear Doris
Day playing on vinyl in the background.

"No, no, Gus, it's okay. I'm good. What's up?"

"I did a divination as soon as I got home," he said. "I wanted to
get you the results as soon as possible. I hope they will help your investigation."

"What you got for me, Gus?" I was surprised he had actually
done it.

"Well," the tyromancer said, "first of all, Crystal Myth herself is
blocked from view by scrying. It's powerful and old magic, probably
related to her Fae heritage, maybe some kind of talisman or charm."
That made sense. Ankou had scoured the world for his daughter and
had told me he had employed every resource, mundane or occult, at
his disposal, including looking for her in the legendary revealing
waters of Elphyne in the ancient Fae homeland. "However," Gus
continued, "I was able to get a read off of the young man who argued
with Glide at the party we saw Crystal at. He's with her now, and
he has a strange dichotomy about him. He has been ally and nemesis
to the now-late Roland Blue."

None of this was knocking my socks off; however, the fact that
the guy was still with her was helpful. Maybe Blue had put her on
ice somewhere? Maybe the mystery man was one of Blue's men and

had decided to see if he could make his own deal with Ankou for Caern and had rabbited with her. If that was the case, what the hell was he waiting for? It had been years since she had vanished from L.A. Unknown guy's presence just created more questions than answers.

"Thanks, Gus," I said, "I really appreciate—"

"Wait," he said, almost breathless, "I saved the best for last. I got an audible divination!"

"Oh," I said, "okay . . . that's . . . great, Gus, really." Let me give you the 411 on tyromancy. It's divination through the use of cheese. Yeah, sexy, right? There are many different styles of doing it. In Gus's case, he viewed the formation of holes, of curds, of mold, as the cheese coagulated. Then finally he . . . inserted various parts of his body into the fermenting dairy product and listened to the sounds that produced. So "an audible response" . . . eww. Then I think, who am I to judge? What a man and his consenting cheese do in the privacy of their own home isn't any of my damn business. Did I mention all Weathermen are kinda weird?

"It said, very clearly," Gus said, as "Que Sera, Sera" played behind him, "'Leucadia.'"

"'Leucadia'?" I said. "Gus, what the fuck does that even mean?"

"Leucadia?" the back of the cab driver's head said. "It's down south, on the coast; it's a less-developed section of Encinitas. A little over two hours from here. Nice place, Encinitas. Me and my buddies used to hit the beach down there in college to surf. It was mostly farms and some horse ranches back then."

"No shit?" I asked.

"No shit," the driver said without missing a beat. I could hear Gus's grin over the line.

"I do good?" Gus asked.

"Gus, you did great," I said. "I owe you one."

"Wow, no kidding? Laytham Ballard owes me one."

I chuckled.

"Got to run. Tell the boys next time I'm in town we will wreck it. Drinks on me."

"Will do. Go get 'em, Laytham, but be careful. I . . . I saw some death coming. I'm sorry."

"It's okay," I said. "Take care, Gus." I hung up the phone. I slid another hundred to the driver.

"What's your name?" I asked.

"Santos," he said, "Jon Santos." He took the bill without looking back.

"Encinitas, Santos?"

"It's like five in the morning," Santos said. "I'm off shift in an hour. My wife, Rose, she's gonna kill me . . . but sure, why the hell not. This has been the most lucrative night of my career, so far, and you are definitely the best passenger story I've ever had. All that shit about monsters and supernatural sex clubs, Charles Manson . . . you really some kind of occult . . . whatever?"

I leaned back in the seat and pulled up a browser on the smart-phone. "An occult whatever," I said, "yeah, that I am."

I caught an hour's sleep on the ride down I-5 South. Before I crashed, I did a quick web search for doctors, primarily ob-gyn, in Encinitas. I found one that fit all the letters and numbers I needed to spin and complete the puzzle, Pat. Her name was Dr. Patrica Nahn, and I managed to come up with her office and home address with some digging. By seven-thirty, Santos and I were in the parking lot of her practice when she drove up in a forest-green Jag.

I recognized her from her Facebook picture, blond hair to her shoulders, thick, black glasses. She dressed like a soccer mom. Dr. Nahn headed toward the locked doors of her lobby, looking a little oddly at Santo's L.A. cab. I stepped out into the morning light and felt the nausea of an all-nighter catch up to me. I looked like a drowned rat that had managed to find a dry hole for a spell. I was not at my most charming. "Dr. Nahn?" She had her keys out and turned to me, slipping the door key between her index and middle finger, ready to use as a weapon if need be against my sketchy presence fucking up her nice morning commute of Starbucks and NPR.

"Yes, can I help you?"

"Crystal Myth," I said. "Karen, Caern." The recognition was undeniable. She knew. The doc turned and crossed to the door, her sensible heels clicking on the pavement.

"I have no idea what you're talking about." She was fumbling with her keys, which rattled hard in her shaking hand. "Now please leave. This is private property and for patients only." The door clicked open. "If you don't go, I'm calling the police."

"Please do," I said, walking toward her. "We can swap stories about how you're doing abortion work for porn stars. I'm sure your other clientele will get a kick out of that." The doc spun, angry, as she looked around to see if anyone had heard me.

"I've done no such thing!" she said, and I believed her. "Caern was a patient of mine. It's none of your damned business! Hasn't that girl been through enough?"

"Yeah, I think she has," I said, "and there is more trouble headed her way if you don't help me."

"Why should I trust you?" she said, looking me up and down.

"You're not catching me at my best," I said. "Actually, that's not true. I'm pretty much always a hot mess. I was hired by friends of hers to make sure she's alive and okay."

"Like a private detective?" she asked.

"Yeah, something like that," I said. "She's alive, happy, and wants to stay anonymous, I'll honor that."

"She is," Nahn said.

"I need to see her to be sure," I said. "There are some evil bastards back in L.A. who wanted to use her, and they were going to kill her. They're still out there."

"I know," the doctor said. "She came to me a disaster, a junkie, three and a half months pregnant. At the verge of a nervous breakdown, the things they did to her." A car pulled in next to her Jag, the office manager I suspected. It was coming up on eight. "Tell me, how do I know you're not one of these evil bastards from L.A.?"

"I am an evil bastard," I said. "I guarantee you I'm the worst you'll ever meet, but I'm not *their* evil bastard."

E ight-fifteen and Santos's cab pulled to the curb across the street from a pale-blue, shingled rancher on Cathy Lane. A few of the yards in this quiet little suburb were dotted with palm trees. There were swing sets and aboveground pools you'd buy at Walmart. Grills and boats under blue plastic tarps. It looked like a really nice place to live, to grow up, to grow old, as far away from L.A.'s porn scene or the Life as you could possibly find. I felt like an invader here, a virus. I didn't belong.

"You cool?" Santos asked, sipping his third coffee. I flicked the cigarette out the window and crushed it with my boot as I stepped to the curb.

"Yeah," I said. "Just been a long time getting here."

"I can take you back to L.A.," he said. "You can leave her be."

"I have to," I said. "I have to see if she actually got herself the fuck out of Hell and made it to Candy Land. I need to know." Santos nodded.

"I'll be waiting," he said.

I headed up the walk, avoiding some scattered toys and a garden hose that hadn't been rolled back up, and stood at the door. For a second the nightmare creaking of Crash Cart's wheels filled my imagination, and I thought of walking into another murder scene, blood and flesh sprayed everywhere. I pushed the images, the stench of slaughter, out of my mind. I could go away. I could tell Ankou anything I wanted, and Vigil would back me up, I was sure of that, now. I didn't have to do this.

I knocked on the door for the most selfish of reasons, not to free Torri Lyn from servitude, not to see if this girl was okay, not a hostage, or someone's domestic slave. I knocked because I wanted to believe with all my heart that she had made it out the other side, and I had to see that, had to know it was possible.

The door opened. I heard children's music; I think it was from the Nickelodeon TV channel. The house smelled of breakfast and baby powder. Caern Ankou, in her early twenties and still beautiful, opened the door. She was in a white cami and jeans, barefoot. A baby bump peeked out under the cami. She had scars on her arms, but they had mostly faded to pale, slightly raised shadows. The only jewelry she wore was a bracelet of unevenly shaped purple quartz and silver filigree. Her blond hair was pulled back into a ponytail. She had a beautiful tattoo of a butterfly on her upper right bicep, in hues of purple and gold, and her eyes in the morning sunlight reminded me of stained glass. She looked at me wide-eyed and happy for a second. "Hi," she said, "can I help you?" I paused, just feeling the radiance of her, the life in her. It was like basking in sunlight. Then the clouds smothered the sun. I saw the look of old fear and distrust slide across her face. Her fingers moved to the edge of the door, ready to slam it.

"Hello, Caern," I said.

TWENTY TWO

Caern Ankou gestured for me to enter without another word. She looked sick and frightened. "This way, please. I don't want us to disturb my son." She led me through the airy, bright house, through a den where a little boy with mocha skin, a mop of unruly black curls, and a slight point to the tips of his ears sat in front of a flat-screen TV and watched cartoons, something called *The Aquanauts*. He looked up at me and smiled. I felt his soul pouring out of that simple smile.

"Hi," he said. He looked to be about two, maybe a little younger.

"Hey," I said.

"In here," Caern said to me, an edge in her voice. "Garland, you watch your shows. Mommy and our guest have some things to talk about, okay?"

"Okay," Garland said, already over the novelty of me and back to the adventures of singing aquatic animals. Caern led me to the rear of the house to an open and sun-filled kitchen with an island for dining. We could still see the boy; there were no doors between the two rooms. Caern sat, struggling a bit to get up on a high stool while cradling her belly. I helped her as much as she'd allow and then sat myself in the chair on the other side of the island, which was littered with junk mail, breakfast dishes, brightly colored plastic, children's bowls decorated with Disney characters, and sippy cups. She had coffee but offered me none.

"Who sent you?" she asked, "Roland Blue, Brett, my father?"

"I'm here on my own," I said. "I was hired by your dad to find you and bring you home."

Caern snorted and shook her head.

"It figures," she said. "I've felt him for years, probing, seeking. This," she said, holding up the purple crystal bracelet on her wrist, "was my mother's. It's powerful, from the first land, and it hides me from the far sight. I stole it from her jewelry box after she died, when I left."

"I know you have no reason to believe me, but I'm here to make sure you're okay, not make you go home."

She sighed. "I'm inclined to believe you're not one of my father's men. You knocked, and didn't try to kick the door down, or grab me and Garland and throw a bag over our heads in some parking lot. How long have you been looking for us?"

"A few months," I said.

"You must be good. He's been hunting the globe for me for . . . nine, ten years. Well, his proxies have. He's too busy to do it himself."

"I had a lot of help from my friends," I said. "Is that why you left? You didn't think he had time for you after your mother passed?"

"Look, Mr. . . . ?"

"Ballard, just Ballard."

"Look, Ballard, no matter how much you've dug to get here, you don't know me, you don't know my life, and you surely have no idea about Theodore Ankou."

"You're right, I don't know your life. I took this job for two reasons, one was a reward your dad promised me, and two was because I cut out from home at thirteen too. I had reasons, one of them was a mother so deep up a bottle, she could have been a model ship. I fed myself, looked after myself and her too. I understand not feeling loved."

"You ever patch things up with your mom?" she asked. "Ever go home again?"

"No," I said. "I didn't. She's dead now." I'd told the lie about her death so often now that even I believed it most of the time. I wondered for a moment if maybe she really was dead by now, then I pushed the thought away and focused on the now.

"Well, it wasn't for lack of attention, exactly," she said. She paused and I saw her pushing herself out of the dark vault of memory too. "You want something to drink? Tea? Coffee?"

"Coffee would be great," I said. As she fixed me a cup, opening and closing cabinets as she did, I turned to watch her son, Garland, in the other room. He was transfixed by the TV, most of his chubby little hand covered in drool and popped in a ball between his lips. "He's a beautiful kid. Where's Dad?"

"At work," she said, handing me a cup. "Thank you. He's the most beautiful part of this world, or any other, that I've ever seen." She was concealing something under the table, a weapon, I figured, maybe a kitchen knife. I didn't blame her. "He left not too long before you showed up. I figured you had waited until he was gone."

"You give me too much credit," I said, breathing in the hot, black coffee like it was the secret of life, which, of course, it was. "I just showed up. My cab is still waiting out there, full of sinister-looking Fae gunsels." She smiled at that and it was like the whole universe got a touch warmer, brighter. I sipped my coffee.

"Gunsel? You out of a Humphrey Bogart movie or something?" she asked.

"Close enough," I said. "I'm impressed someone your age even knows who Humphrey Bogart is."

"My mom loved old movies," she said. "When Father was away on work, I'd hole up in her bed with her and we'd watch all the old movies. I loved *The Maltese Falcon* and *The Big Sleep*. *Casablanca* was my favorite Bogie movie."

"Mine too," I said. "I got to your front door mostly through being persistent and some dumb luck, both of which make up about ninety percent of detective work. What happened, why did you take off from home, how'd you got away from Glide? I know some of it, but there are gaps."

"Do you really care?" she asked. "I mean, it's mission accomplished now, right? Grab me, grab Garland, and take us back for that big paycheck. Why would you give a damn?"

"No paycheck," I said. "Someone I love . . . she's trapped in slavery to the Court of the Uncountable Stairs. I owe her to try to get her out of that. He promised to free her if I found you. I told him if I did find you, I wouldn't make you go anywhere you didn't want to go. He has no clue about your life here, about your family, Garland," I nodded toward her belly, "or baby number two."

A look of relief washed over Caern's face. "He doesn't know?" She slumped a little, then looked at me, searching my face, my eyes. "You're sure? Please, you can't tell him about the children, Ballard!" She was trying to stay calm, I could see that, but a desperate, panicked energy was creeping into her voice. Whatever she had hidden under the table she was clutching it like a lifeline. I saw Garland turn his head, as he sensed the same thing I did from his mother.

"Why did you run away, Caern?" I asked, keeping my voice low, putting down the coffee, leaning toward her.

"When Mom was alive everything seemed normal, sane, just . . . life, y'know," she began, hesitantly. "Father was always busy with his work, his political and business battles. It made him happy. He was a good husband to Mom, he was . . . kind to me, generous, but always standoffish, but I didn't find out why until later." She closed her eyes and cradled her coffee mug, like it was giving her warmth, sanctuary, from a bitter cold. She glanced to her boy who was back to watching cartoons. Garland looked at his mom and she smiled at him. He went back to talking platypuses.

"Then Mom was gone," she said, having recovered enough strength from her ghosts and her child to continue, "and everything changed. It was bad. He shipped me back off to those expensive schools I'd spent half my life at. Holidays were . . . I was alone. Since

Garland was born, Joey and I have celebrated every goddamned holiday with him. We go overboard, we decorate the whole house, we make up all these stupid rituals, Joey makes up songs to sing to him." The summer returned to her and I could feel it. It was part of her Fae nature, the world mirrored her moods, when she laughed there was birdsong, when she wept, the rain was cold. "I swore back then, sitting alone at a fucking million-dollar dining table on Christmas Eve—a feast laid out before me, for me to eat by myself, presents to open with no one—that this would never happen to my kid."

I was silent. I tried to recall a holiday that hadn't involved a hotel room and a bottle. I couldn't. Caern sighed and looked to Garland again. Then she went on. "He came to some big event at my school, on Spetses, a few months after I turned thirteen. It was expected all the parents would jet in for it, so, of course he came. I think it was a concert or something. Afterward, we went out to dinner and he was different toward me, he paid attention to what I said, he . . . actually listened, and we had a conversation instead of him just waiting for me to shut up so he could talk. He was engaged; for the first time in my life, he acted like I was more than just an obligation, like a power bill or changing out the litter box." She swallowed hard as the memory played out and her eyes got wet. She choked back a sob with a feeble laugh and sniffed. "I should have fucking known, right?

"That night, when we were alone and away from everyone, he told me how . . . beautiful . . . I was . . . what a beautiful woman I had become, so like . . . Mom." She was fighting hard to stay in the present, and I wished I could say or do anything to help her in this, but I knew I couldn't. This was hers alone. "He'd never talked to me that way, never. Then he tried to . . . touch me. I managed to slip away, get away before, y'know, before he . . ." I thought she was going to fall apart. She didn't. She rubbed her face, rubbed her eyes, exhaled, and sat up straight. "He told me I had a . . . family obligation to him, to our name . . . since Mom hadn't given him an heir fit to take his place. You see, I wasn't good enough to run the empire. I didn't have the requisite equipment, it seems. He told me he had to make sure the Ankou line remained pure, not polluted, tainted, with human blood." She looked at her boy again and the anger made her trembling voice strong. "It was our . . . duty to keep the blood pure. What a crock of shit. He left the next day without saying another word to me. I went home a few months later when I knew he was away and I took a few things that mattered to me, and I never came back. I never will."

"He gave me some line about an arranged marriage, there was some snobby little noble guy there he said was supposed to be your husband?" She made a choked sound that might have been an attempt at a laugh. It got stuck in her throat.

"Yeah, that was the cover. He'd get me pregnant and then he'd marry me off to some house he wanted to control and we'd all claim the baby was from the marriage. Only the really old-school Fae still go in for the incest thing, so we had to keep this our little secret. It makes me sick just thinking about it."

"You fell in with Glide and the Dugpa cult, not too long after you hit L.A.," I said. She nodded.

"They don't call themselves a cult. Everyone just knows everybody in it," she said. "They don't wear robes or dance around pentagrams or anything stupid like that. Brett seemed so nice. I should have known, you'd think I would have learned. Nice-acting guys fuck you over."

"I honestly couldn't say," I said, "never having been one."

"Yeah, I can see that in you," she said. "You feel like a door torn open in a strong wind, Ballard, an empty house, full of winter wind and spinning dead leaves. Why do you think I'm talking to you? You've been nodding a lot. I'm not telling you anything new, am I, nothing you haven't seen, been through?"

"Did Glide ever tell you who ran things, who was above him in the group?"

"I'll take that as a yes," she said. "He never said, just the occasional hushed phone call in the hallway or outside. I sure as hell didn't ask. By the time Brett stopped being nice, I was so strung out, I

would have blown my fucking father if I was told to. I wanted to die,
I was planning it. I tried a few times." She showed me her wrists.
"They always stopped me. It wouldn't get them off for me to just OD
or bleed out, no. They had my disintegration mapped out, just like the
others. We were like a fucking crop to be grown, harvested." She
glanced briefly at my wrists, my scars, then looked back up at me.

"Then I found out about Garland and I just . . . I couldn't let them
do that to me again." Her hand fell to her swelling belly and she
caressed it. "I knew that Brett would as soon as he found out I was
pregnant."

"Dr. Thobias?" I asked. Caern nodded.

"Yeah. They either forced you into an abortion, or to carry the
baby to term, and then they would take it from you. You had no say
in it, either way. A lot of girls in the industry went to Thobias. He's
one of them, y'know, right? Do you smoke? I thought I smelled it
on you."

"I suspected Thobias was," I said. I handed her a cigarette from
my pack. "They took the kids and had them adopted by other Dugpa."

"Yeah," she said. "I'm pretty sure that was what happened to Brett.
He said once he was adopted, said his grandfather was some kind of
big guy in the group back in the sixties. I think they raised him from
a baby to be so fucked up." She tapped the cigarette against her palm
and gestured for me to give her a light as she put it to her lips with
slightly trembling fingers. Before I could get to my Zippo, she ran
her hand over her tummy again and tossed the American Spirit
down on the table. "Shit," she said. "Never mind. Thanks, anyway." I
put the cigarettes away. "Jesus Christ, how could anyone do that to
an innocent little baby? It's . . . evil. The closest I ever came to seeing
God was looking into Garland's smooshed-up little face that first
time."

"It's going to be okay," I said. "I'm shutting them down."

"Good luck," she said. "You wouldn't be the first to try. If they
can't seduce you, they'll fucking obliterate you and everything you
hold dear. They're everywhere, hardwired into the city, into its power.

I was going to kill myself and my baby before they could kill him or steal him. If Joey hadn't been there, Garland and I wouldn't be here now."

"Joey and you met in the business, in the Life?"

"Yeah, he worked for Roland Blue. He was a techie on some of the movies I worked in, early on, and he was sometimes muscle for Roland to make extra money. We were friends, we weren't even fuck-friends, just friends. We didn't fall in love until after we got away from all that shit. Well, he loved me before, and he wanted to get me away from Brett, from Roland, from all of it. He didn't know about the stuff with the babies, the girls being sacrificed . . . the . . . whatever the hell you want to call them—club, group, society, cult, whatever—until I told him later.

"He's the only guy I've ever known that didn't fuck me over. He loves me, loves Garland, he's seen me at my worst, so fucking damaged and broken, hateful, sick, mean, and he still loves me, wants me, wants our baby. We'd be dead without him. He found us a local doctor to help me get off the drugs and then later, she helped us with the baby."

"Dr. Nahn," I said. She nodded.

"I went cold turkey in his uncle's old beach house out in Leucadia, Garland in my belly. He never left my side. Joey's uncle is dead, so no one knew about that old falling-apart place but Joey, so we were safe there. Joey didn't sleep for a month after we ran. He'd sit next to us, with a gun in his lap and jump at every sound. Garland's named for Joey's uncle."

"An old beach house out in Leucadia, huh?" I said. "Well that explains the cheese."

"The what?" Caern said.

I gave her a dismissive wave.

"Nothing," I said. "It's not important."

"Here," she said, climbing off her stool, "let me show you!" She made her way to the living room, checked on Garland, and then plucked one of a dozen or so pictures off the shelves of an entertainment center and handed it to me. The picture was recent. It showed a handsome young black man with long dreadlocks. It was taken at a Chuck-E-Cheese's restaurant, maybe during someone's birthday party. He was holding Garland and had his other arm around Caern. "Joey works at some of the equestrian centers over in Encinitas. His uncle raised him around horses."

I stood, handing the photo back to Caern. "It's a beautiful family," I said and slid the old Polaroid I had of her and her friend Dree at the concert out of my pocket. I handed it to her as well. She gasped, covered her mouth, and made a little squeak.

"You talked to Dree! How is she?"

"She's good. Working at the bank her father works at. She said to tell you she loves you, and misses you, and that your cat is fine."

"Oh my god, Artemis!" she said. "She's okay?"

I nodded and couldn't help but laugh a little at her excitement.

"You keep that picture," I said. "I don't need it anymore."

"You're not going to tell him about me, about us, are you?"

"No, I promised him I'd see if you were okay. You're doing better than okay. The son of a bitch doesn't need to know anything else."

"Thank you," she said and hugged me tight. "Please be careful, he may not take no for an answer."

"It's the only answer he's going to get," I said, "I promise." She hugged me again.

Caern walked me to the front door. We paused by Garland and he looked up at me and his mother. "Garland, this is Ballard, he's Mommy's friend." The boy looked at me and I saw the doubt on his face before he looked to his mom for reassurance. "It's okay," she said. "I feel it too, baby. He's sad inside, but that doesn't mean he's bad." The boy looked at me and I could feel his judgment. I tried to play it off with a wink. Garland would have none of it.

"It's hard for him, for us," Caern said. "We feel everything like it's physical. It's wonderful and it's terrible." I knelt by Garland so we were pretty much eye to eye.

"Good for you, Garland," I said. "Be sure about who you trust, kid." He nodded and gave me a slight smile. There were gaps between his tiny teeth.

"Okay," he said. "You too."

I stood.

"Look after your mom and dad. You got good ones and that's rare."

Caern opened the door for me. "Thank you, Ballard," she said.

"No, thank you," I said.

"For what?"

"I don't know, for making it out, I guess."

She gave me a sad smile.

"The only way out is through," she said, "but you already know that. Good luck, Ballard. Thank you for keeping us safe. Don't take this the wrong way, but I hope I never see you again."

"It's okay," I said. "I get that a lot."

TWENTY-THREE

On the way back to L.A., I called Vigil on the secure cell. "Where the hell are you?" he said, answering his phone.

"I found her," I said. "Caern, I found her. She's alive and she's okay. Happy even."

"What?" he said. "Wait, where? Where is she, Ballard?"

"She's safe and she wants to be left alone," I said. "That's all Ankou gets. It's more than the bastard deserves."

"Okay, okay," Vigil said. "Fair enough. He won't be happy but he did agree to that. Where are you now?"

"Headed to LAX to meet Grinner. He's digging up some stuff for me on the cult. I'm going to close the books on them before we get the hell out of Dodge. Tell Ankou I said he still owes me, I did what he wanted. I expect him to honor his side in this and try to get Torri out of her service." The line was silent.

"I'm not so sure he's going to see it that way," Vigil said. "He may refuse unless you give him more details."

"Yeah, well, that's all he gets, deal or no deal. Meet you at the mansion in a little while."

"Okay . . ." Vigil said. His voice sounded odd. I hung up.

We stopped at a convenience store outside L.A., and I excused myself to the men's room after buying a road map and a Sharpie marker. In the bathroom sink I drew the appropriate symbols on the map and then burned it while incanting a spell of entreatment to IahXaiq, the god of lost travelers and forgotten roads. It was some road magic I had picked up off the mad scrawlings on a truck stop bathroom stall outside of Hartford. The scribbling, in black marker, raved about the glory and the horror of a place called Metropolis-Utopia that I never, ever wanted to visit.

The spell should cover my tracks pretty well if anyone tried to scry where I had been in the last day or so. It also cost me a single memory, don't ask me which one. The gas station attendant bitched at me for the smell when I walked out of the smoking bathroom, a little dazed.

"You're gonna set off the sprinklers, you stupid son of a bitch!" he bellowed. I had the presence of mind to flip him off, I think, still in the fog of the god's kiss.

Santos dropped me off at the LAX main terminal. I handed him the last of the money in my wallet, a few hundreds and some twenties. He handed me a hundred back.

"Nah, man, you keep it," he said. "From what I've seen, you're going to need it."

"Thanks. You ever need any help, you ask around. I owe you. You're a good guy," I said. Santos waved. My cell began to chirp.

"I may need you to explain all this to my wife. You got my number. You need a ride, shout." He drove away and I answered the call.

"Please tell me you are long gone." It was Dragon.

"I'm at LAX," I said, "meeting Grinner."

"Listen, you need to get out of town right now," she said. "The Maven has sent out a pronouncement, not just to L.A., to Nightwise globally. She's put you on the LibMal, you're number one. Congratulations."

The LibMal was the *Libro de Aruspicum Malum*, the Nightwise's most wanted list of scary monsters and super creeps. "For fucking what?" I asked.

"The murder of Roland Blue, for summoning a Nightmare tulpa

that killed a lot of other people before it lost interest and faded, and for all nine of the unsolved ritual murders dating back to 1984. Apparently she got intel that you and Blue were running some kind of grotto-snuff-porn cult together and he was your accomplice until you killed him last night."

"That's bullshit, and you know it." I was lighting a cigarette and looking around for Grinner's rental car. LAX was a small city all its own, but Grinner had told me the general section of the vast parking moat that he'd be in. "I'll talk to Gida and we'll—"

"Laytham," Dragon interrupted. "There is no negotiation about this. You're wanted dead or alive. Any owl that spots you is going to drop you."

"They can try," I said, getting a little pissed. "I can handle them."

"Not all of us, not me," she said, sounding almost panicked. "Damn it, why couldn't you just leave, like she asked you to?"

"Because I wasn't fucking done yet," I said. "I found Crystal. She's alive and okay, case closed. I'm close to having the real identity of the Dugpa cult's leadership."

"You're close to getting busted, killed, or banished," she said. "I know you think you're the baddest ass on the block, but the Nightwise is all the baddest asses, together. You can't fight that, Laytham, and if you try they will most likely kill you. Please, run, now, until I can talk to the Maven and get this all sorted out."

I spotted Grinner's rental, a white Toyota Camry, with the burly hacker squeezed into it behind the wheel. I headed toward the car. "I'll make sure I email Gida whatever I find before I take them down, Lauren," I said. "You guys can take all the fucking credit. I just want them shut down for good."

"You're not fucking listening to me," she said. Her voice was changing, deepening. She was losing control of her human form. "If I see you, I have to take you down, you understand that. It's my job, it's who I am. It's who you used to be, Laytham. Let me bring you in. I can make sure you stay alive."

"You think I did it, don't you?" I said.

"No, of course not, but it's a tight frame," Dragon said, regaining some composure. "Whoever set this up knows you, played to your reputation. I'm the only one who stood by you last time when at least part of the shit you were accused of was true, jackass. Don't you dare accuse me of selling you out. You have every cop in the Life coming down on you now. Not to mention the Janissaries that will come after you for the bounty."

"Bounty hunters too, huh?" I said. "How much they put on me?"

"Do not fuck around with this, Laytham! They are coming for you. All of them are coming for you. Please, give yourself up and let me—"

"I'm not turning myself in to you, to anyone. I'm closing these assholes down."

I hung up on her.

Fuck. All the Nightwise, everywhere. There wasn't anywhere in this world or several others I could hide for long. I had to clear this up or I would be a dead man. I opened the door to the car and slid into the passenger seat. Grinner looked like three hundred pounds of sausage stuffed into a two-hundred-pound casing. I laughed, I couldn't help it. "Where's your fez and the other six Shriners?" I said, shutting the door.

"Ha-fuckin-ha," he said. "I didn't care about anything, color, style, nothing, I said, 'Just give me some leg room, I'm a fluffy motherfucker, just give me leg room.'" He gestured to the cramped compartment trying to eat him. "I get this."

"Wait 'til you see your airplane seat," I said.

Grinner grunted at me and opened a very thin laptop. He tapped a few keys and then leaned over toward me with it. The screen showed an international bank's logo and columns of figures and dates. "Hacked a few accounting firms and a bank or twelve. I followed the money and as usual, it did not disappoint. Brett Glide's company, Red Hat Productions, gets regular infusions of cash from a series of dummies and fronts that lead back to—"

"The Legion of Doom?" I offered. Grinner ignored me.

"Pentacle Studios," he said, "*the* Pentacle Studios, been around since the silent movie days. They fucking built L.A. around them. Pentacle's a media monster."

"Can you give me a specific person or department at Pentacle that is propping up Glide's business?"

"Yeah," Grinner said. "Better than that, and, oh, Brett's name's not really Glide, it's Winder. Brett Winder."

"Winder," I said. "That name sounds familiar."

"It should." Grinner opened a second window on the screen. It showed a *Forbes* article with a picture of an athletic, smiling, older man, perhaps in his late fifties. He had a full mane of silver hair and a neatly trimmed goatee. His eyes were an intense, deep brown in the photo. He reminded me of someone I had seen recently, but I couldn't place it. The title of the article was "Winder's World, Pentacle CEO Brings Hollywood into the Twenty-first Century." "Our boy Brett's old man is Maximilian Winder, the president and CEO of Pentacle Studios. He's the source of the off-the-books cash to Red Hat, along with about a dozen other adult entertainment companies, all tucked away under one of their subsidiaries' independent development budgets."

"I wonder if Disney invests in porn companies on the DL too," I said.

"Ask fucking Hannah Montana. All of the adult entertainment companies Pentacle is secretly funding have one investor in common, Brett Glide."

"So a studio exec is funding his kid's walk on the wild side?"

"His adopted kid," Grinner added. "Brett was adopted by Max Winder in 1984, when Brett was five years old and Max was only in his twenties. Want to guess which adoption agency Winder used?"

"Son of a bitch," I said. "If Brett was a kid in 1984, he wasn't involved in the initial ritual murders. That had to be Max."

"Yeah, it took some doing, but I found some indications that Winder was involved very covertly with the porn industry in the late seventies and early eighties. He may have produced some films back then, had a few ties to the Mob, they were big into porno production back then. Almost all of this is pre-computer era stuff, so it's hard as hell to find anything solid. Hollywood gossip, rumors, scraps. I sifted and didn't come up with enough for anything but a guess. L.A.'s porn scene was the Wild West back then, man. Winder was a ghost in it."

"So Max is the big kahuna of the Dugpa cult and he raised his boy, Brett, in the faith."

"Yeah, after Max got all legit and respectable, he'd be too high profile to rub elbows with the money-shot crowd," Grinner said, "but his son, raised off the grid at various private schools, he could come back with a new identity and slip right in. I found payments to seven out of the nine victims from Red Hat, all paid out the money from Pentacle. I think we found your cult and your cult leader, bubba."

"Keep the old slaughter house going," I said. "How insulated is he, how connected? The Illuminati? The Benefactors? The Glass Gallery? God, help me, the Fae?"

Grinner shook his head.

"Nope. He's nonexistent in the Life. No connections, no patrons or debts. Same with Brett. Looks like Roland Blue was their only exposure there."

"Good," I said. I rubbed my face, felt the stubble of a beard. I wanted a drink, I wanted several. But with the Nightwise on my ass and the Dugpa to hunt, I couldn't afford to fuck this up. I still wanted that drink, bad. I thought of Caern tossing away that cigarette and it gave me a few breaths of reprieve from the screaming ache in my mind. I told Grinner about my phone call with Dragon, that I was now wanted for Roland's murder.

"No fucking way!" he said, his massive fist striking the steering wheel. He hit it a few more times for good measure. "What is wrong with these fucking people!? We got to get the hell out of here now!" He closed the laptop. "I can get you a package, full identity, in less than an hour. That will buy you enough time to get out to bumfuck Egypt. Make it a little harder to track you."

"I'm not going, not just yet," I said.

"Ballard, this is as bad as it gets," he said. "They will roast your ass if you look at them funny. The Nightwise make the LAPD look like the ACLU!"

"Yeah, yeah, I know," I said. "I need to square up with Ankou, and I need to make sure these Dugpa bastards go down hard."

"No way in hell I'm taking off and leaving you behind. What's the plan?"

"The plan is you get on your fucking plane and go back to your family," I said. "Don't fucking argue with me. You know what Christine would do to me if anything happened to you?"

"I've already seen this movie," Grinner said. "You piss off everyone that gives a shit about you, and they leave and you go do your lone gunslinger bit. Well here's a news flash, desperado, you ain't getting any younger. The Nightwise, they're as sneaky as you, as skilled as you, younger and leaner and more full of piss and vinegar than you are, and they will kill you, and that will be the end of the legend of Laytham Ballard, capiche?"

"Not a bad way to go out," I said. "As far as legends go. But I'm in no hurry to check out. I just need to close some deals and get the Nightwise off my ass."

Grinner checked his smart watch. "I got a little under an hour 'til flight time. You sure you don't want me to stay, man?"

"That baby is making you soft," I said.

"Fuck you," he grunted back.

"Yeah, you get all that foul language out before you get home, Daddy," I said. "I need you to do a few things for me, but it shouldn't be anything you can't do and still make your plane."

I told Grinner what I needed and he did it. We said good-bye and he shuffled off toward the terminal and I caught a cab out to Ankou's mansion in Beverly Park. Two of Vigil's security detail met me at the gate when I buzzed to be let in and they drove me up the hill to the house.

"Luuuucy, I'm home!" I called out in my most devastating Ricky Ricardo, my voice echoing off the Venetian tile. I walked into the huge foyer, fumbling in my jeans pocket for a cigarette and my Zippo. I heard the doors click behind me, locked. I heard the sound of oiled steel, bolts and slides snicking into place all around me, above me. There were about a dozen security men in the foyer and on the balcony to the second floor, above, all pointing guns at me. I hadn't had a shiver in my chakras, hadn't sensed the masking enchantments until now, until it was too late.

Lord Theodore Ankou stood before me and I understood why I had sensed nothing. The Fae's magic was most powerful and subtle when it came to spells of misdirection, illusion, and concealment. Vigil stood behind his lord, to his left. He face was as unreadable as it had been the first time I met him.

"Welcome home, Mr. Ballard," Ankou said. "You've got some explaining to do."

TWENTY-FOUR

They tied me to a very comfy chair in a conference room in the basement of Ankou's mansion. There was no roughing me up, no threats, very polite, just lots of guns aimed at me in between the pleases and thank-yous. It was the classiest I had ever gotten jumped. Ankou dismissed the majority of his boys, leaving us with a cozy core of five of his men, all heavily armed, Sir Vigil, the Fae lord himself, and me, the center of attention.

"Those ropes, Mr. Ballard, are woven from the silk of goblin spiders from my homeland. They tangle any magic you may attempt to weave, and they glow emerald as they hinder your workings, giving my men more than enough time to put a rune bullet in your brain."

"It's very thoughtful of you to tell me that," I said. "Thanks for the heads-up. I assume this little rope party means you have no intention of honoring your word to me."

"Oh, Mr. Ballard," Ankou said, as he sat in a high-backed conference chair only a few feet from me, "my word is for those worthy of it. You are not. Your breeding, your race, your reputation all preclude you from worth. You are a knave, Mr. Ballard, a necessary evil that people of my station must traffic with from time to time, a means to an end, a tool, a rather blunt but effective tool."

"Not gonna lie, I kinda feel like a tool right now," I said, testing the silk ropes holding my forearms to the arms of the chair. "Tell me, Theo, did you ever even consider playing straight with me in this? Getting Torri out of her service, letting your daughter live in peace?"

"Did I consider if the amount of political capital I would have to invest to free the Lady Selene—your 'Torri'—from her service was worth your efforts for me? No, never. Your 'Torri' is a shade, a puny human soul granted the glory and the privilege to serve the Fae. She too is a tool, Mr. Ballard. She serves her purpose where she is. Your nostalgic love for the memory of a rotting piece of meat in the earth made you agree to a deal your instincts told you was not to your bene-fit, as did your somewhat narcissistic feeling of connection to my whore of a daughter.

"Your selfishness, your desire to cling to something that had its time in the light and was gone, made your Torri into a slave, Mr. Bal-lard. You bargained with my people to keep her soul, to give her a life of a sort, instead of letting her depart for whatever ineffable halls human shades inhabit. You put her in chains, and this whole misadventure was predicated on the glimmer of a hope that you could free her from that existence, could be the hero of the piece.

"You can't free her, you can't bring her back, and I think the prag-matic part of you knew that, but you let your sentimentality guide you. It's humorous; you pride yourself, the legendary Laytham Bal-lard, on your toughness, your shrewdness, how life has carved you into something hard, jaded, but I could see the moment we met just how soft you are, and how easy it is to manipulate you. You're too selfish to be the hero, and too sentimental to be the villain. You are truly one of the most pathetic creatures I have ever laid eyes upon. I pity you."

"I'll take the pity," I said. "I'll belly-crawl out of here."

"A flippant word to parry the truth," he said. "You are as constant, as predictable as the tides, Mr. Ballard. You can go on your way. I will even pay you handsomely for your time. All I need is Caern's location, if you please."

"No," I said. "Your word may not be worth spit, but mine is." I looked over to Vigil. His eyes slid away from my accusing gaze. "You tried to fuck your own daughter, you sick son of a bitch. Use her like a breeding machine to keep your perverted bloodline pure. That's some real hillbilly shit right there, Theo. Your wife would curse your name, but, thankfully for her, she's gone already, gone for good." Ankou's human guise shredded as he stood, like a sheet ripped from a clothesline in an angry wind. His totality was too much for my human mind to hold.

"You Fae don't carry on after death, do you?" I said. "You just evaporate, like dew, like she did. You're both lucky she didn't live long enough to know what you were capable of, eh, Theo?"

Ankou struck my face with the back of his hand and I felt my skin numb as the force of it snapped my head to the side. When I opened my eyes, he was flesh and blood again. I could feel my eye swelling shut; the flesh on the right side of my face was too-tight pain paper. My head rang from what I suspected was a minor concussion.

"Well, now," I said, spitting out a mouthful of blood, "look who decided to act like an ape. I know the score on you too, Theo. The only things you give a shit about in this world are your family's reputation and your dead wife. Didn't take much to push your buttons and use you either, did it, Lord Ankou?"

Ankou sat back down. He withdrew a silk handkerchief and dabbed his glistening forehead. "What a vicious little mammal you are," he said, dabbing his upper lip and replacing the hankie. "I almost wish I could keep you as a pet. I have made a study of your race and I have to say, Mr. Ballard, you are a shining example of raw, unpretentious humanity. You should be in some gallery somewhere, perhaps a zoo."

"Last chance, asshole," I said. "Cut me loose."

"Or what, pray tell?" Ankou asked, leaning forward in his chair. "You think your little display of common hustling there puts you in a position to demand anything?"

"No," I said. "This does. I figured you'd try to track and trace my activity through that expensive secure cell phone you gave me. I was sure of it when Vigil 'found' me the night I got ahold of Luis Demir at the MS-13 crib. I knew if I ditched it, you'd know I was onto you, and find some other way to track me. So I had my hacker jailbreak it for me, so it was giving you false information on where I was and who I was calling." Ankou glanced at Vigil, giving the knight a sour look. I kept going. "From there he was able to trace it back to your servers, use the phone's connection to hack you." Ankou gestured to one of his men to bring him something. The man pulled a plastic Ziplock freezer bag from under his coat. "So he now has access to your business, to everything. I figure the guys who sent that Carnifex to dust me, House Xana, right, they'd love to get their hands on your books. So if I don't send him word by a specific time that I'm free and clear, he pushes a button and you lose everything you still give a shit about."

Ankou nodded; he looked more amused than anything. "Well, then," he said, tossing the baggie onto my lap, "I suppose it was fortuitous of me to see that your man couldn't push that button." The plastic was smeared with fresh blood, still warm. Inside the bag were eight fingers and two thumbs. I felt dizzy nausea swirl up in me, snowballing into panic. "Your Mr. Shelton, your 'Grinner' as his vulgar argot proclaims him, he never made his plane."

The fear was thick in my mouth, fighting with rage, trying to catch and burn. "You fucking piece of shit, you're dead." I glared at Vigil, and his face was a screen of static. "Your bitch Vigil there, he pointed him out to you?"

"Quite so," Ankou said, looking to Vigil and nodding. "Mr. Shelton has been quite resistant to divulging information. I had thought it best to use him as leverage to get you to tell me where Caern is, but Sir Burris assured me that you would not be moved by such threats. He said Shelton was merely a retainer of yours, a mercenary, and that you care only for yourself. I made Shelton a very generous offer to betray you; he declined. I repeated the offer after each snip. He refused until he lost consciousness from blood loss and shock. Unfortunate, but I thought this demonstration would clarify your situation for you, Mr. Ballard. I am not some common street hustler you are used to outwitting, some stolid mage you can bedazzle with your criminal acumen. Our kind was old when your world was a cooling pebble. In every possible way, I am a god compared to you. You honestly think you will win here, that you will taste victory?" He took the fingers out of my lap and held them before my face. "You will not; however, there may be an opportunity remaining for you to survive this."

"Fuck you," I said as I spat at him. Fear had turned my mouth into a desert. Ankou laughed as he tossed Grinner's digits on the conference room table. It was one of the most horrible sounds I have ever heard, God laughing at your suffering, your fear, knowing how alone in this you really are. My heart was trying to tear itself out of my chest and acid was scratching my mouth and throat. I thought I might piss myself. This was real, this was it. Gun to my head, no way to bullshit my way out, no way to fight my way out. This was it.

"A valiant response," he said. "The hero ascendant. I think it's time I introduced you to yourself, Mr. Ballard. It's a gift long overdue." He turned to one of his men. "The manticore venom, Jammie." The solider picked up a red-and-white Igloo cooler and placed it in Ankou's slender hands. "I hope you appreciate, Mr. Ballard, the courtesy I give you in not resorting to torture. Your reputation preceded you and I know you have been interrogated by some of the best in the world, in and out of the Life, and that your fortitude is legendary. Also, torture is notoriously unreliable in extracting information." He swiveled open the cooler and removed a hypodermic needle. It was filled with an algae-green substance.

"This," he said, holding up the needle and tapping it lightly, "is the venom of a manticore, a creature of the First World, the land of Faerie. It cost the lives of a dozen of my knights to obtain this. The venom will quickly and effectively burn out the majority of your nervous system. It will render you forever unable to work magic, locking away those miraculous places in you from access. Your light will be hidden under a bushel, Mr. Ballard, for the rest of your life. It will also, I'm afraid, reduce your cognitive and motor abilities significantly. No more witty quips, no more, how do you say, 'snappy patter.' You will be a shambling, twitching, husk of a man. I also intend to make sure you are well and truly addicted to my finest, purest heroin before we release you into the wilds of this fine city.

"I will not kill you, Mr. Ballard. To do so would be to give you an escape. Humans like you often long for death as much as you fear it. Again, pathetic. No, if you do not tell me where Caern is, this is what will happen." Ankou turned to address Vigil. "Burris, go to Mr. Shelton and await my word. If Mr. Ballard gives me the information I require, I want you to kill Mr. Shelton, do you understand?"

"What?" Vigil said, genuine confusion and disgust crossing his face.

"You heard me. If Mr. Ballard refuses to give me Caern's location, then take his associate to a hospital, and perhaps they can still save his dwindling life."

"Lord Ankou . . ." Vigil began. Ankou shut him down.

"You have your orders, knight. Go." Vigil walked to the conference room door, opened it. He looked back to me. Burris and I held each other's gaze for a heartbeat, then he walked out, closing the door behind him. My mind was dumb with fear. It swallowed my anger, swallowed everything.

"So the stage is set," Ankou said, pushing up the sleeve of my T-shirt. "Keep the gun to his head, please. Time to look in a mirror, Mr. Ballard. The hero, the hero here would keep his mouth shut, not give me the morsel of information I require. He would save the whore he sees as a fair maiden, save his loyal manservant who refused to betray him even as he was maimed, and sacrifice himself for the good of others. But the villain, ah, the true villain would never have gotten himself here in the first place. He would have done his job and been on his way, richer for his treachery. But you, Mr. Ballard, you as a bumbling villain, have a choice now to salvage this mess you have created for yourself. Tell me where my daughter is, tell me and I will release you, unmolested, and let you go on your way in the world, free to make up any lie you need to tell yourself and the world to preserve the illusion that somewhere in you is a good man." He raised the needle, brought it toward my arm. "What will it be?"

No one was coming. I had worked hard for a long time to make sure everyone knew I didn't need them, and now, at the end of it, I was going out alone. Ankou's face was close to mine. He was smug and in control. He knew me, he knew the real me, and he loved the terror, the indecision in my eyes, like a trapped animal. The needle came closer, its cold steel touching my skin. Ankou's thumb was poised to push the plunger once the needle was in.

I was going to lose me, lose all the parts of me I was proudest of, the things that mattered most, that made me special. Without them I would be nothing, no one. I could imagine the pity on my friends' faces. I would exist at the kindness of others, and this world, even at its best was far from kind. And to have my story end this way? In a fight, in a blaze of glory, maybe, but not strapped to a chair, not a meaningless, common death, not me, never for me. I closed my eyes. I began to feel the needle rip into my skin. One second, one solitary second. It was the longest of my life.

"Stop," I said.

The needle was taken away from my arm. I opened my eyes and looked into the prisms of Ankou's. I told him, I gave him Caern's address. He nodded, the arrogance slipped from his face like tension leaving, like he was forgiving a pet that shit on the rug.

"Now you understand," he said. "You know who you are now, don't you, Mr. Ballard?"

I began to answer him, answer myself, when the door exploded. Vigil, wounded, bleeding, pistols blasting, dove into the room. He shot one of Ankou's other knights, a bloom of red spreading across the man's chest as he fell and died. The other three were firing back almost at once; one of them pulled Ankou away from me and headed toward the back of the room.

Vigil took a bullet to the side of the chest as he tumbled into the middle of the knights, each trained as he had been, each equally as deadly. He drove a pistol's barrel into one of the men's faces with a crunch, and pulled the trigger. Burris fired at another of the shooters with his other gun, but the knight grabbed Vigil's arm and jerked the gun to the side as it fired, blowing a big hole in the conference room wall. Vigil pivoted, bent his arm in and down, and shot the guy grappling with him in the side of the face. The third man, still standing, jammed his pistol low into Vigil's gut and fired. The gunshot tore a hole clean through him, staggering Burris backward. Vigil returned fire as he fell against the wall and slid down onto his ass, winging his shooter in the shoulder.

Two of the men were still up, staggered and bleeding. Ankou's bodyguard rushed the Fae noble out of the conference room, shouting for backup down the hall. Ankou looked back at me, a strange look of serenity still on his face, then he was out of sight.

I opened the furnace of my Manipura chakra, stoked it with unbearable guilt and rage and let it vomit out of me with almost no focus. The enchanted ropes flared green a second before they became ash. I stood as the guard Vigil had shot in the side of the face turned to shoot me. He turned to ash too, as did part of the conference table and the wall behind him. The last knight standing with a bleeding shoulder had me dead-bang, he raised his gun, began to squeeze the trigger. The message to pull the trigger never made it to his finger as his brain exploded. Vigil tracked the headless body with his smoking gun until it thudded onto the floor. Then he slumped, his eyes closing. I knelt by him, slapping his face.

"Come on, come on, we got to go before the rest—"

"No others," Vigil said. "I took care of them, all of them. Grinner's alive, down the hall. He's . . . in . . . bad shape, but he's . . ."

He drifted off.

"Come on, goddamn it, hang on! You're supposed to be a badass knight!"

Vigil's lips opened even though his eyes didn't. "Not . . . anymore, burned it all down, not . . . anymore."

He went silent.

I found a working cell phone in the carnage and called Anna. "Get over here," I said when she answered. I gave her the mansion's address. "Vigil and Grinner are down. It should be safe here, but get ahold of Dwayne and have him meet you here. Call ambulances, call cops. Hurry!"

"Laytham, are you okay? You sound—"

I hung up. I grabbed a few things from the room and sprinted back toward the garage on the upper level. I took the first car I could find. I don't remember what it was; it didn't matter. I noticed the limo that had been in the garage was gone. I cursed as I roared down the drive, through the already open gate, and onto the freeway.

I did over a hundred the whole way to Encinitas, to Caern's door. I wished I knew the secrets of the road magic that let viamancers bend space, but I didn't, and even if I did, I don't think I had the focus, the calm, to do any working that required clear thought. My mind was a wildfire, there was no reason in it, no plan, just the highway and the sick guilt and dread eating the core of me.

I screeched to a stop at Caern Ankou's house, sprinted up the sidewalk, and through the shattered remains of the front door. There was the smell of gunpowder and ozone, the jagged afterimage of sudden violence humming in the now still, silent air.

Caern's body was in the hallway, near the shelf of family photos— her new family, her only real family. She was splayed on her stomach, like she had been running down the hall when they got her. She had been shot in the back several times. I dropped down beside her, no strength left in my legs, felt her warm blood pooling around her. Her eyes looked up at me, empty—no accusations, no fear—nothing. I closed them.

She was clutching one of the photos of her, Joey, and Garland, like a drowning woman might clutch at a life preserver. It was the same photo she had shown me, her favorite one. As I sat next to her, I saw that she had been shot several times in the belly by someone at point-blank range. There were wounds on her hand that made me think she had tried with her last breath to protect the child in her stomach. She was dead, the baby was dead, and I was still living. I wanted to cry, to scream, to tear at my own face and skin, but I had no fucking right to any of it. I didn't even think I was capable of crying anymore.

She was beautiful, even now. Crystal Myth, Caern Ankou, mother, wife . . . daughter.

I searched the house. There were no other bodies, no loving husband, no little, now-motherless boy. There were no signs of a struggle, only a brutish, hasty search. One of the family pictures from the wall in the hallway was missing. The purple crystal bracelet was still around Caern's wrist. I took it off and put it in my pocket. I took the photo she was clutching too. I held her still-warm hand for a moment.

I walked out of the house, vaguely aware of the neighbors gawking and pointing, some snapping pictures with cell phone cameras. Sirens threatened off in the distance. I got in the car and I drove away.

TWENTY FIVE

The executive offices of Pentacle Studios were off Santa Monica Boulevard. Their security was good, even a few tricks and traps for those in the Life. I bypassed most of it with a lifetime worth of skills cultivated toward getting into and out of locked places. The Harryhausen animates, the IMAX tesseract, and the Trebek sphinx proved a little more time-intensive, but I was very focused on getting my face time with the CEO.

I burst into a conference room full of Pentacle execs, yes men, pitchmen, money guys, and gofers. At the head of the table, looking like a dark, slumming Borgia king, sat Max Winder in a wine-colored button-up with no tie and a black Isabel Marant blazer. His long white hair and goatee were perfect, flawless.

"Hi," I said. "Sorry I'm late. I'm the asshole you've been trying to kill for a while." Everyone in the room shut up. They all looked to Winder, whose face remained serene, save for an arched eyebrow.

"Ah, Laytham," Winder said, standing. He was a few inches taller than me and I sensed no tension or menace in him whatsoever. He strode to me and extended a hand for me to shake. I declined. "I didn't know that our meeting was today, but no worries, please have a seat. Espresso? Clif Bar? Bottled water?"

Winder's executive secretary rushed into the room, breathless. "I'm so sorry, Mr. Winder, he just ran right past me. He came out of the executive elevator somehow! I'll call security."

"They might take a while to answer," I chimed in.

"That won't be necessary, Glenys," Winder said. "If you could please make that other call for me, and tell our friend that Mr. Ballard is here now for our appointment?"

Glenys looked at me like I was contagious and then nodded to her boss. "Of course, sir." She closed the door behind her. Winder returned to his chair at the head of the table. I remained standing, the door to my back.

"I know what brings you here, Laytham," he said. "You don't have to worry about talking out of school. Everyone here is on the same page. We all travel in the same social circle, or summoning circle if you prefer." Laughter came from all corners of the room.

"Makes sense," I said. "Why meet in some dingy cave when you can have your human sacrifices catered?"

"Blunt, but essentially accurate," Winder said. "We're a Los Angeles tradition, Laytham. We've been here since the beginning, through the good times and the bad. We're bankers and politicians, dream makers, and working stiffs, the homeless and the one percent. We cross all the lines, all the barriers. We are explorers in sensation, we breathe in the universe and it breathes us in."

"You're murderers and molesters," I said, walking around the table, looking from face to face, some amused, others guarded, most of them bland. "You destroy lives and you poison souls. There's nothing noble in what you do, nothing enlightening. You're self-centered bastards who muck in people's lives and don't give a damn about the consequences."

"Sound familiar to you at all?" Winder asked. "Like you, Laytham, we take the universe as it is, not as we wish it to be. We use whatever works, we know the only sin is to miss out on something, some scrap of experience. Can you honestly say you're any different than us?"

"You corrupt souls and then you devour them," I said. "You can't justify that."

"Nor do we see any reason to," Winder said. "Laytham, my senses are as acute as yours. I see the scars and the stains on your aura. You have done everything you are accusing us of, yourself."

I paused. I hadn't slept or had a drink in over two days. I felt thin and full of holes. Winder's words hit me hard, as hard as Ankou's accusation. I kept getting locked in rooms full of mirrors and I wished I couldn't see.

"This world is a moral vacuum," he said, standing again, walking toward me. "We, those like you and I, those who follow us, possess the power and the wisdom to move through it like gods." He stood before me, still placid. "Who can stand in judgment of gods, Laytham?"

"The Nightwise," I said, feeling my resolve return. "They can, and they do. They stand between all the sick, twisted, hungry things in the darkness and the Jane Does, the Crystal Myths of this world. All the connections to the murdered women and you, to your companies and your sick little club, everything that we dug up, I had it all sent electronically to the Maven of the Nightwise. They know about all of you now and they are going to shut your asses down."

The door, still to my back, clicked open. I turned to see why Winder was smiling. Gida Templeton, the High Maven of the Nightwise, returned Winder's smile. "Hello, Max, Laytham," Gida said. She paused to kiss me deeply as she passed me and then took an unclaimed seat at the conference table beside Winder's. "I hope he hasn't been too disruptive, Max," she said. "He's good at making messes. I know, I've had to clean up enough of them."

Max patted me on the shoulder and then crossed to give Gida a peck on the cheek before he sat down. "Not at all. We've been having a nice chat. Can I get you anything, my dear?"

"Tea, please," she said. One of the hangers-on in the room fetched Gida a hot cup and saucer. She regarded me. "Bewilderment does not suit you well, Laytham," she said. "The unflappable detective struck mute. No witty quip? No lighting a cigarette with an accusing 'ah-ha'?"

Another flutter of laughter from the room.

"How long?" I said to Gida. My throat was dry.

"Since before I recruited you, my dear boy," Gida said, then sipped her tea and held up the cup. "A touch more cream, if you please?" The gofer obeyed as Gida continued. "I met Max back in . . . 1978, was it Max? We were so young! We crossed swords a few times when I was an investigator in the field. I dealt with some of his early efforts and made it my business to delve deeper into his background. Within a few years, I knew about his father and the cult, and that was when he made me his sales pitch. It was very convincing."

"So you kept the Nightwise away from the Dugpa, from the murders," I said.

Gida nodded.

"And from poor Roland Blue," she continued. "He was our weak link, our necessary vulnerability, I'm afraid. Rolly knew it, though, and he accepted that he might be disposable one day. At least I like to think he understood that."

"He found Crystal for us," Winder said as Gida sipped her tea again. "He and my son, Brett. They recognized how powerful an . . . asset a full-blooded Fae would be."

"Asset," I said, shaking my head. "Why don't you just call her what she was to you? A *mchod pa,* an offering, a sacrifice."

"The strongest we'd ever hoped to have," Winder said. "Even greater than the high workings my father orchestrated for the group in the late sixties."

"Your father?" I said.

"Yes," Winder said, "you met him at Corcoran, at the prison."

"Manson," I said. "Your father is Charles Manson."

"Yes," Winder said. "The group, they called themselves the Process Church back then, they hid me away in the early sixties. I was a *mchod pa* in a sense, myself. I was given to the group, by my father, raised in wealth, power, and privilege among other members, given a bulletproof name, the keys to the Hollywood kingdom, taught the true nature of reality, the jagged path to enlightenment. I was raised just as I have raised Brett."

"So Helter Skelter, those murders were more sacrifices for you bastards," I said.

"Yes," Winder said with a chuckle. "The group has always had so many agents, knowing and unknowing in Hollywood. We control this city and all the power within it. My father may be a coarse man, like you, Laytham, but in his own way, he is a savant, just as you are."

"Which brings us full circle," Gida said.

"You're going to try to kill me," I said, "as a reminder of what happens when someone meddles in your business?"

"Furthest thing from it," Winder said. "We want you to join us."

"Are you kidding me?" I said.

"Laytham, I didn't recruit you for the Nightwise," Gida said. "I recruited you for us, for the group. You'd be perfect."

"Why do you think you're still alive?" Winder said. "We had opportunities to kill you back in the eighties when you began poking around in the sacrifices. Gida said you were worth salvaging and found other ways to keep you off our trail."

I looked at Gida's painfully sky-blue eyes, as guiltless as infancy. "You. You're the one who set the frame on me back then. You set me up."

"Don't be so melodramatic," she said. "You were in descent after Nico died. You were on your way to being a dirty cop. I just moved that process along a bit."

"Did you have Nico killed when he wouldn't drop looking into the killings too?" I asked. Gida pursed her lips and sighed. She ran a hand through her fine, silver hair.

"Yes. I tried to aim him toward the same path you were staggering down, avoid anything so messy and sad, but he wouldn't have it and he began to suspect me, so I had Roland kill him."

"The only reason we tried to eliminate you at Roland Blue's club," Winder said, "was we couldn't be certain if you'd accept our offer and we couldn't allow you to compromise the integrity of the group. When you blackmailed Roland, we had to do something to shut him up. You would have just been collateral damage in that. You understand, Laytham. How many times have you thrown someone under the bus to serve your own interest? It was nothing personal. Crash Cart is an excellent tool, but I'm afraid he gets a bit too exuberant in his work."

"Manson, your dad, he taught you how to dredge that thing up, didn't he?" I said, walking to the wall-length window that gave an inspiring view of the studio grounds and past that, the city. From up here everything looked clean and ordered. It was a great special effect.

Winder smiled. "Yes," he said, "and I taught Brett. My father was unable to be very present in my life for reasons both practical and psychological, but he did his best to impart to me his truths, and I have found him to be very wise. In a different age, a different world, he would be an oracle, a sage. A Wisdom, like you and your grandmother."

I turned from the window and it began to crack, a wide, radial spiderweb with me at its center. The room dropped several degrees and many of the faithful suddenly looked less smug, more frightened.

"You," I said, "never mention her again. She's too good for your toilet of a mind, your filthy fucking tongue, to ever even acknowledge her existence. I will turn you inside out and keep you awake while I do it."

Winder's smile never left his lips. "Of course, my apologies. I know how sensitive that subject is for you. We cultivate our children, show them the wisdom we have culled from our experience, and set their feet upon the path. They are the future, our future. While it is regrettable that Crystal's father caught up to her before we could, her child will find sanctuary with us."

"What did you say?" I asked, narrowing my gaze at Winder.

"Max, you think Laytham and I could have a moment alone?" Gida asked.

"Of course," Winder said. "Let's take five, everyone. Give our new potential recruit a few moments to process all this." The conference room began to clear; there were murmurs of normal water cooler conversations, the game last night, the big joke on the latest sitcom, plans for the weekend, not the kind of things you'd ever expect soul-corrupting and ritual-sacrificing dark tantric sorcerers to discuss.

Winder was the last out to ensure the room cleared fully. He put a hand on my shoulder and spoke to me as earnestly as a preacher at a funeral. "Think about our offer, Laytham, please. We can give you a place to belong. We can be your family." He nodded to Gida and then ambled out of the conference room door and shut it behind him.

"He's right," Gida said, "about everything. You'd be so good here, with us, we'd be so good together again."

"Were you ever really what you pretended to be?" I asked as she pulled me close to her. She had the faintest scent of Clive Christian No. 1 and alcohol. Her hair smelled of wind shivering through wild-flowers. Her voice was intimate, close to my skin.

"Were you?" she said. "All that talk of nobility, agonizing over honor and duty. I tried to show you when you came to my office. We are animals, Laytham, delusional animals. We stumble between what we believe is right and wrong and then try to justify our every action to ourselves, to some fairy-tale god, to each other. That is an exhausting way to live. It wore me out." She brushed my fallen hair out of my eyes. "I know it wears you out too."

Her lips pressed gently to my throat. I was back in that conference room, that frozen moment with the metal stinger of the syringe to my flesh, the wildfire panic, the scramble to survive, undamaged, no matter the cost. Ankou's words, now Gida's words. "What happens if I refuse?" I said, stepping back from her. It was harder to do than it should have been. Gida sighed.

"You'd be committing suicide," she said. "The Nightwise will hunt you down wherever you go; no one will believe you if you try to tell them about me. Your reputation is less than dirt, mine is immaculate. Best case scenario: they capture you, convict you of our crimes and send you into the Hollow Lands, you never see Earth or another living soul again. Since I know you, I am fairly certain you'd go down fighting before you'd let the order banish you from Earth. Either way, you die."

"Can you give me some time to think about it?" I asked.

"No," she said. "You walk out that door without committing to us, then you are going to die, Laytham. No threat, no hyperbole. Just a fact. For once in your life, do the right thing."

"What makes you so sure that Crystal had a child?"

"Our people got onto the crime scene," she said. "I saw the photos on the wall. Yours too, from the neighbors' cameras. Don't worry, I swept up after you with the regular cops, had the amber alerts and the BOLOs canceled. We gathered the little boy's hair, a few other sympathetic items. We'll track him soon, bring him into the fold."

"What about his father?" I asked. Gida gave me a pissed-off look.

"Don't insult me with that question and I won't insult you with my answer. The boy's father is nothing exceptional, one of Roland's old goons. We have no need for him. The official version will be that he killed Crystal in a tawdry and common domestic dispute and was brought to justice, dead or alive. The poor little boy will placed in a good home, one of ours."

Gida looked at me and I saw an idea blossom behind those beautiful eyes. "You could be his father, Laytham. Raise the boy, convince yourself you're keeping him safe from our evil influence if that makes you feel better. When he's old enough he will rise and destroy his grandfather, claim the House of Ankou for his own, for us. You can be by his side, his wisdom, his protector, his voice of compassion. You can make sure he doesn't grow up without a father like you did."

I didn't know what to say; my words, my thoughts, were breaking into one another, tumbling, like icebergs crashing. I had no instruments, no radar. I acted, not thinking. I was good at that. I walked to the door and looked back at Gida one last time.

"Pull the trigger," I said. "I'm taking as many of you with me as I can."

"So a glorious death, going down swinging against the assembled

Nightwise," she said. "That is a fitting method of suicide for Laytham Ballard."

"Death by cop? Something like that, yeah," I said. I began to open the door.

"We had a child," she said, "you, and I." I stopped, looked back to her again. "I found out after you left L.A., left the Nightwise. She's powerful, Laytham, like you, like me, maybe even stronger than both of us together. She's your blood. You could still meet her, still be part of her life if you join us."

"She's better off without me," I said, and walked out the door.

There's always a drink when you need one, some dark dive, or pub, a mom-and-pop corner watering hole, or an expensive club where the drunks hide behind craft beers and expensive wine. You've got the brightly colored chain restaurants with their island bars when you can watch the drunk in a facsimile of his native environment while you enjoy your potato skins and sliders. There's liquor stores where the faithful pull up twenty minutes before the place opens and grab their bottle while still in sweatpants and a robe. Hotel and airport bars, where lost, wandering souls gather trying to pantomime at real life or soothe the ache of being away from home. Bowling alleys, with the ubiquitous plastic pitchers and clear disposable cups; convenience stores and drugstores with yummy bottles of cough medicine; alleys; in your car in a parking lot; the shade of an underpass, cars roaring above you, the smell of diesel in the dark air. Pick a city, any city, and you'll find yourself a drink. The truth is, for a real, Olympic-level drunk the where is irrelevant, all that matters is the when.

I sat on a bar stool and looked at myself in the mirror, my face welled in shadows above the necks of bottles, a city of glass and distilled annihilated memories. This bar was in an old Chinese restaurant that catered to Hollywood tourists, neighborhood regulars, and a smattering of hipster college kids looking to slum safely. It was all scenery, like on some back lot of a studio; none of it mattered, none of it was real. The bartender was as tired and disinterested in me as I was in him. He paused in his orbit, gave me a steady look, and waited for me to say my line.

"You're not the Devil, are you?" I asked. The guy narrowed his eyes, already pissed at my inclusion in his world. "Scotch and soda," I said. He started to walk off to fill my order as quickly as he could and get back to the business of ignoring me.

"Hey," I said. He sighed as he turned. "Hold the scotch."

Anna was sitting in the hospital room beside Vigil's bed. She was curled up in her chair, legs folded up, reading a book on her tablet. She looked up and saw me in the doorway.

"Laytham!" she said, standing. "You shouldn't be here. The Nightwise have guards posted to protect Vigil and Grinner; there are detection spells!"

I pointed to the purple quartz Fae bracelet wrapped tightly about my wrist. "We're clear, at least for a few minutes. This thing is powerful as hell." She hugged me and kissed me, it felt sweet and soft and good. I pulled away. The last thing I deserved was comfort. "How is he? How's Grinner?"

Anna looked at me like she hardly recognized me. "When was the last time you slept or ate? Your face is all bruised up. You look terrible."

"Anna, how are they?"

"Grinner was in surgery for fourteen hours. They reattached everything; they will have to wait to see how much mobility he retains, if any. His wife, Christine, and baby got here in the middle of the night. They are in the ICU with him now; would you like to see her?" I rubbed my face. I felt very tired and a little dizzy.

"No. I can't."

"Laytham, whatever happened at that mansion, it's not your—"

"Don't," I said. "Please don't say that." Anna nodded. She took my hand. I nodded to Vigil. The knight was covered in bandages, drains, and tubes, and was breathing with the help of a machine. "How about him?"

She sighed and shrugged.

"He's a hard case," she said. "They pulled nine magic bullets out of him—what do they call those damned things?"

"Rune bullets," I said. "Enchanted for maximum effect, maximum damage."

"Well, the doctors didn't know any of that, but they did say he was fighting very hard to stay alive. They said it's up to him now." I nodded and headed back toward the door.

"Stay with him. He doesn't have anyone else."

"Where are you going?"

I didn't answer her.

"Laytham, what are you doing?"

"Making this right," I said, "as right as I can. Tell Grinner and Christine I'm sorry. Tell him to take all the rest of the money out of the dummy accounts he's set up for me. It's his now."

Anna shook her head slowly. "No. No, you're not doing that, you're not going out in some stupid blaze of glory. I don't care if you believe it or not, but there are a lot of people who love you . . ."

"I know," I said. "I'm doing this for them. No more people dying for me, no more people sacrificed on my altar. You tell Lauren . . ." I couldn't fit the words in my mouth. They were for real people, real boys with a whole soul and no blood on their hands. "Anna . . ."

She nodded. "Come back and tell us, tell us both."

"Hell, tell that fat sack of a hacker I'm sorry. There have been so few things in my life that were . . . real. You, you were all real."

I walked through the halls of the temple of suffering, each room a gallery of pain. I stole a few things I'd need from a nurses' station and found my way outside.

Theodore Ankou's eyes fluttered open. He was tangled in fifteen-hundred-thread-count Egyptian cotton sheets. His hotel suite window burned from the light of a million counterfeit stars in the heart of the city. My hand was on his throat. His eyes snapped to full predatory awareness, obviously shocked that I had been able to sneak up on him, to get this close. He was about to shrug off his mortal guise and send me flying across the room when he felt the hypodermic needle resting against the plump, pulsing jugular vein in his neck.

"So, Mr. Ballard," he whispered, careful to not move too suddenly against the needle, "to soothe your damaged ego at your failure to keep poor dead Caern safe, you are now the avenger, is that it? Pathetic. Didn't you learn anything from my little lesson? You did what you always do. You kept yourself alive, hale and hearty. You preserved your legend, even if good people had to die to do it."

"Yeah," I said, "I did, and you're right, I've done it before, screwed over people, had them die so I didn't have to. It's funny, there was a time, it seems like a million lives ago, when I would rather die than do something like that. What happened to that me? Was he real, is this me real? So, you see, your lesson was more of a refresher course than a revelation, Theo. I wanted to thank you properly for it all the same."

"My men are trained to sense a whisper of power, a hushed word, even a violent thought. They will be in here any moment," he said.

"No, they won't," I said. "I killed them. Caern had a little gift from her mother, an artifact from the old country. It hides one from scrying and detection spells very well. They never knew what hit them, just like you, Theo. You're alone with an unwashed, savage ape at your throat. How does that feel? I want to know."

Ankou swallowed hard, and his artery squirmed against the surgical steel of the needle. He was sweating a little too. "You think I'll behave as you did? I am Fae, a superior being. How do you know that manticore venom will even affect me?"

"If it didn't turn you into a vegetable, you'd have become a hurricane and shredded me by now," I said. "You wouldn't be sweating. You wouldn't be afraid."

"If you leave now, I'll pay you what you're due for the service you rendered me," Ankou said.

"You wouldn't be bargaining, would you?" I said. Anger darkened his eyes, but the fear remained.

"I have money," he said, "a large amount, bearer bonds in a case with me. In the safe in this room. It's been enchanted to destroy everything in the safe unless the proper code is entered as the password. You can't magically bypass it. I'll give it all to you if you leave me unmolested."

"Combination?" I said. Ankou's face changed just slightly. He felt on steadier control now, was using me again, as it should be.

"How do I know you won't inject me and then just take the money?"

"How do I know you won't kill me the second I take this hypo away?"

"I give you my word," he said. "I swear upon the singing star of the First World. I swear upon my family name. What assurance can you give me that is worth anything to you, Ballard?"

I thought for a moment, then I said, "I swear on the soul of your daughter. You have my word, on Caern's soul."

Ankou was silent for a moment. "You thought she was your salvation, didn't you? Thought that if she could leave behind all her pain and all her failures, you could too. She climbed out of the pit, so you thought you could as well. She was your hope. I see. Very sentimental, very in keeping with who you are. Very well, on Caern's soul."

He gave me the combination to the safe. I felt him relax a little, the tension of his demise leaving him with my payoff.

"You didn't have to kill her," I said, my voice cold shale. "Why did you?"

"It was always my intent," Ankou said. "She would never give me the heir I needed, never submit to her proper place in the scheme of things. And she had tainted her womb with human seed, produced a half-breed bastard as the only one to carry on my family name, and another abomination stewing in her belly . . . disgusting. The thought of my blood out in the monkey world being diluted down to nothing . . . no. You are a prideful man, you understand, even if you wish you didn't. No, Mr. Ballard, you were always to be the instrument of her death. I just had to embellish it for you, appeal to your tattered illusion of being a good man, of being the hero."

I gestured with my free hand. *"Sit Manus Mea."* The closet opened. The wall panel slid aside and the proper buttons on the keypad pushed themselves. There was a soft electronic beep and the safe door swung open as well.

"Now, your turn," Ankou said.

"Yeah," I said. "My turn." I slid the needle into his neck and pushed the plunger down hard. Ankou began to try to sit up. He made a faint popping sound in his throat, like he was fighting to get air and slumped back onto the bed.

"I want the last thing you can comprehend to be this," I said. "You plan to hunt that little boy down, and kill him, as easily as you killed Caern."

Ankou's form shivered between his mortal self and his true Fae nature, like a switch was being flipped by some mad, spasming god, snapping him back and forth between his real self and the diminished mortal illusion.

"I gave her my word too," I said. "That didn't work out too good for her either."

The Fae lord's polychromatic eyes dimmed and rolled back in his skull as his body thrashed, fighting the invading poison. Drool spilled from his mouth, gasping like a fish out of water.

"You're right. I'm a son of a bitch," I said. "You reminded me there's a cost to trying to play at being anything else." He shriveled back into his mortal guise and lay on the bed shuddering with each breath. "As to breaking my word, Fae have no souls for me to swear on. Everything Caern was is gone now, thanks to you. And when you leave this world after however long you exist in that tortured prison of a body, you will be scattered on the wind, gone forever. I wanted those to be the last words in your ear that made any sense to you as your brain was set on fire. You fucked with the wrong monkey, Theo."

Ankou made a whistling noise and his eyes rolled wildly around, searching, fighting to remain still, to focus on anything. He was gone.

"Nice doing business with you, Lord Ankou," I said, dropping the empty needle on the edge of his bed. "Enjoy your early retirement."

TWENTY-SIX

It took me a day to find the old ranch in Leucadia that had belonged to Joey's late uncle. The hunt was complicated by the fact I didn't know Joey's last name, or his uncle's. I knew Caern's son, Garland, was named after the dead man, but that was it.

I decided not to use magic to find Garland because the Dugpa or the Nightwise were out there, sniffing for him and for me. A shiver of a power, especially from me, might catch their attention. The Fae artifact, Caern's mother's necklace, was hiding me quite effectively, and I saw no reason to do anything to change that. I figured I had given House Ankou enough to keep them busy, so I didn't worry about them making this more of a cluster fuck than it already was.

The scant intel I had would have been more than enough for Grinner to find the place, but Grinner was down, maimed. I searched the old way, the hard way. I did title searches at the county courthouse, looking for any Garlands, or even the first initial G. I looked for properties maybe far behind on their property taxes, just scraping by. I also looked for transfers of property within families, and finally for condemned properties in Encinitas. Then I drove around, talked to farmers, ranchers, surfers, convenience store clerks, even a few wandering cops. I had lies for all of them. I finally found it on a lonely, rocky, wooded lot off east Neptune Avenue. It was a run-down

California-style beach house. The yard was kept up somewhat, but just on the verge of being overgrown. It was off from the road a bit, with walls of foliage separating it from its more affluent peers, taking up the better part of a large corner lot. The whole neighborhood was a mixture of wealth, middle class, retirees, and blue collar. The late Uncle Garland's house probably saw its heyday in the late sixties, when this area was most likely more working class and surfer.

After scouting around a bit, I found a 7-Eleven. I thought about calling Dwayne for some backup and muscle in case things got rough. Then Grinner and Vigil punched my memory and I decided if it got rough I'd deal with it on my own. I also considered buying a forty of some malt liquor; I managed to pass that up too, but it was even harder. No fuck-ups, not now. Too many sharks circling.

I came back after dark to the old house. There were no cars parked in the driveway that wound up the hill, no lights on in any of the windows, in fact, no indication of active electricity or habitation at all as I drove by. I parked Ankou's stolen sports car down Neptune, and walked back up, heading into the brush at the edge of the wooded lot, about a half acre from the ramshackle house.

Skirting through the darkness of the stand of trees, I could hear the ocean waves off to my left and below the cliffs. Stray gulls, hurrying home after dark, challenged the surf's roar with their lonely screeches. I could smell fresh mint and sea salt. I felt my body relax in spite of itself. Dwayne would have moved through the lot without making a sound, like poisoned thought. I am not Dwayne. Still, I've done my share of B and E's in my time and I managed to get close enough to the edge of the tree line to see the dark house and the backyard without tripping and falling on my face or making too much noise.

I sat on a stump and watched for a while. Nothing. Dark on dark. Occasionally light and shadow thrown off Neptune from the distant street on the other side of the house would twist into view as a car turned and its lights grazed the house for a moment. As my eyes adjusted to the darkness, I saw what I suspected was a path off to my left that started in the backyard and most likely led down through the rocky slope to the beach at my back.

If you spend enough time waiting and watching your internal clock gets pretty accurate, especially when you've been sober for days. My best guess was that it was nine o'clock now. No signs of any activity, any life. I had deliberately avoided buying cigarettes at the 7-Eleven so I couldn't be overcome by the urge I was having right now for a smoke.

Maybe I was wrong, maybe Joey wasn't pushing his luck twice. He may have bundled Garland up and took off in a car headed for anywhere but here. That's what I'd do, run like hell and keep running. That's a hell of a way to raise a kid, though, and Garland would be reeling from the death of his mother. Shit, I didn't know. I couldn't take care of myself, let alone a kid, I wasn't sure what he'd do. This was just my best hunch and my last scrap of a clue in this long trail that started in Greece.

A slit of soft yellow light appeared at the edge of one of the back windows. Just for a second. There were thick blankets hung over all the windows and someone had opened one just a peek. I stood up, my knees creaking a bit as I did. Okay, maybe risk an invisibility spell to . . .

I saw white light behind my eyes as the blow caught me in the back of the skull. I went down, face-first into the dirt and leaves. I rolled over to see a twelve-gauge combat shotgun pointed at me. The man behind the gun had a grim, tired face and long dreadlocks. He was dressed in a black T-shirt, black hoodie, and jeans. I recognized him from the picture Caern had shown me. It was Joey.

"How many with you?" he muttered quietly.

"Just me," I said. "I'm not with Ankou, I'm not with anyone. I'm here to help you and your son."

"Bullshit," he said. "How did you find us?"

"I spoke with Caern before she died. I was hired by Ankou to find her, but after I talked to her, and saw Garland, I couldn't. He must have had me followed or something. I tried to stop what happened, but I was too late. I want to help you, I swear it."

"You're lying," Joey said. "Get your ass up. We're walking inside. I don't want to make a lot of noise out here, but you try anything and I'll cut you in half." I nodded and got to my feet with a groan. As I stood I threw a handful of sand and dirt into Joey's eyes. I pushed his arms and the gun down toward the ground as I drove a forearm into his face. I felt his nose break and followed the arm bar with a southpaw uppercut. He fell down on his ass, dropping the shotgun. I picked it up and aimed it at him. Joey looked more scared than anything and I knew it was for his son in the house, not for himself.

"Sorry about the nose," I said. "Yeah, I am lying. The truth is Ankou threatened to do worse than kill me and I told him where to find Caern. I was chickenshit, trying to save my own ass. I'd say I'm sorry, but I figure that would be like spitting on her and the baby's grave." The sadness and the anger warred in his eyes. "I'm here to help you, Joey, you and Garland. I took care of Ankou, but that fucked-up cult that you got Caern away from in L.A., they want Garland and I'll be damned if I let them get him.

"I've got money, a lot of money, and some fake IDs for both of you. A friend of mine cooked them up before I nearly got him killed. They're good enough to get you two into Mexico, through TSA to anywhere. I'm here to help. I swear it." I dropped the shotgun at Joey's feet. "You want to kill me, I wouldn't blame you. If you do punch my ticket, the car keys in my pocket are to a Trevita parked about four blocks down. There's a case in the car with the bearer bonds and the IDs. Hell, keep the car too. Ankou won't be needing it."

Joey got to his feet. He wiped the blood from his broken nose. He left the shotgun in the dirt. "We weren't there," he said, more to the night than to me. "I wasn't there. We had a stupid argument about fucking dishwasher detergent. Can you imagine that shit? Goddamned soap. I was tired and I didn't want to go get it and she said she would and I got pissed and we yelled at each other and I headed out the door and Garland, hell, Garland, he wanted to ride along with his daddy. So the last thing I said to her was 'Be right back,' and I slammed the fucking door.

"She was the best thing that ever came into my fucked-up life and I wasn't there to help her, to save her, I let her slip away not knowing how much I loved her, thinking I was pissed at her. Goddamned soap."

"She knew, she told me," I said. "I know that doesn't mean shit right now, but maybe one day you'll feel it. She loved you. You were her hero, you saved her life a long time ago. Don't forget that."

Joey picked up the shotgun. "Come on," he said. "Let's get Garland and get the hell out of here." We broke the tree line and entered the backyard. Garland was standing next to a plastic jungle gym designed to look like a tree house with a slide. The boy was in an old, faded, and too-big L.A. Lakers jersey over footie pajamas.

"Dad?" the boy said. "They're coming. Hi, Ballard."

"Who, son?" Joey asked, looking around.

"Bad men," the boy said. "Real bad men." I opened my Ajna, my third eye and I sensed them too.

"The Dugpa," I said to Joey. "Coming from the beach." I knelt by Garland and unwrapped Caern's purple quartz bracelet from my wrist. I put it around the boy's neck, like a choker. "Garland, this was your mamma's, and her mamma's before that. It's from Faerie, did your mom tell you about the First World?" He nodded as he examined the jewelry. "It's powerful," I said. "It will hide you from hollow men, from bad people looking for you with the sight, what you and your mamma have. Never take it off, you hear me, you never take this away from your skin, and you stick close to your dad." The boy looked at me with large, wise eyes and nodded. They were Caern's eyes. I stood and turned to Joey. "You two get in the house. Hide."

"You'll need help," he said.

"That shotgun won't make a difference," I said. "Your son needs you. If anything happens to me, Garland will know. If it does, you make a run for the car. Get the fuck out of the country and do it fast, y'hear?"

Joey nodded and led his son toward the back door of the dark house. The boy looked back at me and then they both disappeared inside. I cleared the cobwebs of pain and fear from my body with some cleansing breaths and ran toward the beach down the old worn path through the stand of trees. I cleared the tree line and found myself at the edge of the rocky cliff. There were old, worn, concrete stairs with rusted metal rails that led down to the rocky beach below. The moon was hidden behind clouds and I could sense that will had placed those clouds there, so I brushed them aside.

"Iam celare, tacere sororis," I whispered, and the bright, pilfered light of the moon came out of hiding and illuminated the sea and the beach. There were six men. They had landed in a large rubber raft with a muffled outboard motor on it. The raft had been dragged onto the land. All the men wore black tactical gear, black ski masks, and night-vision goggles that made them look vaguely insect-like as they spread across the beach, moving toward the cliff face and the stairs. They were all armed. A second raft, with six more assassins, was closing with the shore.

As the accusing moonlight pinned them, I pulled energy from the air, sifting it through my seething Muladhara lens and gestured downward as the waters roughened and the dark clouds swirled. *"Ignis caeli ardebit inimicos meos,"* I called up to the winds, even as the men heard me and raised their weapons. Lightning, like an angry serpent, crashed down from the sky. It struck and killed two of the men, tossing their bodies into the air. I felt another's magic deflect my lightning and send it dancing across the now-choppy ocean until it dispersed.

"Shit" was all I had time to say as I scrambled back away from the edge of the cliff, toward the trees. There was a hiss and whine of angry bullets as the surviving killers and the landing occupants of the second raft fired their silenced weapons up the cliff at me. I felt a hot iron burn itself into my shoulder with the force of a freight train. I fell back onto the ground from the shot. Before I had time to regroup, I felt the mystical attack on top of me. Foul, poisoned Manipura-driven force engulfed me and tried to smother me, snuff out my life force. It was brazen, reckless magic driven by a level of power I had seldom encountered in a mortal magician. My first instinct was an animal one, to shake myself loose, but I quickly sensed, as my lungs began to seize, that was exactly what my opponent wanted me to do, and the spell coiled tighter about my aura, like a massive python of black cracking energy.

I was on the ground struggling to breathe, to stay conscious, and I knew the Dugpa's assassins were hustling up the stairs while their patron kept me busy. I had less than a minute until they could pump my twitching body full of bullets and then move against Joey and Garland. No. That was not going to happen, damn it.

I forced my body, my instincts, to shut the fuck up. I accepted the spell, its twisted harmony, its mad entropy. I let the monster play, if it killed me it killed me; if this was my last breath, then it was. There was no future, no "next," there was pure crystalline breath, the mind of the infinite, the sun, radiating from my core.

The coils of the spell loosened. I was water, I became my Svadhisthana chakra; pure life force; pure, clean, fluid, slowly eroding the hungry, insistent magic wanting to devour me. I let it devour me and in doing so I devoured it. I slipped loose from the spell. It was a hell of a trap, and it had been built just for me. My life force, my soul was my weakest spot, and the last thing I would have ever relied on to overcome such an attack. Another few seconds of resisting and I'd be dead. As it was, I was feeling pretty rough as I crouched. I saw the masked face of the first Dugpa to reach the top of the stairs. I let the monster slither away and guided it toward the killer. He seized and fell back down the stairs as the spell devoured him. I heard his companions shout as he crashed into them. He was no wizard and he had no mystic aikido to employ against the black tantric spell.

I placed my hand on the ground and anchored myself, becoming the earth. I sent pulse after pulse of root Muladhara energy through the cliff. My head swam from the concussion I was pretty sure Joey had given me when he coldcocked me with the shotgun. My lungs burned and my body ached from the spell I had narrowly escaped.

What I was trying to do now, most wizards in the world, in history, couldn't do on the fly. The enormity of it threatened to eclipse my mind, my will.

Too big, it's too big . . .

But not my fucking ego. *I am Laytham-motherfucking-Ballard, and I am the greatest wizard to ever stride this earth, I am an ass-kicking, pillar-of-salt-turning, motherfucking god, a goddamned rock star, I'm fucking Thulsa Doom with a better agent.* The immovable object quivered, shook.

I stalled. It was too big, it was too much. The next Dugpa's head came into view, then his chest, his raised gun. There was another appearing behind him and another after that. All black-clad, like the night itself was sending its army to kill me, to kill . . . Garland. Garland, his eyes, his mother's eyes. *You are all that stands between that little boy who never hurt a soul, and the hungry night. You're it. If you die, they take him.*

I was no rock star, sure as fuck no god. I was a tired, guilty, selfish, old man running from his fears, from his failures. I was ready, this was as good as it was going to get. That boy was going to live a good life, and that was worth the bad one I had wasted. I released a single breath, felt my Sahasrara chakra take over, gently pushing instead of violently pulling. I begged, instead of ordered, and I felt the world open and yield, felt the other mage's attempt to stop what I was doing crumble like a sand castle.

A large section of the rocky cliff face, including the stairs, collapsed, crashing and tumbling down on the beach below. I heard the shouts and screams of the Dugpa assassins as they fell and then only the sound of the settling earth and the relentless waves.

I stood, shaking. My whole body felt twitchy and weak, as if I had physically pushed the weight. Each breath was fire. It was only then that I realized I had been hit again. I was bleeding from my chest as well as from my shoulder. I walked back to the edge of the cliff, carefully looking over the side. I got dizzy for a second but didn't fall, couldn't fall. Below there were boulders and debris everywhere along the beach. In the silver light, bodies were scattered about the rock-slide, unmoving. The two rafts sat alone at the edge of the encroaching sea. That was easier than . . . I . . . thought it . . . *The Dugpa work through misdirection, they never come at you straight on.*

"Damn it!" I said. I immediately started hacking for my effort. My lungs felt like they were made of molten lead, I couldn't get a good breath. My cough brought up bright red blood. I spit over the cliff and headed back toward the house and the yard as quickly as I could.

The back door was locked. I kicked it open and nearly puked and passed out for my effort. I stumbled into the nearly demolished 1950s-style kitchen. Cabinet doors were reduced to splinters, their hinges partly melted as if by terrible heat. The oven was crushed, crumpled like a tin can. Every drawer had launched itself across the room and the cracked, stained tile floor was littered with old rusted cutlery and now fat, dark drops of my blood. Some of the knives and forks were impaled in the walls, still vibrating from the impact.

"Joey!" I called out as I moved through the debris and into the darkness of the hall connected to the kitchen. "Garland!" The house was cold, colder than outside, and the place smelled of stale piss and something else, something familiar to some corner of my awareness. I saw scraps of light ahead, hidden under thick plastic shower curtains, hung before a doorway. I pushed the curtain aside, focusing my strained concentration, raising my defenses, preparing to fight.

The living room was lit by several battery-powered lanterns. Joey braced against a wall, his body partly hidden by shadow. He was panting and wincing in pain, bleeding from a deep, ugly gut wound.

I turned and saw Garland, his face slack with fear, and before the boy, in the harsh LED light, was Crash Cart, its multiple cabled arms sprouting scalpels and whirring circular bone saws, dripping with Joey's blood. It turned its mangled half-face toward me, and beneath the blood-clotted surgical mask I thought I saw it grin. Two of the tulpa's oil- and blood-slick tentacles were obscenely wrapped around the boy's chest, but it hadn't hurt him. Joey struggled to bend over and pick up the still-smoking shotgun off the floor; its barrel had been cut in two. "You can't have him," the father growled, fighting to hold his insides in.

Garland looked to me, pleading. Everything was dimming. I could hear my blood swelling in my veins, in my skull. I fought to remain present in this nightmare.

"Glad to see you still on your feet, Ballard," Brett Glide said, stepping into the light. "Better late than never, I always say." The Dugpa was dressed all in black, like his men on the beach. "Those were some impressive workings back on the beach. You are as good as they say you are, almost as good as you think you are. Even if you have mastered the technique to keep Crash Cart from affecting you, the boy and his father are not so lucky, and you're barely on your feet."

"Still got a little hitch in my giddy-up," I said, filling my body with Manipura energy. "Unless you want what your boys on the beach got, Big Kahuna, you call off your monster. Leave the boy be."

"Wow," Glide said, smiling and shaking his head. I wanted to kick in his perfect teeth. "I have to tell you, you got style, I'll give you points for that. Bleeding out, exhausted, and beat to hell and you still act like you're going to win this. God, it's a shame you didn't join us."

"You wouldn't have liked it if I had," I said. "I would have gotten rid of you and your bat-shit crazy-ass stepdad day one." Glide chuckled. "Runs in the blood, I guess. He's as fucked-up as his old man. I had a nice long chat with step-granddad in the joint."

"My grandfather is a prophet, a messiah," Glide said, some of the fake Hollywood smile sliding off his face. "You don't deserve to breathe the same air as he."

"To be honest, Brett, I didn't want to. Manson could've used a shower, or some patchouli—the hippie stuff—maybe a little Febreze, at least."

"Shut your fucking sewer of a mouth, you old fucking relic!" Glide shouted, the facade gone. He was red-faced with rage and his voice made Garland jump. Crash Cart's "arms" slid more tightly around the boy, like snakes covered in blood clots. I held up a hand to Glide.

"Mellow, dude, mellow," I said. "Your karma is already fucked up pretty good, no need to push it to eleven." Glide got a grip on himself. I could feel his defenses wavering a bit as he attempted to chill. If Garland wasn't in the line of fire, I would have gone for it then. Glide patted down his hair and put his smiling mask back on.

"Garland?" Glide said to the boy in his best hippie Mr. Rogers voice. "My name is Brett and you're going to come with Crash Cart and me now. It will all be okay, son. I promise. We're going to take you somewhere safe where you will be loved and cared for and in time all these nightmares from before will fade away."

"Damn you, Glide," Joey said, forcing himself to stand. He was soaked in blood, sweating, fighting to say conscious. It was pure love, pure desire to save his son, that was keeping him from dropping. "You leave him alone, you son of a bitch, or I'll kill you!" He took a step away from the blood-painted wall, toward the Dugpa. "Garland . . ." He collapsed, unmoving.

"Do you like Xbox?" Glide said to the boy. "You can have every Xbox game they ever made and some special ones too, just for you, programmed by some of my family."

Garland looked to me. "Bad man," the boy said, nodding at Glide.

"Yep," I said. "Very, very bad. He's talking about you forgetting your mom and dad, kid." I grunted as I knelt to look Garland eye to eye. I sat on the floor, cross-legged in a full lotus position, ignoring the screaming pain in my chest as I folded my legs. I almost passed out but I didn't. "Don't worry, Garland, you and your dad are going to walk out of here and I'm going to make the bad man and the monster go away, and you're going to help me."

Glide chuckled. "You really need to rein in that ego, Ballard. It's over. You've got nothing left. Garland, if you come with me right now, we'll get your daddy some help, get him to a hospital, to a doctor. You don't want Daddy to die like Mommy did, do you? It would be your fault if you didn't come along willingly right now. You don't want to kill Daddy, do you buddy?"

"Look at me," I said. My fingers were already beginning to make the motions, the complex new mudras I hadn't had much of a chance to practice. They had to be perfect for this to work, my form had to be perfect. No goddamn D.T. shakes, no fear, no pain, perfect, or the boy was gone. *Just once, just goddamned once, don't fuck it up.* "Ignore him, kid, he's the fucking boogeyman. He can't hurt you or your dad, neither can that ugly, gross thing holding you. See, the hollow man wants you to give in to him yourself. It gives him more power, and old Crash Cart there, well, he really is just a bad dream. We can take 'em, kid. Look at me, listen to me."

"I'm sorry to say you're killing your daddy, Garland," Glide said. I could feel him building a working aimed right at me. "This old bum, he's lying to you. He doesn't want to help you. He got your mommy killed."

Garland looked at me and I saw the doubt enter those young-old eyes. I completed the first key and my fingers began the second series of mudras; the twisting and the shaping of my fingers was even more difficult than the first. I kept working and I matched the little boy's gaze. It was harder than I thought it would be.

I thought about my grandmother, how she used to talk to me when I wasn't much older than Garland, her gentle voice, her kindness, and most of all, her honesty. I tried to think what Granny would say. "I messed up," I said. "I got scared and I did something bad because I was scared. Your mom got hurt, got killed, because I messed up, Garland. I'm sorry."

"Mamma said you were her friend, that it was okay that you're sad inside," the child with Caern Ankou's eyes said to me as sagely as any guru, as any mystic master I had ever met. "Mamma told me it's okay. She told me we all get scared and we all mess up sometimes. We just got to try again to do good. Mamma was sad inside too, for a long time. She messed up too, but she said me and Dad made her happy inside again. She told me after you left that she could see the good in you, trying to peek out from all that sad and bad. She liked you, Ballard."

"I liked her too," I said. I was almost done with the second key, my fingers were flying. If I hadn't fucked it up this should get Brett's attention. I couldn't fuck this up. "I need you to think of your mamma right now, kid, see her, don't close your eyes, don't be afraid of the monster or the bad man. Think about all the good things about your mamma. See her."

"Okay, this is too fucking sweet for words," Glide said. "And you think *I'm* smarmy, please. Say night-night, old man." He raised his hand to obliterate me with a channel of Muladhara energy. I completed the second key and my hands came together, steepled with a too-loud clap. A halo of violet light surrounded Garland and it slowly drifted away from him as it grew larger, shifted in shape, and began to take on substance. "What did you do?" Glide said, incredulous as he finally began to comprehend what I had been working at. Crimson energy flared like a bloody star from his hand straight toward my heart.

A slender, pale hand stopped it harmlessly, refracted it into a million shards of twinkling, jeweled light. The hand was connected to a wrist crisscrossed with old scars. Garland looked up into the fading lavender light and smiled into the face of his mother.

"It's all right, Garland," the tulpa of Caern Ankou said as she effortlessly pulled Crash Cart's slippery steel cables away from Garland. "Mamma's going to make the bad dream go away now." The tiny little Fae girl shoved back the hulking stainless steel nightmare and Crash Cart smashed back into a wall, sending down a rain of plaster dust and debris.

"That's not possible," Glide said, as he slipped to the floor and assumed a Burmese position. His fingers linked and began to shift and move frantically. "It took my father years, me, decades, to master the formation formulas to build a tulpa. How could you . . ."

"Your granddad Chuck taught me in one day," I said, "for a carton of smokes. I've always been a quick learner, at least as far as magic goes." Glide was working to strengthen Crash Cart's physicality in the waking world. He was working off stale formula and rote visualization. Caern's projection was fueled by the dynamo of a child's imagination and a son's love. Crash Cart tried to roll back toward the boy and Caern stopped him cold with one hand on his boxlike chest. The nightmare began to become a little blurry at the edges.

"Leave my family alone," she said. A fierceness set in her jaw. I saw Joey's head come up, the look of amazement on his face.

I shouted to him even as I began a new combination of mudras, a riff off what Manson had taught me, an improvisation. It was something else I was actually kind of good at, one of the few things. "Joey! Think of Caern, remember her, all your love, all your memories, now!"

Caern became even more substantial, more solid. The detail of her face, her clothes, everything brightened and sharpened, even as Crash Cart was losing detail. I completed my new mudra just as the monstrous tulpa rolled away from Caern, who now was radiant in all her true Fae glory, beautiful, powerful, a goddess, protecting her child. At my direction, Crash Cart grabbed Brett off the floor, gathering him up in his viscous tendrils. The Dugpa screamed and struggled in shock and horror.

"No! No! What are you doing? Stop, you can't do this! I'm your master!" Glide shouted as Crash Cart wrapped the black tantric wizard tighter in his inhuman embrace. The horrible, mangled head turned in my direction. Eyes, one leaking bloody jelly, the other a metal and glass lens embedded in meat, regarded me.

"Go back where you came from," I said to Crash Cart. "Take him with you, he's yours now." The outline of a smile again under the stained, bloody mask. The wall behind the tulpa folded in upon itself, a toothed maw gnawing a hole into our world. The last of Charles Manson's living nightmares rolled backward into the festering wound in space, one of its rubber wheels squeaking and shaking as it did. It dragged Brett Glide, aka Brett Winder, into its realm, the place behind our eyelids we thrash and struggle to flee in deepest sleep. Brett begged, and when begging did nothing, he cursed my name with the last shreds of sanity his charred soul possessed. The mouth closed and became just a wall again. The stench of rancid blood and engine oil faded. Caern's tulpa became her mortal self again. She knelt down and pulled Garland tight.

"Mamma, you a ghost?" the boy asked. "Can you stay with us?"

"Oh baby, Mamma's a memory now," Caern said, "and I'll be with you every day, all day. Anytime you need me, you remember. I'll be there."

"But I'll miss you, Mamma." Garland's voice was quavering, "I miss your kisses and your hugs, and, and . . . it's not fair."

"It is fair," she said. "I know it doesn't make sense to you now, baby boy, but it will in time." The child hugged the tulpa with all his might. Tears ran down son and mother's faces. "It will in time, baby."

I groaned as I made my way to my feet. I was really dizzy from losing blood. I managed to help Joey up, and we leaned on each other like two staggering drunks. Joey wrapped his arms around his son and his dead wife. They held each other, never wanting the next moment to come, never wanting this sliver of time to end. Caern kissed her little boy on the head and her husband on the lips. She looked over to me and that same sad, almost pitying look she had given me only a couple days ago was on her face.

"Thank you for this," she said. "You gave me a chance to say goodbye. You did right by me, by them." She kissed Joey again on the cheek. "Please get him to a hospital."

"I will," I said and stepped away. I knew what was happening, and I knew she didn't have long.

"I love you," Joey said. "I'm sorry I got mad and—"

Caern kissed him again to quiet him.

"You know in your heart how much I love you," she said. "You are the only man who ever kept all his promises to me. I want you to be happy and take good care of our boy. I know you will. I love you, Joey, and I always will."

Garland was crying, the sobs shaking his whole body. Caern lifted him into her arms and wiped the tears away. "Don't go, Mamma, please!"

"We don't get a say in that, Garland," Caern said, kissing his eyes and tickling his tummy. "Don't let that make you sad, or angry inside, honey, please try. Life's beautiful and it's a present, every day you're here. Mamma wishes she had more time with you and Daddy too, but I'm so grateful for every second I had with you. Think about what you have, Garland, not what you lose."

Again, my grandmother's words in my ears. I understood Garland's panic, his fear and how that simmering fear could boil into a lifetime of anger and resentment. I wish I had listened harder to what Granny had tried to teach me.

"Promise Mamma you'll try to not get sad inside? It's okay to be sad inside sometimes, but don't let it eat you up, baby. You end up hollow and Mamma never wants that for you."

"I promise, Mamma," Garland said, wiping his own tears away. He hugged her neck tightly. I knew he was smelling her hair, trying to remember every bit of this moment to sustain him for the long years to come.

"Daddy will help you," she said, "and Ballard too. They'll be there for you when it gets hard and they'll understand."

Caern kissed her boy one last time and set him down. She was already fading, losing detail. Garland clung to his father's leg and hip; he didn't seem to notice the blood. Joey didn't seem to feel his wounds in this moment. Caern became caught in a swirling mass of tiny, indigo lights like fireflies as the tulpa continued to fade away. "I'll find you in dreams," Caern Ankou said to her family. "I love you two. You're the best thing that ever happened . . ." She was so thin now you could see through her like glass. ". . . to me."

She was gone. Her two men, Joey and Garland, stood silently, lost in their thoughts and their pain.

"Your mom's right," I said to the boy as I picked him up. "Don't let all that yucky bad stuff stay in you, kid. You'll end up like that asshole . . . that bad man, Brett."

"Is that what happened to you?" Garland asked, sliding one arm around my neck.

"Something like that," I said. "Don't end up like me, be like your mom."

"Mom liked you," he said. "I like you too, but you smell like smoke." The kid scrunched up his face and pinched his nose. "Yuck!"

I looked to Joey. "You can walk a little farther?"

"Yeah," he said. "Thank you."

"You never have to thank me for a damn thing," I said. "Come on, let's get you some help. I know a street doc that can patch us both up."

We made our way back through the wrecked kitchen and out the broken back door. I was still carrying Garland in spite of the pain and the dizziness. Just a little farther. All three of us stopped at what was waiting for us in the yard.

I counted at least ten of them that I could see, the whole contingent here in L.A. The most powerful wizards in all the worlds, they all had spells ready, boiling at the tips of their fingers. I could sense them and their energies now since Gida was dropping the masking glamour she had been running to keep me from sensing their approach. Dragon was at Gida's side. To everyone else she might look pissed, but I knew Lauren better than most and she was dying inside with sadness and conflict.

"Laytham Ballard," Gida said, "you are under arrest by the Order of the Nightwise for your heinous crimes within our city. By the power of the Silver Seals, and the Compact of Shiva, by the sacrifice of the Bodhisattva, by the secret saint, Alice Weinstein of Fort Worth Texas—destroyer of monsters and guardian of life—by the Court of the Uncountable Stairs, you are bound to stand down."

"I didn't kill those women," I called out to the faceless shadows of my mage peers, ready to destroy me if I made a false move. "You know that, Gida."

"You'll get to have your say at the tribunal, prior to execution or banishment," Gida said calmly. "Now step away from the boy and his father. I'll make sure they are cared for."

"The hell you will," I said. I looked at Dragon. "The Maven is part of the Dugpa cult that has been operating under your noses for a long, long time. They have been committing the ritual murders, and she's been covering for them since before she became Maven. She's sold you out!"

Dragon's frown deepened. There was a murmur from the assembled Nightwise, but not a single destructive spell wavered in its focus on me.

"Ballard, you're not helping yourself here," Lauren said. My former partner took a step toward me. "You're injured, badly. Release those two so they don't get hurt in this. You just . . . you need . . . you need to come along quietly."

"Never a day in my life, darlin'." I said to Dragon. "Handing Joey and Garland over to the Maven is the same as giving them to the Dugpa." I turned and handed Garland to Joey, who held his son tightly despite how much of his own life was leaking out of him by the minute. "If this gets ugly, you two run," I said softly. I moved so that father and son were at my back.

"Yes, the mythical 'Dugpa cult,'" Gida said. "The one you and Roland Blue participated in since you were one of us, before your fall."

"The one you covered up from me and Nico," I said, "and then from Dragon, from all of the Nightwise. The one you are a high-ranking member of, Maven. The one that used Roland Blue as an agent in the Life. Didn't you guys ever wonder why in all the years Blue's been in business you were never able to nail him, shut him down? He was protected, by the Maven."

"Don't listen to him!" It was my old buddy Luke, from the elevator. His partner, Bridgette, was also in the crowd, targeting me with a deadly spell, a look of predatory anticipation on her face. "Ballard's a fraud, a con man. He attacked me and Bridgette! He's as dirty as they come!"

"I swear I'm telling the truth, I . . . I give my word!"

I regretted it as soon as I said it.

"Your word?" Bridgette sneered. "Everyone here knows what your word, your oath, is worth. You betrayed the order and now you're trying to hustle us to get away with murder."

"You reputation does make it hard for you to be believed, Laytham," Gida said. "You were driven from our number because of the things you'd done, the compromises you made. You have reveled in your debauchery and your delinquent behavior your whole life, everyone knows that. You are no longer Nightwise, Laytham Ballard, no longer one of us. You have no code, no honor. You no longer live by the Brilliant Badge, nor can you even summon it. You don't stand for the weak and the innocent, you prey on them, hurt them, and now you're under arrest." The shadow of a smug smile crossed Gida's face for just a second. Only I saw it. "I'm sorry, Laytham."

I felt them all preparing, waiting for me to stand down or to fight. I'd die, there was no hustle, no shit I could pull out of my ass here. I'd die, Joey would die and Garland . . . I looked back at the boy and he looked at me with eyes as big as an owl's. They were his mother's eyes too.

I raised my hand. I thought of Garland, of Joey, of Peggy, of Grinner, of Jane Doe, of all the Jane Does, and most of all of Caern, sweet, sad, Crystal Myth, Caern. I took the bitterness of my failures and I hammered them about me like armor. I had made so many mistakes, authored so many tragedies. I had let so many people down. Not today, not the kid. Garland's words were in my mind as I sifted the formula, went through the routes of the simple ritual and laid myself bare before it in judgment. *She told me we all get scared and we all mess up sometimes. We just got to try again to do good.* I took a shaky, burning, painful breath and I tried one more time to do good.

The Brilliant Badge burned in the night, hovering above my hand. It was strong, and it was steady, and it did not waver. The light of it illuminated the faces of the circle of wizards and I could see the shock on those faces. The best look of all was Gida's. I saw fear there, and maybe a little remorse, some sadness.

Dragon smiled and walked away from the Maven to stand by my side; she summoned the Badge as well. One by one, each Nightwise called their Badge to them and the night was pushed back, held at bay by the joined radiance. Gida stood alone now, circled by wizards, their spells leveled at her, not me. No Badge hovered above her palm. She raised her hands in surrender. Her eyes never left me.

"You're under arrest," I said.

TWENTY-SEVEN

The waves reached for the heavens, then tumbled under their own weight, crashing, falling into white, hissing foam as they rushed across the wet sand. Garland laughed as the water tickled and pulled at his feet. The child squealed in delight and some seagulls gave a shrill reply. The boy ran along the beach and his father ran with him, playing tag with the endless ocean. Joey had lost some weight while he was in the hospital, but he looked good and he scooped Garland up and spun him around. I stood at the rocky edge of the beach, which was off of Third Street, in Encinitas. Vigil, finally up and out of the hospital himself, stood beside me, his arms crossed. I could feel Garland's aura reaching out, teasing at the water, at the gulls. The colors coming off him were brighter than the late-morning sun. Garland saw us and called out to his dad who set the boy back on the wet sand and then raced him to us. Garland won.

"Ballard! Vigil!" Garland shouted as he crashed into our legs. Vigil held out a stabilizing hand to keep the little bundle of speed from falling on his ass.

"Easy," Vigil said, "you'll knock us old men down." The kid grinned and I noticed he had lost another baby tooth. "That's quite a gap there," Vigil said, kneeling to Garland's level. "Perhaps the Tooth

Fairy will leave you a little something for that." I snorted and Burris looked up at me.

"Don't get me started on the Tooth Fairy," I said. "When he's not creeping around between Arcadia and Earth, he runs an odonto-philia fetish website out of Copenhagen."

"Copenhagen, huh," Vigil remarked as he ruffled the kid's hair and stood back up. "I would have figured Great Britain for that."

"I know, right?"

Joey walked up. He shook Vigil's hand. He didn't offer and I didn't attempt. "You both look better than when you were in the hospital," he said. "You wanted to meet up, Ballard? What's going on?"

"Hey kid, take a hike," I said to Garland. The kid grinned again and shook a fist at me. Vigil put his hand on Garland's shoulder. Caern's charmed bracelet, now a necklace, was visible for a second beneath the Marvel's Black Panther T-shirt Garland was wearing.

"Come on, little lord," Vigil said. "Let's go find some shells for your dad and Ballard." After they had wandered down the beach out of earshot, Joey and I took a walk among the rocks.

"How is he?" I asked.

"He misses her," Joey said. "He's sleeping better, now. He talks to a therapist a few times a week."

"How about you?"

Joey paused when I asked.

"Breathing," he said. "Thankful as hell for him. It's hard, but it will be okay. It has to be, right? For his sake."

"Yeah," I said, "it has to be, for him. You're all he's got now." I paused. I wanted to say it again, but Joey shook his head.

"He'd be dead without you, so would I," he said. "Let it go."

"Have you?"

"No," he said. "Most days I want to bash your skull in, usually when things are really bad for him. I can't say I hate you—he thinks so much of you—you're his hero and you didn't have to come back for us, you didn't have to do a damn bit of what you did at the end. You could have gone on your way, and said to hell with Garland and me, but you didn't. That counts for something."

I didn't answer. We walked a little farther. Behind us, Vigil and Garland were playing. "You're leaving, aren't you?" Joey finally asked. I nodded. "You got that look about you. Caern had it for a long time too. She just got antsy at the thought of staying put. After Garland, it passed. Where you going?"

"Away," I said. "I'm not really sure where. I seldom am. A guy I know in Canada with the RCMP emailed me about some wendigos wandering around Yellowknife in an old VW microbus. He asked for help. I may wander that way eventually. You guys good on money?"

"Yeah," he said. "He's rich now, thanks to the money you got off Theo, set for the rest of his life." Joey looked back toward Garland, who was showing Vigil a shell. "He's going to miss you a lot, y'know? You remind him of her."

"No, he won't," I said. "I'll make sure of that. I'll be around if he needs me. Vigil, or Anna, or Dragon can reach me. He's a hell of a kid and he's got a bright future ahead of him."

"It would have been a damn sight brighter if he'd never met you," Joey said. The waves crashed and neither of us spoke. Finally, Joey found his voice again. "I'm sorry," he added. "It's . . . it's just hard."

"I understand," I said, "and you're right. Either of you need anything, *anything*, call and I'm here."

We walked back toward Garland and Vigil. They came up to meet us and Garland handed me a little shell. "For you!" he said proudly.

"Thanks, man," I said and examined the shell. "I'll hang on to it."

"Me 'n' Vigil picked it out special for you," he said. I looked at Burris. The knight shrugged.

"Well, you guys got a good eye," I said.

"Vigil said you got to go help some other people, like you helped us. This will give you good luck 'til you're back," Garland said seriously. "You hang on to it and be good, Ballard. Come back soon. You promise?"

"I promise," I said. "What are you and Pop up to today?"

"Library for story time," he said, "and then we're gonna visit Mamma at the cemetery, and then McDonald's."

"Sounds like a fine day," I said and nodded to Joey.

"You want to come with us, Ballard?" Garland asked. I smiled and shook my head.

"Thanks, buddy, but I got to get back." I knelt down. "Would you say hey to your mamma for me?"

"I will," he said, hugging me tight. "I always do."

Vigil and I were quiet on the drive back to L.A. The radio in the car was playing "Lost Cause" by Beck on some alt satellite station. Finally, Vigil spoke. "You know you could stay."

"Yeah," I said. "I know. Why are you staying?"

"Mostly for Garland," he said. "He's the heir to House Ankou now. A lot of long ears are not going to like that when he reveals himself. He'll need training and counsel if he decides to take up that fight. I still feel . . . an obligation."

I shook my head.

"You can take the man out of the house, but you can't take the house out of the man . . . Sir Vigil."

"No longer," he said. "Just a humble member of the Nightwise now."

"Those ass clowns are lucky to have you," I said. "So's the kid."

"He could use a powerful wizard in his corner too," he said, carefully keeping his eyes on the highway.

"He'll have that, if and when he ever needs me," I said. "So now, I'm a mighty wizard, huh? See, I knew I'd grow on you."

"Like mold," Vigil said. We drove again with only the wind and music for a long time.

"Are we . . . good, you and I?" he asked.

"Yeah," I said. "You were doing what you thought was your duty. I was trying to save my skin. You fucked up, I fucked up."

"We fucked up," Vigil said.

"Sounds square to me. Just look after the kid, okay?"

"You have my word, if that still means anything to you."

"Better than gold," I said.

We drove again for a while. Seafret's "Oceans" filled in the silence. "Did you even consider the Maven's offer?" Vigil asked. "She wants you back with the order. You proved yourself to her, to all of them."

I looked out at the countryside streaking past us. "I'm . . . not much at sticking around. Besides"—I glanced over to him—"they couldn't afford me." We laughed for what it was worth. The city grew up around us. In time it grew quiet again.

"If . . . you ever . . ." he began and then stalled. Some things there really are no words for. We locked eyes for a moment. He nodded and I returned the nod.

"Yeah, man," I said, "you too."

I stood at the door to Grinner's hospital room. He was asleep in the bed, his hands still heavily bandaged and a full beard covering his face. Christine, his tiny bird of a wife, was asleep next to him in one of those shitty recliners every hospital room had. She wore a Scooby-Doo T-shirt and had earbuds in. I could hear her phone playing music lightly. Little Turing, their baby son, was in a traveling crib near the windows. The lights were off and the TV was showing an old *Star Trek* with Captain Kirk fighting some jack-off in a giant lizard costume. I walked in and stood at the foot of the bed. I felt lead in my stomach. I looked at the crib, at Christine. I carefully laid a manila envelope on Grinner's lap and then walked back to the door.

"Hey asshole," Grinner rumbled. "'Bout fucking time you showed up. This caper have a happy ending?"

I turned.

"Better than my average, I have to say," I said quietly.

"Yeah, you wake up Turing, Christine will have your ass." He nodded toward the envelope. "What's that?"

"The rest of your payment," I said. "Bearer bonds, about twenty-five million in paper. Go out and buy yourself a new razor."

He picked up the envelope and I saw a little frustration that he couldn't open it. He set it down. "Okay," he said. "You're paid up 'til next job."

"No next job," I said. "No more. We're quits, you and I."

"Bullshit, what the fuck you talking about?" he said, still trying to keep it down to keep from waking Christine or the baby.

"Look at you," I said. "You're damaged fucking goods. What the fuck do you think I need with a hacker with no fucking hands? I got no more use for you." I turned and headed out the door.

"Hey," he said. I stopped, turned again. "It's not your fault. No one put a fucking gun to my head to come out here, no one made me tell the guy with the gardening shears to go fuck himself. You and me, we're solid, okay?"

"What about them?" I said. "What if fucking Ankou had come after them to get to me? What if you were sitting next to a crib looking at stumps where your baby's hands should be? We solid then?"

Grinner shook his head. "You know, it's a good thing the universe gave you all that power, because you are one dumb son of a bitch." I frowned. "You still don't get it, do you, asshole? You're family. We're family. We look out for each other, we keep each other safe best we can, and we don't bail on one another. Shitty as this world can be, you take what you can get, y'know." I stood there and I did feel pretty dumb.

"Would you guys stop arguing and kiss already," Christine whispered in her sweet, lilting voice, "before you wake up the baby and I have to fucking kill both of you."

"Besides," Grinner said, picking up the envelope again, "this feels a little light." We stood there for a second; neither us knew how to say it. Finally Grinner said, "Get the fuck out. You still owe me, hillbilly, don't forget that."

"Yeah," I said, "I guess I do." I walked over and kissed Christine on the forehead. She didn't open her eyes, just made kissy lips at me.

I walked back out the door. "Good luck jerking off," I said. "See you around."

"Count on it, asshole," Grinner said.

I took a cab to LAX. The radio played "Under the Bridge" by the Red Hot Chili Peppers. The city was beautiful at night, black glass and white light. If you didn't look into the darkness too hard, you wouldn't see the cracks. We drove by a porn theater, its sidewalk hustlers washed out in the buttery light of the marquee. I thought I saw Bambi for just a second, in her cheerleader costume. She blew me a kiss.

In the terminal I stuffed my canvas working bag in one of my storage lockers, one of my homes. No way I wanted to explain the shit in that bag to the TSA. I swapped out IDs and shut the locker. I found myself looking into the eyes of the Dragon.

"Just going to slink back off into the night, huh?" Lauren said. Anna was with her.

"Better than having you busting my balls about that job," I said.

"Do you realize how many wizards all over the world would gnaw off their own arm for the chance to join the Nightwise?" she asked.

"Getting chosen to be the new Maven has really gone to your head," I said. "Fine," I sighed, "offer me the job."

"Okay, you want the job?" she asked. I nodded.

"I'll take it," I said.

"Really?"

"Sure," I said. "Now, I quit. That finally fucking settles that, doesn't it?"

"Asshole," she said shaking her head and smiling.

"You round up the rest of the Dugpa?" I asked.

"Once Gida rolled over on them, it was easy to pick them up and break up their networks," Lauren said. "She and Max Winder were both exiled off Earth yesterday. There are a few minor operators that ran, and our other branches are looking into cults in other parts of the country, but they are finally shut down in L.A. Gida was one of the greatest mages of the age; what a waste."

"Power doesn't guarantee wisdom," I said. "I'm the poster boy for that. Did she mention . . . a child that she had while in the cult, probably raised by another member?" Dragon gave me a cop-scan, sensing there was more to the question. She nodded warily.

"Yeah, she did say she had a kid, but that she managed somehow to not turn her over to the cult. She refused to tell us anything more about the kid or where she was right up until she was banished." I kept my mouth shut but I was wondering where Gida had taken our daughter and who she had left her with to raise. She'd be in her thirties now, and I'd be a stranger.

"The Nightwise could really use you, Laytham," Lauren said, "seriously."

"Darlin', with my reputation, I'd be more of a hurt than a help," I said. "Half the order still want me dead or banished for all the other shit I *did* do over the years."

"You summoned the Brilliant Badge," she said. "You showed everyone you still believe in the cause, in what the order stands for. They'll forgive in time."

"Or maybe I just figured out a way to hack the ritual," I said with a smug grin. "Maybe the Brilliant Badge is no match for the ratfuckery of Laytham Ballard."

"You are so full of bullshit," she said. Then I saw a little doubt cross her face. "You . . . are bullshitting me, right?"

"I got a plane to somewhere to catch," I said.

"If you change your mind," Lauren said, "you know how to find me."

"If you need me . . . on a consulting basis, you holler," I said. "I'm going to miss you both."

"Not if you stay," Anna said. Dragon nodded as the three of us held each other's hands.

"You don't have to keep running away," Dragon said. "You have something here . . ."

". . . Something real," Anna finished. We got a few looks as we kissed each other. I could care less, there was only the three of us. It almost felt like it used to. I was the one to let go of their hands, to step away.

"I gotta go," I said.

"You really don't," Dragon said.

"You run long enough, you forget how to stop," I said. "I'm sorry."

"That much running is exhausting," Anna said. "When you need to rest, you'll come home."

"I will," I said. It felt like a lie when I said it. I wanted to say the part I hadn't said thirty years ago, the most important part, the part Joey regretted never having said one more time, the part that should always be the words on your lips, even after good-bye. I tried and they saw me struggle. Anna smiled. It was a little sad and it reminded me of how Caern had looked at me.

"We love you too," she said.

I took my first-class aisle seat. The guy in the window seat gave me a guarded smile. He looked like a corporate trainer type, someone who spent most of his week in the air or in hotels. He already had earbuds at the ready to wall himself off from the rest of the world, which was fine by me.

We got underway and I felt myself sink deeper into my seat as the plane lifted. The trainer put on his music and entered his own little world. I envied him that. Once in the air, the flight attendant began making her rounds, getting drink orders.

The grid of lights below, the city proper, and all the towns and cities that huddled around her would eventually give way to the deep desert, to yawning desolation. I remember coming to L.A. so long ago, passing over deserts for the first time. I thought they were beautiful. Now they just looked empty and vast.

I was alone, again, just the way I wanted it. I had no idea where I was going when I got off this plane, no purpose, no reason, but I had been in a big goddamn hurry to get here. Running *was* exhausting, especially when you brought the thing you were running from with you wherever you go. At least I knew how to put it to sleep. I gestured for the attendant.

"Scotch and soda," I said.

I was burning for this drink. I had been holding off for so long, so many weeks, maybe months? I had been so desperate not to fuck up again, at first to prove Gida wrong about me, then, after Caern, to minimize, to atone for the damage I create. But now there was no one to disappoint but me, no one to fuck up or damage or kill but me. I was running again, running above the night, through it, and I could feel the desolation approaching, the desert inside and out.

The attendant was returning, and I dug in my pockets for some fake plastic to buy the booze. I fished out my wallet, and with it came Garland's seashell. It was tiny in my palm.

When you've walked the desert so long you no longer really see it, when you've wandered darkness with no light, no warmth, what do you do when you suddenly discover a tiny burning ember still exists in you? Do you stoke it, try again to make the crossing, knowing more likely than not you'll fail, fuck up like you have again and again and again? Or do you snuff it out, put it out of its misery, and stay in the dark and the cold that's come to be your comfort, your banner, your nation?

The shell was small. Garland was so happy when he handed it to me, not a fucking clue about what I really am, and what hell I had damned him to, what he'd suffer because of me for the rest of his life. He saw a different me than I would ever see, would ever know. He believed in that me, like Grinner, and Anna and Dragon did, like Torri and Magdalena had. Time wears our crystalline selves—our hopes and aspirations, our dreams, and our better natures—down to sand. In time, this shell in my hand would be dust.

The attendant returned and offered me the drink. I closed my

fingers around the little shell. I couldn't see it, but I felt it. I remembered the half-assed promise I made to that little boy, to be good. I
looked at the drink in the plastic cup and licked my lips, swallowed,
ached.

"Could you . . . make that just a soda," I said. The attendant
looked annoyed at first but then she seemed to get it. I was betting
I wasn't the first drunk she'd ever had on a plane.

It was a tiny shell, but it felt good in hands that had been empty
for so long. I held on to it as the wasteland beckoned, far below.

ACKNOWLEDGMENTS

It's summer in the south and it's hot as Hell. I wrote *The Night Dahlia* last summer with no AC, my fan blowing tepid air. So it was written, essentially, in a sweat lodge. I'm thankful for that discomfort. The Nightwise stories have always had a strong emotional tie to me. I think you see more of me in these books than anything else I write. Make of that what you will, good or bad. Pulling things out of you should be uncomfortable. Holding them up and then daring to bind them to words on paper, to show them to other people, is a kind of magic, a summoning of a sorts, and an exorcism.

I like to think that it's never too late for redemption, to salvage some tiny glittering scrap of your soul, but my time in the sweat lodge has shown me that redemption is painful, not just to yourself but to others. You hurt them in your failure and then you hurt them again in the reliving, the retelling. It's easier to run from yourself, your mistakes, than to own them. You don't get clean sometimes unless you scour with steel wool and there is no magical catharsis, no music rising like the dawn to tell you that you did the right thing, that the pain was worth it. You just get scars and a vague sense of uneasy change.

I'm in the cool comfort of AC right now, writing these words, but I still feel the same unease, the same uncertainty, that I felt in the lodge. I stumble daily, hourly, between right and wrong, good and evil, harm and care. We build a life out of our comfortable facades, our public faces, and we hope that no one realizes how haunted our houses truly are.

As Ballard has pointed out to me, we rise and we fall. Hopefully, the understanding comes somewhere in that climb. I would like to say I'm sorry to all of those who I grabbed, flailing, on my way down, and thank you to all those who helped me stand again and begin the climb anew. Hopefully, there is wisdom discovered in that cycle.

Thank you to Bruce A. Cutthroat, for winning the "Name Ballard's Band" contest on my Facebook page. Thank you, also, to my daughter, Emily, for her band name that I used as well. I wish I had the space to name all the hundreds of contestants here. Thank you to everyone! I have the most wonderful, twisted readers in this dimension or any other.

Thank you to my dear friends, the League of Extraordinary Beta Readers and Editors: Susan Lystlund, David Lystlund, and Faye Jefferies, for their tireless work and invaluable support. I could not do this without you.

Thank you to the fantastic people I have the privilege to work with at Tor: Tom Doherty, Patty Garcia, Marco Palmieri, Desirae Friesen, Christopher Morgan, Stacy Hill, and my fantastic editor, Greg Cox, who I owe so very much to for his good nature, his patience, his imagination, and his talent. Thank you to my brilliant, nurturing agent, Lucienne Diver, of The Knight Agency, and to all the remarkable people at Knight I have had the opportunity to meet.

And as always, thank you to my children, for being the reason I stand, and the reason I keep climbing. I love you.